O9-AIC-977

"What could be so terrible that a child would stop speaking?" Sophie asked. "I can't imagine."

Something flickered in Kade's stolid expression, a twitch of muscle, the narrowing of coffee-colored eyes in a hard face. "I plan to find out," he said.

"Your police experience should help us find Davey's family," Sophie said.

"Us?"

"Well…" She'd been there when Davey was found and she didn't intend to walk away and leave him with all these unanswered questions. "I know the community really well. People trust me. They'll talk to me. I don't know the first thing about investigating a missing boy." She stopped, frowned. Davey wasn't missing exactly. "Or rather, a found boy. But I know how to deal with people."

Kade raised a palm. "Let's not get ahead of ourselves. It's early yet. Someone may come home from work tonight, find their son gone and call in. Problem solved."

"Do you think they will?" she asked hopefully.

"To be honest?" He dropped his arms to his sides, shot a look toward the living room. "No."

Something in the sudden clip of his voice chilled Sophie's bones.

Linda Goodnight, a *New York Times* bestselling author and winner of a RITA® Award in inspirational fiction, has appeared on the Christian bestseller list. Her novels have been translated into more than a dozen languages. Active in orphan ministry, Linda enjoys writing fiction that carries a message of hope in a sometimes dark world. She and her husband live in Oklahoma. Visit her website, lindagoodnight.com, for more information.

Lois Richer loves traveling, swimming and quilting, but mostly she loves writing stories that show God's boundless love for His precious children. As she says, "His love never changes or gives up. It's always waiting for me. My stories feature imperfect characters learning that love doesn't mean attaining perfection. Love is about keeping on keeping on." You can contact Lois via email, loisricher@gmail.com, or on Facebook (loisricherauthor).

If you purchased this book without a cover you should be aware that this book is stolen property. It was reported as "unsold and destroyed" to the publisher, and neither the author nor the publisher has received any payment for this "stripped book."

LOVE INSPIRED®

INSPIRATIONAL ROMANCE

Recycling programs for this product may not exist in your area.

ISBN-13: 978-1-335-28498-3

The Christmas Child & Gift-Wrapped Family

Copyright © 2020 by Harlequin Books S.A.

The Christmas Child
First published in 2011. This edition published in 2020.
Copyright © 2011 by Linda Goodnight

Gift-Wrapped Family
First published in 2015. This edition published in 2020.
Copyright © 2015 by Lois M. Richer

All rights reserved. No part of this book may be used or reproduced in any manner whatsoever without written permission except in the case of brief quotations embodied in critical articles and reviews.

This is a work of fiction. Names, characters, places and incidents are either the product of the author's imagination or are used fictitiously. Any resemblance to actual persons, living or dead, businesses, companies, events or locales is entirely coincidental.

This edition published by arrangement with Harlequin Books S.A.

For questions and comments about the quality of this book, please contact us at CustomerService@Harlequin.com.

Love Inspired
22 Adelaide St. West, 40th Floor
Toronto, Ontario M5H 4E3, Canada
www.Harlequin.com

Printed in U.S.A.

The Christmas Child

New York Times Bestselling Author

Linda Goodnight

&

Gift-Wrapped Family

Lois Richer

LOVE INSPIRED
INSPIRATIONAL ROMANCE

CONTENTS

THE CHRISTMAS CHILD

Linda Goodnight

For Diane in Dallas, who makes me laugh and cheers me on, as well as all you other dependable, wonderful readers. You know who you are—and I treasure each of you. Thank you for your letters and emails, your Facebook messages and blog comments. This book is for you!

For unto us a child is born, unto us a son is given.

—*Isaiah* 9:6

Chapter One

In twenty years of Dumpster diving, Popbottle Jones had found his share of surprises in other people's trash. But nothing prepared him for what he discovered one chilly November dawn.

Agile as a monkey at seventy-two, Popbottle hopped over the side of the giant bin located downwind of Redemption's municipal building and dropped lightly onto a mound of battered cardboard boxes. The usual garbage and old-food smells rose to greet him, odors he'd trained his nose to ignore in pursuit of more profitable treasures. After all, he and his business partner, GI Jack, were in the recycling business.

From one corner of the dimly lit bin came a scratching sound. His heart sank. Rats or kittens, he suspected. Rats he shooed. The kittens, though, troubled him. He'd never leave domestic creatures to be scooped into a compactor and bulldozed at a landfill.

Gingerly picking his way through the mess, Popbottle directed his steps and his miner's lamp toward the sound. His stomach plummeted. Not rats. Not kittens, though two eyes stared out. Blue eyes. Frightened eyes. The eyes of a child.

Taking a bullet would have been easier, cleaner, quicker. Dying slowly wasted a lot of time.

Kade McKendrick dropped one hand to the golden retriever sitting patiently beside him along the riverbank and tried to relax.

Even now, when he'd been shipped off to Redemption, Oklahoma, for R & R, he wielded a fishing rod like a weapon, fingers tight on the reel's trigger. He'd become too paranoid to go anywhere unarmed.

Memories swamped him. Faces swam up from the muddy red river to accuse. Kade shifted his gaze to the far bank where straggling pale brown weeds poked up from the early winter landscape, hopeless sprouts with nothing in their future but more of the same. Feathery frost tipped the dead grass, shiny in the breaking dawn.

"Might as well give it up, Sheba." Kade reeled in the ten-pound test line, mocking his ambitious tackle. The clerk at the bait and tackle warned him that fish weren't biting this time of year.

He slammed the metal tackle box, startling the dog and a red-tailed hawk still napping on a nearby branch. The bird took flight, wings flapping like billows over the calm, cold waters. Sheba looked on, quivering with intense longing. Together, man and dog watched the hawk soar with lazy grace toward the rising sun. Other than a rare car passing on the bridge, all was quiet and peaceful here on the predawn river. The place drew him like a two-ton magnet in those dark hours when sleep, the vicious tease, evaded him.

Kade sniffed. His nose was cold, but the morning

air, with crisp, clean sharpness, invigorated more than chilled. He picked up the scent of someone's fireplace, a cozy home, he surmised, with two-point-five kids, a Betty Crocker mom and a dad who rose early to feed the fire with fragrant hickory wood.

His lip curled, cynic that he was. Happy ever after was a Hallmark movie.

He, too, had risen early, but not for a cozy fire and a loving family. Although gritty-eyed with fatigue, he hadn't slept a full eight hours in months. But the shrink said he was making progress.

Kade huffed, breath a gray cloud. The shrink probably didn't wake up when his dog barked.

Gathering his gear, Kade started toward his car, a red Mazda Miata parked at an angle near the edge of the Redemption River Bridge. Sheba padded softly at his side, a loyal, undemanding companion who never complained about the nocturnal ramblings.

His great-aunt, on the other hand...

Ida June rose early and she'd be waiting for his return, spouting sluggard quotes, her favorite being, "The field of the sluggard is overtaken by weeds." There were no weeds in Aunt Ida June's fields. One positive aspect of visiting his feisty great-aunt was that she kept him too busy all day to think. Days were all right. Nights were killing him.

Sophie Bartholomew bebopped out the door of the *Redemption Register,* a happy tune on her lips and an order for six dozen cookies on her notepad. She stopped on the sidewalk and danced a little boogie to celebrate the sale. Her students would be pumped, too.

Sophie loved mornings, especially this time of year

with Christmas right around the corner. Already, Redemption geared up for the monthlong celebration.

This crisp morning when the town was just awakening, the scent of fresh doughnuts tantalized the streets in front of the Sugar Shack bakery and café. Sophie headed there next to round up more orders for the annual fifth-grade charity cookie sale. Miriam, owner of the Sugar Shack, never minded, even though the sales cut into her business.

Down the block a city worker dangled from a bucket truck to lace white lights along the front of the town's historic bank building. Sophie gave a little wave. Christmas was unofficially here, and no one was happier about that than Sophie.

She loved everything about Christmas, from the celebrations and festivities to church and decorated cookies and gaily wrapped gifts. Even the commercialism didn't bother her. Christmas, she'd long ago decided, meant joy and love and Jesus, in whatever form it was celebrated.

Across the street on the town square, Ida June Click, octogenarian handywoman, pounded on a half-erected stable while a lean, dark man unloaded lumber from a truck, his navy plaid shirt open over a white T-shirt. Sophia recognized him as Kade McKendrick, Ida June's nephew, although Sophie didn't know him well. He was new in town, but her single friends and several not-so-singles noticed his comings and goings. He mostly stayed to himself. His quiet aloofness made everyone wonder, including her. But he was a looker, as her close friend Jilly Fairmont said. A mysterious looker. What could be more intriguing to a female? Not that Sophie thought all that much about her single status. She was too busy teaching kids and loving the life the Lord had given her.

She had one hand on the glass door of the Sugar Shack when she heard a shout. Over on the curb by the buff-brick municipal building, GI Jack, the eccentric old Dumpster diver who ran a recycling business and created junk art, waved his arms and yelled for help.

"Ida June," he called to the twig of woman in bright red overalls and a man's work jacket. "Get over here quick."

"Here" was a spot right next to an industrial-size trash bin.

"Not another cat. My cup runneth over already." But the feisty eightysomething woman hustled toward him just the same.

So did Sophie. GI Jack was not an alarmist, and one quick glance told her Popbottle Jones, the other eccentric Dumpster diver, was nowhere to be seen.

Traffic was slow this time of day, and Sophie darted across the street with barely a glance. Had something happened to Popbottle Jones?

"What can we do? Shall we call for an ambulance? I have my cell phone." Ida June, still a little breathless from the jog, whipped a modern smartphone from the bib of her overalls. "We must get him out of that Dumpster ASAP. He who hesitates is lost."

Confusion clouded GI Jack's face. "Well, yes, ma'am, I reckon so, but we don't need no ambulance."

"If Popbottle is hurt—"

The funny old man blinked. "Popbottle ain't hurt."

"My friend is correct. I've suffered no ill effect." Ulysses E. "Popbottle" Jones grasped the top of the heavy metal trash bin and peered over the edge, his red miner's hat tipped to one eye. "But we do require assistance."

Curiosity got the better of Sophie and she tiptoed up for a look. The sight she beheld chipped off a piece of her teacher's heart. Cowering against the side of the bin and surrounded by trash, a young boy, maybe eight or nine, clutched a book against his chest and stared out with round blue eyes. Poorly dressed for the cold day, his shaggy blond hair hung limp and dirty around a pale, thin face smeared with something yellow, probably mustard from the piece of old hamburger gripped in his other hand.

"The small fellow won't allow me near him," Popbottle said with some chagrin as he hopped to the street. "Must be my unusual attire or perhaps the miner's lamp. I thought one of you ladies would fare better."

"Probably thought you were an alien from Jupiter," Ida June grumbled. Barely tall enough to see inside, she chinned herself like a gymnast, peered in, then slithered back to earth, muttering. "My nephew will know what to do." Whirling toward the town square she barked loud enough to be heard over the din of a city truck rattling past. "Kade, on the double! We need help."

Sophie, too concerned with the child to wait, said, "GI, boost me up."

The gentle old man, still strong as the soldier he'd been, patted his bent knee. "Foot here."

She grabbed the top of the trash bin and vaulted up and in to slide unceremoniously onto a pile of damp newspapers. She rested there for a few seconds to study the little boy and gauge his reaction to her presence. Dampness soaked through the back of her sweater.

She'd need a trip home before schooltime. Not that her clothes mattered at the moment.

When the little boy didn't scramble away, she slowly moved toward him, picking her way across the junk, careful not to turn an ankle in the heeled boots.

"Hello, there," she said in her kindest voice. "My name is Sophie. What's your name?"

The question was met with a silent stare.

Sophie went into a crouch, inches from the child, but careful not to touch until he was ready. Holding back was hard. She was a toucher, a hugger, believing children needed physical connection. "I'm a nice person, honey. You can talk to me and I'll help you."

Still only that bleak stare.

"I'm a teacher here in Redemption. Fifth grade. What grade are you in?"

Nothing.

Outside the trash bin voices rose and fell—Ida June's spit and vinegar, and a chorus of males. By now, someone had likely called the police station, and Sophie worried the sight of an officer might frighten the boy even more. He was like a wary, wild thing, cornered and ready to bolt at the first opportunity.

Metal scraped against the outer bin. Someone else was scrambling up the side. The boy's gaze shifted to a spot behind Sophie just as that someone dropped to the surface with catlike quiet.

Sophie glanced over one shoulder to see the trim, lithe, dark-as-a-shadow nephew of Ida June Click. His eyes, the same espresso brown as his hair, met hers in a narrow squint. There was something lethal about Kade McKendrick, and she remembered the rumor that he'd been a big-city cop or in the DEA or some such. He looked more like a man who'd been on the wrong side of the law than a police officer.

"The cookie lady," he said with an unsmiling nod.

Sophie offered a cheeky grin. "You'll order some yet. It's a great cause." Every year she and her fifth graders baked and sold Christmas cookies and contributed the proceeds to charity.

He went to his heels beside her and hitched his chin toward the child. In the bin, large as it was, three was a crowd. "Who's your friend?"

She tilted her face toward his, noticed the tense lines around his eyes and mouth. "One frightened boy."

Kade turned a quiet look on the child. "Hey, buddy, what's your name?"

Sophie waited, but when the child's response was more silence, she said, "He's not said a word to me, either."

"What's that he's holding?" Kade gestured, stirring the scent of warm, working male and clean cotton shirt, a welcome respite from the stink of trash.

"A book."

"Good work, Sherlock," he said, lightly enough that Sophie would have laughed if she hadn't been so concerned for the child. "What kind of book and why is he gripping it like a lifeline?"

Sophie wondered the same thing.

To the boy, she said, "I'm a teacher, honey. I love books. What kind of story are you reading?"

He shifted slightly, his gaze flickering to the oversize book.

"Will you show it to me? Maybe we can read it together over breakfast? Are you hungry?" She extended an upturned palm and waited. She was surprisingly aware of Kade squatted in the trash next to her. She knew little about him, other than rumors and that he was good-looking in a black panther kind of way. An interesting energy simmered, in this of all places, as his arm brushed hers.

She ignored the sensation and smiled encouragement at the little boy, all the while praying for guidance and a way to connect.

Slowly, with stark hope and a dose of anxiety, the towheaded boy relinquished the picture book. Sophie shifted nearer, relaxing some and moving easily into teacher mode. She knew books, knew kids, knew how to relate.

"This is beautiful." She touched the brightly colored cover. "Is it your favorite?"

For the first time, the boy responded. His head bobbed up and down. He scooted closer and opened the cover of the popular Christmas tale. Sophie shot a glance at Kade, who offered a quick, approving hitch of his chin. For some reason, his encouragement pleased her. Not that she wanted to impress Ida June's great-nephew, but they *were* in this crowded Dumpster together. The thought made her giggle. The males gave her identical, bewildered looks.

"Look what we have here," Sophie said, her finger on the flyleaf inscription. "*To Davey. Happy Birthday. Love, Mama.* You must be Davey."

Eagerly, the child nodded, his face lighting up.

Someone rapped sharply on the side of the trash bin. The sound echoed like a metallic gong. Davey jumped, then shrank back into himself.

"Are you two taking up residence in there?"

Sophie glanced up. Three pairs of eyes peered back from above the edge, watching the scene below.

"Ida June has the patience of a housefly," Kade muttered, but rose and offered a hand to the little boy. "Come on, Davey, I'm hungry. Let's get some pancakes."

Davey hesitated only a moment before putting his small hand in Kade's much larger one. Then, with eyes wide and unsure, he reached for Sophie on the other side. Body tense, his fingers trembled. Over his head, Kade and Sophie exchanged glances. She wasn't sure what she expected from Kade McKendrick, but anger burned from eyes dark with a devastation she couldn't understand.

In that one look, Sophie received a stunning message. Davey was lost and alone. So was Kade McKendrick.

Chapter Two

Davey sat in Police Chief Jesse Rainmaker's desk chair, swiveling back and forth, while the adults—Sophie, Ida June and Kade—discussed his situation. The Dumpster divers had come and gone, promising to "spread the word" and find where Davey belonged.

Kade hoped they could, but he wasn't holding his breath. He'd seen this before, although finding a kid in a trash can was a new low. A kid, tossed away like tissue. Use once and discard. Yeah, he'd seen plenty of that. Only they got used more than once before they ran or were discarded.

Kade's gut burned with the implication. He hoped he was wrong. He turned his back to the sad little scene and perused the faxes and photos on a bulletin board. Creeps, losers, scum. Somebody somewhere knew who this kid was and what had happened to him.

"Has he told you anything at all? Where he's from, his name, his parents. Anything?" Police Chief Jesse Rainmaker was a solid man. In a few short weeks, Kade had come to respect the understaffed officer and his handful of deputies. They were small-town but efficient and smart. Good cops.

"Nothing," Sophie said. "Even over breakfast, he didn't say a word. I'm starting to wonder if he can speak."

The sweet-faced schoolteacher had drawn a chair up next to Davey. She was good with the kid, calmed him, gave him a sense of security. For a fraction of a minute in the Dumpster, she'd done the same for him. It was a weird feeling.

Kade pivoted. "Why don't we ask him? Obviously, he can hear."

"Or he reads lips," Sophie said.

Chief Rainmaker tilted his head. "Hadn't thought of that."

"I know sign language. I can try that, too," Sophie said, moving round in front of Davey. "Davey."

The dirty little boy focused on her face. Some of his fear had dissipated, but he remained edgy, watchful, uncertain.

With a grace Kade found beautiful, the woman moved her hands in silent communication. Davey stared but didn't respond.

"Well, that didn't work. Davey, can you hear me?"

An eager head bob.

"Why won't you talk to me?"

Davey shrugged, one hand moving to his throat.

"Let's send him over to the clinic," Rainmaker said. "Have him checked out. Either he won't talk for some reason or he can't."

Restless in the small office Kade paced from the bulletin board to the boy and back again. Someone had put an automatic air freshener on top of the file cabinet to counteract the smell of burned coffee and stale shoes. Every few minutes, a spurt of fragrance hissed a girly scent into the air. Jesse either had a wife or secretary. No self-respecting cop would buy—Kade squinted at the can—white tea and roses. Smelled pretty good, though.

"Then what happens to him?" he asked.

Rainmaker rounded his desk, a long metal structure overflowing with paperwork. Kade empathized. Paperwork was the bane of cops.

The chief shuffled through some messages, pulled a stack of faxes from the basket. "Nothing on the wires about a missing child in the area, but I'll make more calls and get the word out. We'll hear something soon."

Kade didn't let it go. Couldn't. "If you don't?"

"Child protective services will take over. I'll have to notify them anyway. Someone is responsible for letting this boy get in this situation. Finding them is my job. Taking care of the child isn't."

Kade grunted. Shoulders tense, he shoved his hands into the pockets of his leather jacket. He'd told himself the same thing once. It was a lie. Taking care of the kids was everyone's job.

Ida June, who'd remained amazingly silent for a full ten minutes, piped up in her take-no-guff tone. "We'll take the boy home with us. No need to call anyone."

His aunt's idea took Kade by surprise, but he didn't object. He wanted to keep an eye on Davey, just as he wanted to find out who'd left him in such a condition. Someone needed to pay big-time. And Kade was in the mood to be the collector.

"Now, Miss Ida June, you know I have to follow the law," Jesse said patiently.

"Please, Jesse," Sophie said, voice as sweet as her

face. "I'd take him myself, but I have to get to school. I'm already late and an aide is watching my class, but Davey's too fragile to go with another stranger right now."

If Rainmaker could resist that face and tone, he was a strong man.

"Girl's right," Ida June announced with a slap to the desktop. Davey jumped, blue eyes blinking rapidly. Sophie placed a soothing hand on his knee. "We'll take Davey to the clinic, me and my nephew here, and then home to clean up. I figure the little man is tuckered plum out. He can rest up for a few hours at my place, and then if you haven't found his mama and daddy, you can call Howard Prichard."

Jesse rubbed the back of his neck. "Tell you what, Miss Ida June, I'll give Howard a call and apprise him of the situation. If he agrees, it's a deal."

Good luck with that, Kade thought.

"Well, get to it." Ida June crossed her arms over the front of her overalls. "Time wasted is gone forever and Lord knows, at my age, I can't afford to lose any."

Mouth twitching, Jesse made the phone call. When the social worker agreed with Ida June's plan, Kade was amazed. Small towns worked differently than the city where the letter of the law was followed, regardless. Here, apparently, human beings took precedence over protocol. Interesting.

They prepared to load Davey and his book into Kade's truck. Ida June had wanted him to ride with her, but Kade and Jesse both said, "No!" with such force that Ida June puffed up like an adder and stalked off. *Kade* didn't ride with her. He sure wasn't putting a child in the truck with her.

"She cut across the street yesterday, slapped a U-turn as if there weren't cars coming both ways, all because there was a parking spot on the other side."

Rainmaker nodded sagely. "I think she got her driver's license out of a cereal box."

Kade arched an eyebrow. "She has one?"

Both men chuckled.

"Come on, Davey," Kade said, taking the boy by the hand.

Davey hopped obediently from the chair and reached for Sophie. Her face crumbled. "Oh, honey, I can't go with you. I have to go to work."

Davey wrenched away from Kade to throw both arms around Sophie's middle. With a helpless look toward Kade, she hugged Davey close against a long blue sweater. Kade got a funny kick in the gut and fought off the urge to join the hug fest.

"You'll come to the house after school." His was a statement, not a question. He knew she'd come.

She nodded, gray eyes distressed. "I'll be there right after three." She held Davey back from her a little, hands on his shoulders. "Do you hear me, Davey? Go with Kade to Miss Ida June's house. They'll take good care of you, and as soon as school is out, I'll be there. We'll read your book as many times as you want. Okay?"

Looking from her to Kade and back as if he thought the pair of them went together, Davey thought over the proposition. Then, he retrieved the book he'd dropped, clasped Kade's hand and followed him to the truck.

Sophie's school day started out shaky, but she, an eternal optimist, was certain things would get better. They didn't.

After rushing home for a quick clothing change, she arrived to find her class in chaos. Emily Baker had suffered a seizure and had to go to the hospital. Even though everyone knew about Emily's disorder, witnessing a seizure frightened the class. Even Zoey Bowman, the vet's daughter whose blindness only increased her compassion and wisdom, had not known how to react. She and best friend, blonde and bouncy Delaney Markham, huddled together holding hands, desks scooted close.

By the time Sophie settled the group down with assurances that Emily was not going to die and a promise to get Mrs. Baker on the speakerphone in a few hours so they all could hear an update for themselves, lunchtime arrived.

"Academics took a backseat this morning," Carmen, the teacher's aide, said as she slid her lunch tray onto the cafeteria table next to Sophie. A fortysomething bleached blonde with an extra twenty pounds, Carmen floated between classrooms doing whatever was needed.

"Caring for people is more important sometimes," Sophie said. She sniffed a forkful of mystery casserole, a combination of tomato and meat scent with sticky pasta in the mix. Or was that rice?

"Don't say that to Mr. Gruber."

"I already have." Sophie jabbed a fork into the glob and took a bite. Not bad. Not good. She reached for the salt and pepper.

"Only you could get away with talking like that to the principal."

"Oh, that's not true. He's fair to everyone. Here, try salt on that." She offered the shakers to her seatmate.

"Anything to hide the taste," Carmen said with a wry grin.

The clatter and din of kids in a cafeteria made talking tough, but Carmen had the kind of voice that could be heard by thirty rowdy kids in a noisy gym. "Come on, Sophie, everyone knows Mr. Gruber has a thing for you."

"Shh. Not so loud." Sophie glanced around, hoping no one had heard. Carmen chuckled, the sound of a woman who enjoyed teasing and gossip, not necessarily in that order. Biff Gruber was a decent man and a good, if uptight, principal. Sophie respected his leadership.

She scooped another bite of the bland casserole, eyeing it suspiciously. "What is this anyway?"

Carmen laughed at the common refrain as the glass double doors swept open. Noise gushed in like a sudden wind. A flurry of overzealous teens, shuffling their feet and jockeying for position in line, pushed inside. Over the din, Carmen said, "There's your dad."

Sophie glanced up. Amid the gangly teens, a graying man in white dress shirt and yellow cartoon tie grinned at something one of his students said.

"Oh, good. I was hoping he'd stop for lunch today." Her dad taught science in the high school. Many days he ate at his desk while tutoring kids. She raised a hand, flagged him over to join them.

As his gray plastic tray scraped onto the table across from her and he greeted the other teachers with an easy smile, the familiar pang of fierce love stirred in Sophie's chest. Mark Bartholomew had aged more than the five years since his divorce from Sophie's mother, a divorce he'd never wanted. Worse, Meg Bartholomew had remarried almost immediately. The implication of an affair still stung, a bitter, unexpected betrayal. Sophie could only imagine how humiliated and hurt her father must have felt.

"Hi, Dad. How's your day?"

"Better now that I see your smiling face. How is yours?" He spread a narrow paper napkin on his lap and tucked in his "mad scientist" tie.

"Something crazy happened this morning."

Expression comical, he tilted his head, prematurely graying hair glossy beneath the fluorescent lights. "Crazier than usual? This is a school, remember? The holiday season always stirs up the troops."

Sophie and her father shared this love of teaching and the special hum of energy several hundred kids brought into a building. At Christmas, the energy skyrocketed.

"We found a lost boy in the municipal Dumpster."

Her father lowered his fork, frowning, as she repeated the morning's events. When she finished, he said, "That's tragic, honey. Anything I can do?"

"Pray for him. Pray for Chief Rainmaker to find his family." She shrugged. "Just pray."

He patted the back of her hand. "You got it. Don't get your heart broken."

"Dad," she said gently.

"I know you. You'll get involved up to your ears. Sometimes your heart's too big."

"I take after my dad."

The statement pleased him. He dug into the mystery casserole. "What is this?"

Sophie giggled as she and Carmen exchanged glances. "Inquiring minds want to know."

He chewed, swallowed. "Better than an old bachelor's cooking."

He said the words naturally, without rancor, but Sophie ached for him just the same. Dad alone in their family home without Mom unbalanced the world. Even though Sophie had offered to give up her own place and move in with him, her father had resisted, claiming he wanted his "bachelor pad" all to himself. Sophie knew better. He'd refused for her sake, worried she'd focus on his life instead of hers.

Carmen dug an elbow into Sophie's side. "Mr. Gruber just came in."

"Principals eat, too."

Carmen rolled her eyes. "He's headed this direction."

Sophie's father looked from one woman to the other. "Have I missed something?"

"Nothing, Dad. Pay no mind to Carmen. She's having pre-Christmas fantasies."

"Mr. Gruber is interested in your daughter."

"Carmen! Please. He is not." She didn't want him to be. A picture of the quietly intense face of Kade McKendrick flashed in her head. This morning's encounter had stirred more than her concern for a lost child.

"Gruber's a good man," her dad said. He stopped a moment to turn to the side and point at a pimply boy for throwing a napkin wad. The kid grinned sheepishly, retrieved the wad and sat down. The high schoolers were convinced Mr. Bartholomew had eyes in the back of his head.

"Dad, do not encourage rumors."

Her father lifted both hands in surrender as the principal arrived at their table. Biff Gruber nodded to those gathered, then leaned low next to Sophie's ear. His blue tie sailed dangerously close to the mystery casserole. Sophie suppressed a giggle.

"I need to see you in my office, please. During your plan time is fine."

Without another word, he walked away.

"So much for your romantic theories," Sophie told a wide-eyed Carmen. "That did not sound like an interested man."

"No kidding. Wonder what he wants," Carmen said, watching the principal exit the room. "An ultimatum like that can't be good."

Sophie put aside her fork. "Sure it can. Maybe he wants to order ten-dozen cookies."

Carmen looked toward the ceiling with a sigh. "You'd put a positive spin on it if he fired you."

Well, she'd try. But she couldn't help wondering why her principal had been so abrupt.

She found out two hours later, seated in his tidy, narrow office. The space smelled of men's cologne and the new leather chair behind the unusually neat, polished mahogany desk. It was a smell, she knew, that struck terror in the hearts of sixth-grade boys. A plaque hung on the wall above Biff Gruber's head as warning to all who entered: Attitudes Adjusted While You Wait.

"I understand you're doing the cookie project again this year," he said without preliminary.

Sophie brightened. Maybe he *did* want to place an order. She folded her hands in her lap, relaxed and confident. This was Biff and she was not a sixth-grade rowdy. "I turned in the lesson plan last week. We're off to a promising start already and I hope to raise even more money this year."

Biff positioned his elbows on the desk and bounced his fingertips together. The cuffs of his crisply ironed shirt bobbed up and down against his pale-haired wrists. The light above winked on a silver watch. His expression, usually open and friendly, remained tight and professional. Sophie's hope for a cookie sale dissipated.

"We've had some complaints from parents," he said.

Sophie straightened, the news a complete surprise. No one had ever complained. "About the project? What kind of complaints? Students look forward to this event from the time they're in second and third grade."

In fact, kids begged to participate. Other classes loitered in her doorway, volunteered and occasionally even took orders for her. This project was beloved by all. Wasn't it?

"How many years have you been doing this, Sophie?" The principal's tone was stiff, professional and uneasy.

Suddenly, she felt like one of the students called into the principal's office for making a bad judgment. At the risk of sounding defensive, she said, "This is year five. Last year we donated the proceeds, a very nice amount, I might add, to the local women's shelter. Afterward, Cheyenne Bowman spoke to our class and even volunteered to teach a self-protection seminar to the high-school girls."

Biff, however, had not followed up on that offer from the shelter's director, a former police officer and assault victim.

"I'm aware the project does a good deed, but the worry is academics. Aren't your students losing valuable class time while baking cookies?"

"Not at all. They're learning valuable skills in a real-life situation. I realize my teaching style is not traditional but students learn by doing as well, maybe better, than by using only textbooks."

Biff took a pencil from his desk and tapped the end on a desk calendar. He was unusually fidgety today. Whoever complained must have clout. "Give me some specifics to share with the concerned parent."

"Who is it? Maybe if I spoke with him or her?"

"I don't want my teachers bothered with disgruntled parents. I will handle the situation."

"I appreciate that, Biff. You've always been great support." Which was all the more reason to be concerned this time. Why was he not standing behind her on the cookie project? Who was putting pressure on the principal? "The project utilizes math, economics, life skills, social ethics, research skills, art and science." She ticked them off on her fingers. "There are more. Is that enough?"

Biff scribbled on a notepad. "For now. You may have to articulate exactly how those work at some point, but we'll start here."

"I really don't want to lose this project, Biff. It's a high point for my students."

"As well as for their teacher who loves everything Christmas." With a half smile he bounced the pencil one final time. "Why don't we have dinner tonight and discuss this further?"

The offer caught Sophie as much by surprise as someone's objection to the cookie project. She sputtered a bit before saying, "Thank you, but I have to say no. I'm sorry."

Her thoughts went to Davey and the way he'd clung to her this morning. She couldn't wait to see him again and let him know she kept her promises. She'd phoned after lunch to say hello and see how he was doing. Kade had answered, assured her Davey was doing fine and was at that moment sound asleep on Ida June's couch. The memory of Kade's voice, clipped, cool and intriguing, lingered like a song she couldn't get out of her head.

No, she definitely did not want to have dinner with the principal.

"I've already made other plans."

Biff's face closed up again. He stuffed the pen in his shirt pocket. "Ah. Well, another time, then."

At the risk of encouraging him, Sophie nodded and quickly left his office. The mystery casserole churned in her stomach. As her boot heels tapped rhythmically on highly waxed white tile, she reviewed the unsettling conversation. As much as she wanted to believe Biff's dinner invitation was purely professional, she knew better. Carmen was right. The principal liked her. She liked him, too. It wasn't that. He was a good man, a by-the-book administrator who strove for excellence and expected the same from his staff. As a teacher, she appreciated him. But as a woman? She hadn't thought seriously about her boss, and given the buzz of interest she'd felt for Ida June's nephew, she never would.

Frankly, the concerns about her teaching methods weighed more heavily right now.

Would Biff go as far as vetoing the cookie project?

Chapter Three

Kade pushed back from the laptop perched on Ida June's worn kitchen table and rubbed the strain between his eyes. Hours of poking into every law-enforcement database he could access produced nothing about a missing mute boy named David. He'd chased a rabbit trail for the past hour only to discover the missing child had been found.

Hunching his shoulders high to relieve the tightness, he glanced past the narrow dividing bar into Ida June's living room. Davey still slept, curled beneath a red plaid throw on the 1970s sofa, a psychedelic monstrosity in red, green and yellow swirls that, ugly as sin, proved a napping boy's paradise. In sleep, Davey had released his beloved book to fall in the narrow space between his skinny body and the fat couch cushion. Sheba lay next to him, her golden head snuggled beneath his lax arm. She opened one eye, gave Kade a lazy look and went back to sleep.

"Traitor," he said, softly teasing. The boy had taken one look at the affable dog and melted. Sheba could never resist a kid. When Davey went to his knees in joyful greeting and threw his arms around her neck, Sheba claimed him as her own. He'd shared his lunch with her, a sight that had twisted in Kade's chest. The kid had been hungry, maybe for days, but he'd shared a ham sandwich with the well-fed dog. Whatever had happened to Davey hadn't broken him. It may very well have silenced him, but his soul was still intact.

Kade rubbed a frustrated hand over his whiskered jaw and asked himself for the dozenth time why he'd gotten involved. He knew the answer. He just didn't like it.

Leaving the pair, he poured himself another cup of coffee and went to finish the laundry. At the moment, Davey wore one of Kade's oversize T-shirts and a ridiculously huge pair of sweats tied double at the waist. Now, when he awoke, Davey's clothes would be as clean as he was.

Once the boy had been fed, cleaned and his clothes in the washer, Ida June had barked a few orders and gone to work at the little town square. With Kade's less-than-professional assistance, she'd been erecting a stable for the town's Christmas celebration. She'd promised to have it finished this week, and leaving Kade to "mind the store" and "find that boy's mama," Ida June had marched out the door with a final parting shot: "Promises are like babies squalling in a theater—they should be carried out at once."

He was still smirking over that one. His mother's aunt was a colorful character, a spunky old woman who'd outlived two husbands, built her own business and half of her own house, drove like a maniac and spouted quotes like Bartlett. And if anyone needed a helping hand, she was there, though heaven help the man or woman who said she had a soft heart.

Kade removed Davey's pitiful jeans and sweatshirt from the dryer and folded them next to clean socks and underwear before tossing the washed sneakers into the still-warm drier. He set them on tumble with one of Ida June's fragrant ocean-breeze dryer sheets and left them to thump and bang.

He wasn't much on shopping any more than he was on doing laundry, especially at Christmas when the holly, jolly Muzak and fake everything abounded, but a single man learned to take care of business. The boy needed clothes, and unless Sophie Bartholomew or Ida June offered, he'd volunteer.

Sophie. The wholesome-looking teacher had played around the edges of his thoughts all day, poking in a little too often. Nobody could be that sweet and smiley all the time.

"Probably on crack," he groused, and then snorted at the cynical remark. A woman like Sophie probably wouldn't know crack cocaine if it was in her sugar bowl.

His cell phone jangled and he yanked the device from his pocket to punch Talk. With calls into various law-enforcement agencies all over the region, he hoped to hear something. Even though he was a stranger here, with few contacts and no clout, his federal clearances gave him access to just about anything he wanted to poke his nose into.

It had been a while since he'd wanted to poke into anything. When he turned over rocks, he usually found snakes.

He squeezed his eyes shut. The year undercover had

skewed his perspective. He wasn't looking for snakes this time. He was looking for a boy's family.

One hand to the back of his neck, the other on the phone, he went to the kitchen window and stared blindly out at the gray sky as the voice on the other end gave him the expected news. Nothing.

He figured as much. A dumped kid might be big news in Redemption but to the rest of the world, Davey was another insignificant statistic.

Acid burned his gut—an ulcer, he suspected, though he'd avoided mentioning the hot pain to the shrink. Being forced by his superiors to talk to a head doctor was bad enough. No one was going to shove a scope down his throat and tell him to take pills and live on yogurt. He didn't do pills. Or yogurt. He'd learned the hard way that one pill, one drug, one time could be the end of a man.

He scrubbed his hands over his eyes. He was so tired. He couldn't help envying Davey and Sheba their sound sleep. He ached to sleep, to fall into that wonderful black land of nothingness for more than a restless hour at a time. The coffee kept him moving, but no amount of caffeine replaced a solid sleep. He took a sip, grimaced at the day-old brew and the growing gut burn. Yeah, yeah. Coffee made an ulcer worse. Big deal. It wasn't coffee that was killing him.

In the scrubbed-clean driveway outside the window, a deep purple Ford Focus pulled to a stop. The vehicle, a late-model job, was dirt-splattered from the recent rain, and the whitewalls needed a scrub. Why did women ignore the importance of great-looking wheels? The schoolteacher, brown hair blowing lightly in the breeze, hopped out, opened the back car door and wrestled out a bulging trash bag. Curious, Kade set aside his mug and jogged out to help.

"What's this?" he asked.

The afternoon sun, weak as a twenty-watt bulb, filtered through the low umbrella of stratus clouds and found the teacher's warm smile. There was something about her, a radiance that pierced the bleak day with light. Kade's troubled belly tingled. She attracted him, plain and simple—a surprise, given how dead he felt most of the time.

Her smile widening, Sophie shoved the black trash sack into his arms. She had a pretty mouth, full lips with gentle creases along the edges like sideways smiles. "Davey needs clothes."

"You went shopping?" She'd barely had time to get here from school. And why the hefty bag?

"No." Her laugh danced on the chilly breeze and hit him right in the ulcer. "I know kids, lots of kids, all sizes and shapes, who outgrow clothes faster than their parents can buy them. I made a few phone calls and voilà!" She hunched her shoulders, fingers of one hand spreading in the space between them like a starburst. "Davey is all fixed up." Perky as a puppy, she hoisted another bag. "This has a few toys in it. We were guessing size, so I hope something fits. The rest can go to the shelter."

"Bound to fit better than what he's wearing now." She was going to get a kick out of his impromptu outfit.

"How is he?" she asked as they carried the bags inside.

"Exhausted." Kade dumped his bag in a chair inside the living room and hitched his chin toward the ugly couch. "He's slept like a rock most of the day."

"What did the doctor say? Have we heard any news

on where he came from? Where's Ida June?" Shooting questions like an arcade blaster, Sophie moved past him into the room. A subtle wake of clean perfume trailed behind to tantalize his senses. Sunshine and flowers and—he sniffed once—coconut. She smelled as fresh and wholesome as she looked.

Amused by her chatter, he slouched at the bar and waited for her to wind down. "You finished?"

"For now." She stood over Davey and Sheba, a soft smile tilting her naturally curved lips. "Is this your dog?"

"Was until this morning."

She gave him that happy look again. She was lucky. No one had wiped away her joy. Life must have always been good in Sophie's world.

"A boy and a dog is a powerful combination," she said.

"Sheba's a sucker for kids."

"So is her master."

"Me?" Where did she get such a weird idea? He did his job. Did what he had to. And a dose of retribution was only just.

"So tell me, what did the doctor say?"

"Dehydrated and run-down but otherwise healthy. Nothing rest and nutrition won't fix." He'd been careful to ask the right questions and the child showed no signs of physical abuse. No outward signs.

"What about his voice?"

Kade nodded behind him to the kitchen. "Let's talk in here."

"Sure." Smart Sophie got the message. He didn't want to talk near the boy, not with the suspicions tear-ing at the back of his brain. With a lingering glance at Davey, she followed Kade to the kitchen.

"Want some coffee?" he asked.

"It's cold out." She rubbed her palms together. "A hot cup sounds great if it's already made."

"Coffee's always made."

She raised a dark, tidy eyebrow. "Chain drinker?"

"Safer than chugging Red Bull."

The answer revealed more than he'd intended. He went to the counter, more aware of her than he wanted to be and wondering, even though he didn't want to, what it would be like to be normal again the way she was. Normal and easy in her skin. Maybe that's what made her so pretty. She wasn't movie-star beautiful, although she warmed the room like an unexpected ray of sun across a shadow. Dark, soft, curving hair. Soft gray eyes. Clear, soft skin. Everything about Sophie Bartholomew was soft.

"What did the doctor say about Davey's voice?"

"He found no physical reason for Davey not to speak, though he did recommend a specialist." Kade poured two cups and held up the sugar bowl. Sophie shook her head. Figured. She was sweet enough. Kade loaded his with three spoons and stirred them in. "We'll have to leave that to social services."

Sophie grimaced. He got that. Social services did what they could, but who really *cared* about one little boy?

"Then there must be something mental or emotional, and he doesn't appear mentally handicapped." She accepted the offered cup, sipped with her eyes closed. Kade, a detail man courtesy of his career, tried not to notice the thick curl of mink lashes against pearl skin. "Mmm. Perfect. Thanks."

"Which leaves us with one ugly conclusion." He took a hot gulp and felt the burn before the liquid ever hit his belly. The more he thought about what could have happened to Davey, the more his gut hurt. "Trauma."

"I wondered about that, but was hoping…" Her voice trailed off. She picked at the handle of her cup.

"Yeah, me, too."

Sophie's fingers went to her lips, flat now with concern for the little boy. She painted her fingernails. Bright Christmas red with tiny silver snowflakes. How did a woman do that?

"You think something happened that upset him so much he stopped talking?"

Jaw tight, Kade nodded. "So does the doc."

And if it took him the rest of his life, somebody somewhere was gonna pay.

Sophie studied the trim, fit man leaning against Ida June's mustard-colored wall. In long-sleeved Henley shirt and blue jeans, dark brown hair combed messily to one side, he could be any ordinary man, but she suspected he wasn't. Kade McKendrick was cool to the point of chill with a hard glint to wary eyes that missed nothing. He was tough. Defensive. Dangerous.

Yet, he'd responded to Davey's need with concern, and he had a wry wit beneath the cynical twist of that tight mouth. He didn't smile much but he knew how. Or he once had. Her woman's intuition said he'd been through some trauma himself. Her woman's heart wanted to bake him cookies and fix him.

A little troubled at the direction of her thoughts,

she raised her coffee mug, a shield to hide behind. She didn't even know this guy.

"What could be so terrible that a child would stop speaking?" she asked. "I can't imagine."

Something flickered in the stolid expression, a twitch of muscle, the narrowing of coffee-colored eyes in a hard face.

"I plan to find out."

"I heard you were a cop."

"Listening to gossip?"

She smiled. "Not all of it."

The admission caught him by surprise. He lightened, just a little, but enough for her to see his humor. She didn't know why that pleased her, but it did. Kade needed to lighten up and smile a little.

"I am." He went to the sink and dumped the remaining coffee, rinsed the cup and left it in the sink. "A cop, that is. Special units."

"You don't want to hear about the other rumors?"

He made a huffing noise. "Maybe later. You don't want to hear about the special units?"

"Maybe later." She smiled again, hoping he'd smile, too. He didn't. "The important thing is Davey. Your police experience should help us find his family."

"Us?"

"Well…" She wasn't a person to start something and not follow through. She'd been there when Davey was found and she didn't intend to walk away and leave him with all these unanswered questions. "I know the community really well. People trust me. They'll talk to me. I don't know the first thing about investigating a missing boy." She stopped, frowned. Davey wasn't missing exactly. "Or rather, a found boy, but I know how to deal with people."

Kade raised a palm. "Let's not get ahead of ourselves. It's early yet. Someone may come home from work tonight, find their son gone and call in. Problem solved."

"Do you think they will?" she asked hopefully.

"To be honest?" He dropped his arms to his sides, shot a look toward the living room. "No."

Something in the sudden clip of his voice chilled Sophie's bones. She frowned and leaned forward, propping her arms on the metal dinette. Ida June must have had this thing since the 1950s. "Have you worked in Missing Children before?"

She was almost certain he flinched, but if he did, he covered the emotion quickly.

"In a manner of speaking."

Sophie waited for an explanation, but when none was forthcoming, she asked, "Do you have any ideas? Any thoughts about where he came from or what happened?"

"A few." He crossed his arms again. She recognized the subconscious barrier he raised between them. What had happened to this man to make him so aloof? For a people person, he was a challenge. For a Christian, he was someone to pray for. For a single woman, he was dangerously attractive. What woman wouldn't want to delve behind those dark, mysterious eyes and into that cool heart to fix whatever ailed him?

"Care to share?" she asked.

He cocked his head, listening. "Davey's awake."

Sophie hadn't heard a sound, but she pushed away from the table and hurried past Kade to the sofa and the little boy who'd had her prayers all day. Behind her, a more troubling and troubled presence followed. She was in the company of two mysterious males and they both intrigued her.

"Hi, Davey." She sat on the edge of the couch, the warmth of Davey's sleep-drenched body pleasant against her leg. Kade's big dog, a golden retriever, slid off the sofa and padded to her master. He dropped a hand to her wide skull and stood like a dark slab of granite watching as Davey looked around in that puzzled "Where am I?" manner of someone waking in a strange place.

"Remember me? I'm Sophie. My students call me Miss B."

The towheaded child blinked stubby lashes and rubbed the sleep from his eyes. He sat up, the blanket falling to his waist.

Sophie grinned up at Kade. "Your shirt?"

A wry twist to one side of his mouth, Kade nodded. "My sweats, too. His clothes are in the dryer."

Davey pushed the cover away and stood. The oversize black pants puddled around his feet. Sophie laughed. "I need a camera."

Davey looked down, and then, too serious, glanced from Sophie to Kade and back again, eyes wide and uncertain.

"Guess what? We have some great new clothes for you. You want to look through the bag and find something you like?" She dragged the bag from the chair with a plastic thud against green shag carpet and pulled open the yellow tie. "There's a very cool sweatshirt in here. And wait till you see this awesome jacket with a hood and secret zip-up pockets."

She was rewarded when Davey realized her mission

and went to his knees next to the bag. Sophie held up a T-shirt. "What do you think?"

He nodded eagerly, then plunged his hands into the sack and removed a pair of cowboy boots. His whole body reacted. He hopped up, stumbled on his long pants and would have gone down if Kade, swift as a cat, hadn't caught him. "Easy, pard."

"I think he likes his new duds."

Davey held the boots up for Kade's inspection. Sophie watched with interest as the man pretended to consider before nodding his head. "Shoulda been a cowboy myself."

Davey's face broke into a wide smile. He plopped onto the floor and shoved at the too-long pants to find his feet. Sophie's smile widened. "Here, Davey. I think you could use some help."

Kade moved into action. "Why don't we find some jeans first and then try the boots?"

But Davey was already shoving his small feet into the brown-and-white-stitched footwear. His foot went in with an easy *whoosh* of skin against leather. Thrilled, smile wide enough to crack his cheeks, he leaned in to hug her from the side. Sophie's heart pinched. The boots were obviously too big, but Davey behaved as though she'd given him the best Christmas present of his life.

He levered himself up with her shoulder and attempted to clomp around, still grinning. The sweats puddled on the floor and tripped him up again. Kade reached out to steady him, expression inscrutable. "Grab him some jeans. I'll help him change."

Sophie did as he asked, touched when Kade hoisted Davey under one arm and carted him, boots, jeans and all, sweats flopping in the empty space beneath Davey's feet, to another room. Sheba padded softly behind, her nose inches from Kade.

Minutes later Sophie heard a *clomp, clomp* as the trio returned, Davey dressed in clean jeans, a Dallas Cowboys sweatshirt and the too-big boots. Kade had dampened the child's pale hair and brushed away the bedhead.

"Well, don't you look handsome?"

Davey beamed and clomped to her. Sheba followed, her nose poked beneath his hand as though expecting him to fall at any moment and prepared to catch him.

"I think the clothes are a hit," Kade said.

"The boots are for certain." Sophie dipped in the bag. "Davey, we might as well go through these and see what else you like. You can keep anything that fits."

As they rummaged through the hand-me-downs, Sophie was a little too aware of Kade kneeling beside her, his taut arm brushing hers as they pulled clothes from the sack. There was a stealthy danger about him, a rigid control she assumed came from his work in law enforcement. Special units, he'd said. Now she wondered what he'd meant.

She was holding a blue dress shirt under Davey's chin, his little arms spread wide to test the sleeve length, when they heard a car in the drive.

"Ida June?" she asked.

A minute later, the doorbell chimed. "Apparently not."

Kade shoved to his feet and went to answer. Sophie heard voices but thought nothing of them until Kade returned, trailed by a man in a business suit. Sophie's pleasure seeped away.

"Hello, Howard." She knew the social worker from

school and the times he'd come to interview teachers about a child's well-being. Good at his job, professional and thorough, she'd always been glad to have him in a child's corner. Until today.

"Sophie, how are you?"

"Great." She'd been better. "Is everything okay? Davey's doing fine here, as you can see. We're sorting through some clothes my students donated."

"Nice of you to take an interest. Tell your students thanks. We appreciate all you've done. Both of you."

"No problem. Davey's a good boy."

"The Cunninghams will be glad to hear that."

Dread pulled at Sophie's belly. "The Cunninghams?"

"The foster family. We got lucky. They can take him today."

Sophie made a small sound of distress. "He's doing fine here, Howard. Why not leave him with Kade and Ida June?"

"Neither has foster-parenting credentials or clearances. The Cunninghams are paper-ready."

"You've known Ida June forever and Kade is in law enforcement."

"The system doesn't work that way. Sorry. The Cunninghams are a good family with experience with special-needs children. He'll do well with them." Howard hitched the crease of his navy slacks and went to one knee in front of Davey. "My name is Mr. Prichard, Davey. You'll be coming with me today. There's a family waiting to meet you. You're going to like it at their house."

Davey frowned, bewildered gaze moving from Howard to Sophie and Kade.

"Howard," Sophie said, beseeching.

"I have a job to do, Sophie. Our department comes under enough fire as it is. We have to follow procedures." The social worker rose, matter-of-fact. "If you'd gather his belongings, he can take them along."

"This is all he has." The plastic bag crinkled as she pushed at it. A few hand-me-down clothes and an oversize pair of boots.

"More than most have, sad to say. Come along, Davey." The man grasped Davey's hand and started for the door. Davey jerked away and ran to Kade, throwing his arms around the familiar man's legs. Sheba whined and pushed against Davey's back. He fell against her neck and clung.

"Let him stay." Kade's voice was hard as granite.

Howard ignored the request. "Come now, Davey." When the boy didn't obey, the social worker scooped Davey into his arms and headed to the car. Davey squirmed but didn't make a sound. The silence was more terrible than any amount of crying.

Sophie followed, fighting tears, her throat clogged with emotion. She pushed Davey's beloved book into his hands. "It's okay, Davey. I know the Cunningham family. They're nice people. I'll call you. I'll come over and see you. We'll find your family. I promise. I promise. Don't be afraid."

Tense fingers caught her arm. Kade, face as hard as ice, said, "Don't make promises."

Sophie stopped in the driveway next to the black Taurus and forced an encouraging smile as the social worker buckled the little lost boy into the backseat. Beside her, Kade said nothing, but anger seethed from him, hot against the evening chill. She lifted her hand, waved and held on to the fake smile while the car backed into the street and pulled away.

A cold wind swirled around her, lifted her hair, scattered scratchy brown leaves across the pavement. The dark sedan turned the corner, out of sight now.

Sophie lowered her hand and stood dejected in the bleak afternoon. What a sad way to spend Christmas.

Be with him, Jesus.

Even though her prayer was heartfelt, Sophie knew little comfort. The sight of Davey's tormented face pressed against the window glass with silent tears streaming would stay with her forever.

Chapter Four

Kade wanted to punch something. Fists tight against his sides, he glared at the departing car, shocked by his reaction. He wasn't supposed to get personally involved. But he *was* supposed to protect and serve. With Davey gone to strangers, how could he do that?

Sophie touched him. A gentle hand to his outer elbow. A comforting squeeze and release. His muscles tensed. He turned from staring down Hope Avenue, a useless occupation considering the car was long gone, to meet the teacher's gaze. He didn't say what he was thinking. A woman like her wouldn't want to know, and as the dismayed shrink had discovered, Kade was not one to vomit his emotions all over someone else anyway.

"I don't know what to do," she said.

"Nothing we can do."

"This doesn't feel right. I don't know why exactly. We barely know Davey, but I'm worried about him. He seemed comfortable with us."

"Yeah." Kade pivoted toward the house. "Might as well get out of the wind. Want to come in?"

"No, I should go. I—" She pushed aside a blowing curve of hair, only to let it blow right back across her face.

"Come in. Finish your coffee." He wasn't ready for her to leave. They shared a common concern and a common ache. Sophie was a nice woman, the kind a man didn't blow off and leave standing in his driveway.

She didn't argue but fell in step beside him. Her height was average, as was his, but his stride was longer. She picked up her pace. "I hadn't read the book. I promised to read his book."

He'd told her not to make promises. Promises got broken. He pushed open Ida June's front door, a bright red enameled rectangle festooned with a smelly cedar wreath the size of an inner tube. "He'll be okay."

"The Cunninghams are good people. They live on a farm."

Sheba met them at the door, body language asking about Davey.

Sophie stroked the golden ears. "She didn't want him to leave, either."

"No."

"I'll call Cybil Cunningham tonight and check on him. She won't mind."

"Good." He went to the kitchen, stuck their coffee mugs in the microwave to heat. "This doesn't end here."

The words came out unexpectedly but he meant them. The microwave beeped and he popped the door open to hand Sophie her heated coffee.

She took the mug with both hands and sipped, gray gaze watching him above the rim. "You're going to search for his family?"

"I'm searching for answers. It's what I do. And I'll find them." The stir in his blood was far more potent

than the acid in his belly. Finding answers for Davey
gave him focus, a mission, something to do besides re-
live failure.

"The police will do that, won't they?" She set the
mug on the metal table and drew out a chair.

Kade shrugged. A lot she knew about law enforcement. "They'll try. For a while. But if the trail grows
cold, Davey will go on the back burner."

"And be stuck in the social system."

"Right." Restless, he didn't join her at the table, but
he liked seeing her there, calm to his anxious. How did
she do that? How did she shift into serene gear after
what had just happened? He knew she'd been emotional
when Davey left. He'd watched her struggle, saw her
pull a smile out of her aching heart for Davey's sake.
Now she drew on some inner reserve as though she
trusted everything would work out for the best. "I talked
to Jesse Rainmaker an hour ago. Nothing. Nothing on
the databases, either."

"I don't understand that. If your child was missing,
wouldn't you call the police?"

She was as naive as a baby, a cookie-baking optimist.
The thought tickled the corners of his eyes. "Maybe,
maybe not."

Her cup clinked against the metal top. "I don't know
much about this kind of thing, Kade, but I want to do
something to help Davey find his family. Please tell me
what you're thinking."

He was positive she didn't want to hear it all. "I can
think of a couple of scenarios. One, his family doesn't
know he's missing."

"That's unlikely, isn't it?"

"Sometimes parents are out of the house, at work,

partying. They come home a day or two later and find their kid gone. By tomorrow, someone should raise a shout if they're going to."

"What else?"

"His parents don't want him." He saw by her reaction how hard that was for her to comprehend. "It happens, Sophie."

"I know. Still…" Some of the Christmas cheer leached from her eyes.

"Davey is mute. A family might not be able to deal with that. Or worse, his parents may not be in the picture. Or he could have been missing for so long they aren't actively looking anymore."

A frown wrinkled the smooth place between her fascinating eyebrows. A face like hers shouldn't have to frown.

"Are you saying he might be a kidnap victim?"

"He's a little young to be a runaway. I searched the database of the Center for Missing and Exploited Children and came up with nothing, but that doesn't mean he's not a victim. It only means no one has reported him missing."

"Are you saying a parent would ignore the fact that their child is gone?"

"It happens. Kids are a commodity. You can buy them on the internet."

Sophie lifted a weak hand in surrender. "Don't."

Ignoring the problem didn't make it go away, but he bit back the obvious comment. Sophie was small-town sweet and innocent. She hadn't seen the dark side. She hadn't lived in the back alleys of the underworld.

Kade poured another cup of coffee, then shoved the

mug aside to take milk from the fridge. Something cool and bland might soothe the lava burning his guts.

"Kade?"

He swallowed half a glass of milk before answering. "Yeah?"

"You want to order some fifth-grade cookies to go with that milk?"

In spite of himself, he laughed. She was a piece of work, this cookie lady. "You're going to hound me."

"Gently. Merrily. It's a Christmas project. So," she said, with quiet glee, "how many dozen?"

"What am I going to do with a bunch of cookies?"

"Eat them, give them as gifts, have a Christmas party. The possibilities are limitless."

"I don't do the Christmas thing."

She didn't go there and he was grateful. He wasn't up to explaining all the reasons he couldn't muster any Christmas spirit. Or any kind of spirit for that matter. His faith hadn't survived the dark corners of south Chicago.

"Everyone eats cookies." Her smile tilted the corners of a very nice, unenhanced mouth. He wondered if she had a guy.

"A dozen. Now leave me alone."

His gruff reply seemed to delight, rather than insult. "You old Scrooge. I'll get you for more."

Wouldn't that be a stupid sight? Him with a bunch of Santas and stars and Christmas trees to eat all by himself. Or better yet, he'd stand on the street corner back home and hand them out. See how long before he got arrested.

"We were talking about the boy," he said.

She shrugged, a minimal motion of shoulders and

face. "Your stomach is bothering you. You needed a distraction."

Kade narrowed his eyes at her. "The cookie lady is a mind reader?"

"People watcher."

She *had* distracted him, although the cookie conversation was not as powerful as the woman herself. A less careful man could get lost in all that sugary sweetness.

He tilted his head toward the garage and the clatter of Ida June's old truck engine chugging to a halt. Before he could say "She's here," his inimitable aunt sailed through the back entrance and slammed the door with enough force to make Sheba give one startled yip.

"I heard what happened." Disapproval radiating from every pore, Ida June slapped a sunflower knitting bag the size of his gym bag onto the butcher-top counter. "I'll give Howard Prichard a piece of my mind and he'll know the reason why. Silliest thing I ever heard of. Jerk a terrified child from a perfectly fine place and take him to live with a bunch of strangers."

"We're strangers, too," Kade said mildly. Seeing her riled up cooled him down even though he appreciated her fire.

"Don't sass, nephew. What are you going to do about this?" With a harrumph, she folded her arms across the front of her overalls. Sheba, the peacemaker, nudged her knee.

Kade imitated her crossed arms and slouched against the refrigerator. "Find his family."

"I expected as much. Good to hear it." Ida June gave the dog an absent pat. Then as if she'd just realized someone else occupied the kitchen, she said, "Hello, Sophie. You selling cookies?"

Sophie set her cup to one side. "It's that time of year."

"Put me down for five dozen. Did you get this nephew of mine to buy any?"

The pretty mouth quivered. "A dozen."

Kade was tempted to roll his eyes because he knew what was to come from his incorrigible aunt.

"He'll have to do better than that. Stay after him."

"I plan to."

"I'm still in the room," he said mildly. The refrigerator kicked on, the motor vibrating against his tense back. "The least you can do is wait until I'm gone to gang up on me."

Aunt Ida June gave him a mock-sour look. "Crybaby. Is Sophie staying for supper? I made that lasagna last night and you didn't eat enough of it to feed a gnat. I refuse to feed it to Sheba." When the dog cocked her head, Ida June amended. "Maybe a bite. Well, is Sophie staying or not?"

Kade arched an inquiring eyebrow in Sophie's direction. He didn't mind if she stayed for dinner. Might be interesting to know her better.

He waited for her answer. An insistent, perplexing hope nudged up inside him.

Sophie rose from the table and pushed in the chair, as polite and tidy as he would have expected. Kade liked what he saw, and not just the fact that she was pretty as sunshine and looked good in a sweater. He liked the feminine way her fingertips glided along the top of the chair rung before straightening the hem of her blouse. And the way she met Ida June's gaze with straight-on, clear and honest eye contact.

A student of human nature, Kade could spot pretense in a second. There was nothing false about Sophie Bartholomew.

He hoped she'd stay for dinner.

"Thank you, Miss Ida June," she said. "But I have to say no. I promised to drop by my dad's this evening and help put up his Christmas decorations."

Kade's ulcer mocked him. All right, so she had a life. Other than Davey, she had no reason to stick around here.

"You're a good daughter," Ida June said, smacking her lips together with satisfaction. "You'll make a fine wife."

"I have a great dad." If Sophie thought a thing about Ida June's blatant "wife" remark, she didn't let on. Apparently, the citizens of Redemption were accustomed to his aunt's habit of saying exactly what she thought.

Sophie took her coffee cup to the sink and turned on the warm water. Above the *whoosh,* she asked, "How's the stable coming along?"

"Leave that cup in the sink. Kade's gotta be useful for something around here." Ida June shouldered Kade to the side and yanked a casserole from the refrigerator. She banged the sturdy glass dish on the counter and dug in the cabinets for foil and a spatula. The woman slammed and banged in the kitchen the same way she did on a job. With purpose and sass.

"You'll take your dad some lasagna." From Sophie's quiet acceptance, Kade figured she knew not to argue with Ida June. "Stable's nearly done. Would have been if Kade had been there. Makes me so aggravated not to be able to carry a four-by-eight sheet of plywood by myself." She flexed an arm muscle and gave it a whap. "Puny thing."

"Nobody would accuse you of being puny, Ida June." Kade moved to Sophie's side and reached for the coffee mug.

She scooted but didn't turn loose of the cup. She did, however, flash him that sunny smile, only this one carried a hint of his aunt's sass. "I can do it."

"Yeah?" he arched a brow.

She arched one, too. "Yeah."

Was the cookie lady flirting with him?

They jockeyed for position for a few seconds while Kade examined the interesting simmer of energy buzzing around the pair of them like honeybees in a glass jar, both dangerous and sweet. Danger he understood, but sweet Sophie didn't know what she was bumping up against.

Ten minutes later, he walked her out the front door, leaving Ida June to heat a spicy casserole that would torture him again tonight.

He opened the car door for Sophie, stood with one hand on the handle as she slid gracefully onto the seat. At some point in the day she'd changed her clothes from a long blue sweater to a dark skirt and white blouse. She looked the part of a teacher. Weird that he'd notice. "Don't worry about the kid."

Keys rattled as she dug in the pocket of a black jacket. "I won't. But I *will* pray for him."

His teeth tightened. "You pray. I'll find answers."

A cloud passing overhead shadowed her usual cheer. "We can do both."

"Right." God listened to people like Sophie. Kade still believed that much.

She started the engine and yet he remained in the open car door, wanting to say something reassuring and not knowing how. Life, he knew, did not always turn out the way it should.

"Kade?" she said.

"Yeah?"

She reached out and placed her hand on his sleeve. Her warmth, or maybe the thought of it, seeped through the thick cotton.

"Everything will be all right." Her gray eyes smiled, serious but teasing, too. "I promise."

The tables had turned. She was the one doing the reassuring. For two beats he even believed her.

Then he said, "Don't make promises," and shut the door.

"Dad, have you ever met Kade McKendrick?"

Sophie stood on a stepladder propped against her father's brick house, feeding tiny blue lightbulbs into equally tiny sockets. Next to her, on another stepladder, her dad attached strands of Christmas lights to the gabled eaves.

"Ida June's nephew? Yes, I've run into him a time or two. Why?"

"What was your impression?"

"Polite. Watchful. A man with something on his mind."

"Hmm." Yes, she saw those things. He was wounded, too, and maybe a little sour on the world. Beneath that unhealthy dose of cynicism, she also saw a man who didn't back down, who did what he promised. Although he had this thing about not making any promises at all. "Hmm."

Her father paused, one hand braced against brick

to turn his head toward her. "What does that *hmm* of yours mean?"

"I don't know, Dad. Nothing really." She didn't know how to put into words the curious interest Kade had stirred up. "He says he'll find Davey's family."

"Maybe he will," her dad said. "I heard he was an agent for the DEA."

"He mentioned special units, whatever those are."

"Could be DEA or any of the other highly trained groups. Seems strange, don't you think, for him to be here in Redemption doing odd jobs with a great-aunt?"

She took another bulb from her jacket pocket and snapped it into the tiny slot. "Maybe he's simply a nice guy helping out an older relative."

"Ida June? Older?" Dad snorted and turned back to his task. "I won't tell her you said that."

Sophie laughed. "Thanks."

"So what are you ruminating about?"

"When I mentioned praying for Davey, Kade threw up a wall of resistance. He did the same thing when I mentioned Christmas."

"Lots of non-Christians get uncomfortable with God talk, but Christmas is a different matter. Maybe something bad happened during the holidays?" He paused to take another strand of lights from her outstretched hand. "Or maybe the guy's a jerk."

"I don't think so, Dad. He was kind to Davey. Almost tender. You should have seen the pair of them digging through that bag of clothes."

"You like him, don't you?"

Her heart jumped, a reaction she didn't quite get. She *liked* everyone. "Beyond his kindness to Davey, I barely know him."

"I knew your mother was *the one* the minute I laid eyes on her."

Like a fly on her hamburger, the remark soured Sophie's stomach. How could Dad speak casually and without bitterness when Sophie still felt the disappointment as keenly as she had five years ago?

She pushed one final bulb into a socket and backed down the ladder. "Are we putting the sleigh on the roof this year?"

If Dad noticed the change in subjects, he didn't let on. With a sparkle in his eyes and the nip of wind reddening his cheeks, he asked, "Do elves make toys? Does Santa have a list of naughty and nice?"

Mark Bartholomew was almost as Christmas-crazy as his daughter, and every year they worked for days decorating first his house and then her little cottage. No matter how cold and fierce the wind or how many other activities they had going, this had become their tradition since the divorce. She'd started the practice so that the first holiday without Mom would be easier for him, but now she treasured this special time with her father.

"Did you see the new displays at Case's Hardware Store?"

"Saw them. Bought the praying Santa and the lighted angel." He clattered down the ladder.

Shivering once, Sophie slapped her upper arms for warmth. "The one with the flapping wings?"

"He's in the garage."

"Sweet." They exchanged high fives, the usual slap muffled by Sophie's gloves.

"I think we've done all the damage to the electric bill we can manage for one day," he said and started toward the porch.

Sophie followed her dad past the inflated snowman, through a door decked with green lighted garland and wreath, and into the living room where the old artificial tree their family had used for years now stood proudly in one corner. She knew he put the tree up for her sake, to keep the family tradition alive even with Mother gone. Life wasn't the same, but it was still Christmas.

With a sigh, she settled into Dad's big leather recliner while he fiddled with the switch on the musical bells and set them chiming. Lights blinked frantically to the tune of "Carol of the Bells." Cleo, the resident cat princess, mewed in plaintive protest and wound herself around Sophie's feet.

"Get up here, girl." Sophie patted her leg. The aging family pet blinked long blue eyes. Then to make sure Sophie remembered that *she* was the boss, Cleo ignored the offered lap and leaped easily to the back of the chair and stretched out.

"As independent as ever." Dad made one last adjustment to the lighted tree and stood. Colored lights flickered over his worn University of Oklahoma sweatshirt and reflected a rosy glow on his skin.

"Queen of her domain." Sophie reached over one shoulder to rub the arrogant cat. "The two of you are quite a pair."

"True. She's my buddy."

Cleo batted Sophie's fingers with soft claws and purred. The Siamese had been Mom's cat, but she'd left her pet behind along with her family. Sophie thought, not for the first time, how lonely Dad must be in this once-noisy, active house with only Cleo for company.

"Have you talked to Todd lately?" Her brother and his family were in the military, stationed in Ft. Hood.

Holidays presented a challenge for them, especially with his wife's family in Florida.

"A couple of days ago. They're going to her folks' this year."

"Imagine that," she teased. "Choosing the Sunshine State over cold and blustery Oklahoma."

"I like cold and blustery."

"Me, too. It feels like Christmas."

She had her father, her church, her students and most of all, her Lord. Christmas in Redemption, blustery wind and all, would be blessed and beautiful. If she sometimes wished for a family of her own, especially at Christmas, it was only natural. Thirty, that suspicious benchmark of spinsterhood, was only a few years away. Not that age bothered her all that much. It wasn't age that made her restless sometimes. But the occasional ache for a home filled with love and laughter and a husband and children was undeniably present. Christmas, especially, was family time.

Her thoughts roamed to Davey and then to Kade. What kind of Christmas would they have? Kade said he didn't "do the Christmas thing." What did he mean? Was Dad right? Had some painful event turned him off to the greatest event in history?

Cellophane crinkled as Dad handed her a red-and-white candy cane. The memory of Davey's book flashed in her head. Hadn't there been a candy cane on the front? Cybil Cunningham was a good woman with a heart for disabled children. Sophie hoped she'd read Davey's book to him. Maybe she'd drive out to see him tomorrow if Kade or the police didn't find where he belonged. She prayed they would.

She gave the peppermint a lick, her first taste of the

new Christmas season. "Do I get your special secret-recipe Bartholomew hot cocoa to go with this?"

"I'm on my way to the kitchen." Sophie started to rise, but her Dad waved her back down. "Sit. You're still not old enough to be trusted with the family secret."

With a happy hum, he disappeared around the wall. Sophie heard the clatter of drawers opening and a pot rattle against the stove top. For these few moments, she let herself be Daddy's little girl again, knowing how much pleasure he took in feeling needed.

She kicked off her shoes and curled her chilled feet beneath her, listening to the tinny melody of "Joy to the World" from the Christmas tree.

Her world *was* full of joy. She wished she could package the feeling and share it with those who found no pleasure in the season.

Kade encroached again, his handsome face serious, the brown eyes dark with some secret angst. Had something happened to steal his joy? Or was he just a guy with a negative attitude?

The cool, sweet peppermint melted on her tongue. From the kitchen arose the warm scent of milk and chocolate. The tree sparkled, a candle dripped cinnamon-scented wax, Cleo purred, warm and content against Sophie's neck.

Maybe Kade had never had this. Maybe he didn't know what he was missing.

Sophie took a deep pull on the sweet candy.

Maybe Kade was a Grinch by accident and needed help to find his Christmas spirit.

She offered up a quick prayer, certain the Lord had

something special in mind for Scrooge McKendrick this year.

Why else would a big-city cop show up in a small, Christmas-crazy town just in time for the holidays?

Chapter Five

The telephone rang at six. Kade grabbed the receiver on the first ring.

"McKendrick," Kade snapped before remembering. This was his aunt's home, not his work phone. He scrubbed a hand over his hair.

"I apologize for waking you," the male voice said.

Waking him? Wouldn't that be nice? He'd let Sheba out hours ago. Since then, he'd been lying on the ugly psychedelic sofa twiddling his thumbs.

"I'm up. Who's this?"

"Jesse Rainmaker at the police station."

The man worked long hours. "You have information on Davey?"

A hesitation. "We have a problem."

Kade's fingers tightened on the handset. "With Davey? What kind of problem? Is he all right?"

"I was hoping you'd know. He ran away from the Cunninghams sometime in the night. Mrs. Cunningham got up around three to look in on him and he was gone."

Kade fell back against the couch cushions and

squinted at the shadowy ceiling. "You think he's a runner? He's done this before?"

The furnace kicked on, shuddering in its old age. Faint heat eked from the floor vent to his cool sock feet. It was cold outside. Had Davey worn his new, hand-me-down jacket? The one with the blue race car on the back?

"Maybe. But a boy like that, without a voice, he's in danger wandering around alone." Rainmaker sighed, weariness heavy across the line. "The social worker told me how he reacted at your place. I thought you'd want to know."

Oh, yeah, Davey was in danger, all right. He couldn't ask for help. He couldn't even yell. And Kade definitely wanted to know. Sometime in the long hours of sleeplessness, the defenseless, towheaded boy with the worried face had become personal.

"Did you notify Sophie?" The woman had plagued him all night, too, with her Suzy Snowflake personality and soft gray eyes. Davey had latched on to her, and she'd be upset about this turn of events. He wished he could spare her the worry. Nothing she could do about it, but she'd want to know.

"I'll leave that to you," Rainmaker said. "My deputies are searching around the Cunningham home. We could use some help, someone Davey likes."

"Give me directions." Kade scrambled for a pen and paper, not trusting his memory in strange territory—another hard lesson learned.

Jesse rattled off a series of section lines and local landmarks, then rang off with a "Thanks." Kade needed no thanks. He needed to find that boy.

Already dressed except for boots and coat, he

shrugged into those, debating the phone call to Sophie. He wouldn't mind hearing her voice but not this way, not as the bearer of bad news.

Gritting his teeth, he whipped out his cell phone and punched in her name, glad they'd exchanged numbers, though at the time, he hadn't been thinking about Davey. He'd been thinking about those soft gray eyes and a softer smile.

Wishing for a pot of coffee, he listened in growing dismay at the *brrr* in his ear. This was Saturday. She would sleep late. Her voice mail clicked on.

"Merry Christmas," the recording said in that candy-coated voice. "You've reached Sophie Bartholomew. Please leave a message."

Easier this way, he thought. Much easier. At least for him.

Acid pooled in his belly. He rubbed the spot.

"Sophie, Kade McKendrick. Give me a call when you get this."

Why couldn't he do things the easy way? Why hadn't he just told her the situation and moved on?

He knew why. According to the shrink he had some kind of superhero complex. He could carry the weight. He could save the world.

Right. He snorted derisively. Tell that in the back alleys of Chicago.

When the phone in his hand suddenly rang, he almost dropped it. A quick glance told him Sophie had gotten the message.

"Hey," he said. "Sorry I woke you."

"You didn't. I was in the shower."

He carefully avoided going there. He was, after all, a man. "The police chief called."

"Davey?" Concern laced the word. Kade hated hearing it, hated knowing he'd put the worry there.

"He's run away from the Cunninghams."

She sucked in a gasp. "Oh, no."

"I'm headed out there now to help with the search. Thought you'd want to know."

"I'm coming. I'll meet you there."

"Get ready. I'll pick you up." He hadn't meant to offer, but he liked the idea of Sophie's soothing presence in his car. "You know the way?"

"Yes."

"Good. I don't."

He'd started to hang up when Sophie said quietly, "It's really cold this morning."

He understood her meaning. Davey was out there.

"Yeah." The chill in Ida June's house had kicked on the wheezing furnace numerous times during the night. "We'll find him, Sophie. Don't worry."

"Promise?" Her teasing words warmed him. He could hear her moving around, getting ready as they talked. He should hang up, but he was reluctant to let her go.

"No promises. Just action."

"I like the sound of that. Action and prayer work every time, and I'm already praying. God knows where Davey is."

"You let me know if He tells you."

He expected her to go all defensive on him, but instead she laughed. "I will. Have you had breakfast yet?"

Weird question. "No."

"I have coffee ready in the pot and yogurt in the fridge."

He made a face at the yogurt. "Bring me coffee and I'm your slave forever."

That warm, throaty chuckle filled his head. "I'm going to remember that."

They had a runaway kid to find and he was flirting with a schoolteacher. No wonder he'd lost his edge. Try as he might, he couldn't resist. And he didn't try too hard.

"Kade?"

"Yeah?"

"I'm joking around to keep from being afraid." Her admission softened him. If he wasn't careful he'd never get his edge back. "It's cold and dark and the Cunninghams live several miles out in the country." He heard her swallow. "Davey has to be scared."

"We'll find him."

Phone against his ear, he made his way through the kitchen toward the garage. He flipped the exterior light switch and started down the two steps toward his car.

"Well." He stopped dead still.

"What is it?"

"I don't think we're going to find him."

A pause hummed anxiously over the distance. "Why?"

Curled in the corner on Sheba's fluffy bed, with the big dog wrapped around him protectively, Davey lay fast asleep, his book clasped to his skinny chest. He wore the zippered jacket Sophie had given him.

"He found us first."

Sophie didn't consider anything odd about rushing over to Ida June's house at six in the morning. She pulled into the short concrete drive before the streetlights went out and the first streaks of sun broke the horizon.

Looking lethally male beneath the golden glow of porch light, Kade let her in. A kick of attraction hit Sophie in the empty stomach. Now that she knew Davey was safely in Kade's care, she took the time to explore the feeling. She hadn't been attracted this way in a long time, and considering Kade's dark broodiness, she was a little concerned by her judgment.

He hadn't shaved yet, naturally, given the time of morning, and a scruffy shadow of whiskers outlined his jaw and mouth. The bottom lip was fuller than the top and held in a grim line, as tightly controlled as his emotions. Everything about Kade McKendrick was close to the vest. His hair stuck up here and there, too, a messy look she found deliciously appealing. He looked like the kind of man with a holster under his shirt and a gun in the back of his jeans, the kind of man who'd fight for those he loved.

Be careful, Sophie.

She thrust a carton of yogurt at him. "Breakfast."

Kade lifted an eyebrow but didn't accept her offer. "You said coffee."

His male grumpiness tickled her. She sniffed the air, certain she whiffed fresh coffee already brewing. "Not a morning person?"

Eyes, dark as her favorite chocolate and more secret than the CIA, mocked her.

"*You* obviously are," he said.

"I am." She couldn't help waking up full of energy and happiness. Life was good. Mornings brought a clean slate, an empty new twenty-four hours to enjoy. "I'm also a woman of my word. Try this while yours is brewing." She handed over the thermos. "If it's any consolation, my dad hates yogurt, too."

"Man thing. You could have brought cookies instead." His tone was somewhere between a grouse because she hadn't and a tease. She liked when Kade teased. It was as if having fun was buried somewhere inside and on occasion bubbled to the surface like lava too long compressed. She'd have to work on unearthing his happy side more often.

"We can make cookies later," she said, and suddenly the idea of bumping around in a spice-scented kitchen with Kade sounded like a great way to spend a Saturday.

"Davey might like that."

She wanted to ask if Kade liked the idea, too, but she figured now was a good time to get her runaway brain under control.

"Is he still asleep?" They were standing in the entry, her view into the living area blocked by Kade's lithe, jean-clad body.

Kade nudged his chin to one side. "Back there. He needed a real bed for a change."

The reminder that Davey had likely slept out in the open for some time took her mind off the deadly handsome lawman. "May I look in on him?"

He set the thermos on the table—a sacrifice she knew—and led the way down a short hall to a bedroom. The door was open and Davey lay on his back covered to the chin. A furry dog snout was propped on his chest.

"Sheba won't let him out of her sight," Kade said in an undertone.

Sophie nodded. "As if she knows he needs her."

"She knows."

They watched the sleeping boy and dog for another

minute. Sophie grew more aware of the room, of the masculine trappings. A jacket here, a pair of boots there, the faint, lingering scent of male grooming. In one corner leaned a battered guitar. This was Kade's bedroom, although the covers on the bed were ruffled only where Davey slept. Had Kade not been to bed last night?

Davey squirmed in his sleep, and a frown passed over the small face. Sheba nuzzled his cheek, and Davey, eyes still closed, wrapped both arms around the dog's neck and settled.

Kade tugged Sophie's elbow. Even though she wanted to stay and watch the sweetness that was dog and Davey at rest, she trailed Kade back down the short hall to Ida June's blue-and-yellow kitchen. Colors of the sun and the sky, she thought, as though Kade's aunt wanted the beauty and freshness of a June day year-round. Sophie got that, although Christmas colors were her favorite.

"Have you notified the sheriff and the Cunninghams that Davey is here?" she asked, and then answered just as quickly. "Of course you have. Dumb question. You were a cop."

"Am." Kade poured himself a cup of coffee from her thermos.

"Pardon?"

"I *am* a cop. On R & R for a few months."

"You'll go back, then?"

"To work? Sure. Chicago?" He took a sip of coffee, closed his eyes either to savor the taste or to brace himself for the jolt. "The jury's still out."

She took the thermos from him and poured her own cup. "As in a real jury or metaphorically speaking?"

Kade smirked. "Both, actually. You want cream or sugar with that?"

"Yogurt."

His hand, halfway to his lips with another shot of caffeine, froze. "In your coffee? That's sick."

"I know." She gleefully stirred in a spoon, mostly to watch his reaction. Finally, he'd let his face show his true feelings.

He watched in horrified fascination as if she was about to eat a live snake. "You didn't do that yesterday."

"You didn't have yogurt." She took a satisfied sip.

Kade made a gagging noise.

Sophie giggled, almost spewing the mouthful. "Stop."

His nostrils flared with humor. "You're doing that to mess with my head."

She didn't remember when she'd started spooning yogurt into coffee, probably in college on a silly dare. Discovering she liked the odd, grainy combination had been the real surprise, although she normally reserved her yogurt coffee for quiet, alone times. Others didn't react well, as Kade so perfectly and delightfully demonstrated.

"Mostly. Is Ida June already up and out or are we disturbing her sleep?"

"We won't disturb her. Saturday is sleep day. She pokes earplugs in her ears, slides one of those weird masks over her eyes and threatens to disembowel anyone who opens her bedroom door before noon."

Sophie shook her head, amused. Ida June Click was, as her father said, a pistol. "Have you two always been close?"

"No." The teasing light flickered out. Oddly, abruptly,

he pushed out of the chair, went to the sink where he braced his hands to look out the window. Sophie had a feeling he didn't really see Ida June's backyard. And she wondered what can of worms she'd inadvertently opened inside the terse cop. Whatever had brought Kade to his great-aunt's home and to Redemption had followed him here unresolved.

Unsure where to tread, Sophie quietly sipped her coffee and waited him out. She studied him, lean waist and wedge-shaped torso taut, the leashed strength in his bent arms quivering with some deep emotion.

"I'm going to fight them over Davey," he said softly.

Puzzling, interesting man. "I am, too."

He whirled then as if he'd expected argument and gave one short nod. "Good. We're on the same page. He's not going back. One of us will take him."

"Until his family is found."

The heavy dose of doubt shadowed his secret eyes again. "Nearly eighty percent of runaways and throwaways are never reported missing by their families. Did you know that?" He tossed the numbers out as in challenge, teeth tight, eyes narrowed. "Eighty percent."

Throwaways? Never reported? Did such horrors really happen? "I can't believe Davey is either. He's young and cute and this is Oklahoma!"

She saw the eye roll he held in check and practically heard his thoughts. She was naive, a Pollyanna, sheltered.

"He's also handicapped. Granted, Davey's a little younger than usual, but facts are facts. Sometimes no one cares if a kid disappears."

Sophie didn't want to believe him. Children were a treasure from the Lord, not discardable afterthoughts.

But Kade's adamant anger gave her a peek inside his head. He spoke from experience and that experience had left him bleeding.

Lord, You've put this man and this child in my life for a purpose. What now?

A quiet rustle of movement stopped the conversation as Davey rounded the corner into the kitchen. With sleepy eyes and a bedhead of pale, unruly hair, he was the cutest thing. Heart melting like a hot marshmallow, Sophie hoped he hadn't heard the unsettling conversation. She cut a glance toward Kade and marveled at the instant change in him. He'd gone from Doberman-like fierceness to the gentleness of the golden dog trailing the child into the kitchen.

"Hey, buddy." He went down on one knee in front of the little boy. "Feel better?"

Davey nodded, then walked into Kade's chest and snuggled his chin into his hero's shirt. Kade's eyelids fell closed. One blunt-nailed hand cradled the mussed head as he drew Davey close. Sheba, the shadow, crowded against both males and nudged Davey with her nose.

"Chief Rainmaker should be here any minute." She set her cup aside. "What will we tell him?"

Kade gazed at her over Davey's shoulder. "That's up to Davey." Holding the child by the shoulders, he eased back to make eye contact. "Why did you run away last night?"

The child shrugged, expressive face worried. She recognized that look. The one she'd seen on a number of faces over the years. A boy who knew he'd done wrong and now had to face the consequences.

"Were the Cunninghams nice to you?"

Davey nodded, then pointed, one by one to Kade, Sophie and Sheba. And finally back to himself.

"Oh, my goodness." This little blue-eyed boy was quickly worming his way into her heart. She went to the floor beside him. "I think I understand." She touched his hair, smoothing a lock that sprang right back up. "You want to stay with one of us. With Kade or me. Is that right?"

A huge smile displayed several half-grown permanent teeth. He nodded vigorously before throwing both arms around Sophie in a bear hug. She rubbed her hands up and down his back in a gesture she frequently used with upset students. Touch, she was convinced, relayed emotion words could never speak. Davey's small fingers kneaded in the hair at her shoulders like a motherless kitten.

"Listen, buddy." Kade gently took Davey by the arm and turned him around. The small, sleep-scented boy stood between the adults in a cradle of care and protection. "Sophie and I will try. We can't make any promises, but we'll try. We want you to stay with one of us until we can find your family."

Davey's eyes widened in worry. He shook his head side to side.

"I'm getting confused here," Sophie said. "Either he wants to stay with us or he doesn't."

Kade shot her a look. "Or he doesn't want us to find his family."

Davey whapped an attention-getting hand on Kade's shoulder and nodded. Sophie's heart sunk lower than an open grave.

"That's it, isn't it, Davey?" Kade asked. "You don't want us to find your family."

The saddest expression came over the small, round face and tears welled in cornflower-blue eyes. He lifted his shoulders in a helpless shrug that both confirmed and confused.

"But that doesn't make sense. Why would he not want you to find—" At Kade's expression, Sophie stopped in midsentence.

He had that look again, the one she'd noticed yesterday in the trash bin. Anger and despair.

His bizarre reaction set her imagination into high gear.

Did Kade's moodiness have something to do with kids like Davey?

Chapter Six

Shortly after nine, the social worker arrived along with Chief Rainmaker. By then Kade was ready for a fight. Itching for one. Something was way wrong in Davey's world, and hard as he tried not to go there, Kade imagined the worst.

After sharing kitchen duty with Sophie to prepare a decent breakfast for Davey—an event he'd found pleasantly distracting—they'd settled at Ida June's Chippendale coffee table with a deck of cards Sophie had supplied.

"I'm a teacher," she said when he'd raised a curious eyebrow at some of the things she'd taken from the oversize tote. "What can I say? Always be prepared."

"Better than a Boy Scout," he'd replied. She'd rewarded his joke with a smile.

Now he was teaching Davey the fine art of War, a man's game if ever there was one. Davey, the little wart, had quickly discovered the joys of taking his adult opponents' lower-numbered cards and was amassing quite a pile. The silent, breathy giggle was heartbreakingly cute. Cute enough to make Kade mad all over again. Somebody was gonna pay for this boy's pain. The sooner he could get back into the investigation the better for everyone.

When the doorbell chimed, Kade left his two guests to battle for the remaining dozen cards.

"He's staying," he said to the social worker the minute they shook hands. If the abrupt statement shocked Howard Prichard, he didn't let on.

"Chief Rainmaker filled me in on the details." Prichard ran a speculative gaze over Kade's face. "I'm still curious as to how a little boy who'd been here only once could find his way back."

Kade bristled. Was Prichard making an accusation? "So am I, but he did. Ask him yourself."

He whirled and led them into the living room just as Davey slapped a nine on Sophie's two. Sophie pretended insult, laughing, and Davey's face glowed with pleasure. When he saw Howard Prichard, the pleasure evaporated. He bolted up from his spot on the floor beside the coffee table and looked wildly around. Sophie took his hand and tugged. The boy collapsed against her, clinging.

Kade ground his back teeth in frustration. "Thanks to your red tape he was up half the night, in the cold, and vulnerable to *any* kind of predator." He hoped Prichard had sense enough to understand that predators didn't have to be wild animals. "He stays with me and he stays safe."

Sophie, with more diplomacy than Kade could muster, levered up from the floor and brought Davey with her still clinging. "Why don't you gentlemen sit down so we can discuss Davey's situation? Would you care for some coffee?"

"Nothing for me, Sophie. Thanks." Jesse Rainmaker stood behind Ida June's stuffed chair, his thick brown fingers resting on the green upholstery. He was solid and calm and coolheaded in the way Kade once had been. Stay aloof. Don't let it touch you personally. It's all about the job.

"I'm fine, too. Thank you," Prichard said, waving away her offer as he settled on the sofa.

Good, Kade thought. Much as he respected Rainmaker, he was in no mood to be hospitable. Forget the coffee and niceties. He wasn't letting another kid slip through the cracks.

With a soothing hand on Davey's back and while holding him close to her hip in a protective, motherly manner, Sophie said, "Howard, I'm sure we can work out a reasonable solution to this problem. You've known me for years. My school does background checks on everyone and I've taught in this town long enough for you to know I care about children. Kade McKendrick is a police officer with federal-level clearances living here with Ida June Click, whom you've also known forever. They are certainly capable of caring for Davey until his family is found."

Kade shot her a sour look. He would find Davey's family. Nothing could stop him. But he wasn't expecting them to want Davey back. Miss Optimistic couldn't get it into her happy head that the world wasn't all cookie-nice and Christmas-peaceful.

"I'll take him," he said to Sophie. "You have your job and your Christmas projects."

"As long as he's with one of us." She rubbed the back of Davey's hair as he gazed up at her, listening to every word. The kid was sharp. Had to be to find his way here in the dark. It would sure help if he could talk.

"What do you say, Howard?" Sophie insisted with gentle steel. "Can we work this out?"

The social worker shuffled through a briefcase. Kade's fist tightened at his sides. A boy shouldn't be at the mercy of a piece of paper.

"Chief Rainmaker and I have discussed the situation at length. I also spoke with the foster family. First, though, I'm duty-bound to interview the child."

"The *child* has a name," Kade said with more vehemence than he'd intended.

Prichard gave him a reproving glance. "The chief and I will need to talk to Davey alone."

"No."

"Mr. McKendrick, I'm not the enemy. We all have Davey's best interest in mind. A man in law enforcement should understand the need for cooperation in these matters."

Sophie's soft fingertips grazed his arm. "Kade, let's go in the kitchen and have another cup of coffee." To Davey, she said, "Davey, these men are only going to talk to you. They are not going to take you anywhere. Okay?"

The kid looked doubtful. Kade bent to whisper in his ear. "I'll tackle them if they try. Deal?"

Davey hunched his narrow shoulders in a shy grin and nodded. After a few more words of assurance from both he and Sophie, Kade scooped Davey up in a football hold and planted him in a chair in front of the social worker. Rainmaker came around front and went to a knee beside the chair. Kade felt better knowing Rainmaker was in the room. Rainmaker and Sheba. With a wink, he chucked Davey under the chin before following Sophie into the kitchen.

Sophie held up the carafe. "Do you really want more of this? It smells like burned rubber."

She'd hoped her statement, though basically true, would lighten him up.

"I'll pass." Kade went to the fridge for a glass of milk, his glare focused on the living room.

"They aren't here to hurt him, Kade." She mustered up her best soothe-the-beast voice, the one she used when fifth graders fought to a point of hysteria. Most times Sophie didn't let anything make her anxious for long, but Davey could be an exception. He was so vulnerable, no doubt the reason Kade was wound up tighter than a double Slinky on steroids.

"Sorry to get intense on you." He downed the milk and then plunked the glass in the sink with a frustrated sigh. "I'm a little edgy this morning."

Only this morning? Sophie stifled a snort. When was Kade *not* edgy? "Davey's blessed to have you in his corner."

He rubbed a hand over the back of his neck, shot a glance toward the quiet mutter of voices in the living room. "You, too." He grinned then, a tiny thing, but a grin just the same. "We're quite the pair of crusaders, aren't we?"

They were. He, intense and cynical. She, the eternal optimist. "We're a good balance. And we both care about that little boy in there."

"Someone needs to."

"Agreed. I have a plan. Want to hear it?"

"There's a choice?"

She made a face at him, even though she was pleased at the humor attempt. Maybe she'd lighten him up after all. "I think Howard will go for it."

Howard Prichard appeared in the doorway. "Go for what?"

Davey scooted under the social worker's arm and rushed to Kade. Sheba scooted in behind him, toenails slipping a little on the linoleum in her hurry to keep up.

"Davey needs to be in school, but because it's only three weeks until Christmas break and we aren't sure how long it will take to find his family, I have a somewhat creative suggestion. That is, if you're agreeable to Kade and Ida June being his temporary foster family. Along with Sheba, of course."

"It's all about the dog," Kade muttered.

Sophie shot him an amused glance.

Prichard smiled, too. "Yes, he is fond of the dog. For a child who can't speak, he can make his wishes very clear. I think we can all agree that the best thing for Davey at this point is to be in an environment where he feels comfortable and safe. From all appearances, that's with one of you. So, if the plan is acceptable to all parties, Davey will remain here temporarily. We'll file this as an emergency placement and take care of the details as we go."

Relief came swiftly, a surprise because Sophie hadn't realized how anxious she'd been. God always worked things out, didn't He? "Other than finding Davey safe in Kade's garage, that's the best news of the day. Thank you, Howard."

"What was this plan of yours?"

"School."

"Yes, school is an issue. With his special needs, testing and paperwork will be required. We'll have to start from the beginning and do a complete battery, including IQ, placement, hearing, vision." He sighed and straightened a conservative blue tie. "Everything."

"Let me talk to my principal. I think we can work this out. With only three weeks remaining until Christmas break, I'm going to suggest that Davey be allowed in my classroom to help with the annual cookie project. At various times throughout the day, the special-needs department can pull him out for preliminary placement tests and make suggestions for after the holidays. I can pick him up each morning and bring him back each evening."

Kade shifted toward her, eyeing her curiously. "You don't have to do that."

"I want to. If it's okay with him. What do you say, Davey? Would you like to go to school with me and have fun with some other kids?"

A frown appeared between Davey's blue eyes. He looked to Kade.

Kade lifted his palms in a helpless gesture. "School's a given, buddy. Everyone goes."

Davey shook his head back and forth and shrugged. The adults exchanged looks. Kade bent to the child. "Haven't you been going to school?"

Davey shook his head no.

"Never?"

Another no, accompanied by a very worried expression in eyes as blue as a cornflower crayon.

Kade's jaw flexed. He blew out a gust of air. "Well, that puts a new spin on things." He placed a hand on Davey's shoulder. "No sweat. Sophie will take care of you. Right, Miss B.?"

Sophie smoothed the top of Davey's hair and let her hand rest there. The once-matted moptop was silky smooth and clean, thanks to Kade and Ida June. "Absolutely. You can go to school with me and I'll take care of everything from there. Okay? I don't want you to worry one bit. It's Christmas time! The best time of year. Worrying is against the rules at Christmas." With more cheer than she felt, she playfully tapped his nose. Davey rewarded her with a rubbery, close-lipped grin. "We'll have so much fun, making and decorating cookies and getting ready for the Bethlehem Walk and the Victorian Christmas events. You're going to love those. You might even want to be in the parade."

Davey's eyes widened at the mention of a parade. He nodded eagerly.

"Well, it's all settled, then," the social worker said. "The pair of you seem to have the situation in hand, so I'll leave you to work out the details. Call me if any problems arise." He handed Kade a business card. "I'll be in touch Monday."

As soon as the other two men left and Davey was busy wrestling Sheba for a chew toy, Sophie said, "I should go."

"Why?"

The blunt question surprised her. "I don't know."

"Then stay." He shoved off the doorjamb he'd been holding up. "Davey."

Oh, right, for Davey. Of course, for Davey. What was wrong with her? "Saturdays are normally pretty full, but I can stay awhile until we're sure he's all right."

"I can't believe he's never been to school. Do you think perhaps we misunderstood?"

"No." Kade made a noise of frustration. "I was hoping to trace school records. Easy to find a person that way. Which means the investigation into his identity just got tougher."

"Oh." She hadn't thought of that. She knew nothing about investigating a lost child or anything for that matter. Police work was off her grid. Where would he start? How would he ever discover anything about Davey's past?

They both stared for one silent, concerned beat at the boy happily playing with the affable dog. When Kade pushed a hand against his stomach—a stomach she knew bothered him when he worried—Sophie knew she would stay awhile. There were two males here that needed fixing and she was a fixer.

"There's only one thing we can do at this point," she said.

The cynic raised a doubtful eyebrow. "What?"

She grinned a cheeky grin. "Bake cookies."

The place was chaos. Granted, her classroom was *organized* chaos, but noisy and vibrant just the same. Far different from the quiet Saturday morning spent baking cookies with Davey and Kade. Two males, one terse and one mute, didn't generate a lot of noise. Nonetheless, Sophie couldn't get them out of her head this busy Monday as she and her fifth graders began the cookie project in earnest.

Sophie stole a quick glance toward the narrow window in her classroom door—a tiny space surrounded by bright paper poinsettias and shiny red garland—praying the noise didn't seep out into the hallway and disturb the sixth graders next door. More than that, she hoped the principal didn't decide to pay an unannounced visit to her classroom today.

"Miss B., our group estimates eight pounds of flour." The speaker was Shyla, a red-haired girl with freckles across her nose. Her twin, Skyla, listened in with an identical, perplexed expression. "Zoey's group says we need five. Who's right?"

A babble of voices from surrounding groups all tried to speak at once, defending their estimations. Each year she divided the students into cooperative groups with diverse assignments. Set up in pods around the room, they began with math, estimating and figuring amounts of supplies needed for their groups' baking, costs of the goods, expected gross and net profits. The early days were always the most chaotic as kids got the hang of the project. Sophie, of course, loved every minute of it, even though she went home every evening exhausted.

"I think we have a mistake here somewhere, Shyla." She tapped a finger against Shyla's notebook figures. "Look at your recipes. Take the amount of flour you need for each batch of cookies. Multiply times the number of batches. Then divide that into the number of cups in a pound of flour. Remember, we're using an estimate here to have plenty."

Shyla's eyes glazed over. Sophie laughed and turned the child toward the screen hanging on the wall. "The data is on the SMART Board. Go. Check your figures. Teamwork, sugar doodle. And remind Trevor I'll need his cost estimate once you're done."

Shyla scooted away, a frown between her eyebrows as she and her twin debated the figures. Across the room Zoey, the local vet's daughter, ran her fingers across braille instructions and spoke to her best friend, Delaney Markham. Sophie's heart warmed at the way the two little girls had latched on to Davey and drawn him into their group. In two hours' time, the blind girl and the mute boy had worked out a simple, effective process of communication with bouncy blonde Delaney as their go-between.

Sophie's thoughts drifted to this morning when she'd picked up Davey for school. He had been nervous and uncertain about this new adventure even though she and Kade had reassured him in every way they could think of. It was hard to know what worried a child with no voice to express his feelings. So far, he made no attempt to communicate in writing either, a fact that concerned both Sophie and the special-needs director.

Wanting to be sure he was okay, she made her way to the pod of four children seated around a grouping of desks. "How are things going over here?"

"Good. We have everything done except our grocery list." Zoey typed something on her laptop.

"How about you, Davey? Everything okay?"

He nodded, his gaze moving around the classroom with avid interest.

"He's helping us, Miss B.," Delaney said. "He'll be real good at decorating. See?" She tugged a drawing from beneath Davey's hand and pushed it toward Sophie. "He's drawing and coloring the cookies so we can have a plan of attack when we start working."

Sophie's heart warmed at the obvious attempt to include Davey. "I knew this team was perfect for him."

She leaned down to hug the girls' shoulders.

"You smell good, Miss B."

"Well, thank you, Zoey. So do you."

The dark-haired girl beamed. "Mom let me use her sweet pea spray."

"Mom" Sophie knew was actually her stepmother, Cheyenne Bowman, who ran the local women's shelter. Zoey, already a strong child thanks to her father, had bloomed with Cheyenne in her life.

"Miss Bartholomew?" Delaney said. "There's a man looking in our door."

Sophie's heart clutched. Biff liked order and quiet. He'd been accepting of her plan for Davey, but he was always a little sketchy about her loosely structured activities.

She schooled herself to turn slowly and remain composed as though her classroom was not the loudest in the building. Before her brain could sort out the man's identity, Davey shot up, nearly knocking over his chair, and raced toward the door.

Sophie's heart clutched for a far different reason. Kade McKendrick's brown eyes squinted through the glass. When he caught her eye, he pointed a finger at Davey and raised his eyebrows.

By now, Hannah, the nosy Rosy of fifth grade, had spied the visitor and plowed through her classmates like a bowling ball to open the door.

"Thank you, Hannah." Sophie parted the sea of nosy students.

"Who is he? Davey's dad?" Hannah shoved her glasses up with a wrinkle of her nose and peered intently at Kade. "Are you Davey's dad? Why can't he talk? Is he really in fifth grade? He looks too little to me."

Davey had Kade's legs in a stranglehold. Kade

looked at Sophie with a dazed expression. "You do this all day?"

Sophie chuckled. Everyone asked that.

Irrepressible Hannah hadn't budged. "I'm Hannah. If you're not Davey's dad, who are you? Are you Miss B.'s boyfriend? My mom says she's too pretty to be an old maid, but she never goes out with anyone. Wait till I tell her."

Face heating up faster than a cookie oven, Sophie said more emphatically, "Hannah, please. You may go back to your group now."

The serious tone did the trick. Not the least offended, Hannah returned to her group, but the frequent glances and loud whispers about Miss B. and her boyfriend kept coming.

"Sorry," Sophie said, cold hands to hot cheeks. "Hannah is a gossip columnist in training."

"I shouldn't have interrupted." He pointed back down the hallway, his tan leather jacket pulling open to reveal a black pullover. He looked really good this morning, shaved, hair in an intentional muss, and he smelled even better. She'd yet to distinguish his cologne, but she'd know it anywhere. The musk and spice had tortured her, deliciously so, on Saturday and had stayed in her head all day Sunday. A man had no right to smell better than chocolate-chip cookies.

"I checked in at the office," he was saying. "The security in this building is terrible. No visitor's badge. No ID. Nothing."

"Redemption is a safe town. We trust people."

"I don't."

"Really?" She cocked her head. "What a news flash."

He curled his lip at her, more a cynic's sneer than

a smile. "How's Davey handling all this…this—" he waved a hand around the room "—whatever it is."

"We're doing our groundwork for the project. Zoey, Delaney and Ross have taken him under their wing. He's thriving, aren't you, Davey?"

Davey nodded, though both adults figured he didn't comprehend the word.

"Having fun, eh, buddy?" Kade asked.

Davey nodded again and pointed at his group. The little girls waved while Ross, as blond as Davey and easily the brightest boy in the class, scribbled away at his notebook. His dad was the town physician and Ross already felt the pressure to succeed. A serious kid, Sophie put him in Zoey's group to brighten him up. No one could hang out with Zoey and Delaney and not have a good time.

"How do you actually bake cookies in here?" Kade asked. "No oven."

"We have some volunteer moms who head up the groups on baking days while the cafeteria ladies supervise the ovens. It works."

"Crazy." Expression still wary and a little dazed, he patted Davey's shoulder and said, "Head back to the group, buddy. I need to talk to Miss B."

Davey clung for one more leg hug before doing as he was told.

"He's adjusting," she said, gaze following Davey until he settled again. As she turned back to Kade, the now-familiar tingle of awareness started up again. She tamped it down. This was her classroom and her students were her main focus, not Kade, no matter how appealing or unnerving. "At first, he was very shy, but now that he knows his little group, he's loosening up more."

"Anyone giving him a hard time about his voice?" From the narrow gaze and hard tone, he might have added, "If they are, I'll beat them up."

The thought, of course, was ridiculous. Sophie couldn't quite envision a grown man, a law-enforcement professional, going toe-to-toe with a ten-year-old. But Kade would definitely protect and defend.

She smiled, glad he couldn't read her thoughts. "Kids are curious, but no one is cruel. They're used to Zoey's blindness and I think that helps them accept others with disabilities. But just in case, I put him with a group of very nice children."

"Glad to hear it." He shifted, hesitated, then cleared his throat. "I guess I should go."

He pivoted to leave.

"Wait." Sophie caught the slick leather of his jacket and held on as she cast a practiced glance over the classroom. The students were working cooperatively. Loudly, but without problems. No need for Kade to rush away. Davey was clearly reassured by his visit. Okay, so she was a little juiced to see him, too. No harm in that, was there? "Any progress today on Davey's identity?"

"Nothing concrete. I spent the morning with Jesse Rainmaker. Good man."

"He is."

"He's doing all his small department can do." His expression said that wasn't enough, and she was sure Jesse Rainmaker felt the same. A small-town police department stretched to have the resources and manpower for daily operations.

"So, where do we go from here?" Sophie turned to

watch her class while listening to Kade. Group work could go sour quickly without her watchful eye. "I want to help, but I don't know what to do."

"I'm getting the word out. Rainmaker's men, when they can, are doing a house to house. I put a notice in the paper this morning along with the snapshot you took of Davey and Sheba." He shifted again, boots scuffing on the tile, obviously out of his element in a classroom full of ten-year-olds. Dads almost always reacted this way. Uneasy, watchful, cutely pathetic until they'd acclimated. She loved when dads visited. Not that Kade was anyone's dad, but still…

"What about the surrounding towns?" she asked. "I'm convinced Davey is not from Redemption."

"I'm working on that. I have a list of area newspapers to email or telephone this afternoon. Hopefully, with enough publicity, we can dig up someone who knows something."

From the back of the room, a strident voice called, "Miss B., Jacob is not cooperating. He says the cookie project stinks and I stink." The speaker sniffed his sleeve. "I don't stink and if he doesn't shut up, I'm gonna…"

Sophie lifted a palm up like a stop sign. "Stop. Right there." To Kade, she said, "I have to get back to business."

"Need me to knock a couple of heads?"

She wasn't sure if he was joking. "Maybe later."

"Anytime." He backed out of the room. "See you after school."

Davey saw Kade's intention and rushed his knees again. Sophie, already on the move toward the disagreement in the back, figured Kade could handle Davey. By the time she'd settled the argument and looked up again, Davey was back at the tables with his group, her door was closed and Kade was gone.

Chapter Seven

Kade didn't know why he'd gone by her classroom. Well, other than Davey. He'd wanted to check on the boy, make sure the arrangement was working out. But he could have called.

No. Better to see for himself.

He groaned. He'd never been one to second-guess every decision. He'd been decisive, sure, confident.

Before.

But wasn't that part of the reason his department had sent him to a shrink and put him on extended leave? He'd lost his confidence and with it the edge needed to do what he did.

He snicked the lock on his car, the cherry-red paint job bright and shiny in the cold sunshine.

Who was he trying to fool? After a discouraging morning of following dead ends, he'd wanted to look into Sophie's clear, pure eyes, listen to her soothing voice and try to believe that life wasn't always ugly. With her optimism, she had almost convinced him on Saturday that Davey was simply a lost child and some frantic mother was desperately searching for him. Cold reality had struck him between the eyes in the police chief's office this morning. No one in the state was looking for a blond, blue-eyed boy with no voice.

Still, Saturday had been…nice. Over a batch of lop-sided sugar cookies, formed into shapes without benefit of fancy cutters, Kade had spent a few hours of peace.

The kicker had come when she'd asked him and Davey to church. To her credit, she'd taken his refusal in stride just as she'd done the first time she had tried to sell him cookies, as if she knew she'd win in the end. She wouldn't. He didn't belong in church anymore, but Davey had gone with her and had come home with a red Kool-Aid ring around his happy mouth and a col-ored picture of the baby Jesus. The kid was bursting with pride that left Kade with no choice. He'd taped the purple Jesus to the refrigerator.

A cloud moved over the pale sun, casting a weak shadow. A piece of notebook paper somersaulted across the street to catch in the chain-link fence surround-ing the school. In this quiet residential neighborhood, cars motored slowly past, a dog trotted toward the play-ground and from somewhere he heard the buzz of a chain saw.

People went about the daily business of life oblivi-ous to the lurking danger.

He'd been trained to see it, trained to a paranoia with-out which he would be dead. A week ago, he wouldn't have cared one way or the other. But now—now, he had a purpose named Davey.

Sophie's soft expression flashed behind his eyelids.

One hand on the open car door, Kade squinted back at the elementary school. No gate secured the building from the street, and the school was wide-open, not a security guard anywhere. Anyone could walk in there and execute a tragedy in a matter of seconds. Didn't these small-town people watch the news?

A bell rang and the double doors burst open, spewing out a running, shoving mass of very small children who barreled toward the playground behind the school. Two teachers, neither of them Sophie, followed the pack. One spotted him and said something to the other. He waited to see if either would accost him, demand his name and business. After a moment of staring, they huddled closer into their coats and disappeared around the corner.

Frustrated, he slammed his car door, jabbed the lock remote and headed back inside the school building. Davey and Sophie were in this place. The principal, whoever he was, was about to get a crash course in safety.

Sophie rubbed her hands over her face and took a deep, cleansing breath. She was tired. Good tired. Today had gone well and each group was ready to move forward with the shopping segment of the project. Carefully organized folders filled with data, shopping lists and cost estimates waited on the back shelf for the volunteer mothers who would do the actual shopping.

The stapler *click-clacked* as she added a candy-cane border to the green butcher-papered bulletin board. Except for this last board, she almost had her classroom covered in Christmas decorations. The students had helped, of course, adding their artwork to the room. Shiny red garland draped from corner to corner. Multicolored lights chased one another around the door and window. Mercy Me's Christmas CD spun out a version of "The Little Drummer Boy."

She sighed. Life was good.

A hand tugged on her arm. She looked down into Davey's enormous blue eyes. He pointed at her face and pulled down the corners of his mouth.

"No, I'm not sad. Just tired." She smiled to prove as much.

The kids had made paper elves to hang from hooks on the ceiling and the accordion-pleated legs bounced up and down every time the heater activated. They made her smile. Everything in this room filled her with happiness. She could never be sad here. Tired, yes. Sad, never.

"You know something, Davey?"

His eyebrows arched in question.

"You're a very nice boy. Being sensitive to other people's feelings is a wonderful gift. You have that."

He returned the smile and without being asked began to pick up the stray bits of green paper she'd dropped.

Regardless of Kade's suspicions that Davey had been abused or come from a terrible background, Sophie saw signs that someone had taught him well. She'd studied abused children, had encountered some, too, and he didn't fit the mold.

But then, as Kade said, she was an optimist who believed the best.

Kade. Seeing him had stirred up the memory of last Saturday and she'd been distracted more than once today thinking about him. They'd baked cookies with Davey, and when the child wandered into the backyard to play Frisbee with Sheba, Sophie had lingered longer than she should have. Long enough to know she liked more about Kade McKendrick than his crisp good looks.

Beneath the aloof demeanor lived a good person with a powerful sense of justice. He'd find a way to help Davey.

Finishing touches on the bulletin board complete, she unplugged the cinnamon-scented candle warmer and reached inside a file cabinet for her handbag. A knock sounded at her door. A silly, surprising hope leaped to the fore. Kade? Come to retrieve Davey?

"Come in."

Biff Gruber, as tidy as he'd been eight hours ago, stepped into the room. "Sophie, I'm glad you're still here."

"You just caught me." Vaguely disappointed, she forced a friendly look. She hoped he hadn't come to complain about the noise. "How was your day? I saw the fourth-grade teacher hauling Marcus Prine toward your office after lunch."

Biff's eyes crinkled. "I earn my paycheck with Marcus and his mother."

"Roberta rushed to defend him, I suppose." Roberta Prine, a main-street beautician, gossip and all-round trouble stirrer, was raising two sons much like herself.

"Yes, but Roberta's visit isn't what I want to discuss with you." His tone went serious and he got that stiff I'm-the-principal look. "I am concerned about your friends who pay unexpected visits to school."

Uh-oh. She set down her handbag and stood behind the desk, glad for the three feet of distance between herself and her supervisor. This was her safe zone, the spot she chose when dealing with prickly parents.

"If you are referring to Mr. McKendrick, who

stopped in to see how things were going with Davey, he checked in at the office."

"His classroom visit is not what I wanted to discuss, although from reports he may have overstayed his time limit. Really, Sophie, the classroom is not the place to entertain male guests."

Sophie bristled. "Biff! I can't believe you said such a thing. You know me better than that."

"Yes, well." He jerked his cuff. "Mr. McKendrick seems unduly concerned with your safety and welfare. He barged into my office complaining about the lack of appropriate security and explained how he could have wiped out the entire student body in seventeen seconds."

Sophie's lips quivered. She pressed them in, bit down hard for a second to stifle the laugh. Biff was not in a laughing mood. "He said that? Seventeen seconds?"

"Something to that effect. I was momentarily stunned after he charged in like a ninja."

Oh, no, she *was* going to laugh. Please, Lord, hold me back. "He is rather ninjalike, isn't he?"

"This is not amusing, Sophie. I run a tight ship and we ascribe to the safe schools' programs. We have policies in place to secure our students' welfare in every area of the campus."

"Kade is in law enforcement, Biff. Perhaps he had some useful ideas?"

"Well, yes," Biff conceded, though she could tell he didn't want to. "We can always improve. Every school can, not just us. But frankly, I didn't appreciate the man's attitude."

Sophie had seen Kade's attitude in action. "I'm sorry. He can be a little…foreboding."

His gaze snapped to hers. "Are you seeing him?"

Sophie blinked, more than a little surprised. Was that what this conversation was really about?

Respectfully, softly, she said, "As my supervisor I'm not sure you have the right to ask me that."

Biff relaxed his stance, his gaze searching hers intently. "What about as your friend, Sophie? You have to know I'm interested in you."

A sharp pain started behind her eyes. Sophie fought down the urge to rub the spot. "You're my principal, Biff. It wouldn't seem right."

"There are no rules in our school against dating a colleague."

Biff would know the rules. In fact, he'd probably scanned the handbook and ethical-conduct forms before coming to her classroom. Now, what could she say?

"You're a wonderful principal, Biff, and I respect you tremendously…"

A hint of color appeared on his cheekbones. "Apparently, I've spoken too soon. I've made you uncomfortable."

She inclined her head. He certainly had. "Thank you for understanding."

"Yes, of course." He glanced around at the vibrant display of all things Christmas, stiff, embarrassed and probably hurt. Sophie did not like to see anyone hurt, and she had the awful need to make him feel better. He was a fine man. She had nothing against him. But he wasn't… Kade.

Oh, dear. How had Kade McKendrick invaded her life with such rapid ease?

"Your classroom looks festive," Biff said just as Mercy Me kicked into "Winter Wonderland."

"Thank you. The kids and I enjoy it." She fiddled

with the straps on her purse, hoping he'd leave before her internal fixer said something she'd regret. All the while, her head whirled with thoughts of Kade. What if they *were* seeing each other? How would she feel about that?

"The new boy is doing all right, I suppose?" Biff asked, apparently in no rush to leave. Or maybe he, too, wanted to mend fences and part on a positive note.

Davey, carefully cutting a paper snowflake the way she'd taught him, seemed oblivious to the adult conversation. She was glad. This whole scenario was embarrassing enough as it was.

"Very well. He's a nice child. A little sad at times, though that's to be expected given his strange circumstances," she said. "He's no trouble at all, and I think my class of natural mother hens is exactly the right group for him."

"This arrangement in your classroom is only temporary until he's tested and placed."

She tilted her head in agreement. They'd discussed Davey's placement in detail. Why did he feel the need to beat a dead horse?

"By then, he'll be more comfortable, I'm sure. Or we'll have found his family." She refused to consider that he might have no family, as Kade seemed to think.

"The special-needs director suggested he see an ear, nose and throat doctor."

"I'll pass that information on to his social worker," she said. "The holidays may interfere with appointments until after the New Year."

"Understandable." Biff studied Davey with professional concern. "He's certainly an interesting case."

Davey wasn't a case to her. He was a helpless, vulnerable little boy who'd stolen her heart the moment she'd seen him clutching a day-old hamburger.

"Speaking of holidays, Sophie, I know you're heavily involved in the upcoming community events as well as spending time with Davey. Are you sure you have time for the cookie project this year?"

A little warning bell jingled. "Are there still complaints?"

"I'm afraid so."

She bit back a frustrated groan and tried to joke. "Maybe if I baked this Scrooge a batch of cookies?"

"Probably wouldn't hurt." Biff allowed a smile. "I should let you get home. Your father left an hour ago."

Sophie relaxed at his friendlier tone. Somehow she'd managed to soothe his ruffled ego, and for that she was thankful. "That's because I've already decorated Dad's classroom." She picked up a stack of papers and her handbag. "Are you ready, Davey? Sheba's probably missing you a lot by now."

The little boy bolted upright with an eager nod.

Sophie came out from behind her desk and clicked off the CD player.

"Sheba is Kade's dog," she explained to Biff. "Davey's crazy about her."

"A boy and a dog are a match made in heaven." The principal touched her elbow. "I'll walk you to your car."

At the risk of completely alienating her principal, she didn't argue. After all, he was walking her to the car, not asking her to marry him.

They were almost to the door when a golden dog streaked inside the classroom followed by a lean, athletic form. Sophie didn't have a thing to feel guilty about, but with Biff's fingers tight on her elbow and Kade glaring like the grim reaper, she blushed anyway.

"Excuse me, I didn't mean to interrupt." Kade heard his tone—a cross between a growling dog and a meat grinder—and realized he spoke through clenched teeth. He couldn't say why, but the sight of the school principal in Sophie's classroom set his nerves on edge.

"We were just about to leave." Sophie stepped away from the principal's grasp. "Is everything all right?"

Would have been if he hadn't just been hit with a sharp pain in his solar plexus. "I came to pick up Davey. You're late. Sheba was driving me crazy."

That was true enough. The dog had paced, whined at the door and had dragged Davey's pillow into the living room. The minute they'd barged into the classroom, Sheba had made a beeline for her new charge. Davey had fallen on her neck with obvious adoration. A man could get jealous about losing his dog that way if the sight wasn't so rewarding. Davey needed Sheba in his corner.

"I think you've met my principal, Mr. Gruber."

Kade gave a short nod. "We've met."

"McKendrick." Gruber was stiff as a two-by-four. "Back again so soon?"

"Walked right in." Kade itched to tell the stuffed shirt how easily he'd entered the building with no challenge, no visitor's card, no one to stop him if his intentions were evil.

To Gruber's credit, he only said, "You can be assured, it will not happen again." He turned, again stiffly, to Sophie. "I'll see you tomorrow, Sophie. Good night."

As soon as Gruber was out of hearing range, Sophie

said, "You're full of sunbeams this evening. Want to go Christmas shopping? Santa is making an appearance at Benfield's Department Store. You can tell him your wish."

He glowered at her, but he wasn't annoyed. Not at her anyway. Sophie was the bright spot he needed after a discouraging day. Even though he was glad to be focused and working again, he'd hit enough dead ends to make him wonder if Davey had dropped from the sky. "This school is an open invitation to trouble."

"Biff said he's working on it." Jingle bells dangled from her earlobes and a small reindeer pin blinked from her shoulder. She arched a sassy eyebrow. "Seventeen seconds?"

The muscles in his back relaxed. "He told you?"

"About your ninjalike visit to his office? Uh-huh." Face alight with amusement, she hitched an overstuffed schoolbag over the blinking Rudolph. "You made quite an impression."

"I might have exaggerated a few seconds." He jerked his chin toward the giant clock on the wall. "It's long past three."

She grimaced. "I should have called you. There's so much to do this time of year. I have trouble leaving on time."

"As long as Davey's all right." *And you.*

He felt stupid to have been worried, but after surveying the poorly secured building, his mind had run scenarios all afternoon from black-cloaked teens with AK-47s to kidnappers in cargo vans snatching kids from the soccer field.

"He's done well today, Kade." Sophie lowered her voice, even though Sheba and Davey were several yards ahead, bopping down the hall toward the exit. "The special-needs teacher did some preliminary testing."

He slid her a glance. His eyes wanted to stay right there, focused on that sweet, gentle face. "Bad?"

"He has some basic skills, but he's nowhere near grade level. He tests at late kindergarten, early first grade, although we suspect he should be in second or even third."

"Figures." The kid hadn't been in school. Period. Wherever he'd been, whatever someone had been doing with him, academics had been ignored.

By now, they were outside. The wispy, swirling clouds and tempestuous wind threatened a weather change. They made him edgy, stressed, as if a storm was coming and he couldn't stop it.

He hoped with everything in him that the wrong person didn't discover Davey's whereabouts.

"I'm parked in the teacher's lot," Sophie said, pausing at the place where the chain-link fence opened to the street.

"I'm over there." He motioned needlessly to the sports car parked at an angle next to the curb. She couldn't miss it. Davey was already there, waiting. Kade lifted his remote to open the door and watched as boy and dog clambered inside.

Still, Kade lingered, not quite ready to let her go.

"I'll see the pair of you in the morning," she said, that mile-wide smile lighting her eyes.

"We need to talk."

She stopped, turned, curious. "Okay."

"Do you have dinner plans?" Probably. With Gruber. Although, hadn't the overzealous student in Sophie's classroom said Miss B. didn't date much? Try as he might, Kade couldn't be sad about that little piece of information.

"No."

"We could get a pizza."

Her face brightened. "Sounds good. Pageant practice starts tonight, so an early dinner is perfect. Want to come?"

"For pizza? I invited you, remember?"

Her quick popcorn laugh was exactly the reaction he'd been shooting for. Mt. Vesuvius in his gut settled a little.

"No, silly, to practice," she said. "Tonight is an organizational meeting to determine parts and such."

He sort of knew that. Ida June was building the Nativity scene at town center where the pageant terminated in some kind of town free-for-all, and she kept his ear full of Redemption's Christmas festivities whether he wanted to hear them. The whole idea gave him hives. What was there to celebrate? A bunch of greedy people making a buck in the name of Jesus? Or the upsurge in domestic violence and drunk driving inherent in the holiday? Give him a padded room first.

"I'll pass on the pageant," he said. "Thanks anyway. Meet you at the Pizza Place."

Sophie tried not to feel hurt, but Kade's abrupt departure as well as his gruff refusal had stung. He'd reacted the same way to a church invitation, but this was different. Kind of.

As she'd driven to the restaurant, she'd had a good talk with herself. Whatever gnawed at Kade had nothing to do with her. She just happened to be in the line of fire. Either that or she was unintentionally pushing all the wrong buttons.

Now, as she sat across from him, downing pepperoni pizza and bubbly fountain soda, she decided to clear the air.

"Why do you get prickly every time I mention Christmas?"

He was in midbite, a string of melted mozzarella stretching from a rather attractive mouth to the pizza slice. Okay, so his mouth was *really* attractive. Firm, sculpted, with tiny brackets on either side. Davey sat next to him, the towhead barely reaching Kade's elbow in the deep booth. Kade had dropped Sheba at the house with the promise to both dog and boy to save a slice for her.

He chewed and swallowed, an amazing accomplishment considering how tight his jaw always was. "I told you I'm not much on Christmas."

"Why?"

"Too commercial. Crime rates skyrocket."

"I've heard people say that."

He peered at her over his soda. "But you don't agree."

She intentionally shook her head hard enough to make the bell earrings jingle. "Didn't you have Christmas when you were a boy?"

Something passed over his face but was gone faster than Davey's first pizza slice. "Sure. I was a kid. Kids do Christmas. They don't know any better."

She was certain he wanted to say more. Certain there was a "but" at the end of his sentence. But something had changed him, something had stolen his childlike belief in all things Christmas.

"I believe," she said simply.

"In Christmas?"

"And in the reason for Christmas. Jesus."

"Yeah."

Was that a "yes, he believed in Jesus," or a polite acknowledgment of her faith?

She leaned forward, put a hand on his forearm. It was rock-hard with hewn muscle. "Christmas really is the most wonderful time of the year, Kade. So many good things happen. People give more, reach out more. I know there's trouble in the world. There always has been. There were griefs and heartaches when Jesus was born. He faced plenty of His own, but He never let that stop Him from sharing joy and peace and love."

He made a soft noise, not quite a harrumph or a humbug. More of an interesting-but-I-don't-want-to-talk-about-it sound.

"Did you ever read the *Grinch Who Stole Christmas?*" she asked.

"You saying I'm a Grinch?" Was that a sparkle she spotted behind that scowl?

"No, I'm saying I have the DVD. If you want I can bring it over sometime for Davey to watch. Or he can come to my house." There were lessons to learn in that simple Seuss classic.

Davey leaned forward, eagerly nodding.

"Looks like that's a yes." She handed Davey a napkin. "I'll loan it to you tomorrow. I loved the cartoon version when I was a kid."

"Me, too." Kade's admission was almost as good as an all-out victory. He *had* liked Christmas at one time.

"Christmas at our house was such fun," Sophie said, with a nostalgic smile. "Dad was one of those Santa Claus kind of fathers who made tracks outside our house and jingled bells in the middle of the night. My brother and I would go crazy with excitement."

"Sounds great."

"Yes, it was. The best Christmas we ever had, though, was when I was sixteen. We didn't exchange gifts that year. We spent Christmas Day at the church serving meals and handing out gifts to anyone who needed them." Her heart warmed with remembrance. "I experienced Jesus in a new way that year, and it's stuck with me. I learned giving really is more fulfilling."

Kade gazed at her with a bemused expression. "You must have great parents."

"I do." Or rather did. A shadow passed over the nostalgic mood. "They're divorced now."

She could almost hear his brain cranking out cynical comments. *See,* he was probably thinking, *life really is lousy.* But Sophie would never believe that. Bad things happened, but all in all, life was good and Christmas was better.

"Divorce can't erase those wonderful memories. My brother, Dad and I still talk about them."

"What about your mother?"

"She lives in Tulsa with her new family. I generally see her on Christmas Eve, but it's not the same, of course." In fact, chitchatting with Mom, Edward and his adult children was an evening to endure, not to enjoy. Her brother, Todd, hardly ever came anymore, which made things at Mom's house harder. Mom tried to include her, but Sophie was the fifth wheel, the one who didn't really belong. She'd much rather be here in Redemption with Dad and her friends.

"What was Christmas like in your family?" she asked.

He pushed aside a plate of pizza crusts. Neat little semicircles of leftover bread lined the edges of the dish. Next to him, Davey was beginning to slow down, too.

"Two older sisters. Mom's an executive accountant and Dad's a hotshot lawyer. We had lots of presents."

"Were you the spoiled baby brother?"

His lips curved. "Something like that."

Elbow on the table, she leaned her chin on the heel of her hand, fascinated to think of Kade as a small boy. "Tell me about a typical Christmas at the McKendrick house."

He hitched a shoulder. "Open gifts, maybe go to Grandma and Grandpa's house. Hang with the cousins, play football or torment our sisters."

"I can see you doing that." Which led her right back to the same question. What soured him on Christmas? "Are you going to Chicago for the holidays?"

When Davey stared at him with interest, Kade ruffled his hair. "Don't worry, buddy. I'm not going anywhere."

Kade's gaze found hers and held. She understood. He was here until Davey's mystery was resolved. Sophie appreciated him for that. When Kade started something he finished it, and he did it with a fierce passion.

"Am I being nosy if I ask how you're related to Ida June?" Sophie asked, eager to know more about this man she couldn't get out of her head.

"Nosy? Yes." He softened the answer with twinkling eyes. "But I'll tell you. She's my grandmother's sister."

"Is your grandmother anything like Ida June?"

"If you mean does she drive backward down the street and spout quotations, no. But they are both strong, feisty ladies who can take you down with a hard look."

"You always know where you stand with Ida June."

"Grandma, too. That's why I'm here." As soon as the words leaked out, Kade shut down again. The light in his face evaporated and he shifted uncomfortably in the booth.

"You know I'm dying to ask," Sophie said.

"Long story." Kade wadded a paper napkin and tossed it on the plate. "Ready, Davey?"

Davey slid the leftover pizza and bread sticks into the takeout box and made a petting motion with one hand.

"For Sheba," Sophie interpreted. She reached for the check, but a strong hand trapped hers on the table.

"My treat."

The quiet insistence warmed her. Here was a man whose pride might suffer if she said no. "Okay. Thank you."

Still, he didn't remove his hand and she began to notice the subtle differences in his skin and hers, the long length of his fingers, the leashed strength.

A flutter tickled beneath her ribs. She lifted her gaze to his.

"I should go," she said softly. Regretfully. "Practice."

"Right." He freed her hand, flexed his once before snatching up the check. "What time?"

"You're coming?" She sounded like a ten-year-old elated over a trip to Disney World.

"Davey," he said, pushing up from the padded seat. "He can go."

"I was hoping you'd reconsidered. The pageant is wonderful, Kade. I promise you'll feel more Christmas spirit if you attend." She couldn't keep the disappointment from her voice. He *needed* to get involved. She was sure of it.

"Not this time. Sorry."

Her optimistic spirit soared. *Not this time* could only mean one thing: there was still a chance, and if anyone in town needed a little Christmas spirit this year, it was Kade McKendrick and the mute child he'd taken under his wing.

Chapter Eight

"Who spit in your sandbox?"

Kade slouched in front of the laptop, jabbing keys with enough force to jiggle the table. Ida June stood with one hand on her hip and a chocolate-chip cookie in the other.

Davey was fast asleep, exhausted from his day at school and the excitement of whatever he'd been doing with Sophie.

Ida June poked at his shoulder. "GI Jack saw you eating pizza with Sophie B. You after that girl?"

Sophie. The woman was giving him no peace. Just like his great-aunt.

"Strictly professional."

Ida June made a rude noise. "I didn't think my sister's daughter would raise such a stupid child. 'Who can find a virtuous woman? Her price is above rubies.'"

"I don't think Sophie's for sale, rubies or not. She's all about cookies."

Ida June whacked his shoulder. Cookie crumbs scattered down his shirt. "I'm gonna have to call your mama, boy."

"Tell her I love her."

"Tell her yourself." She slapped a cookie on the table beside him.

Kade closed the laptop with a snap and took up the cookie. No use trying to work with Ida June on him. He'd call his mother in his own good time, when he was ready to give her something besides bad news about her son.

"How was work on the stable?" he asked.

"Slow. I need you back out there tomorrow."

"I can give you a couple of hours." The rest of his hours, both day and night, would be focused on solving this case.

"And then?" The metal chair legs scraped against linoleum as Ida June perched across from him. She stacked three more fat cookies in front of her. "You got any leads on our little guest?"

He sighed in frustration. "None."

"You will. It's early yet."

Much as he appreciated her confidence, he wasn't so sure. "It's as if he fell from the sky."

"Well, maybe he did." She pointed half a cookie at him. Melted chocolate oozed out in a thick glob. "Miracles happened at Christmas."

Kade squinted at her. "You been in the eggnog, Auntie?"

Ida June slapped the table and cackled. "Life is sure perky since you moved in."

"Yeah, I'm a barrel of entertainment."

"You'll be happier when you get involved."

His great-aunt was pushier than his shrink—a shrink he hadn't called since Davey entered his life. He hoped the agency didn't send out the guys in white jackets to see if he'd offed himself.

There was no use denying his unhappiness to Ida June. She was in on the conspiracy to get him out of Chicago, though like his family, she didn't know the complete story. Even his supervisors had only part of the picture. Fine with him. If he let his mind go there, to what he'd seen and done in the name of justice, he'd be a dead man.

For a while he had been. Then a blue-eyed boy with no voice had given him a reason to keep putting one foot in front of the other. Sometimes the voices in his head said he was trying to make amends, but he knew he couldn't. Not ever.

"I am involved." When Ida June lifted an eyebrow, he went on. "With Davey. He matters." The words sounded angry.

"No argument from me. But he's a child and children need Christmas." His aunt patted the back of his hand with her leathery fingers and rose to rummage around in the kitchen cabinet. "Wherever he came from, whether good or bad, Davey has to be full of heartache. If he's lost from his family, he misses them terribly. If something else—" she paused, drew a breath, the wrinkles in her white forehead gathering in concern "—well, all the more reason for him to grieve."

Kade leaned back in the chair to study his aunt. She was eccentric but also wise. "What are you saying?"

"Keep him busy. Redemption is a loving place at Christmas."

"Sophie's taking him to some pageant thing tonight." His belly started to hurt. He shouldn't have eaten the cookie.

"Good. You go, too."

He wished for an antacid. Or anesthesia. "I'll pass."

Ida June snapped around with a glare. A cabinet door banged shut. "Not and live in my house, you won't."

Or maybe a quick poison. "Blackmail, Ida June?"

She gave him a spunky little grin, like a possum. "Your choice, nephew. You could move elsewhere, but think about Davey. He's just now settling in."

Kade rubbed a hand over the back of his neck. Sure, she was wise, but she was also pushy. He didn't *do* Christmas. Why couldn't the females in his life get that through their heads?

His own thoughts circled around to replay. Was Sophie part of his life now? Did he want her to be? The better question was, could he allow her into a life as messed up and confused as his?

"What do you want me to do?" he growled.

"When Sophie B. shows up to get Davey boy, you just pack yourself right on out the door with her."

"You go. Christmas doesn't interest me." Maybe he should record the announcement for playback at the appropriate moment.

"You're going to deny that poor child in there a little holiday happiness?"

Kade clasped his hands over the back of his head and stared at the ceiling in exasperation. Ida June would not back down. She would not give up. At this juncture, he hadn't the inner reserves to fight her. "All right, I'll go, but that's it. Don't ask me to do more."

"Ask her to help you put up a tree, too."

His hands dropped to his sides. "Didn't you hear a word I said?"

She leveled an index finger at his nose and ignored

the protest. "A real tree, too. Not one of those plastic things."

He glowered, hoping to shut her up. He didn't.

"She's a sweetheart, our Sophie B.," Ida June said merrily. "A man couldn't do much better."

Mt. Vesuvius churned to a boil. "I agreed to a Christmas tree for Davey. Leave Sophie out of this."

"You don't think Sophie's pretty?"

Ah, man.

"She's beautiful. And kind and good." All the things he wasn't.

She also lingered in his head like a sweet fragrance, a song he couldn't stop humming. Being around her eased his conscience, calmed the churning in his belly *and* in his soul.

He dropped his head to his hands and rubbed his eyes, tormented and confused. He had no business getting involved with Sophie. But he wanted to more than he'd wanted anything in a long time. So much so that he was tempted to pray. Not that God would listen.

Ida June lightly touched his shoulder and when he didn't look up, she gave him two gentle pats before padding softly from the room.

Davey was a shepherd boy.

A swell of maternal pride rose in Sophie as the towheaded child, along with several others, tried on various robes and headpieces in pursuit of an appropriate costume for the Journey to Bethlehem parade.

They were inside the community center two blocks from the center of town. Dozens had gathered in the wide space for the meeting, some wanting character or singing parts, but most, like Sophie, taking on tasks behind the scenes. The majority of character parts were played by adults, but they'd made an exception for Davey and a few other children. Davey's expressive face was alive with excited pride at being chosen.

Standing next to Sophie, hands shoved deep into his jacket pockets, Kade murmured, "You must have pulled some strings."

"I might have put in a word with the director," she admitted, grinning up into his face. She was still surprised to find Kade here after his earlier refusal.

"How did you get Sheba in on the act?" Kade hitched his chin toward the big dog sitting patiently while Davey placed a halo around her ears and tied angel wings over her back. Catching the adults' attention, Davey pointed at the retriever and laughed his silent laugh.

"Sheba doesn't seem to mind, does she?" Sophie asked.

"She's crazy about him."

"So am I," Sophie admitted.

"I know what you mean. As if he's always been here." And then, half to himself he added, "Wonder why that is."

Since the moment Kade had appeared at Ida June's wreath-laden door behind a spotless, eager Davey, Sophie had had butterflies in her stomach. A few hours ago, they'd been having pizza and getting better acquainted, but she felt as though she'd known him much longer than a few jam-packed days. In reality, she didn't know him at all, but there was something, some indefinable pull between them.

Maybe their mutual love for a lost little boy had connected their hearts.

"Christmas is about a child," she said. "Maybe God sent him."

One corner of Kade's mouth twisted. "Now you sound like my great-aunt."

"She's a very smart lady."

"More than I realized," he said softly, a hint of humor and mystery in the words. "A good woman is worth more than rubies."

"What?" Sophie tilted her head, puzzled. Even though she recognized the proverb, she wasn't quite sure where it fit into the conversation.

"Something Ida June said."

"Ida June and her proverbs." Sophie smiled up at him. "What brought that one on?"

Kade was quiet for a moment, his gaze steady on hers. He gently brushed a strand of hair from the shoulder of her sweater, an innocent gesture that, like a cupid's arrow, went straight to her heart.

"You," he said at last.

Sophie's heart stuttered. Although she didn't quite get what he meant or why he was looking at her so strangely, a mood, strong and fascinating, shimmered in the air.

Their eyes held, a kind of seeking for answers neither of them had. All Sophie had were questions she couldn't ask. So far, every time she'd approached the topic of his life in Chicago, Kade had closed in on upon himself and locked her out.

A good woman above rubies, he'd said. Had he meant her?

"Sophie!" Someone called her name from the other side of the room. She startled. Kade's fingertips skimmed down her arm, steadied her and brought her back to the large, noisy room. Then, he stepped away and broke the curious mood. But for a heartbeat of time, the festive noise of Christmas had faded into the background. And they had connected.

Had Kade felt it, too? Or was Sophie in danger of becoming one of those single women who imagined herself in love with every man five minutes after they met?

No, she wasn't imagining anything.

Something deep and elemental had stirred when Kade McKendrick looked into her eyes.

Flummoxed, face warm enough to blush, she forced a light laugh. "Better get busy before they fire me."

The cynical curl of lips returned and pushed her away again. "What's your part in all this?"

"Refreshments."

She hoped no one had noticed her staring at Kade like a lovesick teenager. She wasn't a teen and she wasn't lovesick. She was…something.

Sophie swallowed down the crazy stir of confusion. "I'm in charge of concessions. Along with some great volunteers, fifth grade sells cookies, coffee and hot chocolate during the event."

Was her voice as strained and tinny as she thought?

If it was, Kade didn't let on. Or he didn't notice. "Cookies," he said, amused. "I should have guessed."

Sophie's tension evaporated. Cookies had a way of calming anyone.

"So," she asked. "Which job do you want?"

He drew back, frowning. "Me?"

"You're here." She raised both palms. "This is a meeting of volunteers."

"I'm with Davey." He jerked a thumb toward the

child, who was now shoving his skinny arms into an oversize brown robe.

"Coward." She made a teasing face.

His scowl deepened. "Don't push me, lady."

She gave his shoulder a playful shove. He growled and bared his teeth. Sophie wasn't the least bit intimidated. She laughed. So did Kade.

The sound shot straight to her center and settled like a melody. Happy and light.

Davey heard it, too, and flapped a hand engulfed by a too-long sleeve in their direction.

"Better rescue our boy," Kade said.

Sophie nodded, caught on that one troubling, inadvertent turn of phrase. Our boy. He'd meant nothing by it, of course. It was simply a light and easy term of endearment.

But suddenly Sophie couldn't get the phrase out of her head. She'd always planned to have children someday.

What would it be like to say "our boy" to Kade and really mean it?

The next week passed in a blur as Sophie taught school, ran the cookie project and volunteered for every Christmas event Redemption had to offer. And there were plenty. When he'd cooperate, Kade came along. He came because of Davey's involvement and perhaps because of Ida June's pushiness, but knowing she wasn't the reason didn't stop Sophie's pulse from jumping or her smile from widening.

Her friends had started to tease her about the time she spent with Ida June's mysterious nephew. Even her father noticed and asked what was going on. All she

could honestly say was that she and Kade shared a mutual concern for Davey. And if they spent more and
more time together because of the lost little child, what
harm was there in that?

Kade was frustrated to the point of fury over the lack
of progress in Davey's case. He blamed himself, though
Sophie didn't understand why. When she'd asked, she'd
gotten one of his black silences in reply. He'd made an
early escape that night, too, now that she thought about
it. The "why" in Kade's life was one of his hot buttons.
Press for details, and he withdrew.

Sophie considered pumping Ida June about her nephew's mercurial moods, but that seemed so junior high.
If Kade wanted Sophie to know about his past, good
or bad, he'd tell her.

Yet, she suspected something bad had gone down, either professionally or personally. Something bad enough
to leave him wary of letting others close.

On this particular night, with the crisp December
air clear enough to see the stars like a billion diamonds
against black velvet, Sophie slapped her gloved hands
together for warmth and stood outside a makeshift concession kiosk. The Journey to Bethlehem procession
wound in slow, stately fashion toward Town Square.

Although her toes tingled from the cold, Sophie's
whole body warmed with pleasure at the sight of a
very serious and proud Davey following the procession. Brown shepherd's robe flowing, he kept one hand
on the shepherd's crook and the other on Sheba.

Beside Sophie, Kade snapped photos with her digi-
tal camera and made pithy comments that reminded
her of his great-aunt.

He gave a thumbs-up as Davey passed.

A quick smile of half-grown teeth flashed in reply. Kade snapped another photo.

Watching the interaction between boy and man touched Sophie. She saw the exchange of glances, the silent communication. She noticed, too, the hero worship in Davey's eyes and the worry in Kade's. He was growing to love the little boy, whether he knew it or not.

So was she.

Man and boy. Boy and man.

Davey's section passed, moving on toward Town Square. Sophie stood on tiptoe, watching until she could no longer see Davey's brown striped headpiece.

Kade lowered the camera and asked, "Can you take a break from the concession?"

She'd been working the booth since the town began filling with people two hours ago. Her toes were numb and her nose was as red as her sweater, but she'd sold plenty of cookies with her fifth graders and their moms.

"My shift is over. From the looks of the crowd, people are focused on the parade now. The rush will come afterward."

He hooked a hand around her elbow. "Good. Let's go."

A local church choir began to sing "Oh Come, All Ye Faithful," a fitting song for the entourage moving in a steady stream down Grace Street. Sophie fell in step next to Kade, glad for his grip on her arm in the thick crowd.

Along the route, they passed vignettes of actors: Joseph and the expectant Mary, the shepherds in the field, the heavenly host of angels, the search for a room, all ending in the crude stable Ida June and Kade had erected at Town Square.

Music swelled the night air and filled downtown with the wonder and beauty of that first Christmas. Goose bumps prickled Sophie's arms, though not from the cold. To her, this night and the retelling of the birth of Christ was the most special of all Redemption's Christmas celebrations.

With only a little imagination, she could see the angelic host hovering above and hear their hallelujah chorus.

The procession would be repeated several times during the evening, but the largest crowd came early and lingered in the town and in the community center to savor the joyous feelings. And spend money, as Kade had cynically reminded her.

She'd made a face at him, but his comment troubled her. He was enjoying the evening, she was certain, if only for Davey's sake.

A familiar woman turned to say hello. Her eyes widened in speculation when Kade slid his grasp from Sophie's elbow to her hand. He tugged lightly, closing the space between them.

"Crowded," he said by way of explanation. "Don't want to lose you."

She didn't want to lose him, either.

Her eyes watered, stung by the cold, but she felt warm all over.

"Cookie sales should be good," he said.

She nodded, delightfully aware of their joined hands. Although hers were gloved by thick knit, his were bare and strong and utterly protective. She was the safest woman in Redemption. Safe from everything except her own rocketing emotions.

"They already are," she said. "If sales continue this way, our donation will really help someone."

"Chosen a charity yet?"

Her hair rustled against the satiny material of her coat as she moved her head side to side. "Not yet. I'm still praying about it." Yet, every time she neared a decision, something held her back. "I think God has something planned. I just don't know what it is yet."

He fell silent, as he always did when she mentioned her relationship with God. The silence hurt, reminding her of the one major reason she shouldn't allow her emotions to run amok. Her faith was number one. Yet, she willingly, happily spent more and more of her spare time with Kade and Davey. Part of her knew they needed her. Another part knew her heart was getting involved. *Really* involved.

She slid a glance at Kade's profile. The tense jaw was smoothly groomed, his hair trimmed and tidy, the face handsomely chiseled. But it wasn't his looks, she realized, that captivated her. Although they'd attracted her first, she now saw deeper within to a man who suffered stomach pain and sleepless nights because of some secret, inner torment. But he continued to put himself out there every day for Davey's sake. He'd searched high and low, driven hundreds of miles, interviewed dozens of people. All the while, he presented a kind and caring face to the little boy who adored him and hid his worry that Davey had no one.

Kade raised her camera in one hand and flashed another photo. While she'd been too busy working the concession kiosk, he'd taken Davey to his place on the parade route and snapped pictures of the festivities as a favor to her. Because she'd bemoaned the fact that she would miss capturing Davey's excitement and pleasure.

Even if she'd been trying, it was hard not to care about a man like that.

They rounded the corner and crossed the street toward Town Square. The trees, dressed in colored lights, illuminated the sidewalk leading up to the stable where a spotlight shone on the sweet and ancient scene. The golden light bathed the Nativity in an almost-holy patina. Sophie sucked in a breath of cold air, touched as always by the display. A donkey shifted restlessly while two sheep from Pastor Parker's farm chewed hay under the watchful eye of a golden retriever and a silent boy.

A lump rose in her chest. "Oh, Kade," she whispered.

He squeezed her hand. "Sweet," he murmured.

She'd known the scene would look this way, had even helped set it up, but she'd not expected to feel so moved by the addition of one small boy and his dog.

Davey, with crook in hand, knelt at a right angle to the manger where a small, warmly bundled baby slept peacefully. Mary, beautifully portrayed by the darkly lovely Cheyenne Bowman, kept one motherly hand on the baby's chest. The soft, loving look on her serene face made Sophie wonder how long it would be until Cheyenne and Trace Bowman welcomed a new baby of their own.

Longing pierced Sophie. Longing for a child, for a family, for the man holding her hand.

Oh, dear Jesus. Dear, dear Jesus.

The strains of "Silent Night" drifted from the carolers positioned behind the stable. Sophie swallowed down the lump of yearning and tried to focus on the holy scene.

Kade snapped another photo and leaned close, whispering something in her ear. His breath was warm and moist and fragrant with the candy cane they'd shared earlier. She didn't catch his words, so she tilted her face to his to ask. He gazed down at her with an expression that could only be described as affectionate. Her heart leaped. For a second—one lovely, breathtaking second—she thought he might kiss her. Then, he rubbed his cold nose against hers, smiled softly and returned his attention to Davey.

Sophie savored the feelings that bubbled inside her like a fresh, sweet fountain cola. She was bemused, bewildered and breathless. And happy.

Considering Davey's situation and Kade's high wall of self-protection, she had no business letting her feelings run wild.

But Sophie believed the glass was not only half-full, it was overflowing. And she was overflowing with love for a mute boy and Kade McKendrick.

Chapter Nine

"**D**ad?" Sophie gave the Christmas bow one last tweak and pushed the red-wrapped gift under her father's Christmas tree. Purchased years ago by her neat-freak mother, who couldn't abide a shedding tree, the old artificial pine was losing its luster. Although she'd regret the loss of the familiar, Sophie had always preferred a real tree.

But the tree wasn't the reason for her visit to the childhood home.

"Hmm?" her dad answered absently. Seated in his favorite chair, he was reading the *Redemption Register* with a pen in hand ready to work the sudoku puzzle on the back page.

Affection expanded in Sophie's throat. With glasses perched on his nose and his graying hair mussed, Mark Bartholomew looked every bit the absentminded science professor. Some called him a nerd, a term he didn't mind in the least. To hear her dad's opinion, a nerd was a pretty smart guy.

"Can I talk to you about something?"

Newsprint rustled noisily as he closed his paper. "Sounds serious."

Still on her knees next to the tree, she twisted toward him with a sigh. "It is."

"I'm all ears." He patted the arm of his chair and smiled. When she was younger, she and Dad had resolved all her childhood and teenage angst with her perched on the arm of his chair. Not once had he failed to soothe whatever dilemma she'd been facing.

Even though she wasn't sure he could help her now, she knew he'd listen. She knew he'd care.

She settled next to him, the padded upholstery thin now over the chair's wooden skeleton. But sitting here again, with the man she'd loved first and longest, put the world into safe mode. "You know the way you loved Mom?"

"Still do." His face was open, honest and a bit nostalgic.

She fought down the protest that always rose when he said those heartbreaking words. Why didn't a man with so much to offer move on and find someone else? Mom had let them all down. How could he still care? Mom wasn't worthy of such devotion.

"I've never been in love before. Not like that, but…" Her voice dwindled away. Dad would understand.

As she expected, he said, "But you're getting there."

"Yes, I think so." She shook her head. "I know so."

"And you're worried."

"Yes again." She leaned in for a side hug. "You're the best dad. You understand me better than I understand myself."

He patted the back of her hand. She noticed, as she always did, that he still wore the plain gold wedding band Mother had given him nearly thirty years ago. She hurt seeing it there, a symbol of one-sided eternal love. They were alike in many ways, father and daughter, and Sophie feared loving as he did. She didn't want to end up rejected and alone.

The thought came out of nowhere. She'd never hesitated to put her heart on the line. Had she? Was she really afraid of love? True, she didn't date much and never had formed a long-term relationship with a man, but she'd consider herself too busy, too happy in her life. Now, she wondered. Had she purposely been avoiding serious attachment until these unexpected feelings for Kade blindsided her?

"Tell me what's going on," Dad said simply. "Would this most fortunate man happen to be Ida June Click's nephew? And do I need to give him a swift kick?"

Sophie smiled, as she knew he'd intended. The idea of her meek Dad giving anyone, especially a lethal lawman like Kade, a swift kick was silly, but she knew he'd try if Sophie needed him.

"Yes, Kade. And no swift kicks needed. Not for him anyway." When Dad raised his eyebrows in question, Sophie admitted, "I don't think he has a clue about my feelings, and the truth is, I can't really explain them to myself. But this is different than anything I've ever experienced. It's like the whole world takes on a brighter color and I can't stop thinking about him and I feel really alive when I'm with him." She made a small derisive sound. "I don't know."

"Poets have been trying to explain love for aeons. But love is from the soul. It's too big for words."

"How can I be in love with him? How can I feel so…"

At a loss, she lifted both hands in the air and let them flop to her lap in surrender.

"Complete? And a little rattled?"

"Yes. Yes, exactly," she said. "It doesn't make sense. I've known him such a short time, but I feel like a missing part of me has finally arrived. It's crazy."

"No, not crazy, honey. God wired us humans that way in the Garden of Eden. A woman for a man. A man for a woman. Two parts of a whole unit knit together by God's own hand."

She knew the story of Adam and Eve, but this was the first time she'd seen the significance. Eve was fashioned from Adam's rib. Eve was part of him and Adam was part of her. God's breath, His love, had joined them together.

And therein lay Sophie's deepest concern. She gnawed at the corner of her thumbnail. A blot of black marker stained the inside of her thumb like the dark blot overriding the joy of falling in love. "Kade's a good man, Dad—"

"Never doubted it. My Sophie's too wise to go for a loser." He made the shape of an L with his thumb and index finger.

Sophie responded to the joke by squeezing her father's fingers together. "But he's not a Christian. Or if he is, if he ever was, he's pulled away from the Lord."

"Hmm. I see. Now, that *is* a problem. Have you discussed your faith with him?"

"I've tried, but when I bring up the subject, he shuts down."

Furrows creased her dad's brow. For him, as for Sophie, shared faith was a no-brainer. With faith in God, anything else could be worked out. "Seems I remember having this discussion with you a while back. Before this got serious."

"He's polite when I mention church or the Lord, but I feel him draw away."

"Then how has he won my little girl's heart?"

"Oh, Dad, in so many ways. The way he loves Davey. He's determined to find the answers to Davey's missing family. His humor, the respect he shows to me." She went on to tell him about Kade's reaction to her school's security. "He wants to keep the whole world safe."

"Especially you and Davey?"

"He hasn't said as much, but I feel it."

"Sounds like he's falling in love, too."

She shook her head. "I don't know. Protecting people is his job and his nature. Maybe I'm just like everyone else to him."

Dad squeezed her shoulder with one hand. "What if you are? What then?"

With a moan, she admitted, "I don't know."

"I do."

"You do?"

"Listen to your old man, Sophie. Love is its own excuse for being. No matter what happens, even if the other person never loves you in return, loving is always a good thing. Love fills you up and makes you a better person every single time."

"You're talking about Mom."

"And you. And your brother. Different kinds of love, but all of them straight from God's heart."

"Oh, Dad. That's beautiful."

"You know what I think?" he asked, tapping her nose the way he'd done when she was ten.

"What?"

"I think you've been mad at your mother long enough. Anger and resentment hurt you, not your mom."

Sophie couldn't hold back a cry of protest. "But she hurt you. And you still love her. You're alone while she went merrily on with her life and a new man."

The bitterness in her tone caught her by surprise. Was she still so terribly angry?

"Do I look or sound unhappy to you?"

"Well, no."

"That's because I'm not. I have a good life, a job I enjoy, friends, a great church family and two terrific kids." Cleo leaped from a windowsill to stare at him as if she understood every word. "Oh, yes, and a bossy Siamese cat. I am a happy, content man."

"I don't understand that," Sophie argued. "How can you be?"

He drew in a deep breath and shifted to cup her face. "I was devastated when your mother left, but a pair of old Dumpster divers came around here every day for a while to remind me that love never fails. Whether the other person accepts it and returns the feelings or not love never fails. They were right, honey."

"How?"

"Doing the right thing by extending love when human nature called for anger healed *me*. The more I focused on letting go of my hurt and loving your mother no matter what she'd done, the happier I became and the fuller my soul and spirit." He kissed her chin and released her. "Choosing to love your mom was the best thing I've ever done for myself. It set me free."

Tears sprang to Sophie's eyes. All this time, she'd considered her dad as wimpy and passive, a doormat for her mother to walk on. Now, as she compared her feelings for Kade and Davey to those of her father for his family, she finally understood. Even after what Mom had done to hurt her father, he had purposely chosen the higher ground. Sophie had harbored unforgiveness and, as Dad said, the only person she'd hurt had been herself. Her resentment toward her mother and the fear of being alone like her dad had made her wary of finding a love of her own. Then, a battle-weary and heart-wounded cop had leaped into a trash bin, and love had found her.

Sophie slid over the chair arm onto her father's lap for a bear hug. He smelled of English Leather and Irish Spring, the scents of childhood—plain, simple, secure. "You're the best dad in the world."

"Always good to hear." He patted her back. "Did I help?"

"Ever so much." She pushed to a stand, basking for a few seconds in the powerful love she felt for her father and to claim the affection he showered on her. "I love you, Dad."

"Same here, honey."

As she reached for her coat and cap, he asked, "Where are you off to so soon?"

"I have an important phone call to make."

Before she could give vent to her feelings for Kade, before she could trust that love would not fail her, she had a fence to mend. She smiled, anticipating her father's pleasure. "I need to call Mom."

Kade hesitated on Sophie's front porch. He knew where she lived. Had driven past on those nights when he couldn't sleep to make sure she was safe in the little white bungalow. Hers was an older house, probably one of those 1900 historic places prevalent in Redemption. With a small wooden porch complete with cheerful yellow shutters and wooden rockers painted in blue and green, the house was undeniably Sophie's. Bright, happy, joyous. The door wreath was the same. Obviously handmade, probably by her class, the wreath was constructed of recycled Christmas cards cut into leaf shapes and topped with a giant, lopsided red bow.

The sight charmed him. So did she.

A knot formed beneath his rib cage. The thing had started up recently, replacing the burn in his belly, though this was almost as annoying. Almost but not quite. The knot said Sophie was nearby. The woman had him twisted in knots.

He lifted the brass knocker and gave three strong taps. A sharp gust of wind whipped around the corner of the porch and shoved cold fingers beneath his jacket. Being from Chicago, he ignored the chill. He'd been colder.

He probably should have phoned first.

He waited a couple of minutes, but Sophie didn't respond so he knocked again. Part of him wanted her to open the door. Being in her presence pushed the shadows away and made him feel normal again. More than normal.

The sensible part of him said he should hit the road and leave her alone.

He snorted softly. He was a mess. A certifiable mess. Kade lifted the knocker and tried again. Sophie even had him thinking about his faith, or lack thereof. He wondered if God ever thought about him. Probably not much.

She wasn't home. Might as well move on.

Disappointed, he'd turned to leave when he heard the metallic click of the doorknob.

"Kade!"

He spun around. Sophie, smile as bright and cheerful as a Christmas gift, was framed in the doorway like a picture. She had a pink towel wrapped around her head.

"Got a minute?" he asked.

"Sure. Come in." She stood aside and allowed him to pass before shutting out the swirling wind. "Sorry I took so long to answer the door. I was washing my hair."

"I see that." He motioned to her head, the scent of wet hair and shampoo strong. She looked pretty with her face scrubbed clean and her eyebrows dark and damp. "Go ahead and do what you need to. I'll wait."

She removed the towel and shook out her hair into a mass of wiggling snakes. "How's this?"

He grinned. "I'm not answering that question."

She laughed, a full, delighted sound. "Smart man. Let me grab a brush and I'll be back."

While she was gone, he glanced around the small, jam-packed living room. Decorated for Christmas, the space sparkled. He could smell the fresh little tree standing in one corner with a mound of gifts beneath it. Nearly a dozen were the size and shape of footballs. Must be for the boys in her class.

A Bible and some sort of book were neatly stacked on an end table next to the telephone and a notepad. A simple silver cross hung above the television. He expected her blatant displays of faith to make him uncomfortable, but they didn't. He felt…comforted. Sophie was Sophie, sweet and real. Her quiet, living faith was who she was.

Where that left him, he still didn't know.

Not ready to go there, nor the least bit comfortable with that line of thought, he resumed his perusal of her cheerful house. His gaze had reached a grouping of framed pictures when she returned.

"There. Tell me I look better." She'd combed the wet hair straight down to touch her shoulders. The color was dark and rich and glossy. Kade secretly thought she would look beautiful no matter what, but he nodded. "Looks good."

Her grin was disbelieving. "Where's Davey?"

"Ida June. Something about GI Jack, Popbottle Jones and a goat."

Sophie chuckled, a motion that crinkled the corners of her eyes and displayed a tiny dimple on one cheekbone. Weird that he'd noticed something that random.

"They have a goat named Prudence," she said. "She's a hoot. Loves people, but has a strong personality. She also makes great cheese. Davey will have fun."

He'd been to GI Jack's place a couple of times. The mishmash of discarded, recycled flotsam and jetsam was interesting to say the least. A little boy would have a fine time exploring. "I thought so, too, though I didn't have much say in the matter. When Ida June speaks I've learned to go with her decision or suffer the quotations."

"I know what you mean," she said, nodding sagely. "Ida June is as much a hoot as Prudence."

"Yeah. Quite a gene pool I come from." He motioned toward the table of photos. "Is that your family?"

"Those are *my* gene pool. The Bartholomews."

"You look like your mother."

"Really?" An emotion, a little sad and a little proud, echoed from that one word.

"She's beautiful."

Her gray eyes narrowed, but her lips curved. Full, pretty lips on a mouth that loved to laugh. "That sounds suspiciously like a compliment."

"It was." Okay, so he'd told her she was beautiful. That was enough. He didn't have to tell her the rest. The only way to keep his sanity and keep her safe was to keep his mouth shut. His gut threatened, just enough to let him know Vesuvius was still in there, waiting for a chance to make him suffer. Keeping things inside was killing him, but Sophie was worth the price.

What had Ida June said about a good woman and the price of rubies? He thought he was beginning to understand.

Sophie crossed the small carpeted floor and detoured around a canvas bag overflowing with schoolbooks to take up a framed photo. "This is the last picture with all of us as a family before Mom left."

Sadness shadowed her beautiful gray eyes. Even now, the separation bothered her.

"Divorce is tough." His parents were still together, but he had buddies who suffered through the humiliation and pain, even though a broken home seemed to go hand in hand with being a cop. Women couldn't take the strain. Or was it the men who buckled beneath the pressure of dealing with the dregs of humanity day in and day out? He had.

He wondered what had happened to Sophie's parents but didn't pry. No use giving her an opening to ask questions he didn't want to answer.

"I was angry at my mother for years," she said softly as she rubbed an index finger over the face in the picture. "Until yesterday."

"What happened yesterday?" There he went, right

where he'd vowed not to, sticking his nose in her private life. "You don't have to tell me."

"No, it's all right. I don't mind. In fact, getting over my anger is such a big relief…" Her voice trailed off. She put the photo back on the table and returned to the small couch. A love seat, he thought. A cushy blue-gray love seat that nearly matched Sophie's eyes.

A soft fragrance wafted to him as she twisted one leg beneath her and settled. Either she washed her hair with coconut or the woman was a walking macaroon. Sweet and delicious.

Kade cleared his throat and scooted to one end. Sitting on something called a love seat with Sophie gave him ideas he shouldn't have.

"So what happened?" he pressed, mostly to take his mind anywhere but on clean-smelling Sophie.

Serene and apparently not as affected by his nearness as he was to hers, she told him about the sudden, stunning, unexpected divorce and her mother's secret infidelity.

"She hurt you," he said, anger rising at a woman he didn't even know.

Sophie placed her fingertips on his arm. "She did, but I hurt myself worse."

"I don't get it."

"By not forgiving her. I know it doesn't make sense," she said.

"No, it doesn't. She made the choice to leave. Not you."

"That's what I thought, too. Then. But my dad taught me something. Being a slow learner I didn't figure it out until last night. Forgiveness is always right. My faith teaches that, but I didn't want to forgive her, so I let the anger fester. She wasn't miserable. I was."

Moved by her generosity, he said softly, "You're a bigger person than most, Sophie B."

"I don't know about that, but I do know I feel much better now that I've resolved things with my mother."

"You told her?"

"Yes. Last night, after Dad and I talked, I called my mom. We had a long, honest conversation. When I told her I forgave her and I loved her, she cried." Sophie plucked at the nap on the love seat. "She cried."

He could see how emotional the issue was for her. She was amazing, his Sophie B. Full of love and forgiveness and decency.

"What about you? Did you cry?"

She looked up, eyes shining with unshed tears. "I did, but they were happy tears that washed away a hard place inside me that I didn't even know was there."

Kade couldn't resist then. He touched her smooth, velvet cheek with the knuckle of his index finger. "There's nothing hard about you. Never could be. You're the softest, kindest—"

He was talking too much. He had to stop before he spilled his guts.

But there was Sophie, gray eyes gentle and accepting, and he felt a wonderful sense of rightness in being with her, here on her love seat on a quiet Sunday afternoon.

"Kade," she whispered, her breath warm against his fingers, "I wouldn't care a bit if you kissed me."

His heart expanded to the point of explosion. He was only a man after all, and he was half-nuts about a woman who'd just asked him to kiss her.

Hadn't he been thinking about exactly that?

He moved in closer, gaze locked on hers, full of wonder and terror and stupid happiness. When his lips touched hers, some of the hard pain inside him melted like wax. She was everything he'd known she would be. Everything he'd dreamed in his restless sleep and waking imaginings. Sweetness, purity, warmth and glory. A fierce emotion burned in him, protective and stunning.

Right before his brain shorted out, he had one sane thought. He was falling in love with a woman he didn't deserve. And he didn't know what to do about it.

Chapter Ten

The next morning, Kade was still reeling in the wild sensation of kissing Sophie, not once but several times. He shouldn't have. He should have cut and run for her sake, but he'd had no self-discipline yesterday afternoon.

He wasn't sure if that was a good thing or not, considering self-control had gotten him into the mess in Chicago. As an undercover agent—a narc—he'd played the part, done his job and lost his soul in the process. Sophie and Redemption—an aptly named town under the circumstances—had stirred a hope that he might actually find his way again.

His cell phone jingled. He plucked it from his pocket and answered. "McKendrick here."

"Mr. McKendrick? My name is James. You don't know me, but I got this number from a newspaper here in Potterville."

Kade sat up straighter in his chair, a tingle of excited hope racing over his skin. Potterville was thirty miles from Redemption. "I put an ad in that paper."

"Yes, sir. That's why I'm calling. I've seen that little

boy you're looking for. He and his mama used to come
into the grocery store where I work."

"You're sure it was him?"

"Pretty sure. Almost positive."

"Do you know where his mother lives?"

"Yes, kind of," the voice said. "They didn't socialize
much, but I remember someone saying they lived in the
old Rogers' place a few miles out of town."

"Give me your name again and how to reach you."
Kade scrambled for a pen and paper, jotting down as
much info as he needed. "Can you give me an address
or directions to the house?"

"I think so."

Kade wrote quickly, his pulse pumping adrenaline
so fast that his head swam. This could be it. This could
be the break he'd been praying for.

Armed with all the information he could pump from
the man named James, he rang off and grabbed his
coat. On the way out the door, he called Chief Jesse
Rainmaker. He had no jurisdiction in Oklahoma, but
Jesse did.

Whoever the woman was who had kept Davey under
lock and key and then dumped him like a sack of garbage was about to feel the full brunt of legal fury.

Sophie was beside herself with excitement. Kade
had left a message on her cell phone saying he'd had
a break in Davey's case and wouldn't be home after
school. Would she look after their boy? Of course she
would. He knew that. He also knew she'd say nothing
to Davey until they had more information.

She touched her cheek, warm from frequent thoughts
of the kiss they'd shared yesterday afternoon. Kade had

stayed until church time, although he'd never told her why he'd come over in the first place. She'd fed him grilled cheese and he'd helped her wrap Christmas gifts, a hilarious project considering he made prettier bows than she did. They'd talked. And he'd kissed her twice more. Once when they'd been laughing at her pitiful attempt to tie a bow and then when he'd left.

She was still a little shell-shocked by that. Shell-shocked in a very good way. Maybe Christmas had come early for Sophie B.

No, not yet, because when church time had arrived, he'd gone home, refusing her invitation to come along. Disappointed but not surprised, she'd pressed for a reason. He'd given the usual joke about the church roof caving in.

Davey tapped her arm to get her attention. As she handed him the silently requested bakery box, she prayed Christmas was coming early for Davey whether it came for her or not.

A tiny selfish regret pinched her heart. She loved being with this sweet little boy, and she'd miss him terribly if Kade had discovered where he belonged. Although Kade kept his words few and his promises nonexistent, he would miss Davey, too. Hopefully Davey had a family who treasured him even more than she and Kade did.

She ruffled the top of Davey's hair and received his crooked smile as reward. Today turned out to be the perfect afternoon for him to hang out with her after school. Fifth grade had baked and decorated cookies all day.

Being too antsy to remain still, the cookies were a perfect reason for Sophie to keep moving and busy. Even her students had noticed her extra energy and had asked if she was excited about Christmas. She gave them an easy and honest affirmation, but nothing could compare with the gift of reestablishing Davey with his loved ones—if that's what was about to happen, and she prayed it was.

In a chef's apron and plastic gloves, and heedless of the drama being played out on his behalf, Davey stood at a table sorting sugar cookies. Sophie slid each colorful dozen into zip bags and placed them into a small, white bakery box before adding the labels her class had designed—a merry little elf holding a banner emblazoned with Fifth Grade and the type of cookie. Later, she and Davey would make deliveries.

"Just a few more and we'll be finished," she said. "Are you getting hungry?"

Davey's eyes cut from side to side before he grinned sheepishly and pointed at the bowl of broken cookies.

Sophie plopped a hand on one hip and pretended dismay. "Chef Davey, have you been filching cookie crumbs when I wasn't looking?"

He nodded, displaying those half-grown teeth stained with crumbs and food coloring.

"All right, then, my friend, I guess I'll have one of Big Bob's burgers all by myself."

Davey made his sign for Sheba, a petting motion.

"Don't worry," she told him. "We'll go by the house and see Sheba before we have dinner. Deal?"

He nodded, but then his eyebrows came together in a worried frown.

"What are you thinking about?" She tied a strip of green ribbon around the packed box, added the label and the buyer's name. Then she checked off the name on her master list.

Davey moved his lips, though no sound came out, shoved his hands into imaginary jacket pockets, slouched his shoulders and narrowed his eyes in what could only be an imitation of Kade.

Sophie giggled. "You're a little mimic, you know it? You have Kade down pat." He also imitated the preacher at church from time to time and had taken to flouncing around with lips pursed to indicate Ida June. "I think Kade is making you ornery."

Davey hunched his shoulders in a silent laugh.

"I don't know what's taking so long, sweetie, but Kade will be here when he finishes his business. You can count on that."

He could always count on Kade, and Sophie instinctively knew she could, too.

They packed up the rest of the cookies and left Sophie's classroom. The building was empty and silent except for the principal's office. When she passed by, he spotted her and beckoned her inside.

"Sophie, do you have a minute?"

What else could she say? "Of course."

Holding back a sigh, she ushered Davey into the principal's office.

"Hello, Davey," Biff said.

Davey, eyes wide and intimidated, nodded and burrowed close to Sophie.

The principal said, "He's getting attached."

"So am I."

He pushed aside a pad of paper and smiled. This was apparently a friendly visit. "You can sit down. I won't bite."

"Thank you, Biff, but Davey and I are headed to Bob's to have some dinner."

As soon as she said the words, she regretted them. Biff would think she was hinting.

Sure enough, he said, "Why don't you let me come along and I'll buy?"

Dismayed, Sophie pressed her lips together, searching for a gentle way to say no.

"Mr. Gruber," she said, holding up the shield of professionalism, "I appreciate the kind offer. Really, I do."

His smile froze. "But?"

"I'm seeing someone." She hadn't meant to say that, wasn't even sure it was true, though Kade held her heart.

The smile was gone now. "McKendrick, I suppose?"

Great. What would Kade think about her announcing a fledgling relationship to the world? "Yes."

"I see." He straightened his shirt cuffs with a quick tug. "Don't let me keep you, then."

"Didn't you want to speak to me about something?" Sophie asked.

"Nothing important." His tone as cold as January, he turned his attention to what looked to be a letter on his desk. "If you'll excuse me…"

Feeling she should say something but not knowing what, Sophie turned to leave, one hand on Davey's shoulder. As she passed through the open door, Biff said softly, "I hope you know what you're doing."

Biff's odd comment nagged at her as she and Davey headed toward Ida June's to pick up the dog. By the time they'd gotten burgers and fries she'd decided Biff had been showing concern or maybe jealously, and let it go. After delivering several dozen cookies, she and Davey headed to her house where they read and watched a kid movie and kept an ear tuned for Kade's car.

When the boy and dog started to doze on the love

seat, Sophie flipped off the television and stared out the window at the silent night. The neighbors' Christmas lights chased each other around the roofline while a blow-up snowman stood sentry on the lighted front porch. Somewhere Kade followed a lead that must have significance or he would have come home by now. She leaned her forehead against the cold windowpane, thinking of him, longing to see him, but longing more to know what was going on.

Please, Lord, let this be a real break, not another dead end that sends Kade into a broody silence and keeps Davey in limbo.

And please, heal whatever is broken inside the man I love.

Kade leaned his back against the cold siding, thankful—so thankful—Sophie and Davey were not with him tonight. Flecks of peeling white paint scratched against the leather of his jacket. He sucked in long drafts of night air, so desperately cold inside that the thirty-degree air warmed him.

He squeezed his eyes closed and rubbed a hand over them, wishing he could wipe away what he'd discovered in the remote, ramshackle dwelling Davey had once called home.

A hand lightly cuffed his shoulder. "Tough thing."

Kade jerked to attention. No use going soft in front of Chief Rainmaker. "I didn't expect this."

"Who would?" Rainmaker rubbed his sandpapery palms together against the night chill. Neither he nor Jesse had jurisdiction in this area, but the county sheriff had granted them courtesy. Already, at his call, a team of investigators crawled over the place, probably the first people to visit Davey's mother in a very long time.

And she was dead.

He ground his teeth together, stomach raging-hot fire. "What do you think killed her?"

The Native American eyed him thoughtfully. "From all appearances, she died of natural causes. No signs of foul play, no forced entry. Nothing to indicate suicide."

"Just a dead woman and a messy house," Kade said grimly.

"Mostly the kitchen. Evidence that Davey was alone with his deceased mother for some time before hunger drove him to seek food and help."

Kade's fist clenched and unclenched. "I don't like thinking about Davey alone in this house with a mother he couldn't wake up."

"Nor do I, but empty cupboards and refrigerator, dirty dishes and spilled milk. They all point to a child fending for himself."

"And trying to take care of his mother." Kade closed his eyes again tightly, fighting the images in the woman's bedroom. He desperately wanted to talk to Sophie. Somehow she'd make him believe everything would work out for the best. She would pray and God would listen.

But he didn't want her here to see this. Knowing would hurt her badly enough. "The mother must have been sick for a while."

"Probably." Jesse shuffled his boots against the hard-packed ground. His equipment rattled. "When she didn't waken, he covered her with blankets."

Yanking a tight rein on his emotions, Kade turned

toward the rickety front porch. "Let's get back in there. We've got a job to do."

Jesse's thoughtful gaze stayed on him. "You don't have to do this, McKendrick. The county boys can handle it."

"I started it," he said grimly. "This time, I finish."

Rainmaker couldn't know what he meant, but he'd been a cop long enough to understand the sentiment. Kade had something to prove, if only to himself.

"Davey is lucky to have you on this in the first place. We might not have found her for months without your extra efforts."

A car door slammed and both men looked toward a technician carrying in a satchel of equipment. Trees surrounding the yard shed eerie, fingerlike shadows over the run-down dwelling and the professionals doing their macabre duty.

"Had to do something, though this doesn't help Davey at all." He spoke through clenched teeth, deeply angry at a situation he could not fix. Once again, he'd been too late to make a difference. "None."

"Even as bad as the outcome," Jesse said with quiet authority, "you did an exceptional job. My timing may be off, but let me say it anyway. I could use you on my force. Granted, we can't compare to Chicago—"

Kade interrupted him with a sour laugh. "I'll think about it. Later."

The answer surprised him a little. He had every intention of returning to Chicago as soon as the shrink released him. Still, Jesse deserved the courtesy of consideration.

The two men stepped onto the old porch, a wooden structure about to cave in.

Rainmaker's heavy boots made hollow sounds on the loose boards. "Walk easy."

"And carry a big stick?" Kade asked wryly.

Jesse huffed softly at the humor, a cop's major protection against the stress that could lead to insanity. "Yeah."

They entered the house. Even though every light blazed and a beehive of uniformed men and woman worked, an empty coldness sucked the warmth from Kade's bones. In his experience, death did that to a place. "Maybe something in this house will give us Davey's full name."

A technician handed them both a pair of gloves. "You know the drill," she said.

Yes, he knew the drill, better than he wanted to. With heart aching for a blue-eyed boy he'd grown to love, he moved through the small dwelling. Davey had lived in this shabby, run-down place. The investigators had to collect every piece of evidence to rule out foul play, but he agreed with Chief Rainmaker. Nothing pointed to homicide. Nothing pointed to anyone living here except Davey and the woman who appeared to be his mother.

Kade stepped on a spongy bit of floor. The weak boards squeaked and gave slightly beneath his weight. "This house is about to fall down."

Jesse, hawk eyes soaking in every detail, nodded. "Can't argue. You going back in the bedroom?"

Back there with the body, he meant. "Yeah. Got to."

Jesse gave him that look again as though trying to see inside his head. Might as well forget that. Even Kade didn't understand, but he felt compelled to be here, compelled to know answers to the questions Davey would someday ask.

A masked and gowned officer, broad as he was tall, shouldered past the two men. "The coroner is on his way. ETA ten minutes." He made a wry face. "Didn't like being woken up. This kind of thing doesn't happen very often around here."

Well, it happened often to Kade. Maybe there was something to the quiet, small-town life.

Wearing the offered masks, he and Jesse entered the room. Several hours ago, Kade had found her. He'd been alone then, with Jesse Rainmaker on the way. He'd knocked, peeked in windows, called out and finally entered the seemingly abandoned house. The moment he'd opened the door, the smell of death had slapped him backward. With terrible knowledge and a dread deeper than the Redemption well, he'd gone inside.

The blanket he'd pulled over her face had now been replaced by a yellow plastic sheet. He'd never found the covering inadequate before. But for Davey's mom, the plastic was too impersonal and cold.

"Did you see the dog?" he asked quietly, gesturing toward the outlined shape of a stuffed animal. "I'm guessing that toy was Davey's favorite, and he left it behind to comfort his mother. He loves dogs."

"Lord, have mercy." The usually unflappable Jesse shuddered. "Grisly situation for a little kid."

Kade had seen worse. Though his heart hurt so badly for Davey, he wanted to hit something. "The doc said some kind of trauma made him stop talking."

Now he realized his idea of what caused the trauma had been way off. Kidnapping, abuse. Under the circumstances, he wasn't sure which was worse. Davey had awakened one morning to find his mother dead.

He'd been hungry, scared, alone. No wonder he couldn't speak.

Jesse's voice was muffled behind the white mask. "Now that we know the cause, we can get him help to deal with the loss. Maybe he'll come out of it and talk again."

Maybe. But maybe he never would.

"How does a kid ever deal with this? How can he erase the memories and terror?" Kade clenched his fist tight, fingers digging into his palms. He would never forget. How could Davey? "Think how helpless he felt. He's a little kid. He could do nothing to stop what happened. Not one single thing."

A flash of young, helpless faces momentarily blinded him. He was projecting, the shrink would say. Forget the shrink. Kade knew how Davey felt, except Kade could have stopped what happened…and hadn't.

Sophie called in a substitute teacher on Tuesday morning. At eight o'clock she was still shaking, though Kade had arrived at daylight with the news about Davey's mother. With Davey still asleep, the adults had sought privacy in Sophie's extra room, a bedroom turned into a study.

Kade looked awful. Unshaved, eyes red and haunted, he looked exhausted to the point of collapse by the news he had to share.

Everything in her wanted to hold him close and comfort him, but he didn't seem to want that. He'd come into the house with his aloof, professional demeanor carefully in place. Now he was perched on the edge of her office chair, bent forward, with elbows on his jean-clad thighs and clenched hands dangling between his knees. His usually polished boots were scuffed and dirty.

"How did he end up in Redemption?" she asked, setting a cup of coffee and a slice of pumpkin bread on the desk in front of him. She was sure he hadn't eaten. Probably not since before finding Davey's mother. "Potterville's thirty miles or more from here!"

"Jesse and I talked about that." Kade cupped both hands around the warm mug but didn't drink. "Potterville is the nearest town to the house where Davey and his mother lived. Back in the woods, down a long, ragged driveway if you could call it that. More like a trail. No reason for anyone to go out there." He looked up. "It's really remote, Sophie. She had no phone. Not even have a mailbox. Apparently she wanted to be alone."

"I wonder why." Sophie rubbed the chill bumps that wouldn't stop shivering down her arms. Kade had to be even more upset by the reality of Davey's deceased mother. He'd been there. He'd seen. And he'd wanted badly to bring a happy resolution to Davey's quandary.

"The investigation into who she was and where she came from should give us some answers about her reclusive lifestyle. Whatever her reasons, she put Davey in the terrible predicament of having no one to turn to when she died."

"He must have been scared and confused," she said, imagining the thoughts that went through an eight-year-old's head.

"We figure he was with her body for several days before he ran out of food." When she shivered again at the word *body,* his hard voice softened the slightest bit. "He probably decided to go into Potterville—familiar territory—for help but got turned around and went the wrong direction."

"Surely he didn't walk all the way to Redemption."

"We think he did." He lifted the cup to his lips and sipped.

"Thirty miles? That could take days for a child who had no idea where he was headed." Days of tramping through dark, scary woods and sleeping in the cold.

Kade's head tilted. He pinched off a bite of warmed pumpkin bread, rolled the moist cake around in his fingers before setting it back on the saucer. Sophie understood. She had no appetite, either. "Now we know why he took shelter in the Dumpster and why he was so gaunt and hungry."

"Oh, Kade. Our poor Davey. What are we going to say to him?"

He pushed the plate away and sat up straighter. "The truth. Once we know what that is."

"It's Christmas. Little kids are supposed to bask in the festivity and make wish lists and eat too much candy, not lose their mothers."

Sophie wanted Kade to agree, and she wanted him to take her in his arms the way he'd done on Sunday. She wanted him to kiss away her sadness and tell her they would work things out for the little boy they both loved. Together.

He didn't.

"Christmas or not, Sophie, he already knows." The chair rollers rattled as he shoved up from his seat and went to the single window. Through clenched teeth, he said, "He always knew. That sweet little kid has carried the terrible knowledge all this time. And he couldn't tell us."

"Oh, Kade." She couldn't stand it any longer. She went to him, slid both arms around his rigid back and pressed her cheek against his flannel shirt.

He gripped each side of the window with a hand as if holding on could keep him from feeling. But she knew people. She knew him. And he was aching inside.

"You did everything you could, Kade."

"Not enough."

"I can't imagine what you went through last night, but it had to be awful."

The muscles of his back tightened. "It's my job."

"You're a man. With a big heart. Who loves that woman's boy." With slow circles of her palm, Sophie rubbed the tension between his shoulder blades and silently prayed for him.

He went right on staring out the window at the bleak December landscape and said nothing for the longest time.

He wanted to be the strong one, even when he was hurting. He was the guardian, the protector.

"You don't have to be strong for me, Kade," she said gently. "I know you're upset."

He turned then and touched her face, a tender look in his eyes. Her heart filled. She was certain he had something more to say, but his cell phone interrupted.

After a glance at the caller ID, he said, "The police chief," and answered.

The conversation was brief and as he slowly slid the phone into his jacket, he said, "He found something in the house he wants me to see. He says it's important."

Chapter Eleven

Kade knew only one way to tell her. Straight-out.

Adrenaline pumping from the discovery, he drew in a deep breath, leaned both palms on her round dining table and said, "Davey was born without a voice."

Sophie's gray eyes widened with shock. "But that doesn't make sense. I thought only deaf children were born mute."

Kade had been as stunned as Sophie when Chief Rainmaker showed him the fat notebook crammed with wide-rule paper and dark, scribbled cursive. He'd spent an hour browsing through the rambling, sometimes erratic writings.

"Apparently not," he said, voice low. Davey and Sheba were only a few feet away in the small living room watching cartoons. Even now, the zippy music of *Tom and Jerry* seeped through the walls, a contrast to the serious discussion going on here. "We don't know the whole story—and we may never—but at least we have some information, thanks to a journal kept by Melissa Stephens, Davey's mother."

"And she wrote that Davey has never spoken?" Sophie slowly withdrew a chair from the table and slumped onto the seat. "Ever?"

"Never."

Stunned, she propped her elbows on the gleaming cherrywood and rested her chin on folded hands. "I can't quite come to grips with that."

Her hair swung forward. Kade resisted the urge to brush it back, to feel the silkiness on his skin. Duty first. Always.

"Neither could she, apparently." He tugged a chair close to hers and straddled it, too juiced to sit for long. Seeing the pieces of an investigative puzzle come together did that to him. "She wrote long, stress-filled pages about his illness, as she termed it. She had some notion her mistakes had caused the problem."

Sophie turned her face toward him. "What had she done?"

Kade shrugged a palm. "She never said. Maybe she never knew."

The journal's discovery had eased his anxiety, as he hoped it would Sophie's once she'd absorbed the shock. Davey had not been abused or mistreated, at least not in the ways he'd imagined. If Melissa Stephens parented poorly, she did so out of ignorance and fear.

"Appears she worried about everything. Worried D.H.S would take him away. Worried he'd be bullied at school. She was phobic about her mute son."

"So she didn't take him out into the world. At least not very much."

"Right. Not even to school. She was terrified of school authorities, although she mentioned homeschooling at one point."

Sophie's folded hands thudded to the tabletop. "I have my doubts about that."

"I think she did her best." He dangled his fingers over the top of the chair and onto Sophie's forearm in a light tickle of reassurance. "In her own way, she loved him, but she was a scared, lonely woman with no apparent support system. She was afraid to go out in public, afraid of people."

In a gesture so natural Kade didn't notice in time to resist, Sophie turned one hand up and laced her fingers with his. "Agoraphobia?"

So much for duty first. Aw, who was he kidding? Sophie and Davey came first, no contest.

"Maybe," he said. "Hard to say because she doesn't appear to have sought treatment."

"What about her family? Didn't she have relatives to help her?"

"The police are checking into that. Into all her background for that matter. But the journal mentions no one but Davey."

"That's incredibly sad."

"Yeah."

He squeezed her fingers, letting her in close now that he'd gotten himself under control. Hard as it was to admit, he needed this, needed her.

Earlier, when the discovery of the body had been so raw inside him, he'd feared imploding right before Sophie's eyes. He wanted to be strong for her. For both of them.

"You're exhausted," she said softly.

He was tired to the marrow, but there would be no sleep today. Probably not tonight, either. "I'm okay."

She rose and came around behind to knead the knotty slope of his shoulders.

He tensed, the hard knots tightening to the breaking point. "You don't have to—"

"I know," she said, a smile in her voice as she stroked along his hairline. "I want to. Relax."

Relax? When his heart had shifted into overdrive?

She karate chopped the top of his shoulders. "I said relax, McKendrick. Don't make me have to hurt you."

Sophie hurt him? He chuckled, and when he did, the cords of stress in his neck eased.

"That's it," Sophie said. "Let go."

Let go? He wanted to grab her and never let go.

But he kept those random thoughts to himself and let his head fall forward in a pendulum sway.

"You're pretty strong for a girl."

She gave him another karate chop. "Watch it, buster."

He chuckled again and let himself relish the surprising strength of Sophie's fingers against his tight, tight muscles.

Last night's ugliness dimmed a bit. Being with Sophie had that power.

Doing his best not to drool, he dropped his head deeper and deeper until his forehead rested on the chair back. Sophie massaged and hummed while in the living room Scooby and Shaggy raced around saving the world.

He wished it was that easy.

After a while, his neck felt like putty and he fought the urge to doze. Sleeping on the job was not allowed.

Reluctantly, he placed a hand on Sophie's to stop the glorious kneading.

"Thanks," he said. The word came out in an embarrassing slur. He cleared his throat and sat up straight.

"Better?" she asked, coming around to his side.

"Much." He drew in a deep, cleansing breath. Her macaroon scent swirled into his brain. A man could get used to this, he thought. With her around, he'd go soft as a marshmallow in record time.

Right now, he couldn't decide if that was a good thing or a bad one.

"What now?" she asked and the simple question jerked him back to the terrible reality of death and an orphaned child.

"We have to tell him."

"Yes. He needs to know, and he needs our assurance that he did everything he could and nothing was his fault."

Raking a hand over his mouth and chin, he sighed a noisy sigh. Reality stunk. "He has bad dreams."

"I'm not surprised," she said. "I doubt if he really understands what transpired. Those awful days are inside him and he can't share what he knows or fears."

Kade pushed up from the chair, heart heavy with dread. So much for the relaxing massage.

"All right, then," he said. "Let's do it."

The conversation went easier than either adult expected. Davey had known his mother was gone, and even though his eyes filled with tears, he seemed relieved when Kade told him he'd done the right things and his mother was simply too sick to get better.

Sophie made comments about heaven and Jesus and how much Davey's mother loved him. Kade cleared his throat a couple of times, moved by her gentle compassion and the way Davey clung to every word. And to Kade's neck.

"She knew how much you loved her, too," Sophie said, touching the place over Davey's heart.

He nodded, fat tears quivering on his pale eyelashes. Kade tightened his hold on the skinny waist and tugged him closer, wishing he could absorb the pain and let Davey go free. Davey's thin arms clung with a desperation that ripped Kade's heart out.

Sheba, with her dog sensibility, nudged close to her favorite child and whined. Davey reached a grubby, nail-bitten hand to Sheba's head. The connection seemed to comfort them both.

The four of them, man and woman, boy and dog, were locked in a circle of grief and love. For all his determination to remain aloof and professional, Kade accepted that he was done for. No matter what happened from here, he was connected by this experience. To these people. Letting go would not be easy. Not now.

Over Davey's head, he met Sophie's questioning gaze. He nodded, signaling agreement. Davey would grieve and process in the hours and days ahead. They'd help him all they could. If there was a chance he could talk again...

"Davey?" Sophie asked, stroking his hair the way she'd stroked Kade's, kneading and tender and comforting all at once.

Davey raised his head from Kade's chest and left a warm spot on his shirtfront, right over his heart.

Sophie handed him a tissue from her pocket, and Kade almost smiled. The teacher was always prepared.

"Have you ever been able to speak?"

The adults knew the answer, but Kade also knew

where Sophie was leading. The sooner they started, the sooner they'd know if Davey could be helped.

Davey scrubbed the tissue over his tearstained cheeks and shook his head no.

"Did your mama ever take you to a doctor to have your throat checked?"

The small face screwed up in thought before he shook his head again.

Sophie and Kade exchanged glances. No big surprise there.

"Add that to your Christmas list," he murmured, tugging Davey back to his chest. For some reason, he couldn't keep his hands off the hurting boy. Though, come to think of it, Davey seemed to be handling things better than the adults.

Of course, he'd been dealing with his mother's death these past few weeks on his own. Amazing kid.

"I'll call the clinic today." Sophie sat back on her heels. "Dr. Stampley didn't discover anything amiss before, but he mentioned more tests. We were going to see an ENT after the first of the year anyway. Maybe we can move things up."

If there was any way to help Davey, Kade was all over it. He'd even pay for the office call. "I'll take him myself. Anywhere, anytime. Name the day."

She placed her hand over his. "I know. Me, too."

A day with Sophie sounded good, even on a trip to a throat specialist.

Davey looked back and forth between the adults, listening intently to the conversation.

"We think a doctor might be able to fix your voice," Sophie told him.

He cocked his head and frowned before touching his

hand to his throat. To a boy who'd never spoken, the notion probably seemed impossible.

Kade hoped not. Life had taken Davey's mother. The least it could do was give him a voice.

Reality, that cruel viper, raised its head and Child-issed. Davey had no one. He was an orphan. A voice would help, but he'd still be alone in a cruel world.

"And then what?" he murmured, suddenly angry at the lousy injustice he couldn't control. Not in Chicago. Not even here.

Sophie shook her head and frowned a warning. Today was not the time. She was right, he knew, but he also knew if no relative was forthcoming, social services would make the decision. Davey would be lost in the system.

News travels fast in a small town and by afternoon, the buzz around Redemption reached a level louder than the church bells playing carols on the quarter hour. Pop-bottle Jones, bundled to the ears against the cold, appeared at Ida June Click's front door. Today wasn't his first stop to check on the child he'd discovered in his trash bin, but this visit carried greater import.

Ida June, a dear but prickly friend, welcomed him inside to a hot, humid kitchen filled with scents he'd not smelled since his mother was living.

"What is that delectable smell?" he asked. His stomach, prone to beg, grumbled.

"Mincemeat," she said as she slid a perfectly browned pie from the oven and placed it on a rack on the counter. "You have a very good nose on you, Ulysses,"

"A wise man does not forget the finer foods of Christmas past."

"Sit down over there and I'll give you a slice." She flapped an oven-gloved hand toward the metal dinette. "Be careful. This is hot. Don't burn yourself and blame me. You'll have milk with it, too. Much better that way."

Hiding his smile, Popbottle shucked his coat and gloves and settled at the table. "Yes, ma'am, I shall, and will be grateful for both."

Ida June sliced the flaky crust, the rich goodness of cinnamon and cloves filling the air as the steaming pie fell apart on the saucer. She set the plate and milk in front of him and then jerked out a chair and plopped down. "I reckon you heard about our Davey's mama."

Popbottle held a fork aloft, waiting for the steam to dissipate. "Indeed. A real tragedy. How is the lad faring?"

"Pretty well, considering he has a funeral to attend and not a relative anywhere to help him say goodbye. Cried awhile last night. Tore my heart right out."

The news saddened him, as well. A child ought not to be subject to such heartache. "Then the rumors are accurate. Davey is alone in the world."

"From all we can tell. A crying shame, too. He's a good boy. Sweet as that pie." She jabbed a finger. "I wish I knew what was to become of him."

"He seems to be thriving here. Perhaps he could remain with you."

"Howard Prichard says I'm too old to take on a handicapped child." She huffed. "Why, the only thing handicapped about Davey is his speech, and if you ask me, silence is golden. The world would be a better place if certain individuals were struck dumb."

Popbottle grinned around the moaningly delicious bite of pie. He felt Ida June's pain. Being considered too old raised his ire, as well. "The only thing old about you, my dear lady, is a number."

"Agreed. I doubt Howard could climb a ladder and repair a roof if his life depended on it, but I certainly can." She flapped a hand in irritation. "I think he's still miffed over the time he was ten and I caught him striking matches behind his daddy's shed. Could have set the whole town on fire in that drought. I marched him right up to the back door and told his daddy. Fred fanned his britches good."

"Yes, well, this time Howard is in charge and he says we're too old."

"You, too?"

Popbottle scooped in another bite of scalding pie. He'd lose a taste bud or two and the proverbial hair off his tongue, but he didn't mind. A hot pie of this caliber was a rare delight, not to be taken lightly.

"Old and unsafe," he said when he could talk.

Ida June fluffed up like a mad hen. That was the thing about Ida. She ruffled easily when her friends were insulted. He smiled a little. Ida June ruffled easily over about anything.

"That is the silliest lie ever told," she said. "Neither you nor GI Jack would hurt a bug."

"Not us, per se, Ida June. Our humble abode. Certainly, I see his point. A recycling business engenders unstable piles of old bicycle parts, bottles, tins, wires, to name a few potentially hazardous elements."

"Perfect situation for a curious boy to use his imagination and be creative."

"Or get injured."

"Well, we have a problem," Ida June said, heavily propping an elbow on the table.

"A conundrum," he concurred.

She shoved a napkin at him and demanded, "Is the pie any good?"

Popbottle smiled behind another forkful. "The best I've had in fifty years."

Ida June slapped the table and let out a bark of laughter. "Well said, my friend. I won't ask how long since your last taste. That nephew of mine won't touch mincemeat, you know."

"All the better for you and me. And speaking of Kade, why doesn't he adopt Davey? He's fond of the child."

"I've been after him about that very thing. Any fool with one eye and half a brain can see he dotes on Davey." She gave a loud huff. "Why, Kade's practically given him that dog of his, and before Davey came along, dog and master were inseparable."

"He's reluctant to adopt?"

"To hear his story, the child needs a father and a mother, not a burned-out cop who might only be around half the time. He's scared spitless, if you ask me. Afraid of loving and losing."

"Rumor says he'll return to Chicago."

"Not if I have a word to say about it." She grinned, a sly, speculative spread of mouth that put a spark of sass in her eyes.

"Why, Miss Ida June, I believe you're up to something."

"Why, Professor Jones, I believe you're exactly correct."

Sophie looked up from her desk to find Ida June Click standing in the doorway of her classroom wear-

ing a visitor's badge on one shoulder of a pair of bright
red insulated coveralls. Hair, white as royal frosting,
neatly curled from beneath an elf-green stocking cap.
Her cheeks were rosy, her eyes were brown and sparkling, and she looked like a character straight out of a
child's library book. If she whipped out an umbrella and
took flight, Sophie wouldn't even blink.

"Ida June, hello. Davey isn't here. Kade picked him
up so I could work late."

"I know that. They're at the house now, racing
around after a football in the backyard like two fools
who don't know it's winter."

Sophie's mouth curved. Beneath Ida June's vine-
gary statement lay a wealth of affection. Sophie liked
the image of a carefree Kade playing with a delighted
Davey. She wished she was with them, but the cookie
project and other Christmas functions had thrown her
behind on her schoolwork. Grades were due in the office before Christmas break.

"Did you come for your cookie order? I'd planned
to deliver later tonight."

Ida June waved her off. "No worry about those cookies, girl. I don't need them until this weekend for the
Victorian Christmas."

Everyone in Redemption and most of the state knew
about Redemption's turn-of-the-century celebration.
Many of Redemption's citizens were heavily involved,
including Sophie and Ida June. Sophie was still working on Kade.

"So what can I do for you?" she asked, curious now
as to the unprecedented visit from Kade's aunt.

Ida June peered intently down the hallway as if worried about being overheard. Then she closed the door

with a snap and marched across the gray carpet, spread her feet in a fighting stance and demanded, "Are you seeing old what's-his-name, the principal?"

Sophie marked her spot in the grade book and closed it. "I suppose you mean Biff Gruber."

"Yes, him," Ida June said, as if speaking Biff's name would give her a sore tongue. "What kind of name is that for a grown man with a master's degree anyway?"

"'A rose by any other name would smell as sweet,'" Sophie answered mildly.

"The Eskimos have fifty-two names for snow because it's important to them. Makes you wonder about old Biff, doesn't it?" Before Sophie could come up with a reasonable response, the older woman insisted, "Well, are you two an item or not?"

Sophie carefully put her pen in the pencil cup on the corner of her desk. Uncertain of where this conversation was headed, she went for honesty. She wasn't interested in Biff, wouldn't be even if Kade had not entered the picture. "No. We never were. To be honest, I'm bewildered that people keep asking me that."

"Small town, small minds. Two singles working together."

"Colleagues. Nothing more." At least not in Sophie's mind.

"I told Ulysses as much. You wear your heart in your eyes, girl. That's what I told him. And your eyes are looking at only one man. My handsome nephew. Spending a lot of time with him, too."

The room grew warmer. Sophie swallowed but managed to keep her voice even. "Are you matchmaking, Ida June?"

"Well, of course I am," Ida June said with a dash

of irritation. "A woman my age has no time for mincing words and waiting on young people to be sensible. Davey needs a mother and a father."

"What?" Sophie's heart bumped. Ida June was moving way too fast. Sophie was still coming to terms with being in love. Jumping to marriage and a family made her head spin. Her heart, too.

"Kade told me about Davey's family, or lack thereof. Not a soul on this earth to stand in the gap for him. No one but you and my nephew."

"And you."

Ida June harrumphed. "Too old to cut the mustard."

Sophie could see how much that bothered the older woman. "Not in my book. You've been wonderful to Davey."

"I can be his great-aunt if a certain pair of adults will cooperate."

"Ida June," she said softly, admonishing, "I'm not sure what you're suggesting." But she had a pretty good idea. If her relationship with Kade moved forward, it would do so on the grounds of faith and love. No other reason. Not even one as precious as Davey could make love happen.

The handywoman clapped a hand on one hip. A tape measure poked out the top of her pocket. "Do you love my boy or not?"

"Which one?" Even though she loved Kade, he had to love her, too, not just Davey.

"Well, both of them."

Sophie pressed her lips together. This was the strangest conversation she'd had in a while, and an elementary-school teacher was no stranger to bizarre talks.

"Kade and I spend a lot of time together because of Davey. We've become good friends."

"Poppycock. There's more between the pair of you than that."

Yes, there was, but a budding love was a fragile thing to be nurtured in private.

Carefully, she shifted the conversation back to Davey. "Social services is still investigating the possibility that Davey has family somewhere. I suppose Kade told you all the details."

"He did, which is why I'm determined to find our Davey a family before it's too late. Before Howard and his cohorts snatch this child away and you never see him again."

So much for distraction. Ida June had a one-track mind. Like Sophie, the older woman had grown attached to Davey and didn't want to lose him.

But what could they do short of something crazy like adoption?

The notion struck a resounding chord in Sophie's head. Adoption? Could she do it? Was she ready to be a mother? Would Davey want her?

The police had uncovered enough information on Melissa Stephens to trace her records. Her story was almost as sad as Davey's. A runaway from foster care, her parents were dead and there were no siblings. Davey's father was unknown. The people of Potterville remembered seeing her a few times, described her as quiet and nervous, but no one remembered her having any friends or social contacts.

"Davey's mother led a very sad and lonely existence," Sophie mused. "Except for one bright spot."

"Her son."

"Yes." Sophie's chest ached for the woman named Melissa and even more for Davey. "I wish I had answers for you, Ida June, but I don't."

Yet the seed had been planted and she couldn't stop thinking about it.

Chapter Twelve

Kade hadn't been this tongue-tied since he was four-teen and his sister's sixteen-year-old friend had kissed him at a birthday party. Sophie B. was killing him—softly and sweetly, but killing him just the same.

When she'd managed to arm-twist him into serving cookies and wassail tonight at the publishing-house mu-seum and talked about dressing for the part, he hadn't expected her clothes to affect him. She was always pretty, but tonight she was a step back in time, a spec-tacular Victorian lady in long blue velvet. With her dark hair swept up and a tiny hat complete with black veil perched on her head, Sophie took his breath away.

"Wow," he murmured when he could speak.

Her cheeks turned pink and her eyes sparkled above the high neckline and cameo broach. "I love dressing up for this."

He glanced down at his pressed gray slacks and black shirt. Twenty minutes ago as he'd splashed on Cool Water cologne and checked the mirror, he'd thought he looked pretty good. But now he was plain vanilla to her blueberry supreme.

As he escorted her to his car her skirt swished against the side of his legs. "Are you going to be embarrassed with an ordinary guy from the twenty-first century?"

"Don't be silly. I'm just glad you agreed to come." She slid onto the passenger seat and tucked her heavy skirts with a feminine grace he found alluring. Chin tilted up toward him, she said, "You're going to love the Victorian Walk, I promise."

He held up a finger to stop the *promise* word, but dropped it again when she laughed. She'd made the promise on purpose to rile him. Nothing could rile him tonight. Nothing except his great-aunt, who'd made kissing noises when he told her he would be with Sophie. The old woman was incorrigible.

Ida June had also stirred the crazy thoughts he'd been fighting of late. Sophie B., her scent, her cookie-sweet voice, her gentle ways lingered in his head even when he was arguing with child protective services about Davey's welfare.

Ida June was pushing him to adopt, but what kind of dad would he be? A messed-up, cynical cop who chafed at Christmas celebrations? Davey didn't need that. Besides, Kade was single. A boy needed a mother. Which brought Kade back full circle to the woman in the passenger's bucket seat.

He had feelings for her. Big-time. She didn't deserve that, either.

"How long is our shift?" He put the car in Reverse and backed from her driveway. The engine rumbled, but he didn't downshift and floor it to show off the powerful engine. Sophie wouldn't be impressed.

"Only an hour. We'll have a fun time, you'll see."

Forget Christmas. Forget cookies and wassail. He

already was, he thought as he drove through the quiet, radiantly decorated neighborhoods toward town center.

Beside him Sophie chattered brightly, filling him in on local color, including a pretty cool story of the town's founder.

"Redemption," she said, "was born during the Land Run of 1889. One day this was nothing but prairie." She made graceful gestures toward the landscape. "The next day, the population exploded with tents and wagons and makeshift structures that became a fledgling town."

"Hard to imagine."

"Exciting," she said, sparkling like a jewel beneath the passing streetlights. "And meaningful, too. The man who founded the center of town and bought up claims to make the rest was Jonas Case."

Kade glanced from the road to her, a pleasant tickle in his chest. "What's meaningful about that?"

Not that he cared, but he liked hearing her enthusiastic recitation.

"Jonas Case squandered his youth as a gunslinger. Purportedly, a very efficient gunslinger."

"My kind of man. Be good at what you do."

She made a noise in the back of her throat. "You would have chased him down and arrested him."

"Probably," he said with a smirk.

"At some point, Jonas saw the error of his ways and gave his heart to the Lord. He stopped shooting people and began to preach."

"He was still sending people to meet their maker, just in a different way."

The comment had the effect he'd hoped for. Sophie's laughter filtered over him like rays of June sun.

"I never thought of it that way, but you're right. He

was." Skirts billowing over the console, she angled toward him. "Apparently, he had a hard time fitting in, even after he cleaned up his act. People shunned him because of his past."

"Figures."

"So he started Redemption for folks like himself. Outcasts, misfits, those looking for a place to belong, a place to start again in peace and acceptance."

Kade had been enjoying the history lesson, but the parallels between his situation and the gunslinger's hit close to home.

"I saw the scripture at the town well."

"'Come unto me, all you who are heavy laden, and I will give you rest,'" she recited. "Jonas dug the well. He and others engraved the stone as a permanent reminder of why Redemption exists."

Redemption. Kade ruminated on the word. Some men didn't deserve Redemption. Maybe he was one of them.

He fell silent, but if Sophie noticed, she was determined to draw him into her celebratory mood.

When they reached the rambling old Newspaper Museum and exited the car, he spotted other ladies in Victorian dress, cowboys, pioneers, and thought he might as well join in. Anything for Sophie.

He offered his elbow. Sophie placed a gloved hand in the crook, a simple, unaffected action, but a fierce protective pride welled in Kade. He might not be a gunslinger, but he took care of his own.

He tugged her close to his side, smiled when she glanced up. Tonight she was with him.

Dangerous ground, a warning voice whispered.

He drew his imaginary six-gun and shot it down.

When they climbed the tall steps, the door swept open and a dapper gent in top hat and a long, fitted coat greeted them. Everyone knew Sophie. Or so it seemed.

"Good evening, sir. Miss Bartholomew," the man said, doffing his hat.

"Evening, Mr. Martinelli."

Sophie's pretty curtsy and happy giggle tickled the inside of Kade's chest.

"Are we in a time machine?" he murmured next to her sweet-smelling ear.

"Maybe." Her eyes shone light gray, dappled blue and gold by the overhead light. "I told you Christmas in Redemption was fun."

They entered a huge space lit by dozens of Christmas trees. The smell of wassail and pine hung in the air, thick and warm, a welcome respite from outdoors.

"Don't you love those trees?" she asked, motioning with arms that rustled satin and velvet. "They're hand-decorated, homemade, the way they would have been in the early days of Redemption."

She led him to a stately pine adorned with lacy white crocheted figures and then to another heavy with spicy-smelling cookie ornaments.

"Don't tell me you made this one?" he joked.

She sparkled at him. "I wish I'd thought of it."

When she looked at him that way, he got lost. He was out of his element, as if his skin didn't quite fit his bones. All these people, all this decency.

"Christmas was simpler then. More personal and caring, I think." With one finger, Sophie tapped a glittery ball of glued yarn. "Someone's hands took the time to make this. To fill this tree with love."

Kade battled the usual cynical thoughts. Anything

was more personal than mass-mailed ecards and mall Santas who charged to take a kid's picture.

But Sophie didn't deserve his bad attitude. Christmas did seem different here in Redemption. Sure, the town glittered and merchants hawked their sales like anywhere else, but there was something else here, too. Something better, gentler, more caring.

That was it, he thought as he watched a smiling teenager twirl a younger child in an impromptu dance. People cared.

It was enough to make a man want to celebrate.

He might even break down and buy a few presents.

Astonished at his thoughts, he let Sophie guide him through the enormous old building. They took a while because Sophie being Sophie greeted everyone along the way and introduced him until his head swam with names and faces he'd never remember.

"Good thing we came early," he said after shaking hands with a firefighter named Zak and the local vet. He would remember those two. Nice guys.

"Can't leave you a stranger," she said, and he didn't stop to wonder why it mattered.

Eventually they arrived at the far end of the room where a section of long tables spread down one wall. In the center a giant punch bowl steamed with what he assumed was wassail, although the smell was suspiciously like apple juice. On either side of the bowl, homemade cookies were piled high on giant platters.

"Fifth-grade cookies?" he asked, mostly joking.

"Some are. The town council bought twenty dozen and others are donated by local bakers. Aren't they beautiful?"

"Can't argue that." The whole place was Christmas-beautiful, though not nearly as pretty as Sophie. She sparkled tonight, more glittery than any gilded ornament. "Let me taste test to be sure."

She poked a cookie in his mouth.

He chewed and swallowed while she laughed at his surprise.

His heart did ridiculous things in his chest.

Whoa, boy. It's only a cookie.

Right, and Sophie was only a woman.

She offered a ridiculously dainty cup of wassail to wash down the peanut butter. He sipped, wondering if he should stick out his pinky and make her laugh some more. He did and Sophie didn't disappoint.

The wassail, however, did. Apple juice and spices. Was that what wassail was?

The trickle of revelers entering the building seemed more enchanted by the juice than he. He found himself dipping and doling nonstop.

Not that he was complaining. A man would be nuttier than he was not to enjoy a date with Sophie.

Together they chatted up the visitors and doled out refreshments. He hadn't talked this much since the last time he'd been on the witness stand and some defense attorney had badgered him for hours. Tonight's conversation was decidedly more pleasant.

Kade was getting into the spirit of the evening when Sophie's principal appeared. Maybe Kade was imagining things, but he had a feeling old stiff-shirt Gruber didn't like him much.

The feeling was mutual.

"McKendrick," Gruber said stiffly, his glance quickly dismissing Kade in favor of Sophie. Kade couldn't fault him for his taste. "Sophie."

"Cookies and wassail, Biff?" she said with more courtesy than Kade felt. What was it about the principal that set his teeth on sandpaper?

"You look lovely tonight."

"Thank you." She dropped a curtsy. Kade wished she wouldn't do that. Not for Gruber anyway. "I see you're into the spirit of Christmas, as well."

Did she have to be nice to everyone?

"Doing my part." Gruber, the peacock, preened in a shiny gold vest. Sissy color, if you asked Kade. A watch chain—a *fob*—dangled from an inner pocket.

Peacock, Kade thought again, this time with more vehemence. Go play in traffic.

But Gruber wanted to linger. Imagine that? "We have a nice night for the festivities."

Kade's small, irritated noise brought a reproving glance from Sophie. He ignored her. Was Gruber a total idiot?

The temperature was freezing.

Painfully agreeable, Sophie said, "As nice as ever."

Why didn't she tell him to buzz off?

The overdressed peacock lingered longer, nibbling at a gingerbread man. He nibbled. Not bit. Not gobbled. Nibbled. Daintily. Like a girl. What kind of a man nibbled?

"Your class made these?" Gruber asked, one imperious eyebrow arched.

No, Kade thought sarcastically. Santa brought them in his sleigh so you could stand here and annoy the prettiest woman in the building.

But Sophie the diplomat said, "They did. Aren't they delicious? We've made almost a thousand dollars profit so far."

"Commendable," the principal murmured with a smile as fake as his mustache. Kade had the juvenile urge to give it a yank.

Instead, he showed his teeth in something less than a smile. More like a dog about to bite. "I think someone over there is waving at you, Gruber." *Way* over there. South of the Mexican border.

"Really?" Biff looked to Sophie, whose cheeks reddened and eyes bugged as though she wanted to laugh. When she managed a weak smile, he set his half-finished punch cup on the table and said with a hint of threat—at least, Kade took it that way—"Enjoy your evening, Sophie. We'll discuss your project further on Monday."

When he'd made a hasty exit, Sophie whirled toward Kade with a hiss of suppressed laughter. "I can't believe you did that."

He lifted a lazy shoulder. "Gone but not forgotten. The gone is all I cared about."

"You're terrible." She whapped his arm for good measure.

He rubbed the spot. "Worse than terrible."

She had no idea.

"I have to admit I'm glad he left," she said. "He was acting a little odd tonight."

"Only tonight?"

"Kade," she admonished but she giggled, too.

All right, so he was jealous. Gruber made no secret of his admiration for Sophie. "He's not going to give you grief at work, is he?"

Her inner light momentarily dimming, Sophie caught her bottom lip between her teeth. "I don't think so."

Kade saw the speck of worry. Old Biff might react

like a peacock spurned and that would not be a good thing for Sophie.

A growl rumbled in his head. At Gruber *and* at himself. He should have kept his mouth shut.

He was glaring daggers at the faraway principal when a voice intruded.

"Lookey here, Popbottle," a gravelly voice said. "Miss Sophie and Kade is serving up refreshments. I do believe I'll have a taste."

"Apple juice," Kade muttered. "Be brave."

GI Jack, looking as derelict as always, took the offered cup and then slipped a pair of cookies into his shirt pocket. Sophie handed him two more. "I thought you and Mr. Jones were caroling."

"Oh, we are, Miss Sophie." GI swigged the warm wassail and smacked his lips. "Loosening up the vocals."

Popbottle Jones, in an ancient tuxedo and shiny top hat, spoke up. "Speaking of vocals, what is the latest word on young Davey? Has he seen the specialist yet?"

"Tuesday morning at nine we have an appointment in Oklahoma City. We're hopeful."

"Excellent. We'll be praying for a positive outcome. Keep us apprised, will you, please?"

"Of course I will." She handed GI another cup of wassail. Kade figured what the heck and handed over several more cookies. This brought a delighted smile to the old man's grizzled face.

"I knew you were a good one the minute you hopped into that trash heap after Miss Sophie." He chortled, spitting cookie crumbs. "Forty years ago, I woulda chased her myself."

Sophie blushed. Kade laughed with the men. GI was simple but had a good heart.

Popbottle, the dignified half of the eccentric duo, set his cup on the table.

"Caroling commences in five minutes," he said with a doff of his hat. "Thank you for the fine refreshments. Off we go."

GI's head bobbed twice. "Off we go."

"Carolers?" Kade asked as he watched them join an assembled group in period dress.

"Wait until you hear them, Kade. Your doubt will disappear faster than cookies in GI's pocket. Those two are quite the singers."

He knew he shouldn't be surprised at anything about GI and Popbottle, but singing? "No kidding?"

"GI Jack sings tenor, if you can imagine that, and Popbottle has a rich baritone. They're really quite amazing."

He watched her watching them and thought, *You're the amazing one.*

"Do you sing?"

"A little," she said. "Nothing special."

He begged to differ. Everything about Sophie was special.

"What about you?"

"I can wrap my tonsils around a note or two."

"Really?"

"Don't look so surprised. Davey and Sheba think I'm pretty good."

"You sing for them?"

He picked a cookie crumb from the lacy tablecloth, then replaced a few empty spaces with napkins loaded with cookies.

"Pick a little guitar, too."

"That's right. I remember seeing the guitar in your bedroom."

"Sheba's used to it. Stopped howling and covering her ears years ago. Davey wants to learn."

"Guitar?"

He gave her a funny look but didn't say the obvious. Davey couldn't sing if he wanted to. "I showed him some chords."

"Kade, I love this idea. Davey needs ways to express himself. You are a genius."

"The wassail's going to your head," he said, both pleased and uncomfortable at her praise. He played guitar. He could carry a tune. So could half the population. Sharing his love of music was no big deal. It didn't make him a hero. Heroes did the right thing. Whatever that was.

Someone came along just then and interrupted the conversation. The night wore on with cookies and wassail and cold air curling around his legs like an icy cat. The old wood floor was pretty but not too energy efficient.

Through the windows fronting the building, Kade could see a trolley car parked at the corner beneath the glow of lights. An occasional horse-drawn buggy clopped slowly down the cobblestone street. Peaceful, pretty, a time warp.

Carolers, Popbottle and GI among them, stood on the street corners, their Christmas sounds silenced by distance, but vapor clouds and glowing faces sang of joy.

They were sucking him in. Slowly. Surely. And he kind of liked the feeling.

"Have you ever seen anything so wonderful?" Sophie asked, seeing the direction of his gaze.

He turned to look into her glowing face, and he could honestly say, "Never."

Sophie B. was more than wonderful. She was a gift he didn't deserve. Like the town and this night, he felt her moving toward him, opening her generous heart to take him in.

A decent man would go ahead and fall in love with Sophie. He wondered anew how she'd managed to remain single this long. The man who won Sophie's heart would have to be special. He'd have to recognize her for the treasure she was. A woman far above rubies.

There was nothing special about him.

He handed her a sugar cookie, more to stop his thoughts than anything. She bit and chewed, laughing with her lips sealed. Tiny crumbs scattered down her chin. He flicked them away with the tips of his fingers, glad for the excuse to touch her velvet skin.

Sophie sparkled up at him. "Our hour is almost up."

"Yeah?" That surprised him. As she'd promised, he'd had a good time, mostly because of Sophie but not entirely. Redemption knew how to throw a party. "What now?"

He wasn't ready to take her home.

She lifted a mutton-sleeved shoulder. "I'd like to see the living Christmas cards. Want to come?"

"Sure." Even though he had no idea what a living Christmas card was, he helped her into her coat and escorted her down the steep steps to the street, proud to be the man at her side.

Cold air jammed his lungs. He shivered. "Brr."

"Thankfully, there are plenty of stops along the way.

All the stores are open. We can pop inside to get warm anytime."

"Like now?"

"Tough Chicago boy." She bumped against him with a grin and then tugged him toward the stoplight on the corner. "The best displays are on this side. If we get too cold, we can hop the trolley to see the rest.

He'd joked about the cold. With Sophie's smile to warm him, he didn't even feel the windchill.

They strolled the streets with the other Victorian walkers and stopped to peer at Christmas scenes behind the large display windows. In one, a motherly woman with an upswept hairdo played the piano while ringlet-haired girls competed in a game of jacks. Behind them a fireplace glowed. A cozy scene that set him to thinking about family.

A teenage vendor in knickers with a box hung around his neck ventured past.

"Hot peanuts," he called. "One dollar. Get your hot peanuts."

Kade fished in his pocket for a dollar and bought a bag, more for the experience and the warmth than the peanuts. And to see Sophie smile.

"You love this stuff, don't you?" Kade asked, handing her the warm bag.

Sophie's face, rosy from the cold, turned upward. "Peanuts or the walk?"

"All of it."

"Yes," she said, happily hugging herself. "I love it."

With a catch in his chest, Kade gazed down into her lovely eyes and thought of how much he'd miss her if— no, when—he returned to Chicago.

He'd expected the pull toward home to increase with the boredom of living in a small community. It hadn't.

He found her free hand and tucked it into his. Even in the fluffy, lined gloves, her fingers felt small and slender and feminine. A man could be a man with Sophie.

This was a dangerous thought, but tonight was all about pretend. Tomorrow was soon enough to remember all the reasons he didn't belong here with someone like Sophie.

"Is that who I think it is?" Sophie asked when they'd gone barely a block.

An old-time lawman in long, Wyatt Earp duster and black hat strode toward them from the other end of the street, his spurs jingling. Kade blinked in amusement.

"Chief Rainmaker?" he asked when the man approached.

The normally smooth-shaven Jesse tweaked a fake handlebar mustache. "I'm under here. What do you think?"

Kade didn't say what he was thinking. That the look was completely out of character for the staid, professional officer of the court. And he doubted a real criminal would take him seriously.

Sophie spoke up, beaming. "I like it, Jesse."

"Let's hope no one calls me out at high noon for a gunfight. My speed's a little rusty."

Kade had been to the shooting range with the chief. He might not be fast, but he was deadly. For a small-town cop, Jesse was first-rate.

"Did you get my email?" Kade asked.

"Haven't had time today. You find something?"

"A few leads. I think you're right, but I'll need more time to investigate."

Sophie lifted curious eyes to his. "Are you working for the police department on other cases?"

"I've convinced him to use his handy computer skills to chase down some information we need," Rainmaker told her. "I hate computers."

"Kade is wonderful at that kind of thing. Just look at the way he found Davey's mother."

The familiar regret tugged at him. "For all the good I accomplished."

Sophie squeezed his hand. "You gave him closure. That's a lot."

"My office could use someone with his investigative skills and clearances," the chief said. "We're understaffed and underfunded, but I could squeeze some money out of the budget for a man like Kade."

Kade shifted uncomfortably. He was doing Jesse a favor and feeling useful at the same time. But he wasn't working. Not really. Not yet.

The idea of joining a small-town force had him wondering if he was ready to get back in the game. Finding Davey's mother dead had been a blow, but in the end he'd felt better instead of worse. Granted, he'd phoned his shrink to talk things over. The first time in weeks. The shocked doc had made him realize he might be moving forward again.

Come to think of it, he'd slept most of last night and his only dreams had been of Sophie.

He exhaled a vapor cloud. Small-town life was supposed to be simpler, but things were getting more complicated by the minute.

At least for him.

Sophie crunched a salty peanut shell with her front teeth. All the heat had dissipated from the small paper bag, but Kade's gesture continued to warm her heart.

He was different tonight. Relaxed and almost happy. The Christmas spirit had overtaken him. How could anyone roam the festive streets of Redemption without being drawn into the mood?

She was always happy at Christmas, although she credited being with Kade for tonight's extra burst of joy. She was in love, and regardless of the outcome, she would enjoy their time together.

She wondered at his reaction to Chief Rainmaker's offer. He'd gone quiet, thoughtful. Was there a chance he'd remain in Redemption?

A horse-drawn carriage clip-clopped to a stop next to the sidewalk and a man climbed out. He reached back for the bustle-clad woman still inside. The woman laughed, threw her arms out wide and fell into the man's embrace. He whirled her around in a circle before setting her feet on the sidewalk for a lingering kiss.

Sophie averted her gaze, pinched by uncharacteristic envy. She wanted to be loved.

A strong hand tugged at her elbow. "Let's take the carriage home."

She pivoted toward him. "But your car is here."

"I can come back for it."

Excitement fluttered. She wanted to. Badly. "It's not too sensible, but…"

The corners of his mouth quivered. With eyes narrowed and a tad ornery, he said, "Live dangerously, Sophie. Ride with me."

Her stomach nosedived. Live dangerously? He was teasing, she knew. The only danger when she was with him was from her own heart.

While she waited in anticipation, he spoke to the driver, handed over some bills and opened the carriage door. When Sophie started to climb inside, his hands came around her waist and he lifted her easily onto the step. She felt light and delicate and protected.

She scooted to the far side of the bench seat and Kade climbed in beside her. After straightening the heavy throw over their laps, all the while fighting down her billowy dress and making her giggle in the process, he tapped on the roof of the carriage. With a jingle of bells, the horse smoothly moved forward.

"How did women manage with all that?" He pushed again, playfully, at her voluminous skirts.

Sophie laughed softly. "I'm glad I'll never have to find out."

"I thought you liked dressing up."

"I do. For one night a year. Every day would be a chore. Do you have any idea the amount of undergarments I have under this dress?" She clapped a hand over her mouth. "Don't answer that."

Kade's laugh rang out, rich and real. To hear him laugh so freely was worth the slip of the tongue. "I'll be a gentleman tonight and pretend I'm not thinking about your undergarments. Those layers must have driven men to distraction."

"Kade!" Heat rushed up the sides of her neck. "Stop!"

He laughed again, dark eyes dancing in the passing glow of streetlamps and Christmas lights. Settling back for the gentle ride, he put an arm around her shoulders and snugged her closer.

"I'll be good," he murmured against her ear, his breath warm and enticing, "if you say so."

"You better," she said, pulse ticking away in her throat.

His lips grazed her ear and she sighed, snuggling into

him. The carriage swayed to the rhythm of hoofbeats on concrete, a melody that matched her happy heart.

Being with Kade felt right in so many ways. Did he feel it, too? Or was he just a man saying sweet things to a gullible woman?

No, she didn't believe that. Even though he was a man with a man's feelings, Kade treated her with a respect and tenderness that made her feel more secure than she ever had. They could tease and flirt—and did—but Kade never crossed her invisible line.

As they rolled along, admiring the lights and Santas and Nativity displays, they made small talk. About the celebration. About Davey. About everything except the thing utmost in Sophie's mind. The two of them.

"Look," he said, his voice quiet, "it's snowing."

Sophie gave a delighted gasp and craned her neck toward the carriage window. "I love snow."

"How did I guess? Miss Suzy Snowflake, Miss Christmas Eve loves snow. Imagine." But she could tell he liked it, too.

They turned the last corner and headed down the street toward her house. She wished the time would stand still, that this night would never end, that she could spend forever with Kade, snuggled close in this carriage with the snow falling around them.

The carriage rattled into her driveway. A layer of snow, like powdered sugar on cake, sprinkled the dry grass of her front lawn. The rare sprinkling wouldn't last, would likely be gone by morning, but for tonight nothing could be more perfect.

"Home," Kade said.

She drew in a long satisfied breath. "I don't want to get out."

His gaze caught hers and he nodded. "I know."

They remained there for long seconds inside the warm carriage that smelled of leather and Kade's cologne.

She memorized him, the firm plane of his face, the tiny scar on his chin.

She wondered if he knew she loved him. And she was sorely tempted to blurt the words here and now.

Didn't Dad say loving was always a good thing? Didn't a person as wonderful as Kade deserve to know he was loved?

The driver opened the carriage door. Frosty wind blew snowflakes inside. "Step easy, Sophie. The concrete is a little icy."

"I've got her," Kade said.

The driver, a man she'd known since childhood, nodded and stepped aside. "I'll wait here for you, sir."

Kade alighted first and reached back for Sophie. She was tempted to leap into his arms the way the woman had done earlier, but considering the damp concrete and the risk of a fall, she refrained. Instead, she leaned forward and was thrilled when Kade grasped her waist and swept her out into his arms and against his chest.

"I saw that in a movie once," he said, grinning down into her face. "Always wanted to try it."

She giggled, hesitant to turn loose of his strong shoulders. "What did you think?"

"I think the old days had something on us modern folks. All these opportunities to hold a pretty girl. Who knew?"

He set her on her feet but didn't turn her loose. Instead he slid an arm around her waist and led her to the front door. Snow swirled around them like wet feathers.

"This is beautiful," she said, turning toward him and the falling snow. "Such a perfect ending to a special night."

"The best I can remember." His answer made her heart sing.

"Ever?" she asked.

"Ever." Then he softly kissed her, the cold snow melting on their warm lips.

When the kiss ended, he cupped her cheek and smiled into her eyes. The urge to declare her love rose like a helium balloon, warm and beautiful. When she opened her mouth to say the words, Kade kissed her again.

Bells jingled as the horse in the driveway moved restlessly. With an embarrassed start, Sophie remembered the driver looking on.

"Your carriage awaits," she said with a soft, breathless laugh.

Kade made a growling sound, but when she shivered, he took her key and unlocked the door. "Good night, Sophie."

"Good night." She started inside but stopped and turned. "Kade?"

He was still standing on the porch waiting until she was safely inside. A surge of love and hope welled up inside her.

"Christmas Eve is candlelight service at church. Will you and Davey go with me? It's such a beautiful, reverent time."

He blinked as though the question caught him off guard. Slowly, heartbreakingly, he shook his head. "Better not."

She studied the troubled expression, the struggle

going on behind his eyes, and wanted to argue, but a quiet voice inside held her protest in check.

Lips pressed together, the memory of his kiss still lingering, Sophie went inside and closed the door.

Chapter Thirteen

Kade didn't sleep much that night. Not for the usual reasons, but because of Sophie. Tonight the truth had hit him in the face like a sucker punch. He loved her. He wanted to give her everything a good life had to offer.

The problem was he had nothing good to give.

All she'd asked of him was a church service and he couldn't even give her that. He was a lot of things but he refused to be a hypocrite. He wouldn't go inside a church and pretend to pay homage to a God who let bad things happen to little kids.

Flopping over to his side, he jabbed the pillow with his fist. Ida June's fluffy old couch groaned but didn't give. The monstrosity was ugly but comfortable enough to sleep on—if a man could sleep. And when he couldn't, he could slip out the door without disturbing the household.

Tonight he wouldn't ramble. He'd done enough of that and the bitter weather served as impediment.

Tonight he'd lie here and torture himself with thoughts. He'd hope the ulcer didn't act up, and if worse came to worse, he'd get up and open the laptop. Criminals didn't sleep. Why should cops?

He heard the tip-tap of Sheba's paws and caught the light reflected in her amber eyes as she left Davey's side to come to the couch. Her wet nose nudged the back of his hand.

Kade flopped again, this time to his back. "Need out, girl?"

The dog dropped to a sit and put her muzzle on his chest. Kade echoed her sigh. She didn't need outside. She'd come, as she'd done in those awful first weeks after the end of the undercover sting, because she felt her master's troubled spirit.

Kade rubbed her ears, grateful for the company of a silent friend. Sheba was like Davey in that respect. Gentle and silent.

He groaned again and Sheba shifted anxiously.

Monday, perhaps Davey would get good news from the specialist. Sophie was praying and Kade had his fingers crossed that something could be done for Davey's voice.

Tuesday, a small boy would bury his mother. Supported by Kade, Sophie, Ida June and a handful of new friends, he'd lay his mother to rest.

The implication twisted Kade in two. No one could ever replace his mother, but Davey needed a family. He shouldn't be resigned to his mother's lonely, tragic fate.

The thought of Sophie intruded. Again. She'd been in his mind since the day they'd met, but tonight the romantic carriage ride had gotten to him. *She* had gotten to him. After he'd watched her enter the snug little house and heard the lock click into place, he'd walked through snowflakes to the carriage and thought how much like the snow she was. Soft and pretty, rare and pure.

When he reached the carriage, the driver said it all. "It's a lucky man that's loved by Sophie B."

Did she love him? He thought she might. With all his being he wanted to be Sophie's "lucky man," but how could he be? He was big-city. She was small-town. He was dark to her light and rain to her sunshine. Sophie had faith while he'd abandoned his during a year of asking where God was when kids were being sold to predators, and facing the ugly truth that he was as much to blame as God. He'd been there and done nothing. Maybe the fault was all his, not God's.

But still, a Christmas Eve service with all the trappings and Sophie yearning for something from him he couldn't give.

He just wasn't ready.

He was ready, however, bright and early Monday morning for the trip to Oklahoma City. He and Davey, spit-shined, combed and overfed on Ida June's pancakes, left the house in plenty of time to test conditions of the roads. Along the way, they picked up Sophie, who insisted on going along. Not that he minded one bit, and her presence soothed Davey, who'd expressed some doubt about being poked and prodded by a doctor.

According to the local doc, Davey was headed for something called a laryngoscope to look at his vocal cords. They'd tried to explain to Davey in simple terms, but all they'd managed to do was make him anxious.

Sophie was in her usual merry Christmas mood, not a trace of the disappointment he'd seen on her face Saturday night. With Davey buckled in the backseat,

Kade was tempted to reach across the console and hold Sophie's hand. He didn't, though. Until he knew where he was headed, he couldn't involve Sophie in his life any deeper than she already was.

They made small talk about the Victorian Walk and how she wished the snow had stayed, about the cookie project and the upcoming Christmas break from school. They both carefully avoided the subject of Davey's mother and tomorrow's funeral, but the event played heavily on Kade's mind. After the funeral, what happened to Davey then?

By the time they entered the tall, many-storied outpatient clinic, Davey's quietness had turned to fidgets.

"You'll be okay, buddy," Kade said as he took Davey's hand and led him into the waiting area. "Look, there are other kids here and toys to play with. Look at the size of that truck!"

Davey was having none of it. He clung to Kade's side and Sophie's hand, refusing to let go of either. As Davey's temporary guardian, Kade filled out the appropriate paperwork with the boy clinging to him like a dog tick.

What would the little guy do if Kade didn't file for guardianship? Who would be there to hold Davey when he was scared?

Over Davey's head, he questioned Sophie with worried eyes.

"Everything will work out," she said softly and patted Davey's back. Kade wished he believed her. Experience had taught him exactly the opposite.

When a scrub-clad nurse called Davey's name, the trio followed her down an immaculate, antiseptic-scented hallway where Davey was readied for the procedure.

He looked small and scared in the hospital gown. When a nurse came at him with an IV, he screamed, but only breath emerged, a pitifully inadequate sound that left his body rigid and damp with perspiration.

Sophie soothed him as best she could, but in the end, the adults betrayed the child by holding him down. Davey fought, his chest heaving until he realized his struggles were in vain. Then he went limp and lay still and helpless. Kade's stomach hurt to look at him.

"You're okay, buddy," he kept murmuring against Davey's ear. "This is the worst of it." He hoped he wasn't lying.

A tear trickled from Davey to Kade, hot and condemning.

Kade squeezed his eyes tight and tried not to remember other children being hurt by adults. This was for Davey's good, not for bad.

But the parallels haunted him just the same.

"Almost done, Davey," Sophie said. She stood on the other side of Davey's head, smoothing the fine, pale hair from his brow. "You're such a brave boy. I'm proud of you."

When the trauma and tears passed and Davey was being wheeled away, Sophie accompanied the gurney down the hallway, murmuring her motherly endearments while holding Davey's pale hand until the very last moment. The sight chipped a piece off Kade's composure.

"We're doing the right thing," he told her when she returned, her smoky eyes glistening with tears.

"I know," she said. "But he doesn't."

Kade pulled her against his chest to both give and

take comfort. After a bit, regrettably, she drew back and sniffled.

"Where's your Suzy Snowflake smile?" he teased gently.

Her lips wobbled upward in effort. He was tempted to kiss her then and there.

"Come on, I'll buy you some coffee," he said. "If you promise not to do the yogurt trick."

That was enough to bring a real smile. "If you're trying to make me feel better, you're succeeding."

Funny how happy that made him.

One cup turned to two and, just when he was ready to beg a nurse for a glass of milk or a spoon of antacid to toss on the volcano, a door swung open and the doctor appeared.

Sophie grabbed for Kade's hand. Like any parents of a sick child—even though they weren't—they eagerly awaited the verdict.

After a quick introduction, Dr. Swimmer said, "Well, folks, I have good news. Great news, actually. Davey's muteness is caused by a posterior glottic web."

"I've never heard of that," Sophie said.

"It's very rare, rarer still not to be diagnosed before this age, though I've read his records and understand the unusual circumstances."

"What is it? Can you repair it? Will he ever speak?"

The doctor smiled at Sophie's gush of questions. "A glottic web, in his case, is congenital. He was born with a webbing of fibrous tissue in his larynx, or voice box. His is so severe that the vocal cords are impeded. So he can't speak. Usually a child with this condition has breathing difficulties, too."

"He snores like a hog," Kade said.

The doctor inclined his head, smiling slightly. "I'm not surprised. His snoring is probably a stridor coming through the constricted tissues."

Medical jargon was lost on Kade. All he wanted to know was "Can you fix him?"

"We can."

A delighted gasp escaped Sophie. "That's wonderful news."

"I agree." The doctor fiddled with the flat surgical mask still tied around his neck. "But there's one problem. This isn't usually something I discuss with patients, but it's Christmas and Davey is a special case."

"Yes, he is," Sophie said. "Very special."

"Davey is not in any distress, so the surgery to repair his glottis web is elective. I'm willing to reduce my fee, but there are still hospital costs to consider, and according to his records Davey has no insurance and no family."

Kade got the message. "How expensive is this procedure?"

The surgeon gave them an estimate that sent Mt. Vesuvius into eruption stage.

Kade tightened his hands into fists.

Money stood between Davey and his voice.

Sophie was never short on hope. Kade may act as if the end had come, but she refused to believe it.

"We will not give up," she told him later that evening when they were alone at her house, Davey safely sleeping off his trying day under the careful watch of Ida June. "We can't."

They were seated in her living room, a domino game

spread on the coffee table. The smell of hot buttered popcorn filled the house and warmed them.

Kade clicked a blank-four onto the board. No points. "Got a wad of money in your Christmas stocking?"

"Maybe." When he lifted one eyebrow, she played a two-six. "Ten points." She marked a giant X on the score sheet under her name. "My class will donate our cookie money."

Kade studied the board and his dominoes, finger and thumb stroking his bottom lip. "Noble, but nowhere near enough."

She knew he'd say that. She'd thought the same at first mention of the expense involved. But if she lived her faith, and she certainly tried to, she had to believe that nothing was impossible with God. "We'll make more. I also plan to hassle social services."

"Christmas is nearly over." With a sly grin, he plopped down a domino and cried, "Give me fifteen, Miss B."

"Cops are so sneaky," she said mildly, marking his score. "You distracted me."

"Narc's are the worst." He leaned across the table and kissed her. "Now we're even. I'm distracted, too."

Sophie's lips tingled. She touched them. "Double distracted."

"What say we go for triple?" He leaned forward as if to kiss her again. She poked a piece of popcorn into his mouth.

"Foiled." He leaned back, smiling broadly, something he did more and more. When they'd first met, she'd wondered about his dark, broody personality, his lack of joy. Now she saw beneath, through the darkness to the incredible, sensitive man. The cynicism was a protective shell covering a tender heart. Sophie still wondered what he needed protecting from. Certainly not from her, and he'd opened his heart to Davey.

The thought of Davey brought her back to the problem of money. "People eat cookies year-round. If we have to we can bake and sell until the money is raised for Davey's surgery, no matter how long it takes." She slapped down a domino, her mind far from the game. "I believe in miracles, Kade, and Davey needs one. He deserves to have a voice like anyone else, the sooner the better. Why not wish for a Christmas miracle?"

"You're something, Sophie," Kade said, thrilling her to the bones. "I almost believe you'll make it happen."

And then he slapped down a domino, chuckled madly and said, "Twenty points."

The conversation with Kade played in Sophie's head days later when a sad Davey sat at the round table in the back of her classroom listlessly drawing red circles on green construction paper.

He had these moments often since the funeral, a sad, cold, painfully short event. Howard Prichard had enlisted the services of a grief counselor but without a voice, Davey could only express his hurt with gestures and pictures.

The other students rallied around, trying to cheer the usually happy boy. Bless his precious soul, he tried, but his heart wasn't in playing. He was sad and hurt and orphaned. More than ever, Sophie prayed for God to give him a miracle. She prayed about a family, too, wondering as she had a dozen times if she should adopt him. She was thinking about it, long and hard.

Yesterday, she'd discussed the possibility with Dad.

True to form, he'd supported her all the way. Still, parenting required more than giving a child clothes, food and a house to live in. A boy needed a father, too, especially a boy like Davey who'd never had one.

She typed in the final edit of a note to parents. The back of her shoulders ached with unusual tension. As much as she loved Christmas, the last days of school before Christmas break were one of a teacher's greatest challenges. Kids, wired up with too much candy and the excitement of presents, vibrated the building with their energy. Add the concerns over Davey and she was tense.

She was glad when her charges headed to the gym for P.E. During this, her prep hour, she printed the note. In it, she'd explained Davey's situation and hoped to gain support for an ongoing cookie project.

Her students had wholeheartedly voted to donate the money to fund Davey's surgery. No surprise there. The trouble was, the budget was still several thousand dollars short. They had to make more.

She clicked her instant message, the principal's preferred method of interschool communication, and typed, Are you available for conference?

I have a few minutes. Come to my office, Biff typed in return.

Sophie rubbed the back of her head where a painful pulse throbbed. She didn't love the idea of discussing an ongoing cookie project with Biff. He'd been prickly since the encounter with Kade over the wassail bowl, but his approval was essential.

The bells on her doorknob jingled as she hurried out and down the hall. For once she didn't stop to admire the silver-and-green garland looped across the hall or the cotton-ball Santas decorating the walls.

She strode into Biff's office and told him her plans.

"I sent you an email this morning, Sophie. Didn't you get it?"

She blinked. His wasn't the response she'd hoped for. "I haven't had time to check. What was it about?"

"We've decided to discontinue the fifth-grade fundraiser after today." His gaze held hers, firm and unyielding.

Sophie's heart sank into her empty stomach. The pulse in the back of her head thudded louder. "Won't you at least let me explain why we should continue?"

"This shouldn't come as a surprise, considering the conversations we've had on the topic. The project is discontinued, Sophie, and this subject is closed." He scribbled something on a pad of paper. Sophie had the insane desire to yank the pen from his fingers and bop him with it. "Furthermore, this is the last day you can tutor Davey Stephens in your class. He is not a fifth grader, nor are you a special-needs teacher. Mrs. Jacobs in the resource room will take over from here."

The words were a slap in the face. He was intentionally trying to upset her. "Why are you doing this? You know I'm a good teacher and my students perform well academically. Having Davey in our classroom has never interfered with that. On the contrary, my students have learned a great deal from the situation. You also know how important that little boy is to me. He just buried his mother!"

Biff flinched but did not relent. "I must do what's best for the students of Redemption Elementary."

"We're in total agreement on that. What we don't agree on is the method. Isn't there something I can do to change your mind? At least about the project?"

His nostrils flared. Whatever she'd done infuriated him. But what? Why wouldn't he tell her?

Surely, *surely,* his actions today were not personal. Were they?

With a flash of intuition, she asked, "Is this about my relationship with Kade?"

A vein flexed in his neck. He leveled her with a glare. "Don't be ridiculous. Now if you'll excuse me, I have a school to run."

He swiveled away to the computer at his side, leaving her staring at the side of his head in disbelief.

Whatever his reasons, Biff had just taken away her favorite project. With it went the money needed to give Davey a voice.

Chapter Fourteen

He had to cheer them up.

The thought was laughable to Kade, a man whose dark, depressed moods had given him an ulcer and sent him to a shrink.

But this afternoon, he felt like Mr. Happy Face compared to Davey and Sophie. As she did every day, Sophie brought Davey home from school. Unlike normal days, she rang the doorbell and when Kade had answered, his heart thumping happy thoughts at seeing her, she'd barely said a word.

He'd never seen Sophie down. It scared him. What would the world do without Sophie's sunshine? What would *he* do without it?

"Talk to me," he said, snagging her coat-encased arm when she started to turn away and head for her car. "What's going on?"

He sounded like his psychiatrist.

She pivoted back toward him and without a word, walked into his arms.

Endorphins flooded his brain. He could handle this. He stroked her silky hair, let himself have the pleasure of a deep inhale of coconut-scented Sophie and warmed her with his body. Okay, and he might have kissed the side of her head. And maybe her ear.

She shivered. He drew her into the narrow entry and kicked the door closed, still holding her. A man would be crazier than he already was to let go now.

From the corner of his eye, he spotted Davey and Sheba flopped on Ida June's braided rug. They weren't wrestling. Davey wasn't giggling. Sheba's gaze looked soulful.

"Tell me who to beat up," he murmured. "Resolve my anger issues for a good cause."

She lightened some and sighed. "You would, wouldn't you?"

"Love to. Say the word."

"Maybe later."

Her response tickled him. "There's always hope."

"That's the problem. There isn't anymore."

The statement, especially coming from her, bewildered him. The trickle of fear pushed at his nerve endings. If Sophie lost hope, they were doomed. *He* was doomed. "What are you saying?"

She told him. Old stuff-shirt Gruber had put an end to her hopes of raising Davey's surgical fee through the school.

"Why?" he asked.

She shrugged, pulling back from him. Much as he wanted her in his arms, he also wanted to see her face. That beautiful, sweet, loving face.

"Why doesn't matter," she said.

"Matters to me."

"I don't know what to do now." She gnawed her bottom lip. Such a waste of lips, he thought and touched his to the spot. Her lips curled upward and the relief that slammed him like a tidal wave. He'd made Sophie smile.

"I'll kiss you forever if you'll be happy. Or I'll beat up Gruber. Either works for me."

The smile widened. "Silly."

Feeling better, though he'd accomplished nothing but a smile, he took her hand and tugged her toward the kitchen. "Stay," he said simply. "We'll figure this out."

Her answer was to sit down at the metal table. "There has to be a way."

He winked. "That's my girl. Miss Suzy Snowflake does not let bad news stop her."

He poured them each a glass of orange juice and left a third in the fridge for Davey.

"Doesn't the acid bother you?" she asked.

"Seeing you upset bothers me more." He took a sip, waiting for the burn. "Know what I think?"

"Most of the time, no." Lips curving over the edge of the glass, she sipped her juice.

"Forget old Biff," he said, suddenly struck with zeal and maybe a little revenge on the stuffy principal. "We'll continue the cookie project outside of school, only on a grander scale." He didn't know where the idea came from, but he ran with it. "Involve your church, the town, your friends."

"Kade!" Sophie sat up straighter. "That's a fabulous idea. This town knows how to work together. We do it all the time. I'm so used to doing this project on my own, I couldn't think outside the box."

His whole life was outside the box. "Put ads in the paper, posters up, send out eblasts."

"Wait, wait, wait. I have an idea, too." She bounced

up and down, nearly levitating with excitement. "A cookie walk."

"Sounds perfect." He was clueless. "What is it?"

"We'll enlist the aid of everyone who's willing to bake cookies. Then instead of door-to-door selling the way we did at school, we'll ask the church to let us use the fellowship hall for a cookie walk. Customers will come to us. We'll set up tables, provide boxes and let customers choose their own cookies. Then we weigh the boxes and charge by the pound or the dozen or whatever."

Kade raised his hand in a high five. Her skin met his in a quick slap.

"We're going to get that Christmas miracle, Kade," she said with excitement. "I just know it."

He wasn't sure what he'd gotten himself into, but he'd succeeded in giving Sophie hope. And he felt like a million bucks.

Three days before Christmas, they were on a roll. Sophie had faith they could reach their goal during the holidays when people were more apt to give and more likely to need lots of cookies. If they didn't, she wouldn't be upset. They'd just keep trying. What she loved was that *Kade* had come up with the idea. *Kade* had told her to never give up.

That afternoon, she and Kade took Davey to the mall to shop for gifts, sat him on Santa's lap even though he might be too old and paid too much money for a photo taken by a teenage girl in an elf costume. Kade grumbled about commercialism and ordered extras.

If she'd not been in love with Kade before, she was now. From the moment they'd formulated the plan, he'd shifted into high gear. Ads appeared in papers, the fellowship hall was booked and cookie bakers signed up for shifts to create mouthwatering delights.

Davey, who'd been told that he could have a voice, was suddenly himself again and excited to the point of drawing pictures of a blond boy with music flowing from his mouth. Kade was teaching him a simple song on the guitar, and the notion of a singing Davey clutched at Sophie's heart.

Hope was everywhere. Especially inside Sophie B.

Two days before Christmas, a coffee klatch of sassy seniors crowded into Ida June's kitchen to teach the youngsters a thing or two about cookie creation. Three ladies argued over recipes for the world's finest raspberry thumbs while doting on Davey and bossing Kade around. The males, badly outnumbered, sneaked freshly baked samples and grinned when a gnarly finger was shaken in their faces.

"You have green frosting on your chin," Kade said, pointing to Davey. The boy smiled, teeth as green as grass.

"He's eating up all the profits," Ida June said and shoved another cookie at him. "Gluttonous child."

Sophie traded laughing glances with Kade. Excited about the fundraiser, about Christmas, about the services at church, about the scary joy of falling in love, tonight she was excited about something else, too.

"You also have frosting on your chin," Kade said to her. "Red."

She swiped futilely at her face. "Where?"

He moved closer, eyes dancing with mischief. "Looks delicious. Shall I?"

"Kade," she warned, sidestepping. As much as she enjoyed flirting and teasing with Kade, she didn't want to give the sassy seniors anything to talk about.

"Oh, Sophie, quit playing hard to get." Ida June flapped her oven glove. "The two of you go somewhere else to play kissy kissy. This kitchen is too small for courtin' lovers."

Sophie was sure her face turned redder than the raspberry jelly. "Ida June!"

"Go on, get out of here."

Three other sassy seniors grinned in speculative delight.

Kade grabbed her hand. "Escape while we can."

Fanning her cheeks with one hand, she let him drag her out of the too-hot kitchen into the backyard. The cool air felt wonderful. Sheba came along, equally eager to escape the heat and noise.

"That was embarrassing."

"No," he said, moving in. "This would have been embarrassing." He kissed the frosting from her chin.

Sophie hugged him, happier than she could remember. Being with Kade filled the empty spaces inside her. Did he, she wondered, feel the same?

"This is the best Christmas." She rested her head on Kade's chest and listened to the steady heartbeat. Dependable. Strong. Like him.

"Close," he said.

She tilted her face to his. "So you *are* doing Christmas?"

"Don't get pushy." But the words were light and teasing. They gave her new hope that the man she loved could be the man she'd always dreamed of. She yearned to admit her love and hear his reaction, but something held her back.

Please, Lord, she thought. He's come so far and he's such a good man. Heal his heart completely.

"You need a coat," he said.

Sophie was tempted to say he could keep her warm. Instead, she said, "I have something exciting to share."

He tilted back, eyebrows raised. "You won a million and Davey's surgery is paid for."

"Sounds good, but no, although this has to do with Davey."

"Okay."

"I talked to the social worker today."

"And?"

She took a deep breath, both excited and scared. "Someone wants to adopt Davey."

The earth shifted beneath Kade's feet. He didn't know whether to shout hurrah or kick something. He'd been giving some thought to adoption himself, not that he could pass muster, considering he was seeing a shrink. Anyway, he didn't figure they'd let a nutcase like him take on a kid.

"Kade?" Sophie's voice intruded. "Did you hear me?"

He cleared his throat, shaky inside as if his volcano had erupted and caused an earthquake. "The family better be a good one. I'm going to check them out. Not just anyone can have him."

She smiled a little. "I feel exactly the same, but this is not a family per se. It's a woman. A single woman." She held her arms out to each side. "Me. I'm applying to adopt Davey."

His heart shifted into arrhythmia, bounding and pounding as if adrenaline shot through every cell. Sophie was adopting Davey? This was good news. Great news actually.

Then why did he feel as if she'd kicked him in the gut?

Needing to regain his bearings, he stepped back to watch Sheba scare a bird from the fence. This was stupid. He should be jubilant.

"He's a lucky kid."

Really lucky. Stupid of him to feel left out. But they'd been a team, a trio of him and her and the quiet little boy. Hadn't they?

Where did he fit in? He scoffed, facing the facts. He didn't.

"I've been praying about it for a while—"

She had? Why hadn't she told him?

"And counseling with Dad and my pastor. Davey likes me and I adore him. He's adjusted to school. I can do this. I want to."

He touched her arm. "You don't have to convince me, Sophie. You'll be fantastic. You already are. Just what he needs."

They'd discussed the boy's future a dozen times. They'd shared their hopes for the right family to come along. Had she ever mentioned adopting him? By herself?

Mentally, he kicked himself. Why should she tell him anything? He was nothing to her. They'd been thrown into this bizarre situation by chance because they both happened to be near a certain Dumpster at the same time.

Just because he'd fallen in love with her didn't mean she returned the feelings.

But she did. He knew she did. And the best thing he could do was wish her happiness and get out of her life. He told himself that every day. And every night, he vowed to move on. Then morning dawned and like an addict, he sought her out because she made him feel human again.

Now he could let go. He had to. He could go back to Chicago comforted knowing Sophie and Davey had each other. They'd be happy and loved and safe here in Redemption.

Sheba barked at something in the corner of the yard. Kade grabbed the sound as an excuse.

"Better check on Sheba," he said, and walked away from the finest woman he'd ever met.

Man, he needed to call his shrink.

Inside Ida June's overheated, overcrowded kitchen Sophie boxed cookies and pondered Kade's reaction to her announcement. He'd said all the right words, but she had a hard time believing he meant them.

"What are you so quiet about?" Ida June asked, elbowing Sophie to one side to take another carton from the yard-high stack. "My nephew do something he shouldn't? I'll box his ears."

Sophie shook her head. What could she answer? Even she didn't understand what had just happened. When he'd walked off toward Sheba, she'd followed. Part of her wanted to ask what was wrong, but he'd pretended everything was the same.

It wasn't. Even though she couldn't put her finger on any one thing, she felt a change in him.

They'd made small talk until her teeth started to

chatter. As if a strange tension hadn't risen between them, Kade had taken her hand and they'd gone inside.

"Just tired," she told Ida June.

Kade took the packed box from her. "Go. We'll finish this."

His gentle, solicitous gesture both confused and touched her. She had the weirdest urge to cry.

With a deep dread in her chest, she studied his beloved face and prayed to understand him better.

"Okay," she said. "I want to tell Davey tomorrow. Will you help me explain?"

An odd expression crossed his face, but he replied, "You know I will."

He followed her to the entryway and helped her into her coat.

"Kade," she said, screwing up her courage, "is something wrong? Did I say something to upset you?"

Out of sight of the sassy seniors, he leaned in and kissed her forehead in a long, lingering, almost sad kiss.

"Sophie," he said, taking both her hands in his so that they formed a bridge between them, "I've never met anyone like you. You're amazing."

Her heart clattered in her chest. "I feel the same about you."

"Shh." He shook his head to stop her from talking. "Not true. You don't even know me. Not really. I just want you to know, when I leave this town, I'll never forget you. If you ever need anything, call me. And no matter what I have to do, Davey will get that surgery."

Shock waves prickled the hair on Sophie's scalp. Now she understood his odd behavior. He was leaving and hadn't known how to tell her. "But it's Christmas. You can't leave now."

You can't leave ever. My heart will break. I love you. Please don't go.

But she didn't say any of that. Playing the drama queen would only embarrass them both. Kade had never said he was staying in Redemption, and apparently she wasn't enough to keep him here. Kade was going back to Chicago and to whatever had ripped him in two.

Chapter Fifteen

Christmas Eve dawned with bright white skies threatening a snow. Throughout the day meteorologists, with *The Nutcracker* music playing in the background, built up expectations of a white Christmas.

Darkness came early this time of year, and by nightfall a few flurries swirled.

"Spittin' snow," Ida June said when Sophie and her dad picked up Davey for candlelight service. "It won't last."

Sophie hoped she was wrong. A white Christmas sounded lovely to her, especially this year when she could use the extra punch of Christmas spirit.

"Is Davey ready?" she asked.

Smiling shyly, the towheaded boy appeared behind Ida June dressed in a dark suit and tie.

"Oh, my, who is this handsome young man?" Sophie leaned in for a hug." A whisper of Kade's cologne on Davey's skin struck her with longing. "And he smells good, too." She straightened, but Kade's scent followed, taunting her. "Thank you for getting him ready, Ida June, and for the suit. That was thoughtful."

"Not me. Kade." Kade again. Sophie fought off the ache. For all her noble talk about loving without expecting anything in return, she'd wanted things to turn out differently.

With her usual bluntness, Ida June tugged a stocking hat over Davey's ears and asked, "What's going on with you and my nephew?"

The truth came easy. "Nothing."

Ida June snorted and rolled her eyes. "Don't spit on my back and tell me it's raining, girl. Give me a little credit for having a brain. Kade's started that roamin' again."

Sophie tugged at her black gloves, instantly concerned. "Roaming? I don't know what you mean."

"Can't sleep. Just like when he first got here. He was doing better for a while and now he's roaming around at night again like some kind of hoot owl. He drives that wild car of his, goes out to the river, walks the yard. He's gonna catch his death if he keeps it up." She sniffed, snappy glare accusing. "I thought you'd fixed him."

Sophie couldn't fix what she didn't understand. "He said he's returning to Chicago soon."

"Told me that, too." She looked back over one shoulder and raised her voice. "I think he's full of baloney, going back there when everything he wants is here. That place nearly killed him the first time around."

If Kade was within hearing range, he'd know Ida June's opinion.

Although amused by the other woman's antics, Sophie had circled this mountain too many times. She didn't know what had happened in Chicago and apparently Kade never intended to share. "He's a grown man."

Ida June grunted. "Didn't know there was such a thing."

The silly statement brought a small smile to Sophie's lips, though she remained adamant. The ball was in Kade's court. She'd done all she could.

Except tell him the truth, a small voice whispered. That she loved him. She'd miss him. She needed him. But Kade had enough stress. She wouldn't weigh him down with guilt over her.

"We have to run, Ida June," she said, touching a hand to the older woman's arm. "The invitation to come with us is still open."

"No, you go on. Mildred Phipps is coming by." She yanked the front door open. A car chugged slowly past on the damp street. Disappointingly, the snow had stopped. "Tell me one thing, though. Do you care that my nephew's leaving?"

"Yes, I do," Sophie answered softly. "Very much."

"I thought so." Ida June smacked a fist into her palm. "The way of a fool is right in his own eyes, but a wise man listens to advice. I'm thinking my nephew needs some sound advice. Right upside his hard head."

Sophie leaned in and hugged Kade's aunt. If advice would break through Kade's wall, he would be the one adopting Davey and he would never mention going back to Chicago. "We'll have Davey home early, but we might stop for ice cream."

Ida June waved her off. "I'm not worried. At least not about Davey. Now go on before you let out all the heat."

The past two days had been harder than Sophie had imagined. Kade was still in Redemption, but he'd distanced himself. She saw him, talked to him, and every time she did, she prayed that whatever drove him would be resolved. Even if he was never hers, she wanted him to be happy and at peace. Ida June's comments had confirmed he was neither of those.

Soft voices and a friendly reverence greeted them inside the foyer of Redemption Fellowship. Piano music floated from the sanctuary on the tune of "Oh, Little Town of Bethlehem."

The church was beautiful this time of year with huge wreaths hung along the sides of the sanctuary and lush green garland tied with red bows looped across the front. In one corner, a glorious ceiling-high tree glittered with angels and stars. Over the carved crèche Sophie had loved since childhood, a banner heralded Light of the World. This year, local wood craftsman Jace Carter had painstakingly restored the figures to their splendor as a gift to the church where he and wife, Kitty, had been married last summer.

Sophie waved at familiar faces as she herded Davey toward a pew with her father right behind. Along the way, an usher distributed thin white candles cupped with drip protectors.

"We'll light this later," she said to Davey's curious, upturned face. The poor lamb had limited experience with church, but he was well-behaved and interested. His mother, despite her emotional fears, had taught him many good attributes. "Don't worry, Grandpa and I will help you. You won't get burned."

Sophie's dad beamed at the new title she'd bestowed upon him. Davey, too, seemed thrilled to have a grandparent, something he'd never had.

"About time I got to be a grandpa," her dad had said when she'd announced her decision to adopt Davey. She'd sought his wisdom and prayers, knowing Davey would need a male role model. As much as the child admired Kade, his hero wouldn't be here.

If she let herself, she'd worry about how Davey would take the news of Kade's departure. He'd had enough losses.

Dad had mentioned as much when she'd told him of Kade's decision to return to Chicago. He knew she, too, was hurting and the protective father in him wanted to make things better for both her and Davey.

Sophie wished he could. But they'd long ago discussed the chance that Kade might not love her the way she loved him, and she clung to Dad's mantra: love was always worth the risk.

Now the new grandpa placed a loving hand on Davey's shoulder and guided him into the pew. Both her men looked so handsome, Sophie's heart swelled with pride and love.

"Is that a new suit, Dad?" she asked, shucking her coat.

"It is. Is that a new dress?"

Sophie laughed and smoothed the hem of the red asymmetrical sheath. The tiny beading on the edges winked beneath the lights. "Dad, I've worn this on Christmas Eve for the last three years."

"You're so beautiful, you make it look new."

Sophie never doubted that he meant every word. Dad didn't see an ordinary, simple schoolteacher who barely wore makeup. He saw a beauty queen. "Thanks, Daddy. I love you."

"Ditto." He squeezed her hand, his gaze searching her face. "You okay?"

"Sure." A little sad perhaps, but Dad knew. She wished Kade was with them on this special night, not only because she loved him, but also because he needed the peace and healing found in God. "I have a lot to be thankful for."

"We both do. A new start, a new family, a son for you and a grandson for me. Pretty nice Christmas gifts." Her dad winked down at Davey. "Christmas is about a child, you know. Davey brings fresh meaning to that."

Yes, Christmas was about a child with no place to lay his head and no home to call his own.

Sophie slipped an arm around Davey's shoulders and squeezed gently. The same had been true for Davey, but not anymore. The Lord had sent him to exactly the right place to find a new family to cherish him.

"I love you, Davey," she whispered. He grinned his crooked grin and nodded. He knew she loved him and he enjoyed hearing it. What would it be like to hear him say those words to her?

Oh, how she prayed for Davey's Christmas miracle.

The piano rendition of "Oh, Holy Night" grew more subtle and Pastor Parker stepped into the pulpit to begin service. With quiet demeanor the blond pastor spoke briefly of the long-ago night when God's love came down to earth and became the light that still shines in a dark world.

When time came to light the candles, the sanctuary went dark except for the star shining over the crèche. A lovely, peaceful reverence filled Sophie's spirit as she lit her candle from her father's and they both shared the flame with a little mute boy. This was the way it would be, her father's eyes told her. As a family, they would raise Davey in the light of God's grace.

With flames flickering and "Silent Night" swelling with glorious beauty, Sophie prayed for the future. She prayed for Davey's miracle. She prayed for Kade, and as she did, she released him and her love for him to God the way her father had released her mother.

"Heal his heart, Lord," she whispered into the candlelit shadows. "Heal his spirit and his soul, and wherever he is, let him feel your love on this most holy night."

A wellspring of peace flooded her being.

God would go with Kade. And so would her love.

When the service ended the trio started out of the church, moving slowly through the hushed crowd. No one spoke much, and she could see the service had blessed others as it had blessed her.

Her father gently caught her elbow. With a jerk of his head, he motioned toward the far corner of the church.

Sophie's heart leaped. She fought down the joyful cry that shot into her throat.

Kade sat alone on the very last pew. Elbows on his knees, eyes closed and forehead propped on clasped hands, he didn't look up even though people moved past him toward the exits.

Sophie turned a questioning look toward her father. He shrugged and shook his head. He didn't know how long Kade had been there, either.

"I'll take Davey home," he said quietly. "I think you're needed here."

Yes, she was sure of it. Kade had come at her invitation and he needed her. Even if they didn't say a word, he needed to know she was here…and that she cared.

She spoke to Davey, gave him a hug and promised to see him tomorrow on Christmas Day. Her soon-to-be son left eagerly when her dad offered a stop at the ice-cream parlor for mint chocolate chip, his favorite.

Pulse hammering in her throat, Sophie made her way toward the man who held her heart. He looked lonely and forlorn sitting there, but she was ecstatic to see him.

Without a word, she slid into the pew next to him. He didn't acknowledge her presence, so she waited, praying silently for wisdom and guidance but mostly for him to find whatever it was he needed.

After a while, without looking her way, he slid his hand to hers and squeezed. His fingers trembled, and Sophie ached for him.

"I never thought I'd ever come inside a church again," he said quietly, as if to himself.

"Why?" she murmured, pulse thudding in her ears. *Help me, Lord, to say the right things.*

Kade drew in a deep breath and exhaled on a gusty sigh. "Some bad things happened. I lost confidence in God. Maybe I was even angry at Him, which is pretty stupid on my part."

"He's a big God. He can handle it."

He turned his head toward her then, those beloved dark eyes full of sorrow. "*I* couldn't."

"What happened?" There. She'd asked. He could tell or not, but at least she'd made the effort.

"I worked undercover narcotics. Special task forces."

"You told me."

"Yeah." He pulled her hand onto his knee and massaged her fingers as if the contact eased him. "I'm not sure I can tell you the rest."

"Nothing you say will change the way I feel about you."

He gazed at her with a question in his eyes but didn't ask. She hoped he could read the love she beamed his way.

"You sure?" he asked.

"Positive. Please tell me what hurt you so badly, Kade. Tell me why you turned away from the Lord."

He tilted his head to stare up at the ceiling and sighed again. "My aunt said you'd feel that way. She also said I needed to find God again, but I wouldn't find him roamin' around like a hoot owl."

Sophie chuckled softly. She couldn't help herself. The feisty old lady had followed through with her threat to knock some sense into her nephew's head. "I love that spunky woman."

For the first time, Kade's face lightened. "Me, too." He recaptured her fingers and said, "I've been sitting here since the second hymn following her advice, asking God to help me."

"And?"

"I thought He'd let me down. Bad things happened to kids and He didn't stop them. I think I get it now. He hated what happened as much as I did."

Kids being harmed? The concept prickled the hair on Sophie's scalp. "I thought you were a *drug* agent."

"I was, but the job went deeper than anyone expected. The drug cartel had branched out." He closed his eyes, swallowed and said, "Into human trafficking."

Sophie's heart stopped beating for a nanosecond. Horror gripped her. "Oh, no. Not children."

"Yes." The grip on her fingers tightened to the unbearable stage. "I reported it to my superiors. They told me to take it deeper, find the source." His lips curled. "Being a good team player I did as I was told, and all the while kids were being used in unspeakable ways." He shook his head. "I don't want to tell you."

"Don't, please. I understand enough." Enough to know what had driven him to the edge. A man of compassion who harbored a guardian's soul, Kade would break at not protecting a child.

"I knew. And I did nothing but gather evidence." He scoffed, self-loathing thick around him.

She shuddered to imagine the horrors he'd likely witnessed. How did a person ever cleanse such images from his mind? "Did you make any arrests?"

"Oh, yeah, we got our bad guys. They're awaiting trial in a cushy prison, but the arrests can't erase what happened to those kids. They'll carry those scars for the rest of their lives."

The implication sickened Sophie. Her stomach roiled. If Kade struggled at remembering, how much greater was the burden on a child?

"I hate myself for that, Sophie," he went on. "I should have done something to save them. They were helpless kids. I should have stopped it."

"Could you have? Think before you answer, Kade. I don't know a lot about drug cartels but enough to know they are powerful. Could you have stood against all of them? Wouldn't you have ended up dead? And then the criminals would never have been stopped. You might not have saved some, but you ended the cycle and saved others in the future."

"You sound like my shrink." When she tilted her head in question, he said wryly, "Told you I'm a nutcase."

"Nothing wrong with seeing a doctor if he's helping you."

"He might if I talked to him more."

"I know another physician you can talk to. No charge." She smiled softly. "The Great Physician."

"Yeah." He nodded, mouth in a soft line of agreement. "That's what I've been doing tonight."

"And?" she urged softly.

"I don't want to go back to Chicago."

Adrenaline shot through Sophie's bloodstream. She sat up straighter, almost afraid to believe the implication. "You don't?"

"I left my soul in Chicago. I found it again in Redemption. I also found something else."

"What's that?"

He shifted on the padded pew and tapped his chest. "My heart."

Sophie thought *her* heart might jump right out to meet his. "I love you, Kade."

He closed his eyes and was quiet for a moment while Sophie's blood raced and her nerve endings jittered. Even if he didn't love her in return, she could go on with her life content and full. Kade had found himself again. He was on the road to recovery and peace.

When he opened his eyes, Kade said, "You blow me away, Sophie. I'm hard and cynical. And I've done and seen things I won't ever tell you about. I don't understand why or how you can love me. I don't deserve you or your amazing love. But you—" he shook his head as if bewildered "—you deserve everything."

"I have everything I want and need," she said. "Everything but you."

He tugged her closer, caressing her face with his fingers and his gaze. She felt his love long before he said the words.

"Then if you really want me, I'm yours. I love you, Sophie B. I'd be a fool not to." His lips curved. "And we know what Ida June has to say about fools."

Sophie returned his smile, the swell of joy a powerful thing.

The scent of candle smoke still lingered in the church and the pastor had long since dimmed the lights. She could hear him moving around somewhere in the back, a wise shepherd who knew when to make himself scarce. He would wait, she knew, as long as necessary. He was, like his Savior, a good shepherd.

In the front of the church, the spotlighted crèche stood out against a dark backdrop. She felt a rightness in declaring her love here in the church with the greatest love of all symbolized in a carved wooden figure asleep in a manger.

Heart full to overflowing, she stood, drawing Kade up with her. "It's Christmas Eve. We should go and let the pastor get home to his family."

"Yeah, I have a stocking to fill myself." A full-blown smile spread across Kade's face as he took her hand. "Or maybe two."

Chapter Sixteen

Christmas morning dawned cold and clear. The snow, as Ida June predicted, had been nothing but a wish and a flurry.

Kade could have cared less. He'd slept fitfully but not because of his troubled soul. Rather, he'd been excited about the new beginning and he'd lain awake dreaming of a future with Sophie.

At six he rose, jittery for the day to begin. Sheba padded in, stretched her long, golden body and shook loose the remains of a solid eight hours. Kade let her out and back in, a fast trip thanks to the chill in the air.

Ida June would roll her eyes at his sentiment, but for Sophie's and Davey's pleasure, Kade tuned the radio to nonstop Christmas music. With a cup of his favorite caffeinated pain in hand, he plugged in the Christmas tree and slipped a few extra gifts beneath.

He loved that tree. Mostly because he loved the woman who'd decorated it. He'd groused about the smelly little pine when Sophie had dragged him off to a tree farm, but he'd secretly been pleased. The tree had never been the problem. He had. He just hadn't believed he could deserve a Christmas with all the joy and love and trimmings.

Weird how messed up a man could get.

At seven, Davey, rubbing his eyes, stumbled into the living room in his blue-and-red superhero pajamas. His shaggy hair stuck up in a dozen places. He looked around, dazed and delighted by the pile of gifts and the bulging stockings.

"Place looks different, huh, buddy?" Kade leaned in for a hug.

Davey nodded, pointing toward the Christmas tree.

"Get dressed first. Sophie will be here soon." He checked his watch. "Very soon."

As Davey dashed away with Sheba close behind, the doorbell rang. Every nerve ending came to life. Who needed caffeine with Sophie around?

He yanked the door open. She'd come. She was here. Last night in the church had really happened.

She walked into his arms.

He enfolded her, basking in the feel and scent and essence of his woman.

She loved him.

"It wasn't a dream." He nuzzled her ear.

"If it was," she said, a smile in her voice, "we had the same one."

Content, he sighed against her coconut-scented hair. "You still love me this morning?"

"More."

He thrilled at her warm lips against his jaw.

"Merry Christmas to me." He pushed her back a little to kiss her properly. "And to you."

A gagging sound came from behind them.

"Please," Ida June grumbled, "I haven't even had my coffee."

Kade whirled around and grabbed his aunt, smacking her cheek in a noisy kiss. The white bun atop her head wiggled. "Love you, too, Auntie."

She pinked up. "Well, look who's been in the eggnog."

"We have something to tell you," he said, ready to shout the good news from a frozen rooftop.

Blue eyes snapping back and forth between Kade and Sophie, his aunt declared, "'Love, and a cough, cannot be hid.'" She smacked her lips in satisfaction. "I've been saving that one."

Grinning, holding hands, Kade and Sophie joined Davey, Sheba and Ida June in the living room and Christmas Day began.

With love in her eyes and enough joy in her heart to burst into a Hallelujah Chorus—which she did a couple of times—Sophie watched Kade hand out Christmas gifts. At some point, he'd done some serious shopping. Even though she and her father had bought Davey several gifts, Kade and Ida June had bought more. Within fifteen minutes, all four of them had a pile of gifts stacked in front of them.

"Are we going to open them or admire them?" Kade asked.

That was the only cue Davey needed. With little-boy greed, he ripped into the bright paper, flinging ribbons and wrappings all over the living room. Sheba sat at his side, amber eyes adoring her boy.

Kade abandoned his Santa post to sit by Sophie. "You're all the present I want."

"Me, too," she said, handing him one anyway while wishing she'd purchased something more personal than a pair of leather gloves. "I bought this before…well, before last night."

He opened it, declared them perfect like her and gave her his gift. The silver paper and royal-blue ribbon were stunning. "I love the wrapping paper."

"You'll laugh at my gift."

"No, I won't." She opened the package and…laughed. "Leather gloves! I love them."

"Great minds think alike," Ida June declared, wagging a similar pair. "I like mine, too."

Kade motioned toward the stack of mail she'd brought with her. "What's all this?"

"Christmas cards, I guess. They were in my mailbox this morning, so I grabbed them before coming over. Some are for Davey. I thought he'd enjoy seeing his name on them."

"Mail doesn't run on Christmas." He gave the stack a curious look.

"Neighbors, probably. Just dropped them in the box. We do that sometimes." She took one up and opened it. A check fell out.

Kade retrieved the slip of paper from the floor. "Look at this. A donation to help with Davey's surgery."

"What a lovely gesture," she said, heart welling.

"Open the rest."

"You don't think—" Sophie shook her head. "Surely not."

But she opened another. And then another. Some were from friends, others from companies or churches or civic groups. Card after card came with a check or cash and a note wishing Davey a Merry Christmas and a vocal New Year.

By the time she opened the last card, tears streaked down her cheeks. Davey, alarmed, rushed to her side and patted her face. His eyes begged her not to cry.

"She's okay, Davey," Kade said, clearing his throat more than once. "Women cry when they're happy."

Ida June shoved a tissue into her hand. "Quit blubbering before I start."

Because Ida June had been sniffing and her eyes watering for the past five minutes, Sophie laughed through her tears. She nearly had her composure back when the doorbell rang.

"Probably Dad," she said. Ida June had invited him for Christmas dinner. "I'll let him in."

The woman at the door was vaguely familiar. "We heard about the little boy who needs an operation. This being Christmas and all, my husband and I wanted to do something." She handed Sophie a check and walked away.

Stunned, all Sophie could say was, "Thank you. Merry Christmas."

The car had no more than pulled out of the drive when another, and then another and another arrived, each one bringing a donation for "the little boy who can't talk."

Each time there was a lull in visitors—some familiar, others strangers who'd read about the need in the *Redemption Register*—Kade reported on the total.

As the donations continued, Sophie's tears of joy turned to astonished jubilation.

The stream of visitors slowed at noon. While all three males played with Davey's race-car track, Sophie helped Ida June prepare the meal. Once in a while Sophie pinched herself to see if today was really happening.

A shout of laughter had her looking into the living room. Sheba, sitting on her bottom next to Davey, moved her head in circles to the motion of a car racing around the track.

The doorbell rang again. Drying her hands on a dish towel, she went to answer, still laughing at the dog and the trio of males she loved best.

Sophie pulled open the door. "Biff!"

Before her next breath, Kade appeared at her side. He didn't say a word. He didn't have to, but he did glower. Sophie knew how upset he'd been when Biff had discontinued her cookie project. Upset for her sake.

She reached for his hand and gave it a reassuring squeeze.

"I figured you'd be here when you weren't at home." Her principal looked as stiff and uncomfortable as she felt. Though bundled against the cold in a long, wool chesterfield, his head was bare, his ears red.

Considering the words they'd had the last day of school, she couldn't imagine what he was doing here.

"Merry Christmas," she said, for lack of anything to say. She refused to hold a grudge at any time, especially Christmas. Biff Gruber was her principal. She *would* get along with him.

"And to you." Biff thrust an envelope into her hands. "Some of us took up a collection for the Stephens boy. We wanted to help."

Sophie required concerted effort not to drop her jaw and gape. Astonished but touched as well, she said,

"Thank you, Mr. Gruber. Really. This is very thoughtful of all of you."

"Yes, well—" he gave a short nod "—Merry Christmas." And he walked away, back stiff and ears as red as Rudolph's nose.

Sophie closed the door and leaned her back against the solid wood. "This is almost too much to comprehend."

Kade moved into her space, his dark eyes alight. "No, sweetheart," he said. "You asked for a miracle. I think you got it."

Awed and touched, she opened the check and started to cry.

As she wept tears of joy, Kade pulled her into his arms and murmured his love over and over again.

A small body shouldered in between the adults. They went to their knees to take him into the circle of love as a golden dog and a grinning aunt looked on.

The miracles had just begun. Not one but many. Davey would get his voice. Kade had found his hope again.

And all of them had found each other.

All because of a lost and lonely boy…

A Christmas child.

* * * * *

GIFT-WRAPPED FAMILY

Lois Richer

You shall love the Lord your God with all your heart, with all your soul, and with all your strength.
—*Deuteronomy* 6:5

Chapter One

"This can't be the place."

Lawyer Caleb Grant matched the address on the paper in his hand with the crooked numbers on a small bungalow that had seen better days in this Canadian neighborhood of Calgary, Alberta, and grimaced.

"Are you sure you gave me the correct address?" he asked into his phone. Having confirmed his location, he opened the rickety gate.

The serious disrepair of the house contrasted with the garden in front, which bloomed in a riot of color. Mia Granger must be a dab hand with plants. How could a woman with this tender gift for gardening ignore his plea to help a bereaved child?

Before Caleb could reach the end of the cobbled path, the weathered front door opened. A slim woman with masses of strawberry blonde hair tumbling around her shoulders stepped outside and reached for the mailbox. Her hand stilled when she saw him.

"C-can I help you?" she asked in a voice so quiet he barely heard it.

"I'm looking for Mia Granger. Does she live here?" Caleb watched her ivory skin pale.

"I'm Mia. Are you another bill collector?" she said in a breathless voice. "I'm sorry but—"

"I'm a lawyer with Family Ties. It's an adoption agency in Buffalo Gap." He saw no recognition on her face. "Someone called you about me."

"No one called," she murmured in a scared voice, golden-red hair shivering in the wash of sunlight sneaking through a few dappled leaves left on a towering poplar tree.

"They should have." Caleb frowned. Mayor Marsha had talked him into coming here. She'd also promised she'd notify widow Granger of his arrival. When a flicker of worry widened Mia's emerald eyes, he decided he could deal with Marsha later. "I'm here about Lily."

"Who?" As hard as Caleb searched her puzzled face, he saw no sign that she was prevaricating. "I think you must have the wrong—"

"She's the five-year-old daughter of your husband, Harlan Granger, and his mistress, Reba Jones." Though Caleb hated to be so blunt, there was no easy way to do this. "Lily lost both her parents in the car accident that took your husband two weeks ago."

"How dare you?" Mia Granger gasped. One hand grabbed onto the shaky wrought iron railing.

"Are you all right?" Troubled by her ashen face, Caleb reached out to steady her, but the woman backed away.

"You've got everything wrong," she insisted in a tearful voice. "Reba was Harlan's *secretary*. They certainly didn't have a child together. Please leave." She turned away.

"I'm so sorry to trouble you." Caleb's instincts told him he couldn't leave now. He had to reach this woman's heart, for Lily's sake.

"Then, don't." Her pale, pinched face implored him to leave her alone. But Caleb couldn't do that.

"I've checked the birth records," he said softly. "Lily *is* their child."

Mia paled even more. She shook her head.

"It's true. Please, may I please come inside and talk to you?"

Her distrust of him showed in the gold sparks that changed her emerald eyes to hazel. Given the deceitful husband she'd married, Caleb didn't blame her for that. But he was also curious. Torn between trying to believe she was truly bewildered but feeling suspicious that she was trying to avoid him as she had his phone calls, Caleb pressed harder.

"I truly do not want to add to your pain." He employed the calming tone he often used with a skittery witness on the stand. "I only want to help this little girl." He pulled a picture from his chest pocket and held it out. "Lily Jones."

Mia looked at the photo. When her eyes widened and her trembling lips parted in a gasp, Caleb knew he was making up lost ground. But then he saw something puzzling in her gaze—yearning?

"She's a beautiful child, isn't she?" Caleb hated causing this gentle woman more grief, but he was determined she understand that Lily's future was at stake.

"The eyes—they're quite startling." Mia's gaze remained riveted on the picture.

"The same color as Harlan Granger's."

"Many people have dark blue eyes." Mia finally handed him the photo with a sigh. "I suppose you'd better come in," she said in obvious resignation. She allowed him through and then closed the door. "This way."

Caleb followed, noting that the interior of the house had probably once been magnificent. Though it hadn't aged gracefully, it was spotless. The Victorian-style sofa Mia indicated with the wave of one hand was as desperately uncomfortable as it looked, but Caleb sat on it anyway, keeping his face impassive.

Mia Granger stood in front of the massive bay window in a puddle of bright October sunshine. She wore a pair of shabby jeans that looked too big and a faded teal sweater that drooped from her lean curves. Her beautiful hair flowed over her shoulders like a pale copper cape. When she caught Caleb staring, she crossed her thin arms across her chest defensively.

Caleb couldn't stop staring. Backlit by the sun, the shape of Mia's face brought memories of his mother, the mother he'd loved so dearly and lost to his murderous father.

"What was your name?" she prodded.

"Caleb Grant. As I said, I represent an adoption agency called Family Ties." Caleb shook off his memories and concentrated on the delicate woman in front of him. *Do your job*, his brain ordered.

"Lily is one of their children waiting to be adopted?" Mia sank onto an armchair that could have sat three of her and nestled against the folds of a colorful quilt draped across the back of it.

"Not exactly. I wanted to explain when I called, but

your phone is always busy or no one answers." He studied her face, surprised by the flush of red in her cheeks.

"Sometimes I take it off the hook. Or I don't answer. I can't take any more calls from those to whom we owe money." Mia stared at her hands.

Owe money? Caleb hadn't expected that. It threw him off, made him wonder if she was trying to con him. He decided to turn the conversation back to Lily because Mia had made a connection with her picture.

"Lily may eventually be adopted. First we have to sort out her custody and what she's owed from her father's estate." Caleb decided that while Mia might look innocent, she wasn't stupid. She immediately straightened.

"Mr. Grant," she began in a regal tone.

"Caleb," he interrupted.

"Caleb," she agreed softly. "You think my late husband is this child's father. I assure you you're wrong." She continued, her voice growing steadily stronger. "I don't have any money to give Lily. If I did, I would certainly help the poor child." She paused for a moment, then murmured, "I never knew Reba had a daughter, but then I didn't know Harlan's staff well."

"Lily was *his* child, too," Caleb insisted. A new stain of red flushed her cheeks, bringing his sympathy. If he'd known Mia was unaware of her husband's affair, he'd have handled this differently.

"I sympathize with Lily because as a child I lost my mother suddenly, too," she said, ignoring his remark. "But I'm sorry, there's nothing I can do for her. I owe money myself." The receding blush returned and deepened. She lowered her gaze.

"But, Mia, your husband's estate must be considerable." Caleb couldn't believe her temerity. He knew from his research that Granger was loaded. He'd dealt with many prevaricators in his career and was oddly disappointed to realize sweet-looking Mia was one of them. But that sweetness wouldn't stop him from seeking Lily's rightful inheritance.

"Why do you assume that?" Mia's gaze made him feel guilty for poking into her private world. "My husband was a lawyer, but we're certainly not wealthy. You can see how we live." She glared at him. "Harlan had to take whatever cases he was offered. In fact, he often had to go out of town to find work."

The certainty in Mia Granger's voice bothered Caleb. She looked and sounded as though she genuinely believed what she was saying. But if they were so hard up, why hadn't her husband moved his office from its expensive downtown location to a less pricey area?

"What about the ranch? There's a lot of land attached to that, valuable land." He studied her intently, surprised when her forehead furrowed.

"What ranch? Harlan and I were married for six years. We never owned a ranch." Caleb figured she saw something in his face, because the last of her words faltered before she whispered, "Have we?"

"What has your lawyer told you?" Caleb figured his best hope was to untie this mess without further alienating her.

"You mean Trent Vilang? Harlan's partner," she explained, as if Caleb didn't already know that. "I've been feeling unwell since Harlan's death, so Trent's only told me the bare bones about the estate."

"And that is?" For Lily's sake, Caleb pressed, ignoring her frown at his inquisitiveness.

"Trent said there was barely enough money to pay off the firm's bills and Harlan's cre—" Mia gulped. The sheen of tears washed her eyes, but she lifted her chin and finished with quiet dignity, "His cremation."

"I see." As Caleb's uncertainty mushroomed he glanced around, searching for a clue to his next step. His glance stalled on the oil painting over the fireplace. "Lovely painting. Who is it?" he asked, as if he didn't know.

"My mother."

"Your mother was Pia Standish?" He was speaking to the daughter of the woman he'd admired most of his life? Now nothing made sense.

"Did you know her?" Mia's curiosity was evident.

"I did." Caleb declined to discuss his childhood inter-action with the legendary legal genius, but he couldn't suppress a smile remembering Pia's potent courtroom condemnation of his father. "I was her client once. I never forgot her."

"I never saw her at work, but I've heard she was a good lawyer." There was something wistful in Mia's voice.

"Pia was beyond merely good," Caleb told her. "Her firm, Standish Law, was the biggest in the province. I remember seeing well-known people in her office."

"I used to think we were well off," Mia mused re-flectively. "At first I thought that's why Harlan agreed to marry me."

"Excuse me?" Caleb stared at her. Who would need to be coerced to marry this lovely woman?

"I was seventeen and in boarding school when I was summoned home. My mother told me she'd been diag-nosed with brain cancer. She told me that for my own protection I was to marry this lawyer who worked for her, Harlan Granger." Mia's voice faltered. "She said he'd take care of me."

"He was much older. Why would he agree?" Caleb asked.

"Money, I suppose. Harlan received my mother's law firm as a kind of dowry." Her green eyes grew troubled. "Mother had a nice house."

"I was there once." Caleb remembered his awe at visiting the huge mansion.

"Harlan sold it after she died," Mia said, staring at something Caleb couldn't see. "I thought it should have brought us plenty of money, but Harlan said Mother had run up large debts trying to find a cure. He sold the house to pay off what she owed." Her lips pinched together. "I was sorry to lose some of our things," she added in a small, hurt voice.

Mia's defenselessness, her sadness touched Caleb. He gave her time to regroup while he shot off a text message to his paralegal. Find out everything about Mia Standish Granger. Stat.

"That's why your claim is so incredible." Mia rose. "I've lived here since I married Harlan. We've had to be very frugal while he revived her firm. We— I'm not rich, Mr. Grant."

"Your mother didn't leave you any money of your own?" He searched her face, no longer certain she was lying.

"I'm afraid not. Everything goes to pay the bills." A tiny smile flitted across her incredibly beautiful face. "Would you like some tea?"

"I would. Thank you." Caleb hated tea, especially herbal tea, but he'd learned the fine art of pretending to drink it when his best friend Lara was alive, because she'd loved tea and he'd wanted to love her. It still rankled that he'd never felt the strong emotion for her that Lara claimed to feel for him, to realize that he couldn't love anyone because of what his father had done.

Caleb shoved those uncomfortable thoughts away and concentrated on Mia. She had to be pretending her marriage was solid, but he was determined she'd admit the truth before he left here, and if that required tea drinking, that was what he'd do.

"Let's go to the kitchen. It's warmer there." Mia waited for his nod, then led the way. "Have a seat," she invited as she pulled out a mismatched chair from the big oak table. "Do you have a particularly favorite tea? I have a good variety."

Caleb blinked when she opened a cupboard door to reveal neatly organized rows of small packages of tea. "Do you ever!"

"My stomach's been upset since Harlan—died." Mia regained her composure. "Trent's been a dear friend. He consulted an herbalist for me and brings home teas for me to try. They haven't helped yet, but…" She shrugged and smiled. "Take your time deciding which you'd like."

"Any kind is fine." A previous investigation on Trent Vilang had left Caleb with tons of questions. "Dear Trent" had befriended widows before and some of those ladies had become very ill. Caleb kept his reservations about the man to himself as Mia moved around her broken-down kitchen.

Anything that could sparkle in this room did, but the house and especially this kitchen needed to be gutted, and no amount of soap or elbow grease could fix that. Then suddenly, beyond the kitchen, he spied bright sunshine.

"Would you rather sit in the sunroom?" Mia asked, noting his interest. "It's quite warm today because the sun's out. That's when I love working there the most."

"What is your work?" Caleb's curiosity built. Her job was one detail he hadn't yet discovered. Mia looked too delicate for any kind of physical work. Cellist. Or maybe pianist, he guessed.

"Oh, it's nothing," she demurred.

Caleb thought that sounded like someone else's assessment. But he said nothing as she rinsed out a small brown china teapot.

"I dream up designs for quilt fabrics," Mia finally said almost apologetically.

"Oh." That fit, Caleb decided, then realized that though he'd just met Mia, he'd instinctively known that employment suited her. *Getting too involved. Maintain your distance*, his brain scolded. That was difficult to do with this intriguing woman.

"When my designs are incorporated into fabric, the company sends me a bolt of each. I then make up several quilts to feature various aspects of the fabric and how to use it. It's nothing like the law," she apologized. "Nothing at all like the important work Harlan did."

"Why should it be like his?" Caleb wished he'd met the man who'd made his wife feel that her work was trivial. "It's just as important to have beautiful things in the world as it is to have the law." She had the tray ready. "Can I carry something?"

"The tea?" Mia smiled her thanks and led the way into a sunroom that took his breath away. Vibrantly painted canvases lay sprawled around the room, flowers in riotous color, a seaside scene, the cool white on white of deepest winter. "I'm sorry it's so crowded. Harlan was always after me to stack these away." Mia gulped, then reached to move one.

"Please leave it. They're beautiful," Caleb said, and meant it.

"Oh." Startled green eyes met his before quickly veering away. "Thank you. Please sit wherever you like." She poured their tea and then sat across from him on a rickety wicker chair whose quilted cushion said it had been well loved. "Mr. Grant—"

"Call me Caleb." Nothing in her expression to suggest she was flirting or playing games, but Caleb clung to his defenses anyway. He had a job to do. He couldn't let her sad situation get to him.

"Very well, Caleb. Well, other than serving you tea, I don't know how I can help you." Mia Granger frowned. He thought it a shame to mar the beauty of her face, but the helplessness in her next words irritated him. "What is it you expect of me?"

"I'm not sure." Caleb remembered Lily's parting words. *Can you find me a home, Uncle Caleb? Please?* That plea from Lara's niece broke his heart. "I came here hoping to learn the truth, but I'm not sure you know it."

"Whose truth? Yours?" Mia sipped her tea. "Like your claim that Harlan had a ranch."

"He did. Riverbend Ranch." Caleb thought her eyes widened for a second.

"We didn't have a ranch. If we had, why would we live here?" she asked with some asperity. "Why would Harlan need to travel for his business?"

"Are you sure he did 'need' to?" Though she tried

to hide it, Caleb had seen Mia's reaction to the word *Riverbend*. Now his senses were on high alert. She was hiding something, and he intended to find out what, despite that gaze of wide-eyed innocence.

In Caleb's experience very few women could carry off a claim of innocence. Lara had been one, but he wasn't totally certain about Mia because there were even fewer women who managed to tug at his compassion, and she did.

Surprised by the emotions she raised in him, Caleb decided he'd best be on guard around Mia Granger. Anything but friendship was impossible.

Caleb Grant was the most handsome man Mia had ever met. Tall, lean and dark, he exuded confidence, something she'd always admired but lacked. At the moment, Mia didn't like the way he studied her with his silver-cold eyes. Nor did she like how his tall muscular body invaded the place where she'd mostly lived alone. She especially didn't like the calculation in his voice, as if he expected to catch her in a lie.

Caleb's suggestion that Harlan had been unfaithful stung. The situation hadn't been ideal, but she'd done her best to be a good wife after a simple ceremony at city hall had joined them in holy matrimony. No, they didn't share a strong, fairy-tale love. But he'd kept her safe after her mother died and she was grateful. Mia mourned his death. Now she was all alone.

But even though they hadn't *really* been married, not the way other couples were, that didn't mean Harlan would have done what Caleb Grant said.

On the tail of those thoughts, snippets of details dawned. Hadn't she always felt uneasy over Harlan's frequent late-night meetings with Reba? And the way Reba touched his shoulder so fondly before jerking her hand away when she realized Mia had come to the office for her one and only visit? That had stuck in Mia's mind for ages, especially after Harlan had ordered her to stay away. But that didn't mean…

She shoved her wayward thoughts out of her mind. She'd think about Harlan and Reba later. Right now Caleb Grant was here. He was a lawyer. Maybe he'd have some advice that could help sort out her pressing financial problems. Inhaling a breath of courage, she dived in.

"Caleb, this land, er, ranch you speak of Harlan owning. Where is it?"

"Riverbend Ranch is outside Buffalo Gap, about thirty-five miles from here." Caleb's innocent gaze turned cunning. "Do you know of it?"

He'd seen her reaction to that name, so there was no point in pretending. Mia rose, walked to her big battered desk and removed a thin file. She held it out.

"What's this?" he asked, taking it from her.

"It's about Harlan's estate, according to Trent, Harlan's partner and also my lawyer." She sat down, lifted her cup and took a refreshing drink. "Go ahead and look. Riverbend is a lawsuit my husband was handling, if I understand those papers correctly."

His eyes searched hers. Mia held it until—there went her stomach again, clenching and whirling as if some flu bug had hold of it. A minute earlier she'd felt perfectly fine, but now she closed her eyes and waited for her stomach to settle.

"Are you all right?" Caleb's eyes bored into hers.

"A little flu. I hope you don't catch it." Mia sat perfectly still, hands in her lap. When he didn't move she said, "Please read it. I'll wait."

She watched him, amazed by the speed with which he scanned the documents she'd taken hours to peruse. Less than two minutes later he looked up, his mouth stretched tight in a grim line.

"You see? There's nothing about a ranch or money," she said, her voice dropping at the stern look on his face. "I'm not lying."

"This is all Trent gave you? Nothing more?"

Mia shook her head.

"Did you sign anything recently?" Caleb voice was tight and sharp.

"Of course. There were a number of papers Trent needed me to sign to deal with my husband's estate." She shivered, intensely disliking this inquisition but not sure how to stop it.

Caleb had said he was a lawyer and she was sure he was a good one, though she'd never heard of this adoption agency, Family Ties. But as a lawyer he would know how to get people to say things—she should be on guard. He might actually be from some collection company.

"Do you have copies of what you signed?" Caleb demanded.

"No. Trent said he'd copy them at the office and bring them back. He hasn't yet returned with them." Something in the frost of his silver-steel eyes made her shiver. "Is—is anything wrong?" she asked hesitantly, and reared back when he nodded.

"Yes. I think quite a lot is wrong." Caleb closed his eyes and rubbed his temples. "Mia, this will be hard to hear, but you must listen because it's the truth. I've been investigating your husband's affairs, for Lily's sake. Nothing I've found indicates he was hard up for money or that he or Trent had taken on a new client in months."

"But that can't be." She struggled to sort it out and looked at him. She saw nothing but honesty in his expression. Could it be true? "Then, what were he and Reba doing on all these trips?"

"That's what we need to discover." Caleb glanced at his ringing phone, read the message and frowned. When he lifted his gaze to hers, the icy anger made her shiver. "Did you know your lawyer filed documents this morning seeking to take over all your affairs because he says you are incompetent?"

"What?" Mia couldn't believe Trent would do such a thing.

"We need to act fast to protect you. Call Trent," Caleb ordered. "Ask him to come here. Beg if that will get him here immediately."

"Why?" She was afraid to trust Caleb, to trust anyone, yet there was something in Caleb's hard, cold eyes that reassured her he would not be part of any wrongdoing.

She didn't truly trust him, but if he was right about Trent, who else could she turn to for help? She picked up the phone and pressed in her lawyer's number.

"Trent, it's Mia. Can you c-come here? P-please? It's urgent." She listened to his gruff excuses but said nothing. Finally he agreed. "Th-thank you." She hung up.

"Well?" Caleb Grant's silver eyes probed hers.

"H-he'll be here in half an hour. But I have no idea what I'll say to him. What do I do?" Even asking the question scared Mia.

"I'll speak for you." Caleb's fierce glare faded

slightly. "I know it hurts and you don't want to think about it right now, but Harlan Granger was not the man you thought he was and neither is his partner. Something's been going on, something more than an affair. I intend to find out what. Okay?"

A picture of Harlan and Reba together, laughing and loving, sharing a child, while she sat alone, would not leave Mia's mind. Her husband had always been cool, distant and businesslike. He'd promised her mother he'd care for her. Surely he couldn't, wouldn't have turned to another... Suddenly her stomach heaved and Mia could think of nothing but escape.

"Excuse me." She hurried to the bathroom, where she was violently sick.

Oh, Lord, I feel so bad. And something is terribly wrong. Please help me.

She'd barely had a chance to regain her breath when *he* rapped on the door.

"I'm all right," she called, irritated by her weak voice. "I'll be out in a minute."

"We need to hurry." Caleb's voice left little room for argument. In fact, he was leaning against the hall table impatiently tapping his foot when she emerged. Feeling disheveled and weaker than she'd ever been, Mia walked slowly to the sunroom and sat down. She reached out to take her cup, but Caleb ordered, "Don't touch that."

Mia flinched and drew her hand away. "Why?"

"I believe there's something in your tea that makes you sick." His tone was harsh.

"Caleb, that's ridiculous," she burst out. Maybe he was wrong about Harlan... "Trent would never—"

"I'm pretty sure he's done it before," he said, certainty in his voice. "You've been drinking the stuff for days and you've felt ill about that long, right?"

"Yes. But—" Mia stared at her cup as frightening scenarios played through her mind.

"That tea should be tested. The police will be here shortly." Caleb's lips tightened. "They can do that. I've also ordered an ambulance."

She felt herself sway and grabbed the table. "Why?"

"To check you out and take blood samples that will discern if something's off in your system." Caleb leaned forward and covered her hand with his. His touch sent ripples of awareness up her arm. "Mia, you won't like what I'm about to say."

"Is it worse than you saying Harlan was having an affair? That he had—a child with his secretary?" She had to force the words out. When Caleb nodded she saw pity on his face. She did not want his pity, so she straightened her spine. "Go ahead, say it."

"I believe that Harlan, along with Trent, was running some kind of scheme to secrete money. After Harlan died in the car accident, I believe Trent saw a way to get that money for himself." Caleb frowned. "I think River-bend Ranch is the reason, though I haven't yet made all the connections. In order to get the ranch, Trent needs you out of the way."

Mia sat in stupefied silence as Caleb explained about the ranch her husband had supposedly bought. He spoke of a petition for divorce Harlan had supposedly filed the day he died and listed a money trail Caleb claimed he was still uncovering.

Dazed and ill, horrified to imagine the man she'd married was capable of such betrayal, Mia tuned out the pain and hurt that threatened to overwhelm her. How could it be possible? How could God have betrayed her trust? She'd believed for so long that He was there, protecting her, comforting her in her lonely marriage. Now it felt as though He'd played a horrible trick, just as Caleb claimed Harlan and Trent had. It was too much to deal with.

Her brain numb, she sat silent as Caleb told the same story to the police when they arrived. They waited in the kitchen when she let Trent inside. Mia could see guilt build in Trent's eyes as Caleb pummeled him with questions. She couldn't bear to believe that this friend, one of the few she had and the only one she'd truly trusted since Harlan's death, had deliberately set out to hurt her.

While Trent scrambled for a defense, Mia held her whirling emotions at bay. For now she'd be strong. But in her heart of hearts she knew she believed Caleb's accusations. So deep was her feeling of betrayal, she couldn't even manage a silent plea to God for help. He'd let this happen. How could she trust Him again?

A detective arrived, showed Trent a warrant for his arrest and after a few questions told the officers to take her lawyer to the station. The detective seemed to know Caleb and the two whispered together before Caleb introduced her to Detective Ed Gray.

"Our police station has been investigating Harlan Granger for several months via a request from the IRS who are tracking what they believe is unreported income," the detective told Mia. "This new information about your lawyer adds to our investigation. For that reason I hope you'll allow these paramedics to take a sample of your blood. Then I'll need to ask you some questions."

"Okay." Mia remained silent when he beckoned the

paramedics forward. They took several vials of blood, which were then handed to an officer, who sealed them in an evidence bag and left with another officer.

"They'll have our lab run tests on your blood," the detective explained. "As a precaution, I'd like the paramedics to check you over now."

Mia nodded and the two medical people got to work.

"Your vitals seem to be getting stronger," they told her sometime later. "You'll be okay." The detective thanked and dismissed them.

Mia was rolling down her sleeve when two men came out of her kitchen carrying evidence bags that contained her teas. Her heart sank a little further. Could it be true—had Trent been trying to poison her?

"Now for the questions." Detective Ed Gray's face tightened.

Mia did her best to answer everything he asked, even though some of his questions puzzled her. From time to time she glanced at Caleb. His gaze never wavered from her. But it was not a flattering look. It was a suspicious look that asked how she could have been so naive.

In retrospect Mia asked herself the same thing as she finally accepted that she'd been incredibly stupid to have trusted her husband. But it had never occurred to her to not trust him because her mother had. In fact, she'd placed Mia's life in his hands. And Trent was Harlan's trusted partner. So why— She silently groaned, tired of trying to make sense of it.

As the weight of her situation settled on her shoulders, Mia wanted to be left alone. And yet she didn't want to be alone to think about Harlan's betrayal. They hadn't had a normal marriage, but to imagine that he'd betray her with Reba—

One word played over and over in her mind. *Betrayed.* And following it—*you can't trust anyone.*

"Mrs. Granger?" The detective touched her shoulder.

"Sorry. What did you say?" She forced herself to concentrate.

"I know all of this must come as a shock, especially right after your husband's death, but one of my officers has phoned to say Trent just admitted to lacing your teas with a substance to make you sick." He gave her a sympathetic smile. "Our medical people advise drinking plenty of fluids to flush it out of your system. You can thank Caleb for acting on his instincts. There should be no long-lasting effects."

"Thank you." Mia looked at the lawyer and the detective, not knowing what else to say. Everything seemed surreal, like being an actor in some horrible play she couldn't escape.

"The total of what Trent and your husband perpetrated isn't yet clear, but we've launched a full investigation," the detective explained.

"Oh." If possible, Mia now felt worse. The rest? There was more betrayal in store for her?

"I suggest you retain new legal counsel who can begin sorting through your husband's affairs." The detective inclined his head toward Caleb. "I can vouch for Caleb. He'll be straightforward with you. And to be frank, I think you're going to need his help."

Relief swamped her. Surely if the detective trusted Caleb, she could, too, if only for a little while, just until things were straightened out. A niggle of hope flickered to life. Maybe with Caleb's help she could finally dare to imagine a future with hope. *Please, Lord?*

"Any questions?" the detective asked.

"Why did Trent want to hurt me?" Mia asked.

"I can't answer that yet." He gave Caleb a sideways glance. "But I will find out, I promise you."

"Thank you," she said again. A thought pricked her brain. "I don't know if it's important, but Trent didn't buy all of those teas. Harlan brought some home from several of his trips. So if Trent did try to hurt me, and I'm still struggling with that, only some of the tea would be affected."

The two men shared a look before the detective nodded, then said goodbye.

"What do I do now?" she asked Caleb, feeling lost, when the detective was gone.

"Were all your bank accounts joint?" When she nodded he said, "Let's go."

"Where?" His hand on her arm urged her to move. Mia grabbed her handbag from the hall table and followed Caleb outside. She jerked her arm free of his grip to lock the door. "Where are we going?"

"To a bank so you can open an account in your own name." He held open the door of a luxurious black car. "A bank where you haven't dealt before. You'll withdraw everything from your old accounts and put it in there."

"Why?" Confused and upset with questions tumbling through her brain, not the least of which had to do with Harlan and a dark blue–eyed little girl named Lily, Mia protested, but Caleb was adamant.

"If my suspicions are right, what you signed were papers giving Trent legal custody of your affairs, which will allow him to drain every resource you have as dry as a stone." He shook his head when she would have protested. "If he is released today, he could make the transactions immediately and you'll be broke until everything's sorted, which could be a very long time."

"I'm broke now," she whispered.

"That's according to Trent, who isn't the best source for the truth." Caleb pulled to a stop in front of a small bank, turned and asked in a harsh tone, "Don't you get it?"

"I get that you believe Trent was stealing from me," she whispered, afraid to believe it but more afraid to disbelieve this man. "I don't get why."

"Greed." Caleb Grant's face softened as he looked at her. Transfixed by the change of his gorgeous eyes from ice to melted silver, Mia barely flinched when his hand lifted to brush the swath of curls off her face. "It was greed, Mia."

"For money that you think Harlan had." She sighed. "Which he didn't. I don't understand."

"I have a hunch greed is something a woman like you could never understand." For a moment Caleb's compassion almost undid Mia. Until his mouth firmed and the frost returned to his eyes. "Here's the bank. Better get the transfer started."

Despite her reservations, Mia had to depend on him; she had no one else. But she had to be careful. Though she knew little about men, she knew that despite the help he'd given her, Caleb Grant didn't suffer naive women like her easily.

It would take a lot for Mia to trust again.

Chapter Two

❧

"I can't be your legal adviser, Mia. I represent Family Ties. Our intent is to seek reparation from your husband's estate for his daughter, Lily Jones." Caleb swallowed. "I have a conflict of interest."

Wasn't that the truth? Caleb had been all gung ho to oppose Mia when he left his office this morning. Somehow in meeting her, hearing her side of the story and seeing how ill Trent had made her, he'd done an about-face. He now wanted to help Mia, but his own legal position combined with the loss and confusion filling her lovely face during their elevator ride to the twelfth floor made him feel utterly powerless.

"What are we doing here?" Mia asked.

"I have a very good friend, a lawyer, who is one of the best. That's who we're going to see. She's straight as an arrow. You can trust her and I promise she'll help you." Caleb wished he could be the one to guide Mia through the difficult parts to come and reassure her each step of the way, though he wasn't clear on why it suddenly seemed imperative for him to protect her. Maybe it was because he hated seeing the innocent conned and Mia was certainly innocent. He now had no doubt about that.

Bella Jourdain was the best in her field. If anyone could get Mia out of the mess her husband and his partner had made, Bella could. Once they were shown into her inner sanctum, he hugged the older woman heartily then leaned back to study her lined face.

"How come you never get older, Bella?" Caleb asked.

"Clean living, kiddo." Her almost black eyes scanned Mia. "This is Pia's daughter?"

Caleb introduced them. Then he laid out the problem for Bella, having received a text confirmation that his office had already faxed her most of the pertinent information on the case so she wouldn't be completely in the dark.

"You believe the partner, Trent, has been embezzling?" Bella mused, scribbling madly.

"I suspect Harlan Granger was doing the same." Caleb wished he could spare Mia when she frowned at him as if he'd betrayed her. He continued because it was the only path he knew to get Mia and Lily justice. "My assistant just dug up old court records indicating that Mia's mother, Pia Standish, left an in-trust account for her daughter to be administered by Granger until Mia was twenty-one."

"But I'm twenty-three and I've never heard of any account," Mia protested.

"Exactly." Caleb glanced at Bella, one eyebrow arched.

The older woman tapped a pencil against her lips for several seconds, then rose. "You'll have to leave now, Caleb."

"But I haven't finished." He glared at his old friend.

"You've finished here. You represent Family Ties and Granger's child. We both know you can't be privy to any further personal conferencing between me and my client. I appreciate your help, but I must protect my client and you. So it's time for you to leave." Bella walked to the door and pulled it open. "Sorry."

Knowing she was right but frustrated that he hadn't yet found the answers he sought for Lily, Caleb walked to the door.

"But he's been helping me. I want Caleb to stay," Mia said.

"Bella is your lawyer, Mia, and she's very good at what she does. Her concern is your interest, and until she's got things sorted out, you must listen to what she says," Caleb reassured her. Funny how quickly he'd come to like Mia, how fast he'd moved from resenting her for Lily's sake to trying to help her. "I'll wait outside."

"Okay." Mia's green gaze chided him for abandoning her.

Bella gave him an arch look before she closed the door behind him.

Caleb sat in the waiting room thinking about how vulnerable Mia seemed seated in that big austere office. Only this morning he'd been planning to try to coerce her into offering money for Lily's care. He knew now that he wouldn't force her into anything.

That change of heart confused Caleb. But one thing was for sure. He might feel empathy for Mia, want to help—even rescue her, but he couldn't let any of those emotional responses sway his goal to obtain justice for Lily. She was the true innocent here. His concern for the lovely Mia, even though she'd been done wrong, could not affect his professional judgment. But why did God always allow the innocent to get hurt?

He texted his office for an update, glad to be away. Hours of fighting legal battles for clients who'd been wronged was the reason he'd chipped in for half the ranch with Lara. He'd seen it as a place to escape his work and since her death he'd been very grateful for the freedom it offered. His birth father's appearance in Buffalo Gap last week had made him even more grateful because too many angry memories from the past now assailed him. The only way Caleb could exorcise his loathing for the man was with long horseback rides into the hills. As a kid he'd always gone out there to clear his mind. Some things never changed.

Only now when he rode the ranch he saw Lara. Would he ever forget her last words to him?

You've let bitterness take over your world so much, I think it's wiped out your ability to love, Caleb. All I can feel is your hate for your father. It's consuming you. Deepening our relationship with your hate for him between us isn't going to work. You need to let forgiveness heal your heart before we can talk about a future together.

Forgiveness? Impossible when Caleb couldn't rid his mind of the image of his father shoving his mom and her falling backward down the stairs. That was his last memory of her. An hour later she was dead, and his world had never been the same. Sometimes late at night, alone on the ranch, he could still hear her telling him about God, how He loved Caleb, how they had to forgive his drunken father as God forgave them.

Caleb couldn't do it. How did a man who killed his wife deserve forgiveness? How could God forgive a sin like that? It didn't matter that scripture insisted that God forgave no matter what. Caleb couldn't forgive. That inability to reconcile with God ate at his soul like an acid that left only bitter wounds in its place.

His past drove Caleb to go beyond mere duty to ensure every child from Family Ties went to a home where love ruled. That was also what compelled him to find justice for sweet Lily, a delightful child whose father never bothered to know her. How could God forgive that?

Caleb's phone chimed. He read the texted answer to his last question, then sent another. The stream of responses piqued his interest. Bella might try to shut him out of Mia's affairs, but Caleb had contacts. He intended to use every one to find out the truth, because somewhere in this mess was Lily's birthright.

"I can go now."

Caleb looked up from his phone, surprised to see Mia standing in front of him. They walked to his car in relative silence, but once they were inside, the intensity of her clear green gaze focused on him.

"Thank you for taking me to Bella. She's quite a character." Mia continued to study him. "Is it rude to ask how you met?"

"I was her law clerk. She taught me a lot." Caleb started the car before realizing he didn't know where to take her. "Do you want to go home?"

"I suppose so." The way Mia said it made Caleb think she did not relish a return to her dowdy home.

"What *would* you like to do?" he asked, curious about her thoughts. She looked slightly dazed, but then who wouldn't after hearing they had a trust fund they'd never heard of, that her husband had betrayed her and that he'd left behind a child? And that wasn't even mentioning the attempt to steal her inheritance, information that had just been confirmed.

"It's kind of you, but I don't want to take up any more of your time," Mia said after a tiny hesitation. "I can take the bus from here. You don't have to drive me home."

"I don't have to, no." Caleb could see there was something on her mind. "I'm offering. Is there something else you'd like to do?"

"Yes." The response spilled out in a rush. "I'd like to see this Riverbend Ranch you mentioned." Her eyes softened to misty green. "A ride out of the city would be lovely. Space, freedom, nothing but green grass, hills and trees—it's been so long since I've been away from home." The light in her eyes faded. "But that's too much to ask."

"The place is yours. You should see it." Caleb felt a smug satisfaction saying that. He wanted to be the one to show Mia Riverbend Ranch, to watch her eyes stretch wide with wonder, hear her breathy gasp when they drove up the circular driveway. Somehow he knew that Mia would appreciate everything about the ranch.

"Of all the things Bella explained to me, I understand this ranch business the least. Why would Harlan buy such a place and keep it a secret from me?" Her voice quavered. "I must have done something."

"No. You did nothing, Mia." Caleb clenched his hands on the wheel, wishing he had more to offer than paltry words to soothe her wounded heart. "It was Harlan. There was something wrong with him that made him go outside his marriage for companionship."

"I can't understand that, either. You're sure he

and Reba—?" Her tone told him she wanted it to be otherwise.

"I'm pretty sure. You saw the resemblance for yourself." Caleb hated saying it, hated the hurt filling her eyes and the wash of tears. But he'd feel bad for any woman in this situation. "I'm sorry."

"Our marriage was a sham." Mia choked out the words. "I'd accepted that it was only because of my mother that he married me, but now I suspect he really married me to get her money."

"Yes," Caleb agreed.

"We had nothing in common. Harlan didn't care about God or keeping His commandments, but this is so far from—" For a few moments she gave way to bitter tears.

Caleb wanted to fold her in his arms and soothe her, but that wouldn't be proper. He barely knew Mia and yet he longed to make her world right? Silly and impossible. His own past had taught him that nothing could erase the betrayal she must be feeling. So he let her cry, knowing she needed the release.

"You said Lily is five?" Mia hiccupped a sob. "That means they've been together about as long as we've been married. Why stay married to me if he was in love with Reba?" She dashed a tear from her cheek. "Why not marry her? Create a family with her?"

"There's no way you'll ever know." Caleb refused to restate the obvious lure of her money. He wasn't sure she had an inkling of how much her mother had left her, but his sources told him the number was high, very high.

"He knew how much I love children," Mia said on a sob. "I would have liked to meet Lily." Suddenly she gulped and her eyes went dead. "I guess he thought I'd hurt—"

Caleb waited, curious about the comment.

Mia paused, licked her lips, then continued in a quieter voice, "Harlan said he never wanted to have children."

"Judging by the amount of attention he paid Lily, I'm guessing that part was true." Caleb frowned. *I'd hurt—?* Mia wouldn't hurt a flea. He knew that for certain, though how he knew it was a question he'd ask himself later.

"If he didn't want a child, then why—?" Her wounded voice died away.

"Maybe it was Reba's idea. Maybe she hoped having Lily would solidify their relationship. Or maybe Lily was an accident." He wanted to lift Mia's spirits and wondered why it seemed so important to do that.

"I don't believe any child is ever an accident," Mia said firmly. "Every birth is a promise from God. I wish—I wish I could have a child." She began to weep as though her heart was broken.

Caleb watched helplessly, thinking what a wonderful mother this caring woman would make. Somehow he knew that Mia was cut from the same cloth as his mother had been. Mia would welcome a child, make it feel loved, the most important person in her world. Mia would intrinsically know how and when to give a hug. Things Caleb lacked. Because of his father.

"May I give you some advice?" he asked when he couldn't stand to watch her weep any longer.

"Of course." Mia blinked away her sadness. Hope fluttered in its place.

"Harlan betrayed you. There's nothing you can do

about that. But he's gone." How odd it was to advise Mia to do what he couldn't. "I'm sure you did your best to be his wife, but now you have to forget all the whys of the past and move on to what's next."

"What is next?" She frowned at him. "I doubt anything's truly changed. I'll continue designing. I like doing that. Maybe I'll have some repairs done on the house if I can afford it."

"Is that all?" Frustrated by her simple response, Caleb wanted Mia to widen her horizons, to think about the possibilities that could fill her life now.

"That's quite a lot for me, actually," Mia said pertly.

"But you could do much more." Caleb turned off the highway toward Buffalo Gap and Riverbend Ranch. "You have opportunities now, Mia. You should take advantage of them." When she didn't immediately answer he glanced her way and found her studying him, a pensive look on her face.

"Opportunities like what?" she asked.

"Do you drive?"

"No. I don't know how." She shook her head, her amazing hair trembling with the motion. "My mother wasn't in favor of me learning."

"You were only seventeen then," he reminded her. "Your mother probably thought she'd get you lessons later."

"Maybe. Harlan didn't want me to drive," she said thoughtfully.

Caleb wasn't surprised by that. Freedom to drive anywhere meant Harlan risked Mia seeing him with Reba.

"Why did you ask?" She studied him, her head tilted to one side.

"Wouldn't now be a good time to take driving lessons? When you get your driver's license you can buy a car." Caleb watched her eyes flare, heard her gasp.

"I can't afford a car!"

"I think if you ask Bella she'll tell you that you can afford to buy a car," he said, hiding his smile. So she still didn't know. "Maybe two of them."

"Why would I need two cars?" Though Mia frowned at him, she was clearly captivated by the possibility of learning to drive wherever she wanted to go. "I suppose I could learn to drive Harlan's car, though it's very big and fancy. I wouldn't want fancy. I might ruin it."

"A car can be fixed," Caleb said, irritated that Mia was so willing to deny herself a simple thing that would bring her freedom. "If you like trees and open spaces, you should consider moving to the ranch."

"I couldn't do that." Mia looked shocked by the idea. "It's not mine."

"It will be." He took pity on her confusion. "I did some investigating. I was trying to figure out how to get some money for Lily from Harlan's estate."

"Oh." Mia frowned at him, obviously troubled by his admission.

"I learned that the ranch is fully paid for. There is no mortgage or lien on it. Harlan is listed as the sole owner, so it will pass to you." He paused for a moment. "If you lived there, you could have Lily visit." He let out his pent-up breath, hoping she wouldn't be repulsed by the idea of seeing her husband's child.

"No, I couldn't. I could never have Lily visit," Mia said in a very firm tone.

Caleb stared, surprised by how adamant she sounded.

He didn't ask why. Mia's world had already been turned upside down. He didn't want to add to that now.

"Anyway, I thought you said she was being adopted?" she added.

"Actually, I didn't say that. Abby Lebret runs Family Ties. She's the one who will find Lily a home," he said in his most calming tone. "I'm just trying to help. Don't worry. Sooner or later Lily will have a family."

"Everything is such a whorl." Her confusion tugged at him. "Nothing is what I believed it to be, especially Harlan having an affair." She blinked furiously. "I didn't see that coming."

"Because he didn't want you to. Because you trusted him," Caleb said. How could he have ever thought her capable of dissembling? "Don't blame yourself. I'm sure he went to great lengths to make sure you didn't suspect him."

"Proof that I've been living in a fairy world." Mia blew out a sigh that ruffled the hairs across her brow. "I feel like Alice in Wonderland after she fell down the rabbit hole. Everything is bewildering." Fear crept across her face. "I should go home and wait until it's all sorted out."

"You can't run away from the truth, Mia." Caleb's heart ached for her. It had to be horribly confusing to have your entire world turned upside down. "This is just a visit. You don't have to decide anything. You're only going to take a look at Riverbend."

"I guess." Mia gazed out the window with appreciation, repeatedly commenting on the glorious colors of the hillside foliage. "I wish I had my camera," she said wistfully. "I'll never remember these exact shades of red and orange."

"Why do you need to?" Then Caleb remembered her paintings. "You can use my phone," he offered, pulling to the side of the road. "I'll email the pictures to you. You do have email?" he asked as an afterthought.

"Of course. I have to. That's how I connect with my employers." Mia's impish grin made his heart rate pick up. "I don't live completely in the Dark Ages, you know."

"I never said—" Caleb took a second look at her face and chuckled. When he'd first met Mia he never expected her to be such a delight.

One that he wanted to know much better.

"I've probably drained your battery and clogged up your data space with all my pictures," Mia said as she handed over Caleb's phone. "But I just can't get enough of these colors."

"How will you transfer them to fabric?" he asked as he helped her back into his car.

"I'm not sure I can." She smiled, feeling more carefree than she had felt in ages. "But I have to try. Those brilliant reds and oranges would make wonderful quilts combined with leafy greens and silvers, and those subtle shades of browns. Maybe if I—"

Realizing she was chattering, Mia went quiet, pretending to ignore Caleb's searching look. He was a nice man, sometimes gruff and grouchy, but she was fairly certain that was a mask to hide his soft inside. She knew no one else who would have dived into her affairs, helped her find a lawyer and then taken her for this ride. With every mile her questions about Caleb Grant grew.

Suddenly Mia's mind went blank as a lovely log home appeared before her, two stories with fence-post railings and a swing on the deck that exactly matched one she'd dreamed about in the days when dreams still seemed possible.

"Welcome to Riverbend Ranch," Caleb said. She felt his stare even though she wasn't looking at him.

"It's so beautiful." Mia gaped at the magnificent house. Set against a stand of dark green evergreens, the log home stood proudly, waiting to welcome whoever stepped through the massive door. She could feel its warmth and hospitality drawing her from here.

"Come on." Caleb waited for her to exit the car, then shoved the door and grabbed her hand. "Let's explore."

Walking beside him, Mia felt funny, odd and yet somehow wonderful with her hand dwarfed in his. Tall, strong, dependable Caleb. Though leery of trusting anyone, she somehow felt Caleb Grant was the kind of man you could always depend on. Still, mistrust had taken root in the past few hours. She wasn't going to depend on Caleb for anything more than some help.

"I grew up in a house like this." He paused to gaze at the structure. "My parents still live there. I'll take you to meet them sometime."

Questions about Caleb's family multiplied. Maybe someday she'd know him well enough to ask them. Her thoughts scattered at the sight of the roses climbing the railings.

"Aren't they glorious?" Mia let go of his hand because his touch made her stomach woozy. She bent to inhale the scent of the whitest bloom. "Persians always smell the best."

"You know roses?" Caleb looked surprised.

"I grow them in my back garden, though never as big as these." She climbed the three front steps, turned and took in the view. "I can see for miles. So beautiful yet so odd."

"Why odd?" Caleb sank down on one of the rockers.

"Harlan hated the outdoors, animals, anything not city. He liked sleek and modern, not oldie moldy, as he called it." She shrugged. "Maybe he bought this place for Reba." She turned to look at him. "Do you think so?"

"Why would he? Reba had a condo in Calgary. Besides, her name isn't on the deed, only his. And he's owned this place for several years." He voiced his theory. "For the past three years there's been an upswing in ranch sales around Buffalo Gap. I wonder if he hoped to resell this place for a nice profit over what he paid for it."

Mia waited, realizing Caleb had something else to say.

"The local real estate agent commented that Harlan never went inside. She said he had a sheaf of papers. He walked the property while consulting his papers, then told her he'd take it."

"Like I said—it's odd." Knowing Harlan hadn't been inside made it easier for Mia to look through the windows. She gasped at the huge stone fireplace covering the end of one wall, a beautiful chandelier that sparkled in the sunlight and a lovely circular staircase. Suddenly conscious of how nosy she must seem, she backed away. "Excuse me," she said, her cheeks burning.

"Why?" Caleb shrugged. "Don't you want a closer look inside?"

Startled, she whirled around and asked, "Can we?"

"While you were soaking in the autumn colors I texted the caregiver and asked her to unlock it." Caleb turned the knob, pushed the door open and waved a hand for her to enter.

"That was kind of you." Mia walked past him, heart thudding. Caleb Grant *was* a very kind man, and very handsome, and very… Forcing her focus off him, she glanced around as the warmth of the house enfolded her like a comfortable quilt.

"Do you like it?" Caleb asked quietly.

"Who wouldn't? This is what a real home feels like." Mia ran her hands along a log, reveling in its satin smoothness. She gazed up at the vaulted ceiling. "The details are spectacular."

"It's big, I'll say that." Caleb strolled through the front room into a dining room and then the kitchen. Mia followed him, mentally placing her few precious items here and there. "Like it?" he asked, stopping in the kitchen.

"What's not to like?" The big sunny room over-looked a backyard with a screened gazebo, a fountain and a child's play set—for Lily, the child Harlan never wanted? The child she could never have. That hurt too much so Mia refocused. "The patio has a place for campfires and picnics." Her mind immediately began envisioning a fall campfire and the scent of burning leaves.

"Look at this room." Realizing Caleb had moved on, Mia followed his voice. "I think it's a family room, but the windows give it amazing light. You could paint in here."

"Plus, there's another fireplace to make it cozy." Riv-erbend was like the house Mia had once cut out of a magazine and dreamed of ever since, though she'd never dared pray for it. That was too much to ask when she didn't have anyone to share it with, not even a husband now. "It's a family home."

"It could be." Caleb insisted she inspect the four upstairs bedrooms. Each boasted a fantastic view. "It's a nice place," he said when they returned to the front porch.

"Nice?" His simple words jerked Mia from her bemusement. She sat on the porch swing and used her toe to push back and forth. "It's amazing. But I can't understand why Harlan bought it. It's not his type of home at all." She glanced at Caleb and felt her cheeks burn. "At least I didn't *think* it was. I guess I didn't really know him at all."

"Forget Harlan. I'm starving. Let's go have lunch." A moment later they were heading down a gravel road into town. Caleb pointed out different houses and named neighbors. "I live about four miles in that direction," he said, pointing.

"On a ranch." Mia heard the squeak in her own voice. Caleb must have heard it, too, but he simply nodded. "I didn't think of you as a rancher," she said. "I guess that makes me a bad judge of character again."

"Actually you're right. I'm not a rancher." He didn't look at her as he said, "I bought the ranch with a friend, as a sort of investment. Lara was Reba's sister."

Mia jerked upright, surprised he'd known Harper's secretary. Some suspicious gremlin in her head warned that Caleb was still a stranger.

"Lara was a veterinarian. The ranch was to be a refuge for injured or displaced animals."

"It's not that now?" Mia asked, sensing something had saddened him.

"It was Lara's dream. I've tried to keep her dream

going, but I'm failing. I finally took my mom's advice and listed the place last week." Caleb pulled into a parking space in the small town. "Brewsters is a good place to eat," he said, his voice flat, emotionless.

Mia got out of the car, her mind trying to piece together the puzzle of Caleb Grant. This Lara must have been important to him. His voice had softened when he said her name, a trace of fondness lingering as he spoke of her.

Brewsters turned out to be a homey diner with tantalizing aromas filling the air. Most of the lunch crowd had left when a woman Caleb introduced as Paula Brewster greeted them and took their orders. Mia was about to sip her tea when an older woman bustled over and swallowed Caleb in a hug.

"You should have told me you'd be here, honey. I'd have changed my plans and shared lunch with you." The woman turned sharp inquisitive eyes on Mia. "Hello."

"This is Mia Granger, Mom. Mia, this is my mother and the town's mayor, Marsha Grant."

"Granger?" The woman frowned. "Any relation to Harlan Granger?"

"Mia was his wife." Caleb shook his head at his mother so subtly that Mia almost missed it. It seemed like a warning. "We were just looking at Riverbend."

"It's a gorgeous place. Too bad no one's living there. It needs a family." Marsha fluttered her hand at someone near the door. "I'd love to stay and visit, but I have a council meeting. Welcome to Buffalo Gap, Mia. I'm sorry about your husband, but I hope you come back again. Bye, dear." She brushed a kiss against Caleb's bristly cheek and then hurried away.

"Your mother seems very nice," Mia said politely.

"She's actually my foster mother and she is nice. Also nosy. I'll be inundated with questions about you later on." Caleb didn't seem worried. In fact, a small smile curved his lips.

Foster mother? Mia hesitated a moment, then asked, "Did your family have problems?"

"You could say that." His harsh laugh shocked her but not as much as his words. "My father murdered my mother. Marsha became my foster mother. She and her husband, Ben, later adopted me. Your mother made sure my father could never get custody of me again."

Caleb watched shock fill Mia's face and wondered why he'd felt the need to tell her the truth so harshly. His personal story was bad enough, but there was no need to couch it in such bitter terms, except that for the third time this week he'd just glimpsed his birth father here in Buffalo Gap, this time right across the street from Brewsters. In a flash the same old anger had bubbled up inside and splashed all over poor Mia.

"I'm sorry." Her lovely green eyes grew misty with suppressed emotion as she touched his hand in a brief gesture of sympathy. "That must have been very hard for you."

"I managed." No way was he going to dump the rest of his sordid life on her. "Marsha and Ben were a godsend. I even got a sister out of the deal. Cindy's a social worker in Calgary. She and Abby have worked together on several cases at Family Ties."

Their food arrived. Caleb dug into his soup and sandwich with gusto until he noticed Mia picking at hers.

"Is something wrong with it?" Feeling helpless at the sight of her tears, he said, "Mia—"

"I'm being silly." She sniffed and forced a smile. "It's just that I haven't eaten out in such a long time. Harlan said we had to save money—" He saw anger flash in those green eyes before she looked down. "Anyway, it's very nice of you to bring me here."

Caleb's heart pinched at those words. She was grateful for a meal out? It emphasized the solitary life Mia had led. How could Harlan Granger have treated this sweet woman so shabbily?

"Now I've ruined your lunch." She groaned. "I'm sorry."

"Nothing's ruined." He studied her for a moment. "I want to ask you something, Mia, but I don't know if I should."

Her smile flickered nervously. "What is it?"

"Since you're here in Buffalo Gap anyway, would you like to visit Lily?" Caleb held his breath as he waited for her answer.

"I don't know." Mia's fearful look returned.

"We wouldn't have to tell her exactly who you are," he reassured her. "It's just that with her mother gone she gets lonely and…" He let it trail away, knowing he was asking too much when Lily was her husband's child with another woman. "Never mind."

"Actually, I think I would like to see her, as long as you'll be there." Mia played with her teacup. "Maybe seeing her would bring some sense to this strange day."

"Great!" Caleb found himself grinning. "Lily's a sweet girl. This was Reba's hometown. She used to come back and visit Lara a lot, so folks in town got to know Lily. In fact, over the years almost everyone in town has taken a turn babysitting her."

"Even you?" Mia studied him from beneath her lashes.

"Even me," he agreed quietly, remembering the fun times he and Lara had spent with Lily. "Her aunt and I used to date so Lily calls me her uncle."

"*Used to* date?" Mia stared at him, waiting.

"Lara died six months ago." He met her gaze and saw questions widening her eyes.

"Oh. Where does Lily live now?" He thought Mia played with her cup to hide her expressions.

"Officially I'm her guardian. Lara and Reba lost their parents years ago, so Lily's staying with a woman named Hilda Vermeer, a foster mother." He grimaced. "She was a real tartar when I was a kid, but she's mellowed a lot since. I think Lily feels safe with her."

"Children should feel safe," Mia murmured almost to herself.

"Your mother said that to me once." Caleb figured it was unlikely that Harlan would talk about his former partner. He thought Mia must feel starved for details about her mother. Again that desire to protect her bloomed inside him.

"She protected you from your father," Mia said thoughtfully. "Maybe that's why she arranged for me to marry Harlan, to keep me safe."

Not Pia's best decision, Caleb mused, *given the jerk Harlan turned out to be.*

"It's past three," he said after checking his watch. "Lily will be home from kindergarten. I could phone Hilda, ask her if we could come over." He waited, certain that if Lily and Mia could form a bond, chances were that Mia might agree to support Harlan's child and legal action against the estate wouldn't be necessary.

And you wouldn't feel so guilty for not adopting Lily yourself.

"I don't know." Hesitation was written all over her face. But something dark and fearful also lurked in her eyes, something Caleb didn't understand.

"It doesn't have to be a long visit," he encouraged. "I drop in to see her most days. You can say hello." She didn't look convinced, so he pushed harder. "Don't you want to see Harlan's child?"

"Yes, but—" A nerve ticked in her cheek "You don't understand." She glanced sideways at him, then sighed heavily. "Today has been full of surprises."

"I know. It hasn't been easy for you and this must have come as quite a shock. But surely meeting a five-year-old girl doesn't scare you." Caleb immediately regretted those words because it was clear Mia was panicking at meeting Lily. "I'll be right there," he soothed. "We can leave whenever you want."

That seemed to ease her fears. "You're sure?"

"It's just a meeting, that's all."

"As long as you stay. I can't be alone with her," Mia said, her voice raspy.

"Hilda and I will both be there." He smiled. "I'm so glad you're doing this. You'll love Lily." Caleb made the call and after a few minutes' drive they were at Hilda's.

Caleb saw Mia's face soften when she caught sight of the little girl sitting in a corner of the porch. She studied Lily intensely, taking in every detail of her stepdaughter.

"Welcome. I've made us some iced tea. It's so lovely today we'll drink it on the porch," Hilda said after Caleb had introduced Mia.

He wasn't surprised to see Lily hang back. Since

her mother's death she'd become unsure and tentative about most things. He hated the way the little girl clung to Hilda's skirt as if fearing she'd be abandoned again. Caleb knew he wasn't capable of giving her what she needed, but he had a hunch Mia could, *if* she would.

"Iced tea would be lovely. Thank you." Mia smiled. The warmth in her words reached Hilda's heart judging by Hilda's wide smile.

"Have a seat. It won't take me a minute." The older woman bustled inside.

Caleb knew Lily would have preferred to follow Hilda, but that would have meant walking in front of Mia, thereby revealing her damaged leg. He felt his heart squeeze with regret, saddened to see the formerly bubbly child now standing silent in the corner, dark blue eyes riveted on Mia. He struggled to find a conversation opener and came up blank.

"It's a lot of hair, isn't it?" Mia mused aloud, reaching a hand to her head. Though she didn't actually look at Lily, it was obvious the child was the target of her remark. "Sometimes I wish it was shorter like yours. Your hair is so pretty. Those ribbons are perfect." Mia caught her own hair in her hand and tried to twist it into a ponytail like Lily's.

"You look like a clown." Lily promptly burst into the giggles.

"I know." Mia pulled out a small tablet and a pen from her purse and began sketching a clown with big curly hair, a bulbous red nose and striped balloon pants. "Like this?" she asked, holding out the pad.

Clever, Caleb silently applauded. Why had Mia been afraid when she was so obviously at ease with children?

Mia held the drawing so that Lily had to move

nearer to get a good look, which meant she awkwardly shifted her leg. Mia didn't seem to notice. Instead, she kept drawing, adding to the sketch. In moments Lily was fully vested in the picture, pointing out areas that needed enhancement.

"Can you draw a dog, a brown one?" Lily asked.

"I'll try." Mia began sketching until under Lily's tutelage the face of a chocolate Lab appeared.

"It's perfect." Lily grinned. "That's the dog I want. And I'm going to call him Mr. Fudge."

"That's a great name," Mia said. "Who doesn't like fudge?"

The air left Caleb's chest in a rush of relief. This relationship was going to be a success. Mia would make it so because that was the kind of woman she was: caring, gentle and full of love just waiting to be expressed. Maybe her fear had to do with Lily's father, and yet he saw no fear in Mia now, just a sweet spirit that Lily was warming to. He'd been right to bring them together.

He studied the two heads, one so dark, one shimmering with light, just like her mother's. He had a hunch that Mia would one day make some lucky child an incredible mother. Some child—like Lily?

Caleb seldom prayed anymore. God seemed too far away. But this afternoon the soundless plea slipped from his heart.

Can You find Lily a new mom, God?

As Lily's giggles filled the air, Caleb couldn't think of anyone he'd rather see her with than sweet, gentle Mia.

Chapter Three

"Lily's an incredible child." Mia couldn't conceal how moved she was after meeting her husband's daughter.

"You didn't feel a barrier because she's, well, your stepchild?"

"Not at all." Her certainty surprised Mia. "It's obvious Harlan was her father. Those eyes and that chin give it away, but Lily is her own person. She isn't responsible for Harlan's betrayal. She's just a little girl who's lost her mother."

"I'm glad you feel that way," Caleb said warmly. The admiration and appreciation in his gaze warmed a lonely place Mia always kept hidden.

Perhaps it also emboldened her because she blurted, "What happened to Lily's leg?"

"A riding accident." Caleb shuddered. "A year ago she was on a horse for the first time and it threw her. Lily broke her leg. It was a complicated break and hasn't healed well."

"Can it be fixed?" Mia asked.

"Reba told Lara she couldn't find a surgeon willing to try another operation." Caleb's forehead furrowed.

"I haven't had time to check into that. Abby Lebret, the woman who runs Family Ties and is trying to find Lily a home, might have more information."

"Family Ties—oh, yes, the adoption agency you mentioned. So you've handed care of Lily over to them?" Mia said, not managing to hide her disapproval.

"It seemed best. I'm not father potential," he said, defensively, Mia thought.

"I thought you were very loving with her, exactly as a father would be." She mentally replayed her meeting with Lily. "She reminds me of myself at her age." She didn't realize she'd spoken her thoughts aloud until she heard Caleb's voice.

"How is that?"

"I was a sickly child. I missed a lot because I was often in hospital or at home recuperating." Wishing she'd kept silent and fearing Caleb would press to hear more, Mia explained, "It was hard socially when I joined school after the others had already made friends."

"You think Lily's missing out like that?" The idea seemed to startle him. "I've been so intent on getting her affairs worked out that I never gave much thought to her social state."

"She seems a bit restrained. That's probably due to just losing her mother, but I have a feeling her leg also holds her back from being more outgoing." Mia shrugged. "I may be way off base. I'm not a child expert." She gave a harsh laugh. "Far from it, in fact."

"Actually you're right. Before the accident, Lily was bubbly, giggling all the time. You're the first one I've heard make her laugh in ages." His frown reappeared. "I should visit her more often. Maybe take her out so she doesn't brood. I'll have to do better."

Caleb's soft voice, his thoughtful words and the gentle goodbye kiss he'd brushed across Lily's cheek all revealed his soft spot for her. Mia found it indescribably attractive that this hard-nosed lawyer became putty in Lily's tiny hands.

"Thank you for taking me to meet her. She's a darling child. It's Harlan's loss that he didn't really know her." It was the first time she'd ever said anything negative about her husband, but after meeting Lily, Mia was annoyed that he'd apparently ignored the sweet little girl, his own daughter.

"You and she seemed to bond." Caleb's mild tone made her check his face. Nothing unusual there, but the way he'd said it, almost smugly...

"Who wouldn't bond with Lily?" Mia was immediately sorry she'd said that because they both knew Harlan hadn't bonded with her. "I wish you the best in finding her a new family to love her," she added, hoping to dissuade him from considering her as a candidate for Lily's mother.

"Thanks." Caleb fell silent.

Mia bit her lip. If Caleb knew about her past, the mistake she'd made that had cost a child his life—she refocused, saw his face alter into that blank-mask look he favored.

"So what's next for you, Mia?" he asked.

"That's the second time you've asked me that question." Wondering at the reason for his query, Mia searched his face for a clue. "Why?"

"Just wondering if you'd come and visit her again," he said.

Visiting Lily alone was the *last* thing she could do.

"I have no way to get out here. I don't drive, remember?" The joke fell flat when Caleb suddenly slowed and turned right. "Wh-where are we going?"

"To do some driver training." He flashed a grin before pulling onto a seldom-used gravel road. "Ready?"

"I can't—" Mia gulped, then swallowed her words when he jumped out of the car. When he opened her door, she reminded him, "I don't have a permit."

"We'll rectify that later. This is my land, so right now you're perfectly legal to drive on it since I'm with you. Trust me. I'm a lawyer." He gave her a cheeky grin. "If you get into trouble, I'll bail you out, or sweet-talk the cops."

Trust wasn't something Mia was ready to give, but what choice did she have?

"You may regret this," she advised. When it became clear he wasn't backing down, she sighed her resignation, walked around the car and climbed in on the driver's side. "Fasten your seat belt," she ordered as if she knew what she was doing.

Caleb obeyed with a deep-throated chuckle. "Yes, ma'am."

"Now what?" She prayed she didn't ruin his vehicle. It looked expensive. She flicked the key as told and flinched when the motor ground too long.

"Twist, then let go," Caleb directed calmly. Mia repeated the action with better results. "Good. Now you need to start moving. Right pedal is the gas." He waited for her nod. "Left is the brake. Keep your foot on that while you put the car into gear and then *gently* press on the gas pedal."

Mia followed his words and gave a little squeal when the car started rolling forward. She froze, her fingers clinging to the wheel as the car headed for the ditch.

"You do have to steer," Caleb said in a mild tone as he turned the wheel so the car returned to the middle of the road. "Don't worry about oncoming traffic. I'm the only one who lives on this road. I moved out here after Lara died."

It took all Mia's concentration to keep the car centered. She knew he was impatient for her to speed up, but she was terrified to do so.

"You can move a little faster," Caleb hinted after she'd driven at a snail's crawl for five minutes.

"I'll try." She pressed the gas, but the wheels felt squishy, so she slowed down until she was comfortable. Well, as comfortable as she could be driving his car. "I like this speed. I don't feel as if I'm losing control," she said when he hissed in a breath of frustration.

"Maybe it's the gravel," he suggested. "I doubt you've driven on that before."

"I've never driven on anything before," she reminded him with an impish smile. "Oh, there's your house." She studied the sprawling ranch home. "It's nice."

"Eyes on the road," he reminded her.

"Oh, dear." Mia jerked the wheel to center the car once more then realized the road turned in a circle. Steering around it wasn't as easy as it looked. When she found herself heading for a massive pine tree, she pressed her foot against the brake pedal with all her strength.

Caleb gave an "oof" as he slammed back against the seat. Mia risked a look at him, disgusted to find he was laughing.

"It's not funny," she said, irritated that he'd put her in this situation.

"Yes, it is." His silver eyes glittered with amusement. "You drive like a scared girl."

"I *am* a scared girl," she growled, but he only laughed harder. "I think it's time for you to take over." She lifted her hand to unclasp her seat belt, but Caleb laid his over it. "What?"

"You're still in gear, Mia."

Too aware of his warm hand on hers, she shifted the lever into Park then glanced at him. "Okay?"

"Uh-uh. One thing you'll learn early on is that when you get in a driving pickle, you have to get yourself out." His gentle voice soothed her skittery nerves. "Don't expect to do everything right at first. You haven't done this before. It's natural to make mistakes." He drew his hand away. "I'm sorry I laughed at you."

"No, you're not," Mia contradicted, frowning as the corners of his lips tipped up.

"No, I'm not," he agreed. A chuckle burst from him. "You're a good sport, Mia."

"Thank you. I think." Her breath caught as she met his gaze. Why did Caleb Grant have to be so good-looking?

"Now try again," he ordered.

She sighed, shifted back into Drive and turned the wheel, slowly easing down the road.

"Very good," he praised. The words sounded like music to her ears.

"I'm sure most women have their driver's license long before they're my age," she said, suddenly awkward in his presence. "I must seem like a dinosaur to you."

"Pretty young dinosaur. Actually, I think you have a lot of guts." The quiet compliment drew her glance his way. Caleb smiled. "Not everyone would meet her husband's daughter and then take on learning to drive after what you've been through today. I don't think Harlan had a clue about what a strong woman you are. You have a lot of courage, Mia."

"Courage?" She shook her head. "I don't know about that. I'm just trying to face everything as best I can." The thought of Harlan driving out here with Reba made her insides shrink into a tight hard ball. She sniffed to stop the tears that lay just below the surface.

"He isn't worth your sympathy, Mia." Caleb's hard tone surprised her. She glanced his way, saw the ice in his eyes. "He married you to get your money. He defrauded you. He lied and he cheated on you. Forget him."

"Harlan was part of my life for six years," she murmured, peering through the windshield. "I can't just wipe out our past, but I wish I could understand why he did it. It hurts that he'd go to those lengths to keep me in the dark. It hurts a lot."

Caleb said nothing, but his mouth clamped shut in a hard line. Mia drove carefully to the end of the road where they'd started, shifted the car into Park and switched off the engine.

"Thus ends your first driving lesson," he said. "Good job."

"Thanks." She smiled, reveling in the achievement, small though it was. "I believe I will see about getting my license," she said after a moment's thought. "The freedom of going where I want when I want will be worth swallowing my fear. I hope."

"I'll ask you about that fear once you've been driving awhile." Caleb's laughter rang out once more when she made a face at him. How she enjoyed hearing that burst of merriment.

Mia got out of his car and walked to the other side, glancing around as she did. She waited until they were both inside the car and he'd driven back onto the highway before speaking.

"Your ranch looks charming against those sloping hills. Why do you want to sell it?" His quick look her way made her wonder if he'd answer. Several moments passed before he spoke.

"I told you, I'm not a rancher. I love horses, but this place was Lara's dream and I can't make that dream work." He sounded regretful.

"And you can't make her dream yours?" she asked in a soft voice.

"No. I'm a lawyer, not a veterinarian." He exhaled heavily. "Whenever I'm there I see Lara, hear her talking about the future, about what she wanted to do. It feels as if any change I make would be like killing her dream. I can't do that, either." He stared through the windshield. His next words were reflective. "I guess I've finally realized that what was her dream isn't what I want in my future. I have to move on."

"Sometimes that's a hard thing to accept." Mia looked at her hands as she remembered the many times she'd tried to learn what drove Harlan so she could become part of his life. And failed.

They rode for a while until Caleb broke the silence.

"You have an amazing talent for drawing. Did your mother approve?"

"She never said." Mia smiled in reminiscence. "But whenever she found me sketching she'd say something like, 'It's good you can amuse yourself.' I don't know what she'd think of my quilt designs now. The law was what she lived for."

"Was she a godly woman?" Caleb asked as he turned up her street.

"She had faith, though she wasn't showy about it. She used to take me to church when I was little. Sunday morning at church was one thing we did together." Mia pushed away the sad thought that now she had nobody in her life. "I think she felt brain cancer was the worst trick God could play on her. She couldn't stand the idea that she would lose her faculties."

"I can understand that," Caleb said.

"She took too much morphine and died in her sleep." Mia paused, then whispered, "I always wondered if she did that intentionally to avoid losing control." She felt Caleb's start of surprise before he braked in front of her house.

"I'm sure it wasn't deliberate. Pia was too strong to take the easy way out." His words sounded soothing, gentle.

"The doctors said the same, but sometimes I still wonder." Mia liked the way Caleb looked directly at her. So many people never made eye contact. "My mother consulted with a minister before she died. Later he told me she had a lot of questions for God."

"I hear that." There was a tightness in Caleb's voice that intrigued Mia. "I have a lot of questions for Him myself."

"You?" She hadn't considered this competent man would question anything.

"Sure. As a kid I wondered why He'd placed me in the home He had, why my mother died as she did, why my father never went to prison." He made a face. "I'm still asking that last one today. It drives me nuts to see him walking free around Buffalo Gap."

Mia's sympathy welled for the young Caleb who'd lost his beloved mother. "He's contacted you?"

"He's tried, but I don't want anything to do with Joel Crane. Ever." As if to end the discussion Caleb got out of the car and walked around to open her door. "It's been a pleasure meeting you, Mia Granger," he said as they walked to her front door.

"You, also, Caleb Grant." So he'd divested himself of the name Crane. Interesting. "It seems as if I've known you more than a single day." She pulled out her key and unlocked the door. "Thank you for everything you've done. I don't know where I'd have been if you hadn't come along."

"Will you be all right now?"

How could she have thought his eyes hard? They glowed now like warm molten silver, chasing away the late afternoon's chill.

"I'm always all right." Mia forced a smile she didn't feel. "I have to be. I'm the only one I have."

"You can call me if you need me." Caleb handed her a business card. "In fact, let's keep in touch."

"I'd like that," she said, and meant it. "Thank you for everything you've done."

"Make sure you get in touch with a driving school," he said. The wink he shot her way made her blush. "You've started now. There's no going back."

Mia's shyness returned full force. She wanted to escape, to be alone while she pondered everything about this unusual day, but especially about this kind, determined, gentle man. She enjoyed his presence in her world very much—because he made her think about the future and not the past?

"No, there is no going back," she repeated. "Goodbye, Caleb."

He nodded. "See you."

As Mia watched him walk down her garden path, she wondered if she'd ever see Caleb again. He'd been so nice to her, saving her from Trent, helping her find Bella, buying her lunch, taking her to see Riverbend Ranch and to meet Lily. It made her realize how lonely she was.

It also made her realize how hungry she was for the companionship he offered. If only her mother had chosen someone like Caleb instead of Harlan... But no, she couldn't think that way. God had a reason for directing things as He had. Still, the only thing her marriage had left her with was a firm determination never to trust anyone again.

Not that she had to worry, Mia decided as she went inside. Caleb was just being nice to her because he wanted money for Lily. He'd been very clear about that.

Why did that make her sad?

"Forgiveness isn't something we get to choose, nor can we ignore it simply because forgiving is hard or because it seems too onerous," Pastor Don said in his Sunday-morning message. "God *commands* us to forgive."

Caleb shifted uncomfortably. He felt as if the minister had seen him glimpse over one shoulder, observed his angry jerk of surprise at the sight of Joel in the back row, head bowed, pretending piousness. Why was he here? What did he want?

Didn't matter, Caleb decided. Nothing was going to

change. If not forgiving was wrong, then he'd just have to deal with God's punishment because there was no way Caleb could stop blaming his father for his mother's death.

When the service was over, Caleb left as quickly as he could, preferring to skip the fellowship potluck dinner so he wouldn't encounter his father. He went home, scrounged together a sandwich for lunch and considered a ride into the hills. But he'd sold Lara's horses. When he couldn't seem to settle on any specific task, he climbed into his vehicle and went for a drive, surprised to realize he was heading toward Calgary.

To see my sister, he mused. His brain scoffed. *To see Mia.*

The image of her lovely face framed by that mass of golden-red curls filled his mind. What was it about her he found so attractive? Her jaunty spirit that refused to be quelled even though she'd been betrayed in the worst possible way? Her tender kindness toward Lily? Her faith in God? All of those, he decided. And more.

At first Caleb had thought Mia too passive, but he'd begun to understand that her hesitation wasn't always due to fear, but more often because she simply didn't know the next step. Yet even with that excuse, he'd been unable to shake the look on her face or her words about being alone with Lily. She'd been afraid, truly afraid, and he couldn't stop wondering why. Had her marriage not been platonic, as he'd assumed? Had she lost a child?

Some inner imp compelled him to turn down Mia's street. Caleb only intended to drive past her house, but before he arrived there he spotted her walking briskly toward him. What else could he do but pull up beside her and roll down his window?

"Want a ride?"

"Hello, Caleb." A smile stretched across Mia's pretty face as the wind caught her glorious hair and tossed it back. "What are you doing here?"

"Out for a Sunday drive. Get in." The genuine pleasure glinting in her green eyes sent a surge of warmth through him that chased away his anger at his father. He waited till she was belted in, then drove the short distance to her home. "How are you, Mia?"

"Doing well. I had a good talk with my pastor and with Bella, which helped clarify some of the issues I've been struggling with." She turned to study him. "And you?"

"Feeling guilty." Seeing her puzzled look, he smiled. "Today's sermon was about forgiveness. My father was there."

"Ah." He liked the way she said nothing more. She waited till he'd parked, then asked, "Are you coming inside?"

"I won't be in the way?" Caleb asked, only then realizing she might have something planned for her day.

"Of course not." She made a face. "I was going to offer you tea, but after the last time—say, why didn't you get sick?"

"I never drank it. Can't stand the stuff." He made a goofy face.

"But your cup was empty."

"I emptied it." He smiled when Mia shot him a quizzical look. "Have you noticed your plants by the table suffering any ill effects?"

"One of them has wilted. I wondered why." Mia's

merry chuckle echoed in the crisp autumn air as she preceded him up the walk. She opened the door and waited for him to enter. "By the way, I received your letter requesting a meeting about Lily. Bella said it was in with a bunch of stuff Trent had."

"Oh." So she hadn't ignored him, Caleb mused. Mia hadn't even seen his letter when he first visited.

"Bella says you want money from Harlan's estate for Lily." She looked directly at him. "But I already knew that."

"I think Lily, as Harlan's daughter, is owed something." Relief that it was out in the open surged through Caleb.

"I do, too, but Bella says I'm not supposed to tell you that. Not yet anyway." She hung up her jacket and his, then led the way to the kitchen. "Have you had lunch?"

"Sort of." He grinned. "Peanut butter and dill pickle sandwich. It's all I had in the fridge."

"Is that good?" Mia asked curiously. When he nodded she said, "I'll have to try it sometime, but for lunch today I'm longing for pizza. Will you share it with me?"

"Sounds great." He sat down at the kitchen table and blinked in surprise when Mia set a knife and a cutting board in front of him. "What's this?"

"You didn't think you'd eat free, did you?" she teased. "You can cut up the pineapple and vegetables."

"You're going to *make* a pizza," he said, finally tweaking to her plan. "*Homemade* pizza?"

"I won't poison you," she promised, and giggled at his eye rolling. "I promise."

They worked together companionably, her mixing and rolling out her dough, him cutting up whatever she handed him. The tiny, dingy kitchen felt comfortable to

Caleb in a way that his own high-priced stainless-steel one did not, but he was fairly certain that was because of Mia and not the appliances. She hummed softly as she worked.

"That's a tune from *The Nutcracker*," he said, recognizing the notes. "I heard it often when I was growing up because my sister was usually the Sugar Plum Fairy in her ballet class."

"It's always been my favorite ballet." Mia took a quick look at him, then went back to kneading. "It's so full of hope and a child's joy. I go to see that ballet every New Year's Eve. It's my way of celebrating a new beginning."

Mia went to the ballet by herself on New Year's, a time when most couples made it a point to be together, to start the year with a kiss. Caleb's heart winced at the loneliness she must have endured. But beneath that curiosity grew. What would it be like to kiss Mia?

"I've never been to a real ballet," he said to chase away his wayward thoughts.

"You should go." Mia smoothed tomato sauce over her crust, then added all the bits he'd chopped topped by cheese. She slid it into the oven and washed her hands. She seemed nervous. Caleb wondered why until she said, "Can I ask you something?"

"Sure." He waited.

"Why is it so important for you to get money for Lily?" The words rushed out, as if she'd been thinking of them for a while. "I mean, what is she to you?

"I've known Lily, through Lara, for a long time. Besides being her guardian, I'm like her uncle. And she's a child in need. I'd do the same for any of the kids that come through Family Ties," he said. "But you're right.

There's something about Lily that compels me to go the extra mile to be certain she's provided for. Maybe it's because she's so alone. She has no home, no family and no support."

"But surely a child her age doesn't need much money." A frown marred Mia's beauty. "She needs love and care, a family, a home. Not a lot of money. At least not yet."

"It's about more than the money." Caleb didn't want to hurt her but he had to tell the truth, so he set his jaw and laid out the hard, cold facts. "It's *Harlan's* money I want, because he never acknowledged Lily as his daughter, never saw her as far as I know and never interacted with her."

"You mean he cheated her of a father, so you want him to pay," Mia said thoughtfully.

"Yes." Caleb reined in his temper. "I'm guessing he didn't provide for her in his will?" He waited a moment before adding, "Or for Reba, either."

"There's no mention of them," Mia confirmed quietly.

A second look at her face made Caleb take a wild shot. "Or you?"

"No. The will is dated long before we were married. There are no benefactors named. Bella said some things will come to me automatically. Everything else will be dispersed from the estate to me because I was married to him." She said it self-consciously, as if she was embarrassed to get what Harlan had owned.

"Your husband's lack of provision for you, his wife, and for his own daughter really annoys me." Caleb accepted the plate she handed him. "But I'm also concerned because I've just learned there's a chance Lily could get specialized treatment for her leg. There will be costs attached."

"Of course," Mia murmured.

"Then later on she might want to go to college or start a business," he continued. "I think she should have money for her future, money that her father should have provided."

"That makes sense." Mia looked at him for several long moments as if assessing his words. She only broke contact when the oven timer dinged. "I guess it's ready."

Caleb watched her set the browned pizza on a table mat. She cut it deftly, slid a lifter under the golden crust and served them each a piece. She brought a pitcher of lemonade to the table and two glasses, then took her seat. She bowed her head and offered a short prayer over the food. When she lifted her head her green eyes met his, wide and clear.

"Let's eat," she said with a smile.

So they did.

"I can't get over how good this tastes," Caleb said for the third time. "You're an amazing cook."

"Thank you." She smiled as she served him the last slice of the pie. "You'd better savor this because I only have a slice of dried-up chocolate cake for dessert."

"Oh, dessert is going to be on me." Caleb left her to guess what that meant as he ate the last slice while Mia restored everything to pristine order. She caught his stare and blushed.

"Harlan hated a mess," she murmured. "I guess I've gotten into the habit—" Her eyes widened when he reached out and tugged on the perfectly straight tea towels that hung from the oven bar, making their hems hang crookedly.

"I saw that in a movie once." He grinned at her, delighted by the burst of musical laughter she couldn't stifle. "Come on. I'm taking you to my favorite dessert place in this town." He held out her jacket, waited for her to slip it on then led the way to his car. "I don't know why, but I somehow thought you'd have a cat," he mused as he drove downtown.

"I'd love a cat, but Harlan is—was allergic." Her eyes grew round. "I guess I could have one now," she said slowly.

"I guess you could." He grinned as he drove, pleased that she was finally seeing possibilities in her future. "What about driving lessons?"

"I've had two already." She grinned. "The first one was such a disaster that the instructor didn't even show up the second time. They sent someone else. He was an excellent teacher. Patient. Kind of like you," she said with a wink. "I'm to take a third lesson tomorrow."

"Good for you." A tug of pure satisfaction filled Caleb. Mia was finally breaking free. He pulled up in front of his favorite ice cream shop. "Your choice. My treat."

"I haven't had ice cream in years." Mia licked her lips as she stood beside him and surveyed the many flavors listed in the window. "Harlan didn't—" She gave a tiny shake of her head and then said, "There are too many choices."

"Over fifty. Do not pick vanilla," he ordered with a pretend glower.

It took a while, but finally Mia chose pistachio. Caleb picked his favorite double chocolate chunk. Cones in hand, they wandered across the road to a small park to enjoy their treat. Mia pointed out the different species of trees and told him which would lose their leaves first.

"You know a lot about trees," Caleb said, secretly impressed by her knowledge. "You could put that to good use at Riverbend Ranch. The back garden needs some care," he hinted, delighted when a rush of excitement lit up her face.

"I love that house. There's lots of space to grow fresh vegetables." Her face took on a faraway look. "Maybe I could add a fruit tree or two."

"Sounds as if you've already moved in," he said.

"I wish I could." She nodded at his surprised look. "I'm serious. I'd love to have that home, though it would mean giving up my church and the convenience of the city."

"There's a very good church in Buffalo Gap," he said, secretly pleased she was talking about a move closer to Lily. "And we have grocery and hardware stores. But if you need something in the city, Calgary's only half an hour away."

"I'm aware of that." Her eyes strayed from him. Her face became pensive.

"What's holding you back?" he asked.

"Bella hasn't got everything straightened out yet," she said. "But if I did move to Riverbend, the one thing I can't escape is that it's a ranch. I have no idea what to do with a ranch, Caleb, no clue how to manage it or what needs to be done."

"So you hire someone to do the handiwork." He saw Mia wasn't convinced. "My mom said that most of the acres that go with the ranch have been rented to the neighbor for pasture for his horses. You could continue to do that."

"I didn't know that." Her face regained its excitement, sending his pulse thudding in response. "So I could live there with a little help for the odd jobs?"

"If you wanted." Caleb swallowed, deeply moved by the look of joy that filled her face. "It's simply a matter of making the decision and doing it."

"You have that philosophy about a lot of things, don't you?" Mia nodded, then licked her cone. "I guess I hesitate too much. I should adopt your approach and stop wavering."

Caleb finished his cone, torn between wanting to know her decision and feeling hesitant to press for an answer. Finally he could wait no longer.

"So leasing the extra land would make it possible for you to move to Riverbend Ranch?"

"Maybe." Mia's voice sounded stronger than he'd ever heard it. In fact, there was a new hint of self-confidence underlying her words that he found very attractive. "I'll have to talk to Bella, but one of these days Buffalo Gap might have a new resident in the community." She grinned at him. "You might have a new neighbor."

"Good," Caleb responded while his heart somersaulted at the prospect of having Mia nearby. Because of Lily, he told himself as they strolled through the park. He was glad because Mia would be nearer to Lily.

Naturally it was nice that Mia would also be close enough to drop in on occasionally. Just in case she needed him for something. But a friend was all Caleb would be to Mia. As Lara had pointed out, he didn't know how to love.

Chapter Four

"I'm glad you could come, though I'm sorry to bother you." A week had passed since Mia had seen Caleb. Now her heart danced as she opened the door wide to welcome him inside her home. "How are you?"

"I'm fine, thanks." Caleb's smile made his silvery eyes glow. To Mia, he looked very fine, but she couldn't let herself get sidetracked.

"Would you like some coffee?" she asked, leading the way into the kitchen.

"Coffee? You?" His silver eyes widened in disbelief. "I thought you were the original tea lady."

"I hope not original." Mia laughed as she turned to get the coffee, hoping to hide her blush. "I don't drink coffee, but I can certainly make it." She did so in the old-fashioned percolator she'd unearthed in the basement after she asked him to come.

"You don't want to sit in the sunroom?" Caleb shot a questioning glance at the closed door.

"It's usually too cool in the autumn without a lot of sun to heat it up," she explained.

"There's no heat?" He frowned when she shook her head. "But where do you work in winter?"

"In here or the living room," she said with a shrug. "When Harlan was alive I mostly waited to do my work until he wasn't here." She motioned to a chair and pulled out two mugs, hoping she could steer the conversation away from herself. "I hope you won't mind if I ask you some questions about Trent. Bella said you'd been investigating him?"

"Earlier this year on another case." Caleb eyed the pecan tarts eagerly. "Did you make these?"

"Yes. Help yourself," Mia invited. "We share coffee and munchies after Bible study. Tonight's my turn."

"I picked the right afternoon, then." Caleb selected a tart, took a bite and complimented her before asking, "What do you want to know about Trent?"

"I've been trying to understand why he would have tried to hurt me." Mia couldn't quite shake the sense of betrayal she still felt.

She felt Caleb hesitating, but then he said, "You can't know his motives, Mia. Maybe it was the money he watched Harlan take, maybe it was because he knew you'd never suspect him, maybe it was simply greed. I can tell you that suspicious circumstances around the deaths of his last two clients have the police investigating him."

"Oh, dear." She silently offered a prayer for others Trent might have hurt.

Caleb shrugged. "Something inside drove him. It's unlikely you'll ever discover what unless he talks, and I doubt his lawyer will allow that now."

Mia sighed, wishing his responses satisfied her.

"It's not really Trent you're asking about, though, is

Gift-Wrapped Family

it?" Caleb said shrewdly, eyes narrowed. "I think you're really asking why *Harlan* did what he did. Am I right?"

"Yes." Mia struggled to quell a rush of tears, irritated that she couldn't shed these feelings of betrayal. "He stole from me. I can forgive that. But he cheated on me. Bella thinks he was probably having an affair even before we married. On top of which he had a child he never even mentioned."

"I'm sorry," Caleb offered quietly.

"Me, too." Mia couldn't hide her anger. Harlan's deceit ate at her like acid, especially because he of all people knew how desperately she longed to love a child and how she mourned the fact that she couldn't. "How am I supposed to understand what he did?"

"I know this is easy to say." Caleb exhaled, then said in a gentle tone, "You have to let it go. There's nothing you can do to change what happened or make it better or figure out why. It's nasty and dirty and hurtful, but all you can do now is move on."

"It's the scope of his betrayal I can't figure out. Why not tell me straight out that he didn't want me, that I wasn't a good wife?" She bit her lip, embarrassed that she'd blurted that out. "Never mind."

Caleb's silence and the softening of his icy gaze made him look infinitely more approachable than the day she'd first met him, Mia decided. It also enhanced his good looks and that killer smile.

"Listen, Mia. It will take time, but you will get over those feelings." Caleb's hand rested on her shoulder in silent comfort, making her very aware of the intimacy building between them. Then he moved away and suddenly she could breathe again. "Were Trent and Harlan's actions the only reason you called me?"

Suddenly tongue-tied, Mia shook her head.

"Then?" He arched one eyebrow, chose another tart and waited while she refilled his coffee. When she was seated once more he leaned forward. "Tell me how I can help you."

"I want to do something with this house. Bella said you could advise me." She shifted under the intensity of his steely stare.

"You want my suggestion? Blow it up." He chuckled at her start of surprise. "Kidding. How can I advise you?"

"Give me the name of a good contractor." Mia saw Caleb's eyes flare as he glanced around the room. "I want to fix this house."

"So you're staying here." He sounded disappointed. "I can tell you that renovations will be expensive." He glanced around. "It looks to me as if there's been a lot of patchwork over the years. That's costly to remove. How far do you want to go?"

"As far as needed to make this a warm, comfortable, safe home." She hurried on before he could object. "I don't want there to be a single problem left, not to mention that I want it to look good."

"Repair the bathroom, gut the kitchen, heat for your solarium, to name a few." Caleb counted them off on his fingers as he spoke. "It's going to be quite a bill."

"I imagine so. But Bella says I have enough money to cover whatever expenses come up." Almost breathless at the possibilities, Mia waited. Somehow she knew Caleb wouldn't let her down. "Well?" she demanded impatiently when he didn't speak.

Mia couldn't explain it, but in that moment she felt

as if a shield fell between them. He no longer studied her, but kept his gaze on a point just past her left ear.

"I thought you were considering a move to Riverbend," he said.

"Still am." Mia almost smiled when Caleb's eyes widened. She had a hunch the lawyer wasn't often surprised. "The renovations won't be for me, but there's no way I want to pass on all my problems for someone else to handle."

Was that admiration? A second later his stony lawyer face was back and Mia was left wondering if she'd imagined his approval. She must have. There was no way Caleb would care whether she moved to Riverbend or not.

"It's a good plan." He nodded. "You'd certainly get more money for the place."

"That's not my primary concern." Mia had to ask the question that had been bugging her. "Why did Bella tell me you'd be able to help?"

"She knows my past." Caleb smiled a funny sardonic grin. "I was working construction before she offered me a job. My foster father taught me a lot about building while I was growing up. I guess he thought I needed to pound something to alleviate my teenage frustration."

Mia smiled.

"It was easy for me to find work renovating and I needed the money to pay off my college loans. A law clerk doesn't make much and I didn't have the funds to start my own office then, so I did what I knew." Caleb shrugged. "I worked on Bella's office."

"It's lovely." She paused. "Your dad sounds like a great father." An angry look flashed across Caleb's face, puzzling Mia. "Wasn't he?"

"Ben was and is a fantastic father. I wish every kid could have a dad like him." The tribute flowed easily, but then Caleb's tone hardened. "As a father Ben is miles above the father I was born to."

"Oh, Caleb." Mia's heart squeezed with sympathy at the tight angry look on his face, but she had no idea how to ease it without prying. "Maybe your mother's death was a mistake and he's sorry it happened."

"I'm sure you're right." Caleb's lips compressed in a tight line. "Doesn't matter if he is. It doesn't change anything. He killed her."

"But he didn't go to prison," she said, trying to puzzle out details he hadn't shared.

"No. He got off." Those silver-gray eyes grew glacial. "I testified against him. Your mother prepared me, explained every step of it, over and over, to make sure the jury would hear what really happened. Pia was adamant that he not get away with murder."

"Yet the jury didn't convict." Mia knew very little about how the law worked, but she did know that her mother would have dotted every *i* and crossed every *t*. "What was the ruling?"

"Accidental death." He sneered. "They believed my father's story that Mom jerked away from him when he reached out and that's what caused her to fall backward down the stairs. She hit her head at the bottom and later died."

"I'm so sorry, Caleb." The bereft look on his face combined with the loss woven through his words gripped Mia's heart. What a horrible burden he carried. "Is it possible that is what happened? I mean, were you young enough that you might have misunderstood?"

"I was seven, but I didn't mistake anything, Mia.

Every detail is still implanted right here." He tapped his temple. His voice hardened. "I can close my eyes and see it as clearly as if it happened five minutes ago. He was not innocent of her death."

"All right," she soothed as she searched for a different way to approach this. "But maybe he's sorry. Maybe he's found you because all he truly wants is your forgiveness."

"Well, he's not getting it." Ice dripped from the words. "Forgiveness is not something I can grant."

"Why?" she dared to ask, hiding the shudder that rippled through her when Caleb's glacial gaze turned on her.

"Because there are some things that cannot be forgiven." His cold, emotionless voice made her cringe.

"By you, you mean," she said in a quiet voice. "But God forgives."

"Some things not even He should forgive," Caleb snarled. "Killing my mother is one of them." He shook his head. "I don't want to talk about this anymore. What is it about this renovation that you need from me?"

"Names of people I should call." Mia stifled her concern for him and focused on her house. "I don't know anything about renovations, so I'll have to depend on contractors who will tell me the truth, give me fair estimates and do the work properly. I should warn you, I don't trust easily."

"No wonder." Caleb sounded sympathetic, but the look on his face revived all the doubts she'd worked so hard to smother.

"Maybe I haven't thought this through enough," Mia murmured. "Maybe a renovation isn't something I should tackle."

"Chickening out already?" Caleb's grin chased the shadows from his face, though remnants lingered in the back of his cloudy eyes. "You'll need guidance, but there's no reason you can't renovate with the right people to help. You managed learning to drive."

"I did. With you cheering me on." She smiled, reveling in the knowledge that she was no longer utterly alone. Caleb would help her. "Can you do that again? Because I'm not sure I can handle this on my own."

"Why don't you walk me through the place so I can get a better idea of what's needed and who'd do the best job for you," Caleb said. "Can I borrow a notepad?"

"Sure." Mia grabbed her smallest sketch pad off the counter, flipped to a clean page and handed it to him. "Where should we start?"

"Let's go from bottom to top," Caleb suggested. He arched one eyebrow. "Basement?"

"This way. Watch your head. The steps are narrow." She felt embarrassed to let this man in his expensive clothes and shoes see her dingy basement, but at least his head wouldn't brush any cobwebs. She'd cleaned as best she could around Harlan's "leave alone" piles. At the bottom of the stairs she grimaced at the disorder.

"What's all this?" Caleb glanced at the stacks of boxes with a frown.

"It's—it was Harlan's. I wasn't allowed to look at it when he was alive. I'm still hesitant to go through his things." She shivered. "He was so adamant that I not touch these boxes. I only ever came down here to do laundry. I don't like it here."

"I wonder why?" he joked. "Dark, dank and dingy. Nobody's favorite place."

"I guess not." The boxes seemed to grow more intimidating until Caleb spoke.

"Do you mind if I glance through a couple of these so I know if they should be stored somewhere or hauled out as junk?"

"Go ahead." Rather him than her, but Mia couldn't keep herself from leaning forward as he opened the first box and pushed back a bunch of tissue. "What is it?" she asked when Caleb didn't move.

"Glass. Old, I think." Using a piece of tissue, he lifted a brilliant blue bowl from the box.

"It's beautiful, even in this dim light." Mia stared as the facets of the bowl caught the overhead light and sparkled even more. Her mind exploded with suspicion, but she masked her thoughts, silently searching the lines of the beautiful bowl for more clues.

"I wonder if all these boxes contain glass." Caleb stored the bowl carefully and moved on, checking through all the boxes. Finally he said, "Three boxes of glass, two of old papers and the rest look like old books."

"Harlan collected books." Mia suddenly remembered him once saying books were his best friends. "I should take them upstairs so I can go through them. I wouldn't want to take the chance of something being damaged by workmen."

But when she bent to lift one, Caleb stopped her.

"I'll do it," he said. "But first let's look around a bit more." He studied the mechanical area and scribbled some notes. "You need a new furnace. I'd also replace the water heater. You don't have air-conditioning?"

"I've often wished we had it in the sunroom," she said. "It's gets very hot in the summer."

"And cold the rest of the year," Caleb said. "A renovation is the time to remedy both. It's cheaper when all that work is done at one time." He surveyed the rest of the space.

Curious, Mia asked, "What are you thinking?"

"This space would make a great family room or kids' play area if it was finished."

"I can't see it," she said with a dubious shudder. "It's ugly down here."

"That could be changed," Caleb said. "Extra finished space would add to the value of the house. You should have plans drawn to see if it's something you want to do."

"Why?" She was intrigued by his vision of potential in this ugly place.

"Because it should be part of the renovation. It could be a great space." He saw her skepticism and grinned. "Trust me."

"I'm trying," she said, but a voice buried deep inside reminded her that she'd trusted two men and come to regret it. Caleb's eyes met hers and held. Something in the depths of those silver eyes made Mia shiver. "If you need to look more, go ahead. I'm going up."

"I'm finished here." He hefted the first box in his arms and followed her up the stairs. "Where shall I put this?"

"Here please. The others can go on the floor over there." Mia waited until Caleb had returned downstairs before she opened the box and lifted out the blue bowl. Lit by a spear of sunshine, it seemed to glow. Gently she turned it upside down and peered at the bottom. She caught her breath at what she saw.

"Anything good?" Caleb's voice startled Mia so that

she lost her grip on the bowl. She froze as it flew downward. Then his arm reached out and snagged the lovely glass just before it hit the floor. "Better look at them on a stable surface," he said calmly, and set the bowl on the counter.

"Isn't it lovely?" She caught her breath at the beautiful object, vaguely aware that Caleb continued to trek up and down the stairs until boxes littered the floor of the small kitchen.

"You're still looking at that?" he said, huffing slightly as he set down the final box and closed the basement door. "Don't you want to see the rest?"

When Mia didn't immediately answer Caleb began removing more glass from the boxes. He lined them up across the counters. They were different shapes, color and sizes, some vases, some bowls, some functional, some simply to look at. And look Mia did. She also picked up several and examined their bases.

"You know what they are, don't you?" Caleb's gaze tracked her movements as she gently set down a flaming orange plate.

"I have an idea, but I'll have to check it out first." She wasn't quite ready to share her suspicions.

"They're certainly colorful. And I've figured out where they came from." Caleb grinned when she turned to look at him. "I think Harlan's mother was a collector. The label on three of the boxes is addressed to a Mrs. Granger."

"Really?" Mia bent, frowned, then rose. Feeling his gaze on her, she walked to a shelf and pulled down a huge family Bible.

"What's wrong? Do you want me to leave?" he asked, clearly perplexed.

"No." She flipped open the heavy cover and slid her finger down the list of names until she came to the one she wanted. "Jane Granger."

"She was his mother?" He shrugged when she nodded. "There you have it, then."

"Do I?" Mia returned the Bible to the shelf and sank onto a chair. "Look at the name on those boxes, Caleb. Look closely." She held her breath as he squatted to get a better look. Then his head jerked. He stared at her over his shoulder.

"Mrs. M. Granger," he said very softly. "You."

"Me." Mia's brain felt swathed in cotton wool. She couldn't make sense of this. "Did Harlan buy them for me?"

"Then, why didn't he give them to you?" Caleb's voice hardened after he'd checked the labels again. "They're date stamped four years ago, received at his office."

"I don't understand this," Mia said helplessly. "I did a quilt design several years ago, which I loosely based on a glass artist named Lalique. I was trying to achieve his sense of movement and fluidity on fabric. I remember because it was the one time Harlan asked about my work." She gulped. "The timeline is right," she whispered to herself.

"So he realized you liked this artist, probably did his own research, found out the pieces were collectable and bought some for you." Caleb frowned. "But why not give them to you? Why not display them?"

"Here?" Mia tried to mask her scorn. "Hardly suitable. Not to mention the insurance he'd need."

"Then—" Caleb's silver gaze narrowed. "Riverbend?"

"I don't think so. It's not his type of place and there are no showcases." Mia fell silent as her brain drew the obvious conclusions. She couldn't quite believe Harlan would have done it to hurt her and yet... "He knew how much I loved Lalique and yet he left these beautiful things sitting down there with orders that I wasn't to touch them. To spite me?"

To spite me?

Caleb flinched at the hurt and confusion in Mia's words. He felt helpless as tears of sorrow trickled down her cheeks. How any man could be so callous of this sweet woman's feelings irritated him beyond measure, especially because Mia went out of her way to be kind and sensitive to everyone. He wanted to help her, to make it better, but what could he do? If he let her get too close, she'd realize he wasn't the man she thought. Then Mia would shed tears over him and the disappointment he'd caused her. The idea of being compared to her jerk of a husband made Caleb feel sick.

"I'm sorry." He touched her shoulder, trying to express his empathy.

"So am I." Mia lifted her chin, tears glittering on her lashes. "I'm sorry he felt he had to go behind my back. I wish my mother had never arranged our marriage. Harlan must have been so unhappy."

"*He* must have been unhappy?" Caleb couldn't stop the angry words. "How can you forgive him? He doesn't deserve your tears."

"Yes, he does." Mia wiped her cheeks and managed a tremulous smile before her gaze slid to admire the lovely glass. "All his secrets and lies must have made his life horrible."

"This Lalique—is it valuable?" Caleb asked mostly to get her to stop weeping over a man who'd never deserved her care and consideration.

"If they're authentic they may be worth a great deal." Mia brushed her hand against her wet eyelashes before summoning a smile. "You'd have to get them appraised."

"No, you would." He grinned. "And the books. They're yours, remember?"

Mia looked stunned. "I guess they are."

"Do you mind if I go through the main floor now? You need to tell me what changes you think should be made here and upstairs."

Caleb was surprised by Mia's acuity as she pointed out areas of concern. Upstairs he gritted his teeth and forced himself not to comment on the shabby state of her room.

"It has to be freezing here in the winter," he said, noting the drafty window.

"It's not bad." Mia smiled. "I make quilts, remember?"

"Maybe you should start making rugs," he muttered to himself, and knew she'd heard by her throaty chuckle. What a good sport she was.

"This was Harlan's room." Mia stood at the doorway as if she was afraid to enter.

"Why don't you use this room?" Caleb asked, noting the expensive furnishings and thick carpet. "It feels much warmer."

"I couldn't do that." Her green eyes stretched wide. "It was his."

Distaste? Fear? Caleb couldn't decipher her expression, so he let it go and followed her to the bathroom.

"Total gut?" she asked.

He nodded, his silver eyes revealing his surprise. "Where did you—?"

"I heard it on TV," she said with a tiny smile. "I've always wanted to say it."

"Gutting this bathroom and simply leaving it that way would be an improvement." He realized immediately that he'd dissed her home and tried to make amends. "It's a lovely old house, though. The wood is superb. If this stairway was restored it would be magnificent. I'm glad you're going to bring her back to her former glory. I only wish you'd been able to live in it that way."

"Knowing someone else is enjoying the improvements will bring me a lot of joy." Mia led the way downstairs. Caleb thought she looked like a regal princess descending the palace staircase.

"You have someone in mind to live here, don't you?" When they reached the kitchen he saw the truth on her lovely face. "Someone special?"

"A wonderful man trying to raise two stepkids in a very trying situation. He's finding it tough to put a roof over their heads and feed them on his limited means." Mia's shy smile said everything he needed to know about this "friend." "I met him at church. His name is Arthur."

"Oh." Caleb pretended concentration as he wrote down the name of a contractor he trusted while trying to ignore the sprout of envy that had sprung to life inside his chest at the mention of this man with children. But how could he be jealous of a man he didn't even know?

Was he resentful because Mia was exactly the type to take on the mothering of two needy kids and do it superbly? Or was it because he feared this man and his children would diminish his chance of getting her to focus on mothering Lily?

It couldn't be for any personal reasons, because Caleb was not getting involved with Mia. His relationship with Lara had proved he was too jaded, too marked by his past to care for someone deeply enough to share his life with them. He was only here to help Mia as a friend.

So as a friend, he was officially worried about this Arthur, Caleb acknowledged privately. Maybe he'd stop by Mia's church on Sunday to vet the guy, make sure he wasn't pulling some kind of con job on her, as her husband had done.

But he was doing it because he was Mia's friend. And because of Lily.

Chapter Five

On the following Sunday, Caleb stood at the back of Mia's church searching for her distinctive strawberry blonde curls. Chagrined when he couldn't immediately spot her, he began to question his decision to bring Lily. He'd hoped to fuel the bond between her and Mia, but if she wasn't even here…

A tug on his hand drew Caleb's attention to Lily. She pointed to an empty pew three rows from the back. He nodded and followed her, smiling when the little girl lifted her pure clear voice to join in a hymn. He'd never known anyone who loved church as much as Lily. She'd only agreed to come with him to this one because she'd coaxed a promise of lunch from him.

Caleb's heart lurched into a gallop when he finally spotted Mia, who had moved forward and now waited at the front while kids' church was announced. Little ones from all over the congregation hurried toward her. Her lovely face glowed as she greeted each one with a bright smile. At Caleb's prompt Lily rose and limped toward Mia, too.

Mia's green eyes widened in surprise when she saw

Lily. She held out a hand toward the child, then scanned the congregation until her gaze rested on Caleb. His pulse rate soared when her smile broadened. She turned her attention back to the children to shush them for the pastor's prayer. Then Mia and the children left.

Feeling better about his decision to come here, Caleb paused a moment to consider her obvious ease with the children. There had been no trace of fear on her face when she urged them from the sanctuary, but then he recalled the other workers who'd accompanied her. So it was only on her own that she became fearful? Puzzled and confused, he turned his attention to the bulletin and grimaced at the sermon title.

"When forgiveness is impossible."

Not again. Caleb consoled himself with the knowledge that at least here his father wasn't sitting behind him, watching and waiting. He'd brought Lily and Mia together again, but now he wished Lily had asked him to accompany her so he could avoid hearing the sermon.

"There is no sin too deep that God's forgiveness can't reach."

Caleb stiffened at the pastor's assertion.

"I said *no sin*. That includes everything you can think of and more besides." The short, bald-headed man chuckled. "God's seen it all, every ugly, dirty, shameful thing humans can do. And still He says we must forgive."

Caleb shifted uncomfortably, fuming that he'd chosen this Sunday to come to this church. Why hadn't he gone to his own church, and come to see Mia later?

"But forgiveness of something that's touched you personally isn't easy."

The words slammed into Caleb in spite of his intention to ignore that booming voice.

"When someone has wronged us, the hurt festers inside us. We grow less and less inclined to forgive."

Each word felt like a dart piercing him, yet Caleb couldn't shut them out.

When the pastor glanced over the congregation, Caleb felt as if his stare penetrated through the layers of bitterness and anger burning inside him and reached out to the kid inside him who still mourned his mother's death.

"What I am saying," the minister continued in a quieter tone, "is that we must get the spotlight off our poor miserable lives, let go of the unforgiving cancer that eats at us so we can become a healthy part of His family. That's when we will finally be free."

Was that how Mia seemed able to forgive her husband's infidelity and cheating? Because she'd turned it over to God? Caleb longed to ignore the rest of the sermon, but the pastor's words kept him nailed to his seat, forcing Caleb to think deeply.

He was jerked from his thoughts when everyone rose to sing a hymn. While the pastor pronounced a benediction and dismissed the congregation, Caleb's brain churned with questions. How could God expect him to forgive the person who should have loved his wife, Caleb's mother, till death did them part?

Several people shook his hand and welcomed him before he saw Mia and Lily heading toward him. Mia's turquoise dress emphasized her lovely figure and glorious hair beautifully. Caleb smiled and pretended he wasn't staring.

"Lily is a very apt pupil." She brushed Lily's cheek tenderly. "It was a pleasure having her in our class."

"It was so fun, Uncle Caleb." Lily's dark blue eyes gleamed. "We went fishing just like Jesus's disciples did, only we didn't have real water."

"Cool." A pang stabbed through him to finally see she'd recaptured some of her joy. Lily was a lot like Mia; both of them found delight in the simplest things. "Did you catch anything?"

"Yes. And I ate it." She giggled.

"Only some fish-shaped crackers." Mia's gaze met his, then dropped. She seemed suddenly uncomfortable. "Well, I'd better go clean up."

"Can Mia come with us for lunch, Uncle Caleb? You promised you'd take me, remember?" Lily's dark blue eyes beseeched him to agree.

Funny how much he wanted to have lunch with Mia. Not seeing her this week felt as if he'd gone without coffee. The fulfillment he usually found in his work had been missing, too.

"Would you like to join us for lunch, Mia?" Caleb asked, expecting her to decline.

"I'd love to, if you're sure it's not an imposition," Mia said quietly. "I don't want to interfere with your time together."

"Me an' Uncle Caleb have lots of times together," Lily informed her. "He takes me for rides up in the hills sometimes."

"Takes you for rides?" Mia's curious gaze studied him.

"I ride in front of him, 'cause of my leg." Lily glanced down, then shrugged. "Me an' Uncle Caleb have a secret place where we go to watch the animals. We can see them, but they can't see us. We take snacks to eat and special glasses to watch them and sometimes we leave food for the animals. But not people food," she explained seriously.

"Of course not." Mia's glance drifted to him. "That's awfully nice of Uncle Caleb."

"Yeah. He's really nice. Don't you think?" Lily hugged his leg.

"I do," Mia agreed.

"Can we help you clean up?" Caleb asked to deflect their praise. She refused, but he and Lily followed her to the kids' center anyway. Some of the other workers had already straightened the room, so there wasn't much left to do but wash the plastic glasses the kids had used. Mia washed and Caleb dried while Lily played with a puppet.

"It's very kind of you to help." Mia's soft floral perfume reminded him of the Persian roses at Riverbend.

"How are things with you?" He found himself eager to catch up with her world.

"I got my driver's license." Her obvious delight in the accomplishment made him chuckle.

"Good for you. I guess the next step is to choose a vehicle. Or were you intending to use Harlan's car?" Caleb wished he hadn't asked when he saw her shudder.

"I'd prefer to sell that," Mia said in a flat tone.

"Then, do it." He frowned at her hesitation. "Why not?"

"I don't know. It seems so wasteful. I mean, I already own it and it works fine according to the garage." When her hand brushed his as she handed him the last glass, a tiny electric jolt speared through Caleb.

"So you sell someone a great car." Where once he

might have felt irritation at her indecision, he now realized that each step Mia was taking on her own was a totally new experience. So he patiently waited as she mulled it over.

"I'd have to buy a new car." Mia drained and rinsed the sink. "Actually I'd like that, to have something all my own. But it's difficult because I have no idea how to choose. All I know is I'd like a red one." She winked at him. "Bright shiny red."

"Red's nice," he agreed, keeping his face solemn as he enjoyed her pleasure.

"But an impractical reason to choose a car." She frowned. "I've done lots of reading about vehicles, but now I'm more confused than before."

"Maybe you should test drive some and see how comfortable you feel in each," he said gently, sensing how overwhelmed she felt.

"Good idea," she applauded. "You always make everything sound so simple, logical."

"My dad Ben always says that if you can break your goal down into steps, you can take one step at a time and then it won't seem so overpowering." He hung up the tea towel on a nearby peg.

"A very sensible man, your dad." Mia's smile coaxed Caleb to agree.

Just then Lily walked over and folded her hand in his.

"What's wrong?" He hunkered down so she could whisper in case she didn't want Mia to hear. But Lily didn't whisper.

"I'm so hungry my stomach is eating my back, Uncle Caleb."

He shouted with laughter, knowing exactly where

that saying came from. "You're copying Grandpa Ben now, aren't you?"

"Yes." She tilted her dark head to one side. "But it's true."

"Then we'd better go eat something. Hamburgers?" She shook her head. "Hot dogs?" Same reaction. Caleb hid his smile. "Pizza, then."

"Uncle Caleb, you promised we could have waffles." Lily frowned.

"Yes, I did." He tapped the end of her nose with his forefinger. "And I always keep my promises. Waffles it is. Okay, Mia?"

"Perfect." Mia picked up her purse and a matching jacket. "I love waffles."

"With strawberries?" Lily asked.

"Or blueberries," Mia agreed. "And whipped cream and maybe some bacon." She turned to Caleb. "I'll pay for half."

He almost laughed until he realized she was perfectly serious. So he simply said, "This is my treat, Mia. I promised Lily."

"Okay. But next time it's my turn." She accepted Lily's hand in hers and the three of them left the church, neither female aware of just how much Caleb wanted there to be a next time.

He drove to the restaurant, letting Lily chat with Mia while he noted every car dealership along the way. It would be an easy matter to stop after lunch to admire his favorite vehicle. Then they could "happen" to test-drive the vehicles in which Mia showed interest.

But Caleb's subterfuge wasn't necessary because after lunch Mia asked him if he'd mind taking her to look at a small SUV she'd admired online. While she spoke with the salesman he did a quick search on his phone. The vehicle was rated highly, had no known major defects and came in the bright Christmas red Mia yearned for.

"What do you think?" she asked him a few minutes later.

"I think you should test-drive it. If it doesn't fit you, you don't want it." Caleb wanted Mia to experience choosing her own car based on her own feelings, hoping it would help her find confidence in her decisions.

When the salesman returned with the keys, he and Mia walked with Lily to the red car. Caleb had to hide his amusement at Mia's worried look as she sat behind the wheel.

"You're a licensed driver now," he murmured in her ear through the open window. "You can handle whatever challenges you meet."

Mia's shoulders went back, she sat a little taller in the seat and her grip on the wheel loosened. After a moment she met his gaze.

"Thank you. I think you're the nicest man I've ever met, Caleb Grant." After tossing him a quick smile she started the car and drove away, leaving him staring after her.

The nicest man? Guilt rushed in. He was trying to get Mia to care for Lily so she'd take over as Lily's benefactor. Was that being nice?

"What are we going to do now, Uncle Caleb?" Lily asked.

"We're going to sit in my car and wait for Mia to come back." He waited till she was settled, then climbed in beside her. "You like Mia, don't you?"

"Uh-huh. She doesn't cluck with her teeth when she looks at my leg," Lily said.

Her words made Caleb do a double take.

"Do lots of people do that?" he asked curiously.

"Uh-huh. Then they look away and say, 'Poor thing.'" She tilted her head and frowned at him. "Am I poor, Uncle Caleb?"

He shook his head immediately and reached over to hug her. "You're not poor, Lily, because your heart is rich with love."

"Oh." She gave him a dubious look. "I don't know e'zackly what that means."

"It means I think you're the best kid in the whole world," he said, and brushed a kiss against the top of her head.

"I love you, too, Uncle Caleb." Lily flung her arms around his neck and hugged him. "I wish you could 'dopt, me but Ms. Vermeer says you won't," she mumbled into his shirtfront. "How come?"

"Well, I can't adopt you, Lily, because I wouldn't be a good daddy. I don't know how." Caleb squeezed the words out around the lump in his throat. He wasn't sure where this overwhelming need to protect Lily had come from. He only knew that he was her godfather, and her godmother, Lara, would have wanted, no, expected him to watch out for her niece.

"I could show you how to be a daddy, Uncle Caleb." Lily's earnest tone nearly undid him.

"I would like that more than anything, sweetheart. But it just can't be." He held her as a rush of sadness filled him. This was why he couldn't forgive his father, because Joel had ruined Caleb's ability to love and care for anyone.

"Is it 'cause you don't have a house?" Lily wiggled free. "Grandma Marsha told Ms. Vermeer you're gonna sell Auntie Lara's ranch."

"I have to, honey," he admitted. "Because I don't know how to love the animals like your aunt did." *I don't know how to love anyone.*

"Oh." Lily sighed. "I'm like Auntie Lara's animals. I don't have a home, either."

"I will find you a home, Lily," he promised for what felt like the hundredth time. "But you have to be patient."

"And I hafta pray. That's what Mia told me." Lily grinned at him. "She said I got to tell God what I want and wait for Him to answer."

"That's good advice." Caleb's heart pinched for this child's sweet heart and for Mia's gentle soul. Maybe if he tried harder he could make her see that she'd be a great mom for Lily.

"I sure hope my mom is happy. Do you think she is, Uncle Caleb?" Lily's sad voice broke through his introspection.

Caleb gulped and searched for the right answer. But he couldn't find one. All he could think of to say was "I'm sure she didn't like leaving you alone, Lily. She loved you very much."

"I know." Lily sighed and laid her head back against her seat. A moment later one fat tear tumbled down her cheek. "Mia said my mom's with God, but I wish she was with me."

Caleb felt useless and helpless as Lily gave way to sobs. He cradled her in his arms, knowing it was only natural for the little girl to miss her mother, but still feeling he should be able to do something to ease her loss. Something more than sitting here, letting her cry.

Was it wrong to feel a surge of relief when Mia came driving back onto the lot?

Sensing something had happened between Caleb and Lily, Mia made an excuse to the salesman and hurried back to the pair in the car. Caleb drove her home without saying a word. Lily was also quiet.

"Will you come in for a few minutes?" she invited. "The house is a mess, but I can offer coffee and juice."

"You've started the renovation already?" Caleb's eyes widened. "I'd like to see it."

"Come in, then." She led them inside hesitantly, wondering if Caleb would approve of the changes she'd asked for. As she feared, his face was tight with disapproval when he finished surveying the main floor. "You don't like it."

"It's going to look amazing, but, Mia, you can't live here during this." He waved a hand at the broken drywall, the half-removed walls and the debris scattered everywhere. "It's a mess."

"I'm managing," she said defensively.

"But you shouldn't have to manage. I should have thought of this earlier," he said, his anger obvious. "I know. Why don't you move into Riverbend and save yourself this aggravation?"

"I wish I could." She dug out a glass for Lily and poured some juice into it. "Here are some cookies, too," she offered, clearing a space at the table for the little girl. Then she started the coffeemaker. "There's some problem with taking possession of Riverbend. Bella said there's a lien on it for unpaid taxes."

"Harlan didn't pay them?" Caleb's confused look mirrored her thoughts.

"Apparently not. I instructed Bella to do that so they're now up-to-date," Mia explained. "But the municipality is demanding what Bella feels is an excessive amount of interest. She's trying to sort it out."

"Well, she needs to hurry because clearly you can't keep living here." His glance held irritation. "Where do you work?"

"In the sunroom."

"But there's no heat! And it's been below freezing the past couple of days." Caleb's lips pinched in a tight line. "I'm going to call Mayor Marsha and see if she can help."

"Your mother?" Confused, Mia watched him pull out his phone. "What can she do? She's mayor of Buffalo Gap, not the municipality."

"She has some sway because Buffalo Gap helped the municipality out a few years ago. Maybe they'll listen to her and expedite the situation." He began speaking into his phone. Mia turned away and chatted with Lily, glimpsing her home through Caleb's critical eyes.

It was a mess. Maybe she shouldn't have brought them in here. But she'd been so proud of the changes in this shabby old house. Even in such disrepair it seemed full of promise.

"Okay, get your things together, Mia." Caleb shoved his phone into his pocket, then held out his hand to accept the coffee she'd poured.

"What do you mean?" she asked in confusion.

"You're leaving here. Mom texted Abby and she says there's room at Family Ties. You can stay there until Bella can get you into Riverbend." He finally noticed her shaking head and moderated his voice. "It's safe there, Mia. You'll have a quiet place to work and you can use the kitchen to cook whatever you need, or you can eat out."

"But—" She gaped at him, unable to imagine walking away from this mess. "I can't just leave my home!"

"Why not?" After a second survey of the room, Caleb shrugged. "You've already moved out most of the furniture. I'm sure the workers would find it much easier to do their jobs with you out of here, too. They wouldn't have to worry about disturbing you or making a mess and you wouldn't have to shiver in that fridge of a workroom. It's the perfect solution."

A warm area to work did sound good, Mia admitted privately. And time to think without constant hammering. Then, too, there was Buffalo Gap's gorgeous landscape to consider. It would be her inspiration for a new project.

"But how will I get around?" she asked. "I doubt there are city buses in Buffalo Gap."

"That is a problem." Caleb thought for a moment. "Maybe you could drive Harlan's car for a day or two, just till you're settled. Then you could sell it and buy what you really want."

Mia suppressed her shudder. She didn't want to even sit in Harlan's car, let alone drive it, but it was a solution she was loath to ignore. Besides, the thought of escaping this mess now excited her.

"What about the women at Family Ties? Will they mind me moving in?" she asked.

"I doubt they'll even notice you're there. Family Ties was once a hotel. It's been renovated, but it's still huge with lots of room. Abby told Mom they're running at less than one-third full, so you're more than welcome. You'll love Abby." Caleb looked supremely confident.

"How can you be sure?" Mia asked curiously.

"Because Abby is exactly like you. Big, generous heart trying to help every needy person who crosses her path." His grin made him look younger. "You could be sisters."

"But I've never even met her. I don't like to just show up," Mia protested. But Caleb had an answer for that, too.

"Call her." He dialed a number, spoke to someone then held out the phone. "Go ahead. You'll see that Abby Lebret has the same soft heart as you."

Ten minutes later, reassured by Abby's warm welcome, Mia sat in the driver's seat of Harlan's car, now packed full of her things, and followed Caleb to Buffalo Gap.

"Lord," she prayed as she drove, "I trust You to direct my path so I'm moving temporarily to Family Ties. Please help me be a light for You. And please help me find a way to help Caleb. After all, he's done a lot for me." A little glow of warmth puddled inside her.

She really liked Caleb. Maybe too much?

Chapter Six

On Friday, a week later, Caleb walked down Main Street on his way to pick up Mia at Family Ties. Crowds attending Buffalo Gap's Harvest Days filled the streets for the annual event in mid-October. Since local retailers stayed open extended hours to run deeply discounted sidewalk sales, hurrying through the throngs of eager shoppers was difficult.

About to cross the street, Caleb stopped in his tracks. Joel Crane, his biological father was heading straight for him. Immediately Caleb's hackles went up, but with half the town mingling around them he refused to make a scene. He despised the gossip and innuendo he'd overheard since his father's arrival, but he wasn't about to back down or run away now, so he stood his ground and waited.

"Caleb." A tentative smile flickered across his father's face. "I was hoping to talk to you."

"I have nothing to say to you." Guilt chewed at his insides when a hurt-puppy-dog look washed across Joel's face.

"But *I* have something to say to *you*, and it's important. Please listen." Joel touched his arm, but Caleb shook off his hand. "I didn't kill her, son. I loved your mother. I wouldn't have hurt her for anything in this world."

"Wouldn't you?" Infuriated, Caleb demanded, "You don't think it hurt her when her husband came home drunk, called her names and bullied her when he didn't get his way? We don't have anything to discuss," he grated. "Stay away from me."

While his father protested, Caleb sidestepped him and continued toward Family Ties, seething.

"Caleb?"

A hand on his arm made him flinch. He whirled around. Mia stood behind him.

"You walked right past me," she said.

"Sorry." He exhaled heavily. "I just had a run-in with my father. You might want to reschedule our lunch. I'm not in a very good mood."

"Why don't we walk for a bit? I've been painting and I need some exercise." She looped her arm through his and tugged on it to get him to move. "Isn't it a gorgeous day? It seems like winter's eons away."

"Don't kid yourself. We often have snow in early October. This year we've been lucky." The mundane subject and Mia's bright cheery tone chased away his dark mood. "What have you been painting? No, don't tell me. Scenery."

"Yes." Her smile caused a flush of heat to warm Caleb's frozen heart. "But not only that. Family Ties is wonderful, full of stories. Abby's amazing. So are the two young women in residence. Their resilience is inspiring. One of them, Jan, is working on a little garden area at the back of the building."

"Fall bulbs, I suppose." Caleb frowned. "But she won't be here to see them bloom."

"Preparing the area makes Jan's heart bloom now." Mia's kindly voice soothed. "Someone else will benefit from her work in the spring."

"If it helps her I'm glad. I've been working with both of those women. Giving up a child isn't easy and Jan in particular feels very guilty. It's even more important to make sure her child has a wonderful home." When Mia moved toward the town park, Caleb matched her steps, noting how the tension had left him. Funny how when he was around Mia his day always seemed brighter.

"You really care about your clients. I like that. What did your father want?"

The unexpected question brought back Caleb's tension. He struggled to suppress his negative feelings but Mia noticed. She stopped beside a park bench, sat down and patted the spot next to her.

"Talk to me, Caleb," she invited in that sensitive way she had.

"I don't—" He stopped, surprised when her eyebrows drew together in a severe line.

"I think we can safely say that you've listened to my problems more than anyone should have to," she said in a firm tone. "It's about time I repaid the favor, so talk."

"There's not much to say. He's looking for forgiveness. I can't offer that." Caleb added, "I doubt I ever will."

"Okay, but couldn't you at least listen to him? You're his son. He misses you, wants to reconnect. You don't have to offer anything," she said when he glared at her. "But you could listen."

"No." Caleb shook his head. "I can't."

"Because?"

"Because he doesn't deserve it." He stiffened when she chuckled. "That's funny?"

"Yes, it's very funny." Mia patted his hand as if to apologize, but her next words astonished him. "None of us deserve anything, Caleb. People say, 'I deserve this,' but we don't *deserve* anything. Thankfully God loves us in spite of our unworthiness."

"That's not right." He stared, confounded by her logic.

"Yes, it is." Mia lifted her face into the sunshine. "God forgives us, not because we deserve it, but because He loves us. So, to me, it seems wrong when we who have been forgiven with such grace won't forgive others."

"So you've forgiven Harlan for deceiving you?" he shot back, and hated himself for saying it when a cloud dimmed the light in her lovely eyes.

"I'm trying." She gave him a reproachful look. "It isn't easy, but I'm trying to remember that he didn't understand love. He was afraid of it. I can't hate him for being afraid."

"I don't think that's a good enough excuse for what he did." Before Caleb could say more, Mia jumped to her feet.

"It's my reason. Can we eat now?" Her loveliness made him catch his breath as she danced from one foot to the other, waiting for him. "I'm starving. And this time I am buying, so no arguments. Got it?"

"Yes, ma'am." Her severe tone couldn't suppress her resurfacing smile, and that amused him. "Where are you taking me?"

"That place over there." She pointed to Eats, the priciest place in town. "Abby said they have the best lasagna, and that is exactly what I've been craving. Make sure you eat enough because you're going to need it."

"I am?" Caleb thought he'd never known anyone who found such sheer delight in life. Mia was embracing everything that came her way and somehow turned it into joy. "Why?"

"Because, Caleb, tomorrow morning I'm moving into Riverbend Ranch, and I'm hoping you'll help me." Ecstatic, Mia grabbed his hands and swung in a circle around him. Her happiness spilled all over him, chasing away the shadows of the past.

"At last. Congratulations," he said. "Of course I'll help." Caught up in the joy of her news, Caleb grasped her waist, lifted her and swung her round, thrilling at her peal of laughter.

Mia's elation and hope was contagious, but suddenly her eyes met his and Caleb realized how intimate the moment had become. Slowly he lowered her to the ground and gently released her, reluctant to let go of this amazing joy-filled woman but knowing he couldn't allow her to burrow into his heart. Because he couldn't bear to see hurt fill her expressive eyes when she realized he had nothing to offer her.

Mia balanced awkwardly for a moment, but before he could reach out an arm for support she righted herself. Her eyes held his, probing, asking questions, waiting.

"I hope you'll be very happy at Riverbend, Mia," he said sincerely.

"I will be. It's going to be my new start," she said in a firm tone. "I'm going to have a wonderful life."

"You deserve it." The words slipped out before he

realized it. He glanced at her, saw her lips twitch and couldn't stop his own chuckle. "Well, you do."

"No, I don't. But I thank God He's given it to me. And I don't want to argue with you, so let's go eat." She grabbed his hand once more.

Caleb followed, content to escape the intimacy of the previous moments but reveling in the pleasure of her company. He liked Mia, liked her spunk, her plucky courage, her determination to find a bright spot in everything. But there could never be more than friendship between them because, although he was certain that Mia was full of love just waiting to be poured out, he was not.

"I suppose you have to get back to the office soon." When Caleb forgot about his father, he was utterly charming. Mia hated to see their time together end.

"Not necessarily." He leaned back in his chair. "Did you have something in mind?"

"No. I'm just enjoying relaxing with you. Hearing about your childhood on the Grants' ranch is interesting." She waited until their server had brought his chocolate cake and he'd tasted it. "I've never been around animals much. I don't think my mother liked the mess they caused. She loved order."

"As a kid I had lots of pets." He grinned at the memories. "A pet raven, a bull. Once I even had a pet snake, though that ended when Marsha found its hiding place. She is deathly afraid of them."

"Me, too." Mia couldn't suppress her chuckle. When Caleb arched one dark eyebrow to ask why, she tapped the side of her cheek. "You look very nice in chocolate icing," she teased, "but not very lawyerly."

He made a face as he dabbed his napkin to remove the spot. "Want a taste?" he asked, holding out his fork loaded with icing.

"No, thanks." She shuddered. "That's enough sugar to add ten pounds."

"With your energy level?" Caleb continued eating, but she knew his brain was dwelling on something else.

"I don't eat a lot of sugar. Harlan's mother died from diabetes and it was something he was always warning me about." Caleb didn't need to know how often she'd eaten sweets in private to avoid those comments.

"You won't hear me putting down this good stuff," Caleb promised, savoring his cake with obvious enjoyment.

"I want to ask you a nosy question, but you may not want to answer it," Mia said, deciding to broach a subject that had been bothering her for a while. Though his eyes narrowed, he didn't immediately shut her down. She liked that.

"You can ask," he invited in that rumbly voice she found so attractive.

"You clearly love Lily. Why don't you adopt her?" She hadn't finished the question before Caleb began shaking his head.

"I can't," he said, his voice bleak.

"Because?" she pressed. Did the flickering in his silver-gray eyes mean he was hiding something from her?

"Well, for starters, I don't have a home anymore." He pushed away the rest of his uneaten cake. "I received an offer on the ranch this morning. I'm accepting it."

"Congratulations." His lack of expression piqued her curiosity. "That's good news, isn't it?"

"Yes and no." He shrugged. "They want possession before winter, so I need to move out fairly soon."

"You must have thought about somewhere else to live in Buffalo Gap when you listed it." Mia tried not to be too obvious in studying his reactions, but she was intrigued by his blunt refusal to consider adoption.

"I've looked at a few places, but I don't want to make any quick decisions. That's kind of what I did when Lara and I bought the ranch," he admitted.

"And you were sorry?" Were those shadows in his eyes regret?

"If Lara had lived, it would have been perfect. I could have helped her achieve her dream. But I never even considered I'd be left to run it. I've failed so miserably I had to have someone take all the animals."

"I'm sure you did your best. I doubt Lara would ask more than that," Mia soothed. "So now you have nowhere to live and that's why you can't adopt Lily?"

"Actually I do have a place to live. My parents have a little cabin on their land, beside the river." A funny little smile twisted Caleb's lips. "Dad used to be an outfitter. Over the years they've had hunters, birdwatchers, fishermen stay there in all seasons. It's a bit primitive and certainly no place for Lily, but I can make do."

"Is that what you want?" There was something in his words she didn't quite understand. Reluctance, perhaps? "To make do?"

"No. I want my own place, a ranch but without cattle. A place with lots of space and freedom." The words died away, as if he didn't want to give away too much.

"So at heart you are a cowboy," she teased.

"Always," he said with a chuckle.

"But it won't have a place for Lily." Immediately his face tightened and Mia knew she'd pushed too hard.

"Look, I'm not the person to raise Lily," he said, lips tightening with his irritation. "She's a great kid, but it would be wrong for me to even try to be her father."

"Wrong?" Mia didn't want to keep pushing, but in her mind Caleb would be the perfect father. "Is it her leg?"

"Her leg?" His eyes widened and then narrowed. "The fact that Lily has a damaged leg has nothing to do with it. It's because of me, because I can't be who she needs. Can we leave now?"

"I'm keeping you from work. I'm sorry." Mia waved to their server and handed him her brand-new credit card. While they waited, she gathered her things, aware of the tension between them. She signed the receipt, added a generous tip and rose.

"Thank you for lunch," Caleb said, sounding slightly mollified.

"Thank you for joining me." Mia walked out of the restaurant and waited until they were walking across the park, some distance from the restaurant before she let out a little whoop. "That felt so good." She grinned, delighted with herself.

"What did?" The mystified look on his face made her burst out laughing.

"Paying for lunch. Independence," she explained. "I've never had a credit card before. Harlan liked to live on cash."

"Harlan liked to have you locked up, without access to any assets," Caleb corrected sourly. "Never mind that they are *your* assets."

"Let it go, Caleb." She held his gaze. "It's the past.

It doesn't matter now. I'm moving into a new home of my own. I don't want to tarnish that with ugly thoughts. Be happy for me?" she begged, touching his arm with her fingertips. "Please?"

He studied her for several wordless moments. Finally his fingers curled around hers, warm and comforting. "Of course I'm happy for you, Mia. I can't think of anyone who deserves a new home more." He smiled, squeezed her hand, then let it go. "Though I still can't help wondering why he bought Riverbend."

"Maybe someday we'll know. I believe God had a hand in it. Oh, look. It's Lily." Mia's heart squeezed tight at the sight of the little girl sitting on a swing in the park's playground, head down, shoulders dropping in a dejected way. "Why is she alone?"

"Hilda's place is right over there. Look, she's sitting on the front porch watching." Caleb lifted a hand and waved. Hilda waved back.

"Lily looks so sad. Let's go cheer her up." Mia started toward the little girl, glad that Caleb followed without question.

"Hi, Lily," she murmured, kneeling by the child. "How are you?"

"Sad." Lily looked up, face streaked with tears. "I'm an orphan."

Behind her, Mia heard Caleb groan.

"Who told you that, honey?" She brushed dark wet strands of hair away from the child's tearstained cheeks.

"Some kids at school. They said orphans get sent to houses where they have to work for their food." Lily sniffed. "My leg hurts sometimes. Maybe I can't work hard enough. I get awful hungry."

"Sweetheart, you're never going to have to work for

your food." Caleb hunkered down beside Mia, his voice warm and tender with reassurance. "I'm going to make sure you're always cared for. And you're not an orphan."

"How come?" Lily frowned at him, her gaze questioning. "My teacher read us a story about orphans. An orphan is a child who doesn't got a family. That's me."

"But you do have a family, darlin'." The tenderness of Caleb's voice sent a rush of sweetness through Mia's heart. What a good man he was. Her heart pinched when he slid an arm around Lily's tiny waist, lifted her from the swing and hugged her against his side. "You have a family who cares about you very much."

"Who?" Lily's voice wobbled, as if she was afraid to believe what he was saying.

"Well, you've got me. *Uncle* Caleb, remember? Uncles are family." He tickled her under the chin. "And you've got Mia. And you've got Ms. Vermeer looking after you, and Grandma Marsha and Grandpa Ben. They're all your family and they love you very much."

"We all care about you, Lily. We love you very much," Mia added, struggling to keep her voice from breaking. "You're not alone."

"But that's not real family." Lily sniffed. "A real family has a mommy and a daddy."

"Listen to me, darlin'." Caleb tipped her chin so she had to look at him. "What makes a family isn't a mommy or a daddy. What makes a family is love." His fingertip smoothed away her tears. His voice oozed compassion and caring. "You are loved so much, my sweet Lily."

Mia wanted to weep at the tenderness of his words and the love glowing in his silver eyes. As Lily's smile peeked out she longed to wrap her arms around both of them and hang on. This big tenderhearted man had put aside his own inhibitions about love to reassure a little lost girl. Caleb would make a wonderful father. If only she could convince him to adopt Lily.

"Why didn't Hilda come with you to the park?" Caleb said when several minutes had passed.

"'Cause I yelled at her an' told her not to. I ran away." An ashamed look turned Lily's face sultry. "I was mad at those kids."

"Hilda cares about you a lot, Lily. See, she's sitting over there all alone." Caleb brushed a tender hand over the little girl's head. "She must be very worried to see you so upset. You need to apologize."

"I know." Lily's head hung with shame.

"I'll go with you." Caleb rose, clasping her tiny hand in his. His eyes met Mia's. "Will you come, too?"

"I'd love to." Mia walked with the somber pair back to Ms. Hilda's, where Lily offered her apology and was quickly tearfully embraced.

"You sure are a lucky girl." Mia watched her as they munched on Hilda's fresh cookies. "A lot of people care about you."

"I know." Lily looked down. "I didn't mean to be bad. I just wanted my mommy back so I could be a family." A lonely tear clung to her eyelashes.

Mia couldn't just sit there and not do something. Caleb was there. Surely nothing bad could happen with him watching, nothing like what had happened before. She wrapped her arm around the little girl and snuggled her against her side.

"Tell me about your mom, Lily."

Lily talked for a while about the things she remembered best. Then she drank her milk and ate her last cookie before asking, "Will you tell me about your mommy, Mia?"

Mia glanced around. Caleb had returned to his office for a meeting, but Ms. Hilda was sitting a few feet away on her porch knitting. She wasn't alone with Lily.

"Please?" Lily begged.

"My mom was a lawyer, kind of like your uncle Caleb," Mia began. "Her job was to help people and she worked very hard to do that."

"What about your daddy?" Lily asked.

"I didn't have one. I asked my mother about him once," Mia murmured, suddenly transplanted back in time to her tenth birthday. "My mom got a very sad look on her face and said he'd gone away and wasn't going to come back. I could see that talking about him made her sad, so I never asked about him again."

"That's like my daddy!" Lily sat up straight, eyes flashing. "When I was little I asked my mom who my daddy was. She said I didn't have one. That night I heard her crying, so I didn't ask about my daddy anymore."

"It's hard to understand grown-ups sometimes, isn't it?" Mia comforted. "But we all have a daddy, one who loves us very much."

"You mean God, don't you, Mia?" Lily nodded. "Auntie Lara talked about Him all the time. My mommy was her sister. Auntie Lara said her and mommy's daddy was God and He was the bestest dad anyone could have."

"Auntie Lara was right," Mia said, thankful for Lara's faith. "God loves us very much. We can talk to Him whenever we want. He doesn't get tired or go away or get too busy to listen. He's always with us."

"I know." Lily snuggled against her side. "God's a

nice daddy, isn't He, Mia? I think He's kind of like Caleb. I love Caleb."

"He loves you, too, sweetheart." Mia reveled in the joy of having the sweet girl tucked against her side as the autumn sun warmed them.

Oh, God, I want a family, too, she prayed silently. *I want a child just like Mia. Please, could You erase the past and make it possible for me to be a mother? Please?*

But even as she prayed, she knew it couldn't be. She'd hurt an innocent child. Unwittingly, true, but that child had died because of her. She couldn't be trusted with another. So the next best thing was to get Caleb Grant to see that he was the perfect father for Lily.

"I think I've worn you out already." Mia chuckled when Caleb blinked his eyes open and pushed away from the kitchen island. "I thought Saturday would be your best day. That's why I chose today to move."

"Huh?" He frowned.

"Because it's your day off," she clarified. "Like you'd have more energy? I guess I should have found more moving helpers for my move to Riverbend."

"You should have bought less stuff," he shot back, enjoying the happy smile she'd been wearing all day. "I'm just thankful that furniture stores deliver. Carrying in all your quilt fabric has aged me ten years, though."

"Poor old man. We're almost finished." She held out a tray of doughnuts. "Have another to give you some energy."

"No, thanks. I'm already on a sugar high." He glanced around the kitchen, a little shocked by how quickly she'd made it look like home. Shiny new copper pots swung from a rack above the massive stove. Bright green accents scattered here and there made it look as if Mia had cooked in this kitchen for years. The whole effect was enhanced by strategic placing of vigorous plants he'd helped her unload from her car. "Are you satisfied with it?"

"Mmm, pretty close," she mused. "Let's take a tour and I'll make notes of what else I need. Starting with my workroom."

"Do I have to go in there again?" he teased. "Your talent scares me a little."

"How?" She turned on him in surprise.

"You do everything so well. It's intimidating." He looked around the room. Her bright paintings hung everywhere, bringing light and happiness. "I think you need another lamp in here for nighttime."

"I have another, but I can't remember where it is." She sounded as if she was concentrating on something else. He'd learned that look in her eyes meant she'd begun visualizing another design for her quilt fabric. "The built-ins are perfect for storing my fabric." She hugged herself. "I'm going to love working here."

"Let's look at the rest." He left and walked to the living room, pushing away the urge to replace her arms with his. "I thought this room was too big, but your interior designer was right. The huge furniture makes it cozy, along with the fire." He sank into the plump cushions with a sigh. "I still think you should have chosen leather, but…"

"Leather's too cold. I've had enough cold to last me a lifetime." Mia inclined her head toward the dining room. "It looks great but it's intimidating. I don't know enough people to fill all those chairs."

"You soon will." Caleb grinned at her frown but didn't pursue the matter. "Upstairs?"

She nodded and preceded him up the winding staircase. "This is my room," she said as she pushed open the double doors.

"It's lovely." Which was an understatement, Caleb decided. Among the azure blues and deep sea greens Mia radiated like a mermaid in her ocean. "I thought maybe you'd choose white and frilly," he mumbled, not intending for her to hear.

Mia laughed. "Frilly? Not my style."

"But this isn't the master bedroom," Caleb exclaimed.

"That's too big for just me." Her cheeks turned an attractive pink. "Besides, I like this view of the garden better." As she led the way down the hall, he saw her glance below to the courtyard at the front of the house. "There are a whole lot of cars arriving," she said in a surprised tone.

"Uh-huh." Caleb grinned at her. "They're here for you, for a housewarming."

"For me?" Mia stared at him. "They don't even know me."

"That's why they're here," he said with a chuckle. "Do you think we should go and greet them?"

"Oh. Yes, of course." Mia led the way downstairs. "I wish I'd had time to change into something less casual."

"You look great. They'll love you. Stop worrying," Caleb said.

"How did they know I was moving in today?" she asked.

"I told them." He grinned, then reached around her to fling the door wide.

Caleb knew Mia's head was whirling as people flowed into her new home bearing dishes of savory goodness and gifts they insisted were simply a welcome to the community.

"We want you to feel at home and free to call on any of us at any time," Mayor Marsha said, speaking for the group. "Everyone's a neighbor in Buffalo Gap." Her gaze moved from the open door to Caleb. *"Everyone,"* she said pointedly.

Not understanding her emphasis on that word, Caleb glanced out the door and saw Joel standing there.

"Why, Mother?" Caleb demanded in a low voice.

"He's a part of our community now, Caleb," she said in a firm tone. "We've never excluded or ostracized anyone and we're not going to start with your biological father."

Acutely aware of the many sets of curious eyes around him, Caleb debated walking out the door, until he glanced at Mia. She'd been so happy moments before. He couldn't ruin this for her, but he wasn't going to talk to Joel Crane either. Not today. Not ever. He stalked away.

The small, older man who watched Caleb walk away with hope dying was the man who'd murdered Caleb's mother? Mia's heart ached for the two as Caleb left and his father's shoulders slumped at the snub. The entire room had fallen silent. She stepped forward.

"Please come in," she invited, holding out her hand. "I'm Mia Granger."

"Thank you," he said so quietly she barely heard him. "I'm Joel Crane. Caleb's—" His chin drooped.

"Father," she finished loud enough for the others to hear. "Welcome here. Thank you for coming."

Marsha began directing operations, and the awkwardness of the moment dissipated as Mia's guests resumed chatting with each other.

"It isn't much but I brought some chips and dip," Joel said. "I'm afraid I'm not a very good cook."

"Among other things." Caleb now stood at her elbow, his glare fierce.

"Caleb, please," she whispered, standing on tiptoe to whisper in his ear. "This is my first real home. I want to enjoy it, for people to feel welcome here. Please don't spoil this for me." Mia slid her arm in his, knowing how deep his aversion for his biological father went and yet desperate to keep the peace. "Please?"

The ice in his silver eyes made her insides quiver. A moment later her heart sank as he nodded and then excused himself.

"I'll go," Joel said, and handed her the bag of chips. "Marsha insisted I come, but she was wrong. I don't belong here."

"You live in Buffalo Gap, don't you?" Mia asked. At his nod she smiled and threaded an arm through his. "Then, you belong here. Let's meet these people."

Actually her guests introduced themselves to her, none of them showing the least bit of anger or judgment that Joel Crane was among them. Except for Caleb. He hung in the background, watching everything with his icy glare. Mia was on her way to talk to him when a shout stopped her.

"Mia!" Lily hobbled across the room and threw herself into Mia's arms. "I came to see your new house."

"I'm glad you did." She hugged the little girl tightly,

then glanced at her other guest. "Welcome, Ms. Hilda. Is that some of your delicious lemon pie?"

Hilda said that it was, then hurried toward the kitchen. That was when Mia heard Lily say, "You're Caleb's dad." Her head tilted to one side when Joel nodded. "He's mad at you," she said.

"Honey, Joel and I are meeting people. Would you like to come along?" Mia intervened.

"Uh-uh. I want to talk to Uncle Caleb about my birthday party." Lily awkwardly hurried away.

"I have apologized to Caleb for causing the accident with his mother, you know," Joel murmured. "Or tried to. He won't hear me."

"I know," Mia whispered, and squeezed his hand. "Caleb is in a lot of pain. We'll just have to keep praying that God will touch his heart."

"That's why I've stayed here," Joel admitted. "I keep praying God will heal the breach between my son and me. Meanwhile I accept whatever jobs I can get and wait."

"I'll pray, too," she promised.

They finished their tour of the room. At the end of it, Mia was certain she'd never remember all the names. Then Mayor Marsha said a short grace and announced that there was enough food for everyone to help themselves. Mia stood in a corner, content to watch and listen, savoring the pleasure of having her friends and neighbors share food in her home.

For the first time in ages she didn't feel left out or on the sidelines. Today she felt as though she had taken the first step to truly belonging. Thanks to Caleb.

"Are you angry at me?" Caleb's quiet voice broke her introspection.

"For what? This?" She waved a hand toward the crowd. "This makes me extremely happy. It's exactly how I wanted Riverbend Ranch to be. Full of friends, fun and happiness. It's an answer to my prayers." She blushed as she said the words that lay on her heart. "You are an answer to prayer, Caleb. I'll never be able to thank you enough for helping me take this step."

"You did it on your own," he said before accepting a cupcake from a tray Abby Lebret was passing around. "But as long as you don't mind me inviting half the town…"

"I'm glad you did," she said. "You're the best friend I ever had."

Best friend?

Caleb smothered his frown. Nothing worse than being a best friend to a lovely woman. Especially one as beautiful as Mia.

"I've never had many friends." Mia's gaze followed Lily as she limped from one person to the next, her eyes dancing with excitement as she chatted. "Not like Lily has. Everyone seems to love her."

"What about the friend from church who's going to live in your other house?" Caleb hoped he didn't sound as disgruntled by the knowledge as he felt.

"You mean Arthur?" Mia blinked at him looking startled. "I guess I never thought of him like that."

"He's *not* a friend, but you're letting him live in your house?" Caleb said.

"Yes, because of his grandchildren." Mia's green eyes darkened. "Their mother's in rehab. Their father abandoned them. Their grandfather is trying to put some stability in their lives. I thought living in the house instead of their tiny apartment could help him do that."

Caleb couldn't speak because of a coughing fit caused by choking on his cupcake. He'd spent all this time being jealous of a *grandfather*? And why was he jealous anyway? Mia was nothing to him but a means to get Lily's future solidified. Right?

Yeah, right, his brain snickered. *It's because of Lily, has nothing to do with the way your soul lifts when you see Mia, or the way she can make you feel that anything is possible if you try hard enough. Your chest gets tight and you can hardly breathe when that sweet scent of hers fills your nostrils because of Lily. Uh-huh.*

Caleb cleared his throat and shut off the mocking voice.

"You should come see my old place," Mia invited, her wide grin revealing how much she approved of the changes. "It's amazing."

"What are you two whispering about in this corner?" Mayor Marsha demanded.

"We're not whispering, Mother," Caleb said.

"Yes, you were." Marsha studied him with a knowing smile. "I can always tell when you're not telling me the truth, Caleb."

"We weren't exactly whispering," Mia said. "I was about to ask Caleb if he thought your family would be available to come for Thanksgiving dinner."

"Well." Caleb choked back a laugh at Marsha's consternation. For once she seemed at a loss for words. "I, um, think we'd be delighted."

"Don't you have to check with Sis and Dad?" He kept his face as innocent looking as possible while silently cheering for Mia. He'd never known anyone to dumbfound his mother.

"I'm sure they'd love to come, but I will check with them and let you know. Will that be all right?" Marsha smiled when Mia nodded. "Good. Well, dear, I have a meeting, so I must leave. I do want to wish you all the best in your new home, though. I hope you'll be very happy."

"Thank you." Mia gracefully conceded to Marsha's effusive hug. "Your mother is a lovely woman," she said as Marsha called her goodbyes to the rest. "You're so lucky."

"Lucky?" Caleb blinked in surprise. No one had ever said that to him before.

"Yes. Lucky, or rather blessed," Mia said in a firm tone. "You could have had far less loving foster parents than the Grants. God certainly looked after you."

Mia left to speak to several others who were following Marsha's lead and leaving. Caleb mused on what she'd said.

He'd never thought of himself as lucky or blessed. Actually in his deepest heart he'd held a grudge against God for breaking up his family, for letting his mother die, for allowing his father to escape just punishment, though he'd always been glad the authorities had made sure he didn't have to live with a drunk who'd never been able to care for him. But blessed?

Years replayed in Caleb's memory of the many kids he'd met in the foster system and the horror stories of the families they'd been sent to. He'd never experienced any hardship, never needed anything. Marsha and Ben had showered him with affection from the moment he arrived. They still did. They loved him and they made sure he knew it.

What had he given them back? Duty? Obedience? He owed them much more, but that was why he couldn't keep on allowing soft thoughts for Mia to grow. Caleb couldn't love. He knew that. Lara had known that. But he didn't want Mia to know it. It would diminish him in her eyes, and Caleb so wanted to be the man she admired.

Chapter Seven

"Caleb, I need your help." Mia wished she hadn't needed to call him at his office. "Actually Meals on Wheels needs your help. It's my day to volunteer, but Abby has an emergency at work, so, well…"

She was babbling and she knew it. Caleb's generosity in organizing her housewarming still gave her a warm feeling inside. His actions had helped ease her way into making friends in Buffalo Gap. But lately she'd realized the community was pairing her with Caleb, which made her nervous and wary. She'd decided to avoid him. Until now.

"Mia? Are you there?"

"Sorry," she apologized, stuffing away her concerns. "What did you say?"

"I said I'd love to help you, but I'm due in court in ten minutes and I can't back out." He sounded rushed. "Maybe if you'd called earlier—"

"No, it's fine. Really. I'll get someone else. Thanks anyway." She hung up before his rumbly voice could cause any more damage to her skittering nerves. Why was it that she only had to hear him speak and her insides trembled?

"Mia? Is anything wrong?" Mayor Marsha stood at her car door. "Nice," she said, admiring the vehicle Mia had finally purchased a few days earlier. "I've always loved red vehicles."

"Me, too." Mia smiled, wondering how it was that the mayor seemed to show up at just the right moment. "You wouldn't have a spare hour, would you?"

"Ah, Meals on Wheels." Marsha shook her head. "I'm sorry. I've a meeting in about five minutes. Maybe Joel could help you."

"Joel?" Mia blanked out for a minute, then followed Marsha's glance to the man sitting on a bench across the street. Caleb's dad.

"He doesn't look busy and he's been here long enough to know where most everybody lives," Marsha said. "He helped me last week with meal deliveries. Maybe you could ask him."

"But Caleb—" Mia didn't want to say it, but it seemed important to consider his aversion to his father.

"Forget Caleb. You need help, and Joel's available," Marsha said firmly. "I'll ask him if you're shy. Joel!" She waved her hand to beckon him. The older man rose, walking toward them with a quizzical look on his face.

"I'm not sure—" Mia swallowed the rest of her objections because Joel was too near.

"Mia needs help delivering meals," Marsha explained. "Are you available?"

"Yes. Nobody seems to need a handyman today." He looked directly at Mia. "Are you sure you want me to help you?"

Swallowing her reservations, she nodded. "I'd appreciate it. Otherwise I'm going to be late because I'll have to do it alone. I don't know most of the people on my list. Not yet," she said with a smile, thinking how little he seemed like the monster Caleb portrayed. "Climb in and let's go pick up the meals." While Joel got in her car Mia smiled at Marsha. "Thanks for your help."

"Have a good day," Marsha said with a nod. Was that glint in her eye satisfaction?

Mia didn't have time to dwell on it as she drove to the hospital kitchen and loaded the meals. Joel had to repeat his directions to the third house because her mind was busy noticing how easy he was to talk to. As they delivered the meals she thought how lonely Joel seemed.

"Three more and then we're finished." Mia checked the car's clock, amazed to see an hour had flown by. "I've really enjoyed this. You should add your name to the volunteer list. They could really use more people."

"I'd like to," he said quietly. "But I don't know how much longer I'll be in town."

"You have to move on?" From the downturn of his lips, Mia didn't think Joel wanted to leave Buffalo Gap.

"I haven't been able to find much work and my money's getting low." He sighed. "Turn in here." When she pulled to a stop he got out and delivered the meal.

"You were saying you didn't have work?" she prodded when he returned. If Joel left town, she felt certain he and Caleb would never reconcile and Caleb would never be rid of the anger and bitterness that had built up over the years.

"I was hoping to stay here longer." Joel glanced at her with eyes so like Caleb's. "I'd hoped to get my son to at least talk to me, but…"

"I have some jobs at Riverbend," she blurted. "I

know it's autumn and probably too late to do much in the garden, but I'd like to prepare the area for some work in the spring. There's also the matter of two horses."

"You own horses?" he said with some surprise. "I didn't know you rode."

"I don't." Mia made a face. "A neighbor phoned this morning to say he'd been looking after two horses that belong to Riverbend. He's not able to do it anymore and would like them moved as soon as possible." She sighed. "I didn't know anything about horses coming with the property, but I can't just abandon them. Do you know how to look after horses?"

"I worked on a dude ranch down South for a while. I know the basics." A smile lit up Joel's face, then dissipated in his frown. "Are you sure you want to trust me to work for you? You know about my wife?"

"I know she died in tragic circumstances." Mia followed his directions to the next address. When he returned to the car, she faced him. "I know there's a wall between you and Caleb. I can't guarantee that you staying in town will help break it down but I do think it's important you keep trying."

"He'll be furious with you for hiring me." Joel's sad eyes met her. "I don't want to be the cause of a rift between you."

"Caleb is my friend. I'd like you to be my friend, too," Mia said with a smile. "But more than that, I think it's very important for both of you to find common ground. If you're at the ranch when Caleb visits, maybe he'll be forced to see the past in a different way and come to terms with it. I just want to help him, Joel."

"Thank you for caring about him," Joel said quietly.

Mia took the plunge. "You're welcome to come to

Riverbend with me. I'll show you what I want you to do. There's a little bunkhouse that you could use. Once you see everything you can decide whether or not to accept my offer."

"Thank you." Were those tears in his eyes? "But if at any time you'd like me to leave, you must say so. Agreed?"

"If that's the way you want it." Satisfied, Mia drove to their final stop. With all their meals delivered, she headed for home.

Home. What a lovely word.

On the way she prayed that she was making the right decision. Caleb would be upset, but that wasn't going to stop her from doing what she could to help him reconnect.

But could You step in and ease things a bit, Lord? She shuddered at the thought of Caleb's anger turned on her. She didn't want to hurt him. He'd been good and kind to her and she liked him a lot.

Too much?

Mia reminded herself of Caleb's insistence that he couldn't love. Given his relationship with Lily, she knew he had a lot of love to give. But it wouldn't be for her. If she ever let herself trust a man enough to have a relationship, it would be to have a real marriage, with children.

And that was a dream Mia could never have. She wasn't fit to be a mother. Ever. It was too dangerous. Harlan had made sure she understood the consequences of that long-ago mistake. He'd forgiven her but Mia doubted Caleb would.

In his eyes she'd be a murderer, just like Joel.

* * *

"What, *exactly*, is going on?" Caleb glared at his father, barely able to squeeze out the words around the lump of gall lodged in his throat. "What are *you* doing here?"

"Joel's working for me," Mia said, stepping between father and son. "He's the answer to my prayers, actually."

"Some prayers," Caleb mocked. He crossed his arms across his chest as an iron band tightened inside. "Doing what?"

"Helping me with my horses, for one thing." Her joyful smile sent that familiar yet crazy warmth through his blood.

"Horses?" He listened impatiently while she explained. "Yeah, I remember old man Ness did have a couple of horses when he owned Riverbend. I didn't realize Harlan had boarded them." He faced his father. "But that doesn't explain *your* presence here."

"*I* hired him." There was a steely tone to Mia's voice that Caleb had never heard before.

So mind your own business was implicit in her words. He'd wanted Mia to stand up for herself, Caleb mused in self-mockery. He just hadn't expected she'd do it with him.

"Joel, you go over and explain that we'll take possession of the horses as soon as we can make provision for them," Mia said. "If Mr. Ness has any suggestions about which outbuildings we should use, please take note of them."

Joel nodded and left after a glance at Caleb.

"Are you sure this is a good idea?" he asked when his father was gone.

"You're the one who told me I needed to step out and live," Mia reminded him. "Or words to that effect. Now you're changing your mind?"

"No, but you also need to protect yourself," he warned. "Joel Crane will take advantage of you. That's what he does, Mia. He is not a man who deserves your pity."

"I don't feel pity. I need help. Joel can help me." Her tone changed to reproof. "Everyone deserves a second chance, Caleb."

"Haven't you learned yet to protect yourself?" Exasperated but seeing her implacability, Caleb put away his other objections for another time. He'd have to be the one to protect her from his father.

"I'm going inside for tea. Feel free to join me if you have time." Mia tossed the offer over one shoulder as she headed for the house.

"Can I have coffee? Strong coffee? I need the caffeine." Caleb followed, wondering why he'd chosen to drive out here yet knowing the answer. Mia would listen and understand. She wouldn't say something inane. She'd address his issue head-on.

Sure enough she asked, "What's wrong, Caleb?" once the coffeemaker was dripping water through the grounds.

"You got a new coffeemaker—just for me?" He grinned, enjoying her flushed face as he sat on a stool at the breakfast bar.

"For anyone who visits and wants coffee," Mia corrected, flushing more deeply as she lowered her head to avoid looking at him. "New house, new coffeemaker. Now, what's bothering you?"

"You met Bethany, the newest girl at Family Ties?" he asked.

"Last week. She had her baby yesterday, didn't she?" Mia nodded. "I'm going to stop by tomorrow with a gift for her."

"Don't bother." When she lifted her head from arranging a plate of cookies, Caleb told her the rest. "Her parents arrived and took her and her baby boy home."

"But she was adamant about giving him for adoption when I spoke to her last." Mia studied him. "You couldn't stop it?"

"I wish I could have. She's very mature, but it turns out she's underage and they don't want their grandchild given to strangers." Caleb clamped his jaw shut, remembering Bethany's shame, pain and hurt. He should have been able to protect her.

"If they want her home, that's good, isn't it?" Mia poured his coffee and nudged the plate of cookies forward before sitting beside him.

"No. They want Bethany to keep her baby to force her to 'face up to her sins,'" he said with disgust. "Can you imagine the life she and her child will have in such an unforgiving house, where she's reminded every moment that she's sinned and made to pay for the rest of her life?"

"It sounds horrible," Mia agreed thoughtfully.

From her look Caleb guessed she was thinking of Joel, but surely she knew his sin was far different from Bethany's. "It isn't the same as with my father," he said.

"Isn't it? Sin is sin. And God forgives." She kept a bead on him for several moments. Then suddenly a dimple appeared in one cheek. "How much underage is Bethany?"

"Three months. Why?" Mia's cunning smile shocked him. "What are you thinking?"

"I'm sure there's some follow-up legal work you have to do with Bethany," she said. When Caleb shook his head, she narrowed her gaze. "No sign-offs on a detail that necessitates a meeting where you, as her lawyer, would be duty bound to advise her that if, after three months, she still feels she can't raise her child, she could return to Family Ties? Being of legal age and all," she hinted with a wink.

"It would be hard for her to give up her baby after three months, but if that's what she truly wanted—" He mulled it over, then grinned. For the first time that day, Caleb felt as if the sun had come out. But then that was always the effect Mia had on him.

"Well?" she asked, tongue in cheek.

"I do believe there is one detail I overlooked," he murmured. "As an officer of the court, I'd be remiss to let that pass. I must speak to Bethany privately."

"Good." Mia sipped her tea, but from the way she peered into the amber liquid, it was clear she something else bothered her.

"What's wrong?"

"I was at our quilting group this morning, which, by the way, I love. They asked me to design a Christmas quilt to be raffled off. We're all working on it communally and it is going to be gorgeous."

"Uh-huh." Caleb was utterly out of his depth.

"Anyway, we talk as we stitch and this morning the talk was about Lily and some new tests she had." Mia looked at him reproachfully. "You didn't tell me."

"I didn't want to say anything until I got some more

answers." Caleb kept his eyes on his coffee mug. He didn't want to tell her the rest.

"What is it, Caleb? Is there anything to be done for her?"

He loved the concern in Mia's voice for the little girl he adored.

"Caleb?" Maybe it was the weight of her hand on his arm, or the gentleness of her question, or perhaps it was the glow of her emerald eyes. Whatever the reason, it suddenly became easy for Caleb to reveal his heart.

"There is something that can be done for Lily," he said carefully. "There is a specialist who comes to Calgary who could see her, but he's not scheduled for a visit there for another three months, and the cost of his work is not covered by our government health care plan."

"Money is not the issue here, Caleb. Lily must have the best we can get, no matter what the cost." Mia pulled forward a pad of paper and a pen. "What is this surgeon's name?"

"Dr. Peter Frank. But, Mia, he won't make a special trip just for—"

"Have some faith, Caleb." She grinned at him and then, to his amazement, winked. "One of the members in my Calgary church was a doctor whose son was in my Sunday-school class. I'm going to talk to him and see if he can help us."

Caleb watched Mia make her phone call, hardly daring to hope. Yesterday he'd been defeated by the information he received about Lily, certain there was little more he could do. But as Mia spoke to her friend, a flicker of hope flamed to life. Despite his intention to remain unmoved by the lovely textile artist, his appreciation of Mia and her refusal to take no when it came to Lily's welfare soared. How could he ever have thought Mia fragile?

As she crossed each barrier in reaching her goal to speak to Dr. Frank, Caleb realized how much had changed in the shy, reticent woman he'd met a few months ago. Or maybe her determination had always been there. Whatever it was, Caleb was inordinately glad that he hadn't walked away that first day he'd met Mia.

Several times Caleb noticed Mia's eyes close when she was put on hold. He realized she was praying. Mia's faith in God's love for His children continually intrigued Caleb. Unlike him, she seemed to have no questions about God. Caleb envied her that. He'd seen her gentle, loving manner win over crotchety folks at church and bitter young women at Family Ties. Nobody was immune to Mia's warmth.

Including him? Most of all him, Caleb's heart insisted.

Within half an hour Mia was speaking personally to Dr. Frank, laying out Lily's case before asking him to make a special concession to see her. Caleb couldn't tell from her face after she hung up the phone what the decision was.

"Well?" he asked impatiently when she doodled on her notepad.

"He'll see her, but only if we can get her to Sick Kids Hospital in Toronto by Friday." Mia's calm pronouncement stunned Caleb.

"Friday?" He blinked. "But—that's only three days from now."

"So we'd better get to work." Mia shot him a grin, then pulled forward her laptop and punched in an airline's website. Fingers hovering above the keyboard, she turned to him and asked, "You are coming, aren't you?"

"Oh, I'm coming," he assured her, reaching for his wallet. "You can charge our two tickets on my card."

"Two? You don't think I'd let that little girl go without me, do you?" Mia glared at him. "I will be with Lily through whatever comes, Caleb. Don't even try to stop me."

"I wasn't going to," he said, delighted by her response. Mia ignored his outstretched card.

"Thank you, but not necessary." She kept her eyes on her keyboard. "I guess this is a good time to tell you. I have set up a trust fund for Lily."

Caleb felt bemused, befuddled, as if he'd missed something. "You did?"

"Well, actually Bella did, at my request. It will cover any expenses we incur." She did look at him then. "Of course, you'll have to sign off on the expenses because you'll be the administrator."

"But—" He struggled to find words. This woman. This marvelous, wonderful woman. Caleb's heart expanded until he could hardly breathe. "Mia, that's so kind of you. It's amazing." Her generosity toward Lily humbled him. "Are you sure you want to use your personal funds—"

"They're not *my* funds. That glass you found in my basement turned out to be genuine Lalique and worth quite a bit." She chuckled when his eyes opened wide. "I loved four of those pieces, so I kept them. They're displayed in my bedroom."

"And the rest?" he asked, hardly daring to believe he'd finally achieved his goal for Lily.

"Bella contacted an art dealer friend who was delighted to find homes in museums for the most special pieces. The rest were sold. That's Lily's fund. Bella will get the information to you as soon as everything is settled." Mia told him the amount.

Caleb's jaw dropped in shock. Mia returned to booking the airline tickets, then paused. "Do you think Hilda should come along?"

"No. She hates flying. The man she was once engaged to died piloting an airplane. She hasn't flown since." Caleb still couldn't believe it. "Mia, are you sure?"

"Yes." She looked across the breakfast bar at something he couldn't see. "I've prayed for weeks about that glass. Harlan meant its use for something else, but God had other plans. Harlan's rare old books were sold to set up a fund for needy women who come to Family Ties." She shrugged. "You'll have to administer that, too, I'm afraid. Along with Abby, of course."

Caleb couldn't find the words. Mia had taken a negative in her life, her husband's miserly trick against her, and turned it into something wonderful.

"You know that verse 'All things work together for good'?" she asked, face upturned. "Well, I believe that's what God is doing in my life. He's working things out. Like this ranch, like your dad helping me, like providing funds for Lily and helping Abby's outreach at Family Ties. It's all part of His plan."

Caleb blinked. What could he say to that? Nothing but a heartfelt thank-you.

They spent the next hour planning details like which hotel would be easiest to reach from the hospital and whether they should stay an extra day to let Lily relax. No detail seemed too small to escape Mia's attention.

By the time darkness had fallen and the aroma of roasting chicken filled the kitchen, Caleb knew that if ever he could love someone, he'd want that person to be Mia.

But then his father returned and Caleb put away those wayward thoughts. Love wasn't for him—he knew that. But when had he begun to long for the right to hug Mia close, to grasp her hand and share her joy in planning wonderful things for the future?

Even if he could let go of the past, Caleb was pretty sure Mia couldn't be part of his future.

Chapter Eight

Determined not to let Lily fret over the visit with Dr. Frank, Mia kept the little girl busy with games and puzzles during the flight to Toronto.

"You thought of everything," Caleb said when Lily's head nodded onto his shoulder and she fell asleep. "She hasn't had time to worry."

"That was the goal." Mia tucked the computer Lily had used in her bag.

"It hasn't stopped me worrying," Caleb admitted. "What happens if he can't do anything for her? What if—"

"Caleb." Mia reached across Lily and threaded her hand in his. The touch made her stomach wobble, but she held on anyway. This was not the time to let her personal feelings get in the way. This was the time to join together and support this little girl. "This morning I read a scripture. 'The Lord will provide.' Let's hang on to that."

He squeezed her hand. "I am continually shamed by the strength of your faith."

"Shamed?" she asked, pleased by the compliment but

too aware of her own personal struggles to trust God, of her ache to hold her own child when she knew that wasn't His will. "Part of being in God's family means supporting each other."

Mia drew her hand away. Contact with Caleb always made her wish for more, but she simply couldn't imagine ever again depending on another man. It felt utterly humiliating to remember how she'd been hoodwinked by Harlan and hadn't even suspected it, to recall her blind obedience to his edicts as if she had no mind of her own when all the time he'd been using her to get the inheritance her mother had left. Bella had summarized the totality of his nefarious schemes on the phone last night, leaving Mia feeling stupidly naive.

But at least she'd learned from her miserable marriage. She'd learned to listen to the still, small voice inside her. She'd learned to ask questions, a lot of questions, and to look for answers from more than one person. Most of all she'd learned that the freedom of choice was worthy of staying independent. So far anyway.

"Wake up, sweetheart. We're landing now." Caleb brushed Lily's cheek with his knuckles and smiled when her long dark lashes lifted. "Is your seat belt fastened?"

"Uh-huh." Lily peered at him, trust glowing in her dark blue eyes. "Will it hurt, Uncle Caleb?"

"I don't think it will hurt today. The doctor just wants to look at your leg to see if he can help you," Caleb explained.

"What if he can't, Uncle Caleb?"

Mia's heart broke as shadows moved into Caleb's silver eyes. He opened his mouth but clearly had no words, so when he looked to her, she smiled at him and then Lily.

"You mean what if he can't fix your leg?" Mia said softly.

Lily nodded. "I'll be the same then, won't I?" she asked.

"I don't know. None of knows what God has planned for us, honey." Mia cupped the child's chin in her palm. "Six months ago I didn't even imagine I'd be living at Riverbend. But God had other plans. We have to trust that He'll do what's best for us because He loves us so much. Can you do that?" she asked as the plane taxied to the terminal.

"I'll try." Lily's shoulders straightened.

Mia's heart bumped with pride as the little girl moved regally down the aisle and out of the plane. Though people turned to watch her, it wasn't her limp they were looking at. It was Lily's beautiful smile. Most of them smiled back.

So did Dr. Frank. It took less than half an hour to reach the hospital thanks to a very capable cab driver. They were immediately shown into a room where Dr. Frank probed and pressed, assessing everything with shrewd eyes as he teased Lily with a bunch of goofy jokes. When he was finished he didn't send Lily from the room as Mia had anticipated. She moved closer to Caleb, seeking his support as they waited.

"Well, Miss Lily." Dr. Frank sat in a chair, putting his eye level even with hers. "You've had some problems with your leg since you broke it, haven't you?"

"That's why we came to see you," Lily said. "Can you fix my leg, Dr. Frank?"

"I'm not sure." Mia listened intently as Dr. Frank explained how the bones had grown together wrong. "It would take a lot of operating to take the bones apart and put them back together the right way," he warned.

"That would hurt." Lily paled.

"It will hurt for a while, until your bones get used to being in the new way," Dr. Frank said honestly.

"And then I wouldn't limp?" Lily asked. "I hate limping."

"I think if we did the operation, you wouldn't limp as much, but I can't say for sure that you wouldn't limp at all, Lily." Dr. Frank leaned back in his chair. "We won't know that till after the operation."

"How much would it hurt?" Fear filled Lily's voice. Mia moved to comfort her, but Dr. Frank made a motion that asked her to stay where she was.

"It would hurt a lot at first," he said quietly. "We would give you some medicine to make it hurt less, but it will hurt. And it will hurt while you learn to walk."

"I already know how to walk," Lily said indignantly.

"Yes, now you do, but after the operation your leg has to learn all over again. It won't want to." Dr. Frank explained every detail, answered every question to prepare Lily for what lay ahead.

Mia's head whirled. She couldn't imagine how Lily was able to understand it all, but to her surprise, the child sat straight and tall, paying close attention. Caleb looked just as focused.

"So what do you think, Lily?" Dr. Frank finally asked. "Do you think you want to have the operation on your leg or are you afraid it will hurt too much?"

Lily's forehead furrowed as she considered what he'd said. Mia wanted to go to her and lend support, but she knew it was important that the little girl make this decision herself. If Lily asked for help, she and Caleb would gladly offer it. But the choice was Lily's.

"My mom died. That hurt a lot." A tear trickled down her velvet cheek. "It still hurts."

"It probably always will," Dr. Frank said in a soft voice. "But after a while it will get easier."

And so it went. Lily asked every question she could think of and Dr. Frank patiently answered each, repeating if he needed to, easing her fears but making no attempt to mask the truth. Mia felt as though she were on pins and needles, waiting for the little girl to make her decision. At last Lily stretched out a hand toward her. Mia stepped forward and clasped it tightly. On Lily's other side Caleb did the same.

"What should I do, Mia?" Lily asked.

"I can't tell you that, honey." Mia brushed her hair off her forehead. "I can only tell you that I think Dr. Frank is very good at operating and I believe he would do his very best for you. Do you want some time to think it over and pray about it?"

"No." Lily shook her head. "I already prayed. A lot."

"Then, what does your heart say?" Mia asked softly.

"It says yes," she said firmly. "Is that okay, Uncle Caleb?"

"It's very okay." Caleb drew them both into the security of his arms. Mia could have stayed there forever, but there were details to see to. Besides, if she stayed tucked in his embrace for much longer, it would only be more painful to leave and harder to resist the craving to return to that weakling she'd been and allow someone else to be strong for her.

That could not happen. She focused on Lily.

"When?" Mia asked the doctor.

"I'd like to do the surgery as soon as possible, and I'd rather do it in Calgary," Dr. Frank said to them. "That way Lily won't have to go through a long return flight. And she'll be closer to her friends during her recovery. I know she has a lot of those." He and Lily shared a smile, but then his face grew serious. "It will be quite costly," he warned in a low voice. "I'll gladly donate my fees to help her, but the hospital will require payment for the specialized care Lily will require, and they'll want a large part of the payment up front."

"Cost is not a barrier," Mia said firmly. "Lily must have whatever she needs."

"Are you sure?" He named a figure that made Caleb's eyes widen. Mia only nodded.

"Whatever," she insisted, certain that the money she'd set aside for Lily's future could not find a better use. "Do you have a date in mind?"

"Wednesday next week." Dr. Frank smiled at her surprise. "That is, provided Calgary can set it up. It has to be then because I'll be leaving for a mission trip to Africa after Christmas and I want Lily well on the way to recovery before I go."

"Is next Wednesday okay for the operation, Lily?" Mia watched as fear fought faith in Lily's dark blue eyes. "That gives us lots of time to pray," she whispered in the child's ear. When Lily nodded, Mia hugged her.

"Will you be with me, Mia? You and Uncle Caleb?" she asked in a wobbly voice.

"Of course we'll be there. The nurses will probably have to throw us out of the hospital we'll be there so much." Mia let out a pent-up breath as Lily giggled. A glance at Caleb revealed tears glossing his eyes. When he turned his head to brush them away, Mia felt that pinch on her heart again. He was such a good man.

"Okay, I'll set it up and send you the details." Dr. Frank tweaked Lily's nose. "I'll be checking on you. You have email?" He pretended amazement when she said no. "Well, you'll have to get it. I can't go without talking to my favorite patient for a whole week!"

"I can borrow Mia's computer," Lily assured him. "Or Uncle Caleb's. They both look after me."

"You're a pretty lucky little girl to have such good people caring for you, Lily." Dr. Frank rose. "I have to go. You keep praying." His glance included all of them. "I like knowing God's been asked to attend my operations."

"I'll pray really hard," Lily promised.

"Me, too." Dr. Frank beckoned Caleb into the hallway, leaving Mia with Lily.

Although she yearned to hear what was being said, Mia accepted that as Lily's guardian, Caleb was in charge. She waited until after lunch. They walked to a nearby park where Lily could play. Then Mia asked what had been said in the hallway at the hospital.

"Dr. Frank shared some details about her aftercare," he told her. "I'm concerned about that. I don't think Ms. Hilda can manage everything."

"I've noticed she's getting less mobile. Why is that?" Mia asked.

"Hilda fell last year and reinjured her knee when she was looking after the son of a friend of mine, a little boy named Henry. The doctors recommended Hilda have a knee replacement this fall, but then Lily needed a place to stay and…" He let the rest of it trail away.

Mia knew what was coming, but she also knew it

couldn't happen. She steeled herself against his anxious voice.

"You've already done so much, Mia. I hate to ask this. But would it be possible for you to have Lily stay at your place to recuperate—"

She had to stop him.

"I'd like nothing more than for Lily to come to Riverbend, Caleb. Goodness knows I certainly have the room. But I can't do it." She turned her head away from his probing gaze and studied the little girl working so hard to climb up the stairs to the slide. "It just isn't possible. I'm sorry."

"Can you tell me why?" His voice, soft, patient, soothed that part inside her that yearned for tenderness. "Please? I won't judge."

Perhaps that promise was why Mia gave in to the urge to tell the story she'd kept secreted inside for five long years.

"You call your father a murderer," she began. "Well, I am, too. I'm responsible for a child's death. He's dead because of me." There—she'd said it. Mia looked at Caleb, steeling herself for the disgust and loathing she knew she'd see there.

But Caleb's silver-gray eyes held neither disgust nor abhorrence, only surprise and compassion mixed with sadness. He glanced over to make sure Lily was all right, then lifted Mia's hand and folded it into his.

"Tell me what happened, Mia." His kindness was her undoing.

"His name was Bobby Janzen," she said, unable to stop the gush of words or tears. "He was three years old and I loved him."

Harlan had never let her explain, never wanted to

hear the details of that horrible time. He'd "cleaned up her mess," as he'd put it, then forbade her to ever babysit another child again. He couldn't afford the scandal of her ineptitude, he'd said.

"Go on." Caleb tightened his grip on her hand when she would have pulled away. "Lily's chatting with that little boy," he said when she glanced away. "She's fine. Tell me the rest of the story."

"Bobby's parents were our neighbors," Mia explained after a deep breath. "I was bored that first year I was married to Harlan. I was used to school and people and things filling my day. Then my mother was gone and there was nothing but grief. I had to do something, and since Harlan didn't want me to work, I started going to the park. I met Bobby." She closed her eyes and let the memories fill her mind.

"You befriended him?"

"Yes. He was a darling child. I never got tired of sketching him. I gave him one. His parents thanked me for it." Her voice wobbled. Mia paused to regain control. "After a while his nanny and I would meet in the park. When she'd chat about him I'd soak in every detail. That little boy held my heart in his hands. I'd have done anything for him."

"Something happened." There was no question in Caleb's voice.

"One day his nanny told me it was her last day caring for Bobby," Mia said softly. "She was getting married, moving away."

"So you took over for her." Caleb nodded. "Understandable."

"Not exactly." Mia shook her head. "Harlan would never have agreed to that. But I did begin babysitting

Bobby at night, when his parents wanted to go out. They'd always have him ready for bed. All I had to do was give him his bottle and tuck him in." She stopped, suddenly grief filled at the memory of holding that sweet, warm child and singing to him, of knowing he'd never smile or chortle that funny laugh of his again. The pain never went away.

"Say it, Mia." Caleb put an arm around her shoulder and drew her against his side. "What happened?"

"I didn't put him to bed right." She choked out the words. "I thought I had. But when I went to check on him an hour after I put him down he wasn't breathing. Harlan told me later that Bobby had choked and died because I wasn't careful enough," she whispered, heart wrenching at the memory.

"Careful enough? But he wasn't an infant," Caleb said with a frown. "So…?"

"I'd given Bobby a little bear for Christmas. He was always rubbing it against his face. It was soft and it made a little noise." She gulped at the memory of Bobby's joy in the silly little gift. "Usually the bear sat on his nightstand, but that night he was fussing and I let him take it to bed with him. Harlan said the bear came apart and he choked on a part. Bobby died because of me, Caleb. I gave him the toy and then let him have it in bed. It was only because Harlan pleaded with Bobby's parents that I wasn't charged with his death."

"So now you won't be alone with any child," Caleb's lips murmured against her hair.

"I can't allow it." Mia turned to look at him, surprised to find his face so near hers. "That's the promise I made Bobby's parents. Harlan said it was the reason they didn't have me charged with his death. I had to promise I'd never be in a position to endanger another young child."

"Oh, Mia, what a lot of grief you've carried." Both Caleb's arms went around her then. His lips pressed against her forehead. "I know you'd never hurt a child. I'm so sorry this happened to you."

"So am I." How wonderful to be held so tenderly, to feel his touch against her skin. Caleb hadn't reacted at all as she'd expected. Maybe he didn't understand. Hating to break contact, she drew back so she could gaze into his eyes. "I would love to have Lily stay with me, but I can't, Caleb. I will never put another child in danger."

Caleb could hardly stand the grief in her voice.

"Mia, Lily's older. She won't choke. She—" But Mia interrupted him.

"What if she fell and I wasn't there to catch her?" She turned her head to study the little girl. "What if she climbed to the top of that slide at Riverbend and somehow fell off?"

"That wouldn't be your fault!"

"Yes, Caleb, it would, because I'd have broken my promise." She bit her lip as one lonely tear dribbled down her cheek. "I know God has forgiven me, but I can't forgive myself."

Caleb tried to argue, but he could see his protests did no good. Mia had lived with her guilt for far too long. She explained that she loved children, hence her Sunday-school class at the Calgary church, but that there had always been others there to make sure nothing happened.

Somehow the more Mia explained, the more a feeling grew inside him, a kind of hunch that Harlan had somehow used Bobby's death to keep Mia bound to him and that ugly house she'd lived in. Guilt and fear were the perfect tools to stop activities he didn't control.

"I'll do anything I can for Lily. I love her very much." Mia rose. Her gaze slid from the child to him, determination lifting her chin. "But I can't keep her at Riverbend."

There was no more time for discussion because Lily came over limping wearily. Caleb treated both his ladies to a special dinner, but after they returned to their suite at the hotel, both Mia and Lily seemed subdued and soon retired to their rooms. Left alone in the living room, Caleb phoned Marsha. Ever since that day so long ago when he'd first met her as a foster child, she'd been there for him. Now he needed her advice.

True to form, Marsha listened carefully to everything he had to say.

"The operation is wonderful news, dear. How amazing that Mia would do that for Lily. Such a sweet woman. But why do you think she won't take Lily to Riverbend?"

"It was a personal confidence, Mother. I can't say." Caleb would not betray Mia's trust in him. "Let's just say she's afraid to be alone with Lily in case something happens."

"Then, it seems to me your path is clear." Caleb could almost see Marsha's eyes glow as her firm voice transmitted into his ear. "You need to find someone who will stay at Riverbend with Mia. Perhaps then she'll reconsider."

"Maybe." The more he thought about it, the more Caleb believed that was his answer. "But who?"

"Ordinarily I'd have a dozen names for you," Marsha said in a troubled tone. "But half the church has signed up for that gospel cruise with Pastor Don. It starts next week. I don't think most of those left would be much help with an invalid child. I'd offer, but your father is so looking forward to our yearly trip to Montana that I'd hate to see him disappointed. Still," she said, "if it's a matter of a child's health—"

"No, Marsha. You have a hectic schedule. You and Dad need that time away together. I'll think of someone. Oh, I know. Ms. Hilda." Caleb barely had a moment to savor his solution before his mother ended that.

"I heard via the grapevine today that the doctors are pressing her to get that knee operation as soon as possible," Marsha said quietly. "She's put it off because of Lily, but it's getting to the state where she needs to have it done or…"

"So we've got two folks who need care." Caleb sighed, frustrated by the news.

"Seems to me you need to seek the Lord's help on this one, son. That's my best advice." Marsha caught him up on some other local news, but Caleb knew the odd silences interspersing her words were because Marsha was yawning.

"Thanks, Mom. Get some sleep. I'll see you tomorrow."

"Caleb, have you spoken with your father?" By her tone he knew she was referring to Joel.

"I have nothing to say to him." He couldn't help the anger in those words.

"As long as you keep that attitude, you'll never be able to move on," Marsha said in a gently reproving voice. "And I think you need to move on, don't you?"

"What do you mean?" he asked, confused by her words.

"There's a certain widow newly moved into River-bend for whom you seem to have great affection. Don't make the same mistake you made with Lara, Caleb. Don't let anger over your past ruin what could be something special with Mia. Good night, dear. I'll be praying." Marsha hung up before he could respond.

Caleb sat in the dark room overlooking Toronto's night sky, musing on her words. Did he have a special fondness for Mia? Of course. The remembered pleasure of holding her in his arms kept intruding, though he tried to suppress it.

In the silence of the night he began to examine what lay behind his need to make sure Mia didn't feel alone, why Caleb wanted to be there for her, to make sure each moment in her life was filled with the joy she'd been denied too long.

It wasn't because he loved her, though some strong emotion inside flared whenever she was near. But that wasn't love.

Was it?

Chapter Nine

"We'll be right here waiting for you." Caleb bent and pressed a kiss against Lily's cheek, ignoring the others gathered around the little girl in her hospital room. Mia's heart squeezed as emotion overwhelmed him. He couldn't say the words, but there was no doubt he loved this child.

"We'll be praying, sweetheart," she whispered in Lily's ear, then relinquished her grip of the small hand as the nurses wheeled Lily's gurney from the room. "We love you."

"Love you, too" came the drowsy response.

And then she was gone and Mia was alone with Caleb.

"I hate this," he said, his jaw clenched tight. His hand sought hers and held on as if it were a lifeline.

"Of course you do. So do I. Because we're not in control." She smiled at the teddy bears and balloons that so many from Buffalo Gap had sent to encourage Lily.

"Dr. Frank better be as good as his reputation," Caleb growled.

"We're not depending on Dr. Frank. Our trust is in

God." Mia couldn't sit in this empty room and wait. She needed to move. "Let's go for a walk."

"But—"

"He said at least four hours, Caleb." She tugged on his hand. "There's nothing we can do here. Come on."

After a bit more persuasion Caleb agreed to leave Lily's room. In the crisp autumn sunshine, Mia drew in deep breaths, trying to quell the sense of worry plaguing her. A passage from Isaiah's thirtieth chapter filled her thoughts. "The Lord will be very gracious to you at the sound of your cry." *I'm crying to You, Lord*, she prayed silently. *Please help Lily.*

"It's going to snow soon." Caleb lifted his face into the light breeze.

"How can you tell?" Mia matched her step to his until he realized she was almost running and modulated his pace.

"Believe it or not, it's the one good thing my old man taught me before he screwed up my life." Caleb's fingers tightened on hers. She squeezed back. He turned his head and grinned at her. "Too tight? Sorry."

"Tell me about this thing Joel taught you." She wanted him to dwell on this first positive thing she'd ever heard him say about Joel. "Can Ben do it, too?"

"No. Ben is a born rancher, but he could never sense a weather change the way I can." Caleb shook his head. "My dad's better at it than me, though. He doesn't even have to stick his head outside. Somehow the barometric pressure changes and Joel just knows what's coming. I can't explain it."

"That's amazing." Mia pointed out a cloud formation over the tips of the distant Rockies. "Looks as if you're right. Joel isn't just good at weather, though. He's also amazing with Lily. She says he's building a rocking horse for her. She's ecstatic that I own horses. You do know she wants to ride again?"

"I know, and it scares me to death." Caleb let go of her hand and wrapped his arm around her waist, drawing her closer as a strong wind began to buffet them. "Sure you want to keep walking in this?"

"Yes. I like facing off against the elements." And she liked being so close to him, protected, cherished. Where was her hard-won independence now, Mia asked herself. "Did Joel ever make toys for you?" she asked, hoping to draw on his pleasant memories.

"He once carved a train set for me for Christmas. I guess he and Mom couldn't afford the real thing, so he made it out of wood. Really intricate work," he remembered, his voice far away. Silence fell between them because the wind gusts made it difficult to speak. Caleb pointed to a fast food place across the street. "Let's go have coffee. Or tea," he added with a grimace.

"Joel's also a great Bible teacher," Mia said, continuing the conversation when they were both seated with a hot drink. "The other day I mentioned Martha—you know the story about Mary and Martha, the two sisters who Jesus visited?"

"You mean the Martha who felt she was doing all the work while Mary enjoyed Jesus's visit? Yeah, I know it." Caleb frowned. "What does Joel have to do with it?"

"I never understood why Jesus rebuked Martha. I've always thought she got the short end of the stick, that she slaved away and her lazy sister let her." Mia chuckled. "Joel helped me see that when Jesus rebuked Martha it wasn't because she was working too hard or that He didn't appreciate it. It was because her focus was wrong. He offered her a golden opportunity to hear what He had to say and instead she focused on trivial things to show she was a good hostess. Joel gave me a new perspective on relationships with God."

"He should practice what he preaches." The hardness in Caleb's voice made her wince.

"He's trying, Caleb. He's really trying to put the past behind him and make his life count," Mia said gently.

"That's too easy. It lets him forget my mom," Caleb snapped.

"He hasn't forgotten, Caleb. She's constantly in his thoughts. 'My wife was a great baker,' he told me the other day when I made an apple pie. And he mentioned that she would have enjoyed our quilting group." Mia nodded. "In fact, he speaks of her often."

"That doesn't change what he did," Caleb said coldly.

"Are you sure he's guilty of murder?" Mia couldn't let it rest. Somehow she had to help Caleb let this go. Maybe if he could get past the barriers…

"Are you sure he isn't?" Caleb's glare pinned her in place. "I was there. I saw it happen. He pushed her."

"Or he reached out and she backed away." He didn't like that, evidenced by the flare of anger in his eyes. Mia tried again. "Or perhaps he did reach out to push her away as she advanced on him. And perhaps that's why she fell. Or perhaps— What does it matter now, Caleb? It won't bring your mother back."

"Exactly." He crossed his arms over his chest and leaned back, jaw rock hard.

"Joel told me your mother was a godly woman." Mia decided to try one last time. "Wouldn't she have forgiven him if he'd asked?"

The nerve in Caleb's left cheek twitched as he

worked to control his resentment. Strangely Mia didn't feel afraid. She only felt sympathy. Well, she also felt a deep desperate need to wrap her arms around him and hold him close, taking his pain.

If only she could. Because she loved him.

The self-realization stunned Mia so much she barely heard him say they needed to return to the hospital. It took Caleb pointing out the tiny snowflakes for her to notice that the sun had disappeared and winter was on its way.

You can't love Caleb. It's a mistake to let any man get close. He'll want to tell you what to do, try to bend you to his will, just as Harlan did. He might even try to trick you to adopt Lily. You can't love him.

"Why is it so important to you that I forgive my father, Mia?" As they walked into the hospital, Caleb's quiet question drew her from her introspection.

She stared at him, mentally noting all the things she most admired about him. He was tall and strong and principled. He had integrity that he wasn't willing to breach. He loved Lily, did everything he could to make sure her life would get better. Almost everything.

"If you could forgive your father…" she began, feeling her way as she spoke. "If the two of you could come together, reunite your family—" She stopped. Dared she say it?

"Not going to happen," he insisted firmly. Then he lifted one eyebrow. "But say it did. So what? Why does this matter to you?"

"Because it would make you happy," she whispered, staring at him. "It would end your self-imposed suffering. And Joel's. The two of you could find some common ground."

"And?" he pressed when she hesitated.

"Then you could make a home for Lily," Mia said in a rush.

Caleb's eyes stretched wide in astonishment. He stared at her, blinked, clearly stunned. Finally he shook his head.

"Also not going to happen, Mia. But let me ask the same of you. When are you going to get past your fear? When will you stop letting what Harlan said and did affect the rest of your life?"

"I'm trying to do that," she whispered.

"Are you?" His eyes seemed to drill into her, exposing her secrets. "So when are you going to let go of your guilt over Bobby and adopt Lily as your own child? You are meant to be a mother."

The thought of it was so attractive that Mia got caught up in imagining all the things she and Lily could do together. Funny how Caleb always figured into those plans. It took a moment to remember it couldn't happen.

"I'm rebuilding my life the best I can." A sense of vulnerability swept over her. "I'm trying to break through all the barriers Harlan caused."

"Are you enjoying your new life?" he asked.

"Of course I love having my own home where I can indulge my style. I love having my own car and driving where I want to go." She exhaled and glared at him. "I know you think there's nothing to stop me from doing all the things I've only dreamed of except my fear, but that fear is as real to me as your hatred toward your father."

"I don't hate him," Caleb said, but she ignored him.

"I wish that one day I could have a child of my own." Mia saw his eyes flare and knew what he was hoping, but she had to dash those hopes. "I wish that so much. But that's not going to happen. It can't."

"Why?" Caleb followed her into Lily's empty room. When she stood by the window and didn't respond, he took her arm, forcing her to face him. "Why can't you be a mother?"

"Because I couldn't survive if something happened," she murmured, heart aching. She loved the way his silver eyes softened when they looked at her, thrilled to the touch of his fingers as they sought out her hand and held it.

With Caleb near she felt strong, capable. But Caleb wouldn't always be there. She had to depend on herself.

"You're stronger than you think, Mia," he murmured. "And I don't believe you'd ever let anything happen to a child." His arms slid around her waist and he drew her close. "You're too full of love."

Even through her coat Mia could feel the strength in him, solid and dependable. She needed that strength right now, needed desperately to make him understand. For a moment she gave in to her heart's yearning and laid her head against his chest, relishing the tenderness she had not known in six years of marriage.

"I love Lily with all my heart, Caleb. If I had a daughter, I'd want her to be exactly like that little girl." She lifted her head just enough to gaze into his eyes. "What will we do if—"

"She's going to be fine," he said, his lips millimeters from hers. "God wouldn't let anything happen to a sweet kid like Lily. Have faith, Mia." Then his face moved those few millimeters and his mouth touched hers.

Mia had only ever been kissed twice in high school.

She didn't know exactly how to return his embrace. All she did know was that when his lips pressed against hers, joy suffused her. She wanted to show him how much she enjoyed his touch, how deeply moved she was. So she kissed him back as best she knew how, thrilled that he didn't pull away but instead drew her even closer.

She savored every moment, every tiny detail, tucking them into her memory to take out and think about later. Mia wanted that kiss to go on and on, but too soon Caleb drew his lips away. A sense of loss filled her until his big hand snuggled her face against his chest once more.

She could stay here forever, Mia thought, safe in his strong yet tender embrace.

He shouldn't have kissed her, Caleb told himself over and over as he and Mia waited in Lily's room. Mia was inexperienced. She wouldn't understand he'd only been trying to comfort her.

Comfort her or yourself? He shoved the thought away, but his mind immediately drifted to the pleasure he'd found in holding Mia, in letting her lean on him. When he'd finally found enough sense to draw away, her eyes were sparkling, her face shining, and he knew he had to be very careful not to let Mia expect more from him. He couldn't love her. He didn't know how to love.

For the tenth time he checked his watch. Lily had been in surgery for three hours. His whole body clenched when there was a movement by the door. Something had gone wrong. He didn't know whether to groan or grit his teeth when his father walked in.

"I wanted to stay away," Joel said quietly. "But I couldn't. Is there any news?"

Caleb was about to tell Joel to leave but Mia rose and walked toward him. She hugged him.

"Not yet. Come and wait with us," she invited. "We can pray together."

Caleb couldn't watch his father fawn over Mia, fooling her as he seemed to have done to everyone else. He jumped to his feet.

"I'm going to get some coffee," he said, and stalked from the room. But the hospital cafeteria was noisy and he couldn't sort out his thoughts there so he left, searching for some place to be alone, to sort out his miasma of feelings.

There was no one inside the chapel. Soft ambient lighting gave no hint to the time of day. Hymns hummed in the background, enfolding Caleb in their comforting sound. A stained glass window sat center front, its words backlit.

"As I have loved you...you also love one another."

It wasn't a plea or a request. It was an order. Love one another. The question was, how could Caleb love a man he was convinced had killed his mother?

Wouldn't your mother have forgiven him? Mia had asked. And that was the thing. His mom would have, instantly and completely. She'd loved Joel with every fiber of her being. She'd told Caleb that, shown it in every word, every action toward Joel.

"I can't do it," he whispered. And yet he had to. The anger that continually festered inside was eating him up, ruining his life. Caleb knew it could not go on. "Show me how to forgive," he prayed.

His eyes strayed to the right. Another verse, smaller

and less conspicuous hung from a tapestry. *Forgetting those things which are behind, I press on toward the goal.*

The apostle Paul had done awful things. And yet God had forgiven him. How could He have done that?

His mother's favorite verse, which she'd framed and hung on her bedroom wall, suddenly filled his mind. *My grace is sufficient for you.*

Meaning what? That if God could forgive, Caleb had to accept that and move on. Meaning he needed to forgive and move on? Could he do that?

Every fiber of his being yearned to be free of the load of anger he'd carried for so long. And yet—

Caleb checked his watch, then rose to leave. He found himself looking directly into the painted gaze of Jesus holding a child on His knee. The artist had depicted such love in His intense eyes that for a moment Caleb couldn't look away.

"I'll try to forgive him," he promised finally, then left the quiet room. But what to do about Mia?

When Caleb arrived at Lily's room, the door was open. Quiet voices spilled out to him. He stood in the hallway, hesitant to interrupt.

"Mia, being content does not mean being complacent as you were before." His father's voice floated toward Caleb. "It doesn't mean being wary about everyone, either. You trusted your husband. That's what wives are supposed to do. The fault was in him. You can't make up for his faults by protecting yourself, by never caring for anyone again."

Mia murmured something Caleb couldn't hear.

"If only I could change the past, go back to that day and have my wife alive again." Could the sorrow in Joel's words be faked? Caleb wondered. "I'd give my life for hers if I could. But that's not the way it is. I made a terrible mistake. God has forgiven me. I only wish Caleb could."

"I'm not sure I've forgiven Harlan, Joel." As Caleb listened, Mia's voice broke. She cleared her throat and continued, "I wanted my mother's love so badly, but I felt like a nuisance to her. So I tried to stay out of her way even though I was so lonely. Then I married Harlan and I felt just as abandoned. It was so hard to keep trusting God."

"But you did and now here you are." Joel's voice softened. "You've come through the clouds into the light and now you can look to your future with hope. You can pass on what you've learned to Lily."

"I love Lily." The wistfulness in Mia's squeezed Caleb's heart. "Caleb thinks I should adopt her, but I can't."

"Because of Bobby Janzen," his father said. So Mia had told Joel about the little boy who died? She must really trust him.

"His death has never left me. I was responsible for that. If I hadn't been so careless…" A sound puzzled him until he realized it was Mia weeping.

The heartbreak of her sorrow hit Caleb hard. There had to be something he could do to help her. Maybe she hadn't understood everything. Maybe Harlan had lied about the circumstances. He pulled out his phone and texted his paralegal, asking her to find out everything she could about a three-year-old child named Bobby Janzen who'd died less than six years ago. He couldn't love Mia, but maybe he could help her.

Caleb had just completed his call when someone touched his shoulder.

"Let's join the others," Dr. Frank said. "Lily is out of surgery."

Chapter Ten

"You're a gift from God, Joel." Mia hugged him quickly, too aware of Caleb standing nearby, watching with that disapproving glint in his silver-gray eyes.

"Me?" His eyes, so like Caleb's, stretched wide.

"You. I know God arranged Hilda's surgery to happen at just the right time, while Lily was in the hospital. But now, thanks to you, both of them can recuperate here at Riverbend."

Almost two weeks ago, after visiting Lily, Joel had offered an encouraging word to retired nurse Maisie Smith in the hospital cafeteria after noticing how dispirited she seemed. Maisie told him how she was hoping to find temporary work to provide the funds for her grandson to take a longed-for class trip to Spain. Joel had introduced the nurse to Mia, and the two had soon come to an arrangement.

With a live-in nurse available, Mia had lost all her reservations about having Lily stay in her home to recuperate. After hearing about Hilda's surgery, she'd invited Lily's caregiver to recuperate at Riverbend, too.

Both patients were recovering nicely and everything seemed to be working better than Mia had expected.

"I guess with 'your gift' here, you don't need me hanging around," Caleb muttered in a sour tone. He tossed an affronted look at Joel.

"Of course we need you. Joel's got his hands full with the horses. And I have other plans for you, Caleb." Mia looped her arm through his and smiled at him, relishing the sweet wash of happiness that filled her. After his tender kiss the other day—well, how could he not know she'd always need him?

"What plans?" He looked slightly less disgruntled when Joel excused himself and left.

"You once told me your adopted father, Bud, taught you how to build. Well, a builder is exactly what I need. Or rather, what Lily needs." She described the ramp she wanted outside the back door. "Lily and Hilda will both want to go outside."

"Mia, it's snowing. It's been snowing for days. Even if they did go outside, and that's doubtful given that it's November and freezing cold, there's no place for them to go beyond the back porch." He eased away from her touch.

"I know it's snowing. And I know that right now going outside is the last thing on their list. But they are going to get bored in here," she said, waving a hand to encompass the house. "They'll want to be outside if only for a breath of fresh air, and I want there to be no barriers. Anyway, Lily is going to have to learn how to navigate through this winter, unless you've found her a home in a tropical climate?"

"I haven't found her a home at all," Caleb said with a wistful edge to his voice. "There just doesn't seem to be anyone willing to take on a child of her age, especially when they learn she's recently had surgery."

"Abby hasn't had any luck, either?" Mia asked. She knew that since Lily's surgery Abby had placed three other children through the Family Ties Adoption Agency. But though she'd contacted all of her former colleagues at child services in Calgary for help, Abby had found no one who would take Lily. Caleb looked so discouraged when he shook his head that she touched his shoulder. "We'll just have to keep praying."

"It hasn't done her any good so far." His face tightened. "Lily's such a great kid. She just wants to love and be loved. Why is that such a hard prayer to answer?"

"Caleb, God isn't going to abandon her." Mia used as firm a voice as she could muster, stuffing down her own questions. "He has plans for that little girl. But in the meantime it's up to us to help her get as mobile as she can, as fast as she can. Hence building a ramp."

"She wants to go to church tomorrow." Caleb grimaced. "I sort of promised she could."

"Caleb!" Mia glared at him. "I know you love her and you can't deny her a thing she asks for, but her surgery wasn't that long ago."

"Dr. Frank said she needs to use the muscles to get her strength back," he defended with a sheepish look.

"Doing the exercises he prescribed. Not by going to church where she'll be bumped and jostled. She might even fall." Exasperated yet understanding that in his desperate love for this child, Caleb was willing to give Lily the moon if it would make her smile. "I'm going to stop praying that you'll adopt Lily." She made herself a cup of tea. "Because I know perfectly well that if God granted my plea and you became her father, that child would be spoiled rotten."

Silence. Mia gulped at the realization that she'd spoken aloud.

"You pray that I'll be Lily's father?" Caleb's voice oozed astonishment. "But—I—"

"Love her," Mia finished. She was so tired of him pretending it was otherwise.

"I can't love her," he insisted. "I can't love anyone."

She whirled on him, fed up with the excuses.

"That's what you tell yourself, isn't it, Caleb? That you can't love anyone?" She knew from the lines that formed at the corners of his mouth that he was irritated with her, but Mia couldn't stop. "The truth is that you're afraid to love."

"Is that the truth?" His voice emerged tight and clipped.

"Yes, it is," she shot back. "You're afraid to let yourself love because if you did, you might love and lose, just as you lost your mother. And that would hurt. A lot."

"Life hurts." He shrugged and turned away.

"Of course it does. Being alive and open to everything God lets us experience means risking pain. Otherwise we'd be dead." Mia softened her voice, desperate to reach him. "But buried beyond the pain are wonderful memories. Beauty we could not even imagine had we not risked loving."

"Like Bobby?" He faced her then, eyes shooting darts of anger. "Are your memories of him enough to expiate your guilt?"

"Not expiate," she murmured, blanching at the attack. "But was it worth going through what I have to know him?" She nodded. "Yes, a thousand times yes. He came into my life and blessed me. I can never regret loving him—" She choked, unable to say the rest.

Suddenly Caleb was there, wrapping her in his arms and holding her so tenderly. What could she do but lean against this man who'd seen her through the toughest patches of her recent past, despite the cost to himself?

"I'm sorry," he murmured, his lips pressed against her ear. "I'm so sorry, Mia. I shouldn't have said that. I know you loved Bobby, that you only wanted the best for him. What happened was a terrible accident, not your fault."

Mia let herself revel in his words and his touch. His tender embrace was a balm to her battered heart. She wanted so badly to relax against him and just enjoy the moment with this man she loved. But there was more at stake than her happiness here. A terrible weight plagued Caleb and Mia longed to help him break free of it.

"Caleb," she said, not quite certain what she wanted to say because her heart was so full.

"You're wrong about me, Mia. I can't love anyone," he was saying. "I tried so hard to love Lara, but it wasn't there because that part of me shriveled up and died when my father killed my mother. That's why I'll never forgive him." The last words were harsh and bitter; Mia ignored them.

"When Lily was in the hospital, if she needed help what would you have done?" she asked.

"Whatever she needed," he said without hesitation.

"Anything?" she pressed, praying silently for a way to make him see.

"Whatever it took to make her better." He drew back to stare into her eyes, then shook his head as understanding dawned. "That's only natural. Everyone wants to protect a child."

"Do they?" Mia met his gaze and held it, so glad she'd been given the chance to love this wonderful man. "Harlan didn't. Lily was his own flesh and blood, but he felt no compunction to do anything about her injured leg, or her life, or her future. He didn't love her."

"I am not like him," Caleb snapped.

"No, you aren't. Because you love Lily. You want to see her healthy and happy. You want the best for her." She lifted her hand to cup his cheek, mesmerized by the rough, bristly skin that masked a heart as soft as a marshmallow. "That's love, Caleb. That's what love does. 'If you love someone you will be loyal to him no matter what the cost. You will always believe in him, always expect the best of him, and always stand your ground in defending him.'"

"First Corinthians 13," he murmured. His lips brushed her hand as he spoke, sending a sweet shiver of longing straight to her heart.

"Yes." Mia smiled. "You love Lily."

"Yes." Caleb looked stunned yet also thrilled by the admission. "Yes, I do," he said in a firmer voice. He pressed a kiss into Mia's palm. "I love Lily Jones."

"I think you also loved Lara." He opened his mouth to object but she slid her palm from his cheek to his lips and held one finger over them. "I believe you truly loved her, but your love got blocked out by your anger toward your father."

"Why?" he demanded, easing his mouth away from her touch.

"Because love can't stay where there's hate." It was too hard to stand like this, in the circle of Caleb's arms, and not blurt out her love for him. Mia didn't want to do that, not now. This was the time when he needed to understand what his hate cost him. So she eased away from his embrace but grasped his hand to retain contact. "Your hate pushed out your love for Lara. Are you going to let that keep happening, Caleb?"

Your hate pushed out your love. Are you going to let that keep happening?

The words kept circling inside his head, demanding an answer. Even here among the din of kids whom Joel had brought to Riverbend with their Sunday-school teachers so Lily wouldn't have to miss her beloved church—even now the accusation wouldn't leave him alone.

Hate. Was that how Mia saw him—filled with hate? But that was what he was. Even now as Caleb watched his father sitting with the kids, it churned and boiled inside him. He'd told Mia he wouldn't stay in the house with Joel there, stung when she simply nodded.

Caleb tromped through the snow, moving as far from the house as possible, as if that would help. Even deep in the woods he couldn't seem to escape the lilting joy in Lily and her friends' voices as they sang "Jesus Loves Me."

"Don't they sound wonderful?"

Caleb should have known Mia would follow him. She seemed to love the snow. But then Mia loved everything and everyone. She wasn't bitter about her past, like him.

"Did you notice how great Joel is with them? He must have been a wonderful dad—" Mia choked off her sentence and risked a look from beneath her lashes. "Before, I mean."

Obviously embarrassed by her faux pas, she silently simply walked with him ever deeper into the woods until there was no sound save the crunch of their footsteps and the odd "puff" as snow fell from heavily laden boughs.

"I've never had a real Christmas tree." Mia, head lifted, was surveying the pines around them. "This year I will have a real tree."

"Not these, I hope." Caleb chuckled when she blinked her surprise. "Mia, they're far too large to fit inside your house. You have to find a clearing where a younger tree is growing."

"And then chop the sweet innocent little tree down?" She scowled. "That sounds horrible."

"It's not as if there's a shortage. You have acres of trees." Caleb couldn't help shouting with laughter at her aggrieved look.

"That's not the point." Tossing him a glare, she stomped off, then floundered. Caleb reached out and grabbed her arm, hauling her out of the drift.

"Don't step off the path." When her gaze held his Caleb knew she was hinting at a deeper meaning. "To answer your question, my father was a great dad, when he wanted to be. The problem was his drinking started to take more time than his kid."

"He made mistakes," she said. "We all do."

"Most people don't make his 'mistakes.'" Caleb treasured every moment he spent with Mia, loved to listen to her bubbling laughter, to watch her face light up and her emerald eyes dance when she tried to play a trick. She was fun to be with, a pleasure to help and a joy to kiss. But she was fixated on Joel. "Why did you have to hire him?"

"Because I needed help and he is very good at helping." She tilted her head. "Joel is not the father of your childhood, Caleb. He's not the man you remember. He's changed."

"But has he changed enough that he can be trusted around Lily?" Caleb asked.

"Joel would never hurt that little girl, not in a million years, so don't you even imply such a thing." Mia bristled, her eyes like jade chips that flashed with temper. "Lily is desperately lonely and Joel is the closest thing to a grandfather she's ever known. He provides stability and security that she's desperate for."

"*My* father?" He made a face.

"Don't you dare mess with them, Caleb." Mia stomped in front of him and glared. "I will not see that child hurt because you're stuck in the past."

"Adorable Mia. What a mother you are." Caleb couldn't help it. He slid his arms around her waist and hugged her tight, breathing in the scent of pine and snow and sunshine and something indefinably sweet—Mia.

"What are you doing?" She wiggled to get her hands free.

"Hugging you." He tipped his head and pressed his lips to hers. "Kissing you."

She seemed frozen by his kiss. He rubbed his cheek against hers and found it as soft as velvet yet chilly from the winter air.

"Thank you for caring about Lily," he whispered in her ear. "Thank you for being willing to fight for her happiness."

"You're welcome," she managed when she found her voice. A funny look filled her face.

"What are you thinking?" He loved the way she felt in his arms, as if she belonged.

"I was just wondering if you could do that again," she said, her amazing eyes half-hidden by her thick lashes.

Caleb half hoped she meant what he thought she was intimating. But he was afraid to let himself express the feelings building inside him lest he hurt her. He could never tolerate knowing he'd hurt Mia.

To make sure they were thinking along the same lines, he asked, "Do what?"

"Kiss me again. I've never been kissed like that before. I like it," she assured him, twining her arms around his neck.

So did he. Maybe too much. But Caleb's heart swelled inside him as he studied her sweet face. He bent his head and kissed her, slowly and thoroughly, touching her inviting lips with his until she responded and fire built between them. But Mia was an innocent and he didn't want to get her hopes up; despite her assurance, he knew deep inside that he couldn't love her because he hadn't been able to rid himself of his bitterness toward his father. God hadn't answered that prayer.

So after a few moments of pure bliss, he stepped back and let his arms fall away while his head told him he was crazy.

"I don't hear any singing," he said, struggling for composure and avoiding looking at her. "Do you think Sunday school is over?"

"Probably, but they're staying for lunch." Mia slipped her hand into his. "Want to help me make pizza?"

Yeah, he did. In fact, Caleb wanted to help Mia Granger do anything she asked. The only thing he couldn't do was love her. So he walked back to the house, helped her assemble pizzas and reveled in every moment he spent with Mia.

When it was time to eat, the other children quickly came to the table. Thinking he needed to carry Lily, Caleb was about to enter her room when he heard her speaking. The words made him jerk to a stop and listen.

"Why is Uncle Caleb mad at you?"

"I did something very bad and he can't forgive me." The sorrow in Joel's words struck Caleb in a way nothing his father had said before ever had.

"Did you 'pologize?" Lily asked. "Ms. Hilda says you hafta 'pologize when you do something that hurts somebody."

"I tried, Lily. But I guess some things are too hard to forgive."

"Did you 'pologize to God?" the little girl asked.

"Many times." Caleb could hear the smile in those familiar tones.

"An' He forgave you, right?"

"Yes, He did. In fact, the Bible says after He forgives us, He remembers our sin no more." There was a sound like someone rising from a creaky chair—Mia's old rocking chair. Caleb flinched, needing to move away, but strangely transfixed by the humility and sorrow in his father's words.

"Then, I think Uncle Caleb needs to 'pologize," Lily declared firmly. "We're s'posed to forgive those who trespest against us."

"Trespass," Joel corrected with a chuckle.

"Yeah. I'm going to tell Uncle Caleb that."

"No, Lily. Please don't," Joel begged.

"Why?" Poor Lily sounded confused by his rejection of her help. So was Caleb.

"It's very kind of you, but I'd rather you didn't talk to Caleb about it." His father grunted, a sign he was hefting Lily in his arms. "I don't want Caleb to forgive me because someone asks him to. I want him to forgive me because he wants to."

Silence for a moment. Then Lily said, "Like when Ms. Hilda tells me to 'pologize when that nasty Paul Brown makes fun of my leg but inside I'm still mad at him and I only do it because she makes me?"

"Exactly like that," Joel agreed. "Ready for pizza?"

"Yes."

Joel's chuckle reached out and tugged at Caleb's memories. He stepped into Mia's sewing room so they wouldn't know he'd overheard them. Being surrounded by the myriad colors and textures of Mia's work evoked memories of the many times he'd heard his father's hearty laugh when his mother teased him. Or when Joel had teased her, or Caleb.

When Joel had been sober, they'd been a happy family. Why did he ruin it all?

Why did You let it happen? his heart cried.

A sheet of forest-green fabric sat on Mia's worktable. On it was a piece of paper with words. Caleb leaned closer and read, "Now all that I know is hazy and blurred, but then I will see everything clearly, just as clearly as God sees into my heart right now."

He jerked back, suddenly aware that God saw how his anger and hate had festered, overtaken his thoughts and even his prayer life. He saw how Caleb had resisted every overture his father had made, how he'd refused to give the only thing Joel had asked—forgiveness.

Uncomfortable with the shame that thought brought, Caleb stepped back, prepared to leave the room. His gaze fell on a small quilted plaque that hung above Mia's desk. It held one word. *Forgiven.*

Caleb knew it referred to Bobby. He felt his heart break, knowing the pain she still carried. He was certain that nothing she'd done had harmed that child yet still she, an innocent, sought forgiveness.

Which made Caleb consider how he could see himself as the "forgiver" when there was so much he needed to be "forgiven" for.

"Caleb?" Mia's voice called.

"Coming." He stepped out of her studio with his mind whirling. Yes, he needed to reassess his position with regard to Joel. And he would do that later, when he was alone. But he also had to find out about Bobby. If it would help Mia, he needed to do that.

Caleb felt embittered and angry, locked in his world of hate. But Mia wasn't. After seeing her tender care of Lily, every need met, every question answered, every tear comforted, Caleb was positive sweet, innocent Mia had done nothing to any child for which she needed forgiveness.

Chapter Eleven

"It has to be the best Christmas Lily's ever had." Mia glanced from Caleb to Joel. Both were seated at her breakfast bar with coffee mugs in hand and a plate of cookies in front of them. "And I need you to help me make it so, both of you. Can you manage to work together, for Lily's sake?"

"Of course we can." Joel didn't glance at Caleb. "Where shall we start?"

"With a tree." Conscious of Caleb's silence, Mia dived into her list of things to do. "I want a real tree. So we'll all have to make a trip into the forest to choose it. Joel's arranging a sleigh ride for us?"

"Working on it," he promised.

"Good. We'll cut it down two weeks before Christmas. Now, we'll need to decorate that tree," she continued, smothering her mirth at their groans. "Lily and Hilda and I have already started making some decorations, but I want to take them both to the mall in Calgary to buy more. This is a new house. I'm starting with fresh Christmas traditions. That will include some outside decorations that I'll need help to put up. Okay so far?"

"Take them to Calgary—" Caleb's Adam's apple bobbed up and down as he gulped. "How?"

"We'll rent a van," she said, thrilled with her plan. "Hilda is already managing quite well with her walker. We'll take it along. It has a seat on which she can rest if she needs to. Lily will need her wheelchair. Problems with that?"

Silver eyes stretched wide, the men slowly shook their heads.

"Good." Mia knew neither of them understood why she needed to make this Christmas so special for Lily so she relaxed her tone, desperate to gain their help while they forgot their own problems. "I've been speaking with Lily about Christmas. She's had a dream for years. Her mother never baked cookies with her, didn't have a tree and Lily only ever got one gift. I intend to change all that."

"Can I say something?" Caleb frowned when she nodded. "What happens next Christmas when Lily doesn't have all this—hoopla?" he finally managed.

"She will have it. I will make sure that every Christmas Lily has is special." Mia couldn't tell them she was head over heels in love with Lily or that the child's sweet presence in her life seemed an affirmation of God's love. "This year Christmas will be the special time for Lily that I longed for when I was a child."

"You know that after Christmas, Family Ties will initiate a very strong search for a home for Lily?" Caleb must have seen her shock. "She'll be walking much better by then thanks to your hard work. After the holidays Abby feels Lily's chances will have gone up by leaps and bounds."

Mia gulped, stunned by the thought that she might

lose the child she now loved as her own. An idea began to percolate, but she kept it to herself, determined to find out her options before she acted. That was part of managing her own life.

"Lily will love this Christmas." Joel's hand covered hers, transmitting his caring before he let go. "What else can we help with?'

"I want a stack of wood ready for using in the fireplaces over Christmas." Mia paused then clarified, "I'd prefer if we could use only fallen trees or deadwood."

"I can handle that," he promised. "In fact, I'll go get started on it if there's nothing else you need right now."

"Great. Thank you, Joel." She grinned when he finished his coffee, grabbed one last cookie and hurried out the door.

"And me?" Caleb asked.

"I have a very big favor to ask of you." She exhaled then explained. "My house in Calgary is almost complete. I need someone to go through it with me, to make sure the work is as it should be and that nothing's been missed."

"No problem." She loved Caleb's easy acceptance of the job. With him by her side it would be easier to tour the house and not be overcome by the sad memories of the past.

"But that's not all I need." When his eyebrows rose she grinned. "I want to completely decorate the place, down to dish towels and pots and pans, before I hand it over to Arthur. And I want it done so he can move in with his grandkids before Christmas."

"But that's only six weeks away!" Poor Caleb. What a wonderful friend he'd been.

"I know." She reached out and touched his shoulder, needing the contact to remind herself that this man had kissed her passionately and tenderly. He was not aloof and immune. He simply needed to see that giving was a way to heal the heart. "And I have one more even bigger favor."

"Okay." He gulped. "What is it?"

"I need you to go shopping with me." Mia almost laughed as fear filled his silver eyes. He was such a sweetheart.

"Uh, shopping for what?"

"Gifts. For kids." Did his shoulders relax just a bit? "Sixty of them." Nope, he was as tense as before. Mia loved the way he didn't immediately refuse, though he probably wanted to.

"You want to get gifts for s-sixty kids?" Jaw slackened, Caleb gulped when she nodded. "Where did you get to know sixty kids?"

"They're foster kids I've worked with at my church in Calgary," she explained. "Every year I give them a little something to make their Christmas extraspecial. This year I want to do it again."

"So if you've done it before, why do you need me?" he asked, his curiosity apparent.

"Because the majority of them are boys." She nodded at his understanding. "You see the problem. I'm not up on boy interests, but I'm sure you are. Besides, I think they'd appreciate something other than a quilt."

"You've given all these kids quilts?" Caleb's eyes stretched wide at her nod. "More than one quilt to each?" he asked in a shocked voice.

"No, but I've given them different quilted things. Quilting is what I do." Mia shrugged. "I know it's asking an awful lot of you and that you're busy and probably can't—"

"I'll help you."

"—spare the time, but—what did you say?" She paused, startled. "You'll help me? Really?" At his nod, her smile broke out.

"I'd love to see how that dump of a house came together." He made a face at her frown. "I'm sorry, Mia, but it was a dump."

"I know." She pretended sadness for a moment, but her heart was too light at the thought of spending precious hours in the company of this wonderful man. Maybe he'd even kiss her again. "When?"

"It sounds as if you're a lot busier than me," he said with a grin. "I can reschedule wills, estate planning and real estate sales around your schedule."

"Is that all you do?" She wrinkled her nose. "It sounds boring."

"Thanks." He chuckled when heat burned her cheeks. "No, it's not all I do. The work for Family Ties is the most interesting, but there's not much action right now. Abby has only three women there at the moment and their children have already had adoptions arranged. Not much happens there over Christmas."

"But after Christmas you'll start looking for a permanent home for Lily." Deeply moved by the pain she saw in his face, she asked, "You won't consider adopting her yourself?"

"No." Caleb shook his head firmly. "Lily needs a real home with a mom who's like you, someone who knows how to make her world special. You should adopt her. You could handle it, even with all the other things you've got going on. And you certainly do have a lot."

"My busyness is due to you, Caleb." Mia grinned. "That very first day we met, do you remember what you said?" He shook his head. "You told me I was stronger than I imagined, to consider my opportunities. I took that to heart. God has blessed me beyond measure. I have the resources to help people. In fact, it's my duty. So you see, it's your fault."

"Looks as if I unleashed a lion." Caleb chuckled. "When do we start?"

"Is today too soon? I want to choose the gifts before things get picked over. Besides, they'll need to be wrapped and—" When he held up a hand she stopped. "What?"

"Let's go."

"Thank you. Thank you so much, Caleb." Mia gazed at him, ecstatic at the idea of spending an entire day with him. Then she realized he was looking at her with a question in his eyes. Embarrassed, she hurried to tell Maisie they'd be out and to call Joel if she needed anything. Then she grabbed her jacket and her purse. "I'm ready."

"We'll take my car." When she asked why, Caleb grinned. "Bigger trunk."

"Oh." She smiled back. "Right."

As they drove into the city, Mia couldn't suppress the joy inside. For today she wasn't going to wonder about the future, about what would happen when Caleb finally found a home for Lily and she left or if Caleb would ever return the love she felt for him. Just for today she was going to relax and enjoy every minute she spent with this wonderful man.

"Are you sure?" Caleb grimaced at clothing Mia had chosen for a boy on her list. "It's not a gift I'd have wanted as a kid."

"You have all your fancy lawyer clothes." She

rubbed her finger against his leather sleeve to tease. "Eli doesn't, and the older couple he's living with can't afford to provide the kind of things he needs to attend college classes."

"College? You said he was fifteen?" Caleb appreciated the sheen of her lovely hair cascading around the shoulders of her cream-colored coat.

"He is fifteen and far ahead of kids his age. That's why he's taking college courses." She nodded to the clerk, who suggested several more items. "Please include a gift receipt so he can exchange anything that doesn't suit him," she directed as she handed over her credit card. "Trust me, Caleb. I do know what to get *this* kid. I just never had the opportunity before."

"We can't lug all these bags around. I'll take everything out to the car," Caleb said when the transaction was completed. "Where will you be?"

"In the camera store across the way." She brushed his arm the way she had many times before. And he liked it.

As Caleb walked to the car park, he reflected on how much he liked it that Mia was comfortable with him. Actually there was a lot he liked about his relationship with Mia. For one thing, she continually surprised him. Take these kids; she had tons of information about each child and the family each was with. Those families were included in her gift plans.

"Fostering is hard on others in the house," she'd explained. "A little treat now and then can help ease the adjustment."

That was Mia in a nutshell. Nobody was left out of her generosity. Even the merchants in Buffalo Gap.

"People should support the place where they live," she'd insisted on the ride in. "I've ordered something from almost every store there. What we'll buy in Calgary are things the town's stores don't carry."

Her caring and compassion enriched his growing feelings for her. One of these days Caleb was going to have to figure out exactly how to deal with those feelings, but for today he was going to help where he could and enjoy being with her.

He found her listening to a salesman's spiel about the benefits of buying a camera with six lenses. Mia was clearly overwhelmed by the man's aggressive sales pitch.

"Who is it for?" he asked when Mia glanced at him with a silent plea for help.

"Greg. He's ten, loves photography of every kind."

"Thank you," he said to the salesman. "We'll think about it." Then he grabbed Mia's hand and steered her out of the store.

"You have a different idea for Greg?" she asked.

"Yes. A simple, easy-to-use camera with the capability to do more once you learn how to use it. You don't want to frustrate his interest with too fancy. Let's try this place." Caleb drew her toward a very small shop where he knew the owner.

Ten minutes later, after Mia paid for the camera she turned and smiled at him. "See, this is why I wanted your help. It's perfect for Greg."

And so it went. Mia told him about the child and his circumstances and Caleb helped her find the place to build those interests. It became a kind of game where he pushed himself to pose different ideas for her to consider. But by noon he was bone tired and starving.

"I need lunch," he said when it seemed Mia could go on forever. "How about here?"

"Chinese?" She bent to study the menu.

"You don't like Chinese food." He stuffed down his sigh and his longing for moo goo gai pan. "A hamburger, then?"

"Oh, I love Chinese food." Mia licked her lips as if to prove it. "I just haven't had it in years."

Since Harlan came on the scene, Caleb guessed.

"Chinese it is." He drew her inside, their packages banging between them. "Why don't you get a table while I go put these in the car? If they'll fit," he muttered only half under his breath.

"Maybe I should have hired that van today." Mia grinned when he looked at her. "We're only half-finished."

"Don't tell me that before I've eaten," he groaned and shuffled out of the restaurant amid her laughter. But as he stuffed her bags into the car, Caleb noted that there was nothing in any of the packages for Mia. Neither had she mentioned wanting any of the many things they'd looked at.

She was going to extreme lengths to make sure everyone she knew had the best Christmas ever. But who would ensure that Mia's Christmas was special? Because of her, many people would find a special gift under the tree. Would she?

As he walked back to the restaurant, Caleb decided to take particular note of her interest in everything. The least he could do was find a gift for her that was something she truly wanted, not flowers or chocolates but something personal that she would remember him by.

And when did Mia remembering you become so important?

That question nagged at Caleb, but he ignored the

little voice in his head, Later he'd think about it, he promised himself. Much later.

"Are you sure you want to do this now?" Caleb asked as he pulled up in front of her former home. "You've already had a very full day."

"I want to see what they've done. I want to be sure they're finished so I can pay off the contractor. He's been great to work with, quick and understanding about my needs. I don't want him to have to wait for his money." Mia inhaled, tossed a smile at Caleb and got out of the car.

"The exterior lights must be on a timer. Good idea." He walked with her to the gate, opened it for her. It neither wobbled nor squeaked. The wrought iron shone dark against the snow, perfectly straight. It gave the house a dignified, cared-for first look.

"Excellent," Mia said, and mentally ticked one item off her list. "The front door's been refinished," she noted as she unlocked it. "Come on in."

She stepped inside, flicked the light switch and stopped, stunned by the beauty of her former home. Behind her she heard Caleb close the door, then he moved to her side.

"I think you'll want to move back here," he said, breaking the silence that had fallen.

"It's amazing. I didn't know opening it up would make it seem so large. That was his idea and I was wary of it because I thought it would reduce the character, but it doesn't. It looks charming." Mia's heart, tight with sad thoughts of returning to this dreary place, now sang. "Arthur and the kids are going to love this."

"The fireplace is gas. Safer and more efficient."

Caleb followed her through the living room. "I always knew this staircase would be spectacular," he said in a hushed voice. "It's better than that."

He was right. The stately stairs stood proud and regal in their dark rubbed stain. The treads were covered in a broadloom that would silence footsteps rushing up and down. Mia reached out and sought his hand, needing extra support.

"The kitchen will be the real test," she whispered.

Caleb squeezed her icy fingers in his. "Have faith."

"Yes." She walked forward with him, then gasped. "Caleb, look!"

"I'm looking." He stood beside her, as silent as she, soaking in the details of airy white polished cabinets with moldings and trim wrought by a master hand and finessed by sparkly quartz countertops. A breakfast nook occupied the former sunroom, which had been restored with insulated windows. No longer frigid, the room boasted a tiny fireplace that lent it a cheery feel.

"I could work in here," she whispered.

"Anyone could," Caleb agreed. "Look, French doors to your garden. Want to check out the basement?"

Mia found nothing of the house's former dingy basement. Instead, she saw a huge family room begging for a big television and comfy seating. There was a guest bedroom and a bathroom tucked in the back and a small office to one side that might also be used as a workshop.

"Think your Arthur and his kids will use this?" Caleb asked.

Mia gave him a droll look. She wanted to stay, to let furnishing ideas percolate, but her curiosity was too great. "Let's see upstairs."

Nothing could have prepared her. The master bedroom had huge windows, a squishy soft carpet and an en suite that rivaled the one at Riverbend. The other two rooms shared a Jack-and-Jill bath that was equally luxuriously appointed. Crumbling crown moldings, now repaired and repainted, lent an elegant finish.

"Well?" She turned to Caleb, conscious that, somehow, he still held her hand. She drew it away, embarrassed to be so needy. "Do you see anything that he's missed?"

"Are you kidding? This place could be the center spread in a magazine." Caleb followed her downstairs. "All it needs is furniture."

"Yes." A rush of pleasure zipped through her at the prospect of filling these rooms with beauty. "I can hardly wait." She let the pictures flow through her mind. She could make it so lovely—

"May I say something?" The hesitancy in Caleb's voice and the frown on his face caught her attention.

"What's wrong?"

"Nothing. It's a lovely home. You and the contractor have done a wonderful job," he praised, a soft smile lifting his lips.

"But? I can hear a 'but,' so you might as well say it." Mia didn't know why it irritated her that Caleb couldn't congratulate her and let it go. But she respected him too much to not hear him out.

"I don't want to deflate your bubble." He touched her cheek with his forefinger, smoothing the skin as if to soften what he was about to say. "You should be very proud of this place. It's even more praiseworthy that you want a man and his kids to enjoy it. You are a very amazing woman, Mia. Don't you have even the smallest craving to move back here and enjoy the fruits of your labors?"

"No. This isn't home. My home is at Riverbend Ranch." She tilted her head to one side, reconsidering what he hadn't said. "Do you think I should come back here? Is that what you mean?"

"No," Caleb said firmly. "I just wondered if you had regrets."

"None. So?" He was making her nervous. Caleb had never yet hesitated to speak the truth to her.

"This man, Arthur, and his grandchildren." He chose his words carefully. "Do you think it might be overwhelming for him to move from his apartment to such grandeur?"

Mia gaped at him. She'd never even considered how Arthur and his grandchildren would react, except she'd assumed they'd love this place.

"You want to fill it with beautiful things and I understand that, but maybe they have some of their own cherished possessions that they'd like to bring along. Maybe a bed or a table, something that has good memories." He grimaced. "Maybe I'm way off base."

"No, you're not." Mia managed a smile as her dreams dissipated. "You're exactly right. That's the reason I needed you here. I want this to be a home for Arthur and his family. Not a show home but a place they'll be free to relax, not worry they'll mess up something. Thank you, Caleb."

Mia's heart was so glad he'd risked irritating her rather than let her make a huge mistake that without even thinking she wrapped her arms around his waist and leaned her head on his chest.

"Do you know you're the best friend I've ever had?"

she whispered, feeling his heart thud against her cheek. "I love you, Caleb."

Then she stood on tiptoe and pressed her lips against his, trying to show him without words what lay in her heart. His hands came up and gripped her arms and for a moment she thought he would push her away. But a soft groan rumbled somewhere deep inside him and then he was kissing her with a desperation she hadn't expected.

"Oh, Mia," he whispered when at last his lips left hers and pressed to the shell of her ear. "You can't love me."

She tilted her head back to better look at him. "Why not?"

"Because I'm not lovable."

"I think you are. You're kind and generous and concerned about Lily. You go out of your way to help Hilda and you're there whenever Abby needs you for Family Ties. Marsha and Ben can't say enough about the way you've cared for them, made sure they have what they need." She let her fingers trace out the features of his face. "You don't like it but you put up with having Joel around Riverbend because you understand how much I need his help. You care about God and living His way. You're a wonderful man and I do love you, Caleb."

"You shouldn't. You're young and naive. You don't understand the darker side of life. You live in a world of dreams." He stepped back so her arms fell away. "I'm not lovable, Mia. It's no wonder you don't see that. Your goal is to make life better for everyone around you. You make things seem possible but they aren't. I can't love you."

"You don't care about me?" When Caleb didn't answer she stepped closer and spoke as boldly as she dared. "You don't come to Riverbend because you want to see me, to be around me, to laugh with me as I laugh with you?"

"That's not love," he said with a glare.

"Isn't it? Define love for me, Caleb. Tell me what you think it is, because I believe love is sharing good and bad. Love is caring for someone enough to tell him the truth even though you think it will hurt him." She took a breath but refused to stop even though his eyes were getting that frosty look that told her he was annoyed. "Love is holding a little girl while she weeps for her dead mother. Love is agreeing to shop for an entire day and carry packages when you could have ridden with your father up into the hills you love."

She smiled at the surprised look on his face.

"Love is slipping fifty dollars into an old lady's pocket at church because as her lawyer you know she's a little short in paying her heating bill," Mia murmured.

"How did you—?" Caleb stared at her. Then he shook his head. "It wasn't meant to be seen," he muttered.

"Which is also love." Feeling stronger by the moment, Mia smiled at him. "Love is so much bigger than you think, Caleb. You loved your mother, but I believe you love your father, too. In fact, it's not that you don't love Joel. It's that you won't let that love grow. I'm not sure why. Maybe because you see loving him as some kind of betrayal of your mother."

"He killed her!" Caleb said with teeth gritting. "How do you love someone who's done such a thing?"

"You forget about the past and you look at him as God sees us after He's forgiven us, as a new person with nothing from the past to mar us." She slid her hands around his, hoping passionately to finally reach that cold, lonely part of him that couldn't forgive. "You love Joel by giving up the right to be his judge and accepting your role as his son."

Caleb studied her for a long time. Expressions she couldn't understand or define flitted across his face. His eyes softened, lost their ice as he freed one hand to cup her cheek in his palm. Finally he bent and pressed his lips to hers in the most tender kiss Mia had ever received. Tears filled her eyes when he lifted his head and he shook his head.

"I think you are the sweetest, most generous, most kindhearted woman I've ever known, Mia Granger," he murmured. "You shame us all with your generosity of spirit and your bighearted acceptance. I see God in you, in the way you try so hard to extend His love."

"Caleb."

He kissed her silent.

"I wish I could be the man to love you, Mia. To share your amazing world as you bring joy to every life you touch would be a most amazing journey." He kissed her again, then drew away. "But that can't be, because my father would always be between us. To forget what he did to my mother, to dishonor her memory when the only thing she ever did was to love him, to love me—" He shook his head, his eyes brimming with a heartsick sadness. "I wish I could get rid of this lump inside me that demands he pay for what he's done. But I can't. And I won't saddle your life with that."

Mia couldn't say a word. Her heart was breaking and there was nothing she could do about it.

"I'll wait for you in the car. Whenever you're ready," he said quietly.

As she watched him leave, all joy in the day they'd

shared, in the house she'd had transformed, all her hopes and dreams dissipated in the knowledge that the only man she'd ever cared about would not be part of her life.

"Am I always to be alone, Lord?" she prayed when the front door closed behind Caleb. "Is love, real love, only for other people?"

Mia let the tears fall, pouring out her heart to the only one who understood. And when her barren soul could weep no more, she brushed away the tears, composed herself and walked out to Caleb's car with one thought uppermost in her mind.

Caleb had said she was strong. Well, she would have to be to survive this longing in her heart. But she'd made up her mind. If she couldn't have his love, she was not going to bury herself in a corner of sadness.

Mia was going to find a way to adopt Lily. She'd ask Caleb to help her. Maybe then he'd understand that love could grow and push out hate and fear and guilt.

Chapter Twelve

"I thought you'd be happy, Caleb." Abby Lebret sat in his office, brow furrowed as she studied him several days later. "Mia wants to adopt Lily. That child could have a wonderful new home with a woman who clearly loves her very much. Why aren't you smiling?"

Because I won't share it with her. Because I'm jealous of a child Mia is showering with love. Because I want to be part of it.

"Surely you don't object to Mia adopting Lily?" Abby's gaze narrowed. "You're her guardian and of course you can object, but why would you?"

"Because *he's* living there." The words seemed to squeeze out of Caleb despite his intent to keep them to himself.

"From what I've seen, Joel is adding immensely to Lily's life." Abby shook her head. "I've done a thorough assessment, Caleb. I've talked to everyone involved and looked at this adoption from every angle. I can't think of anything better than Mia's adoption of Lily, and for Joel to be part of it."

"I thought you'd say that," he admitted.

"It's not just me. I have a hunch that if you tried to stop this adoption and Mia went to court, a judge would see it my way, too. Joel has done nothing wrong," Abby insisted.

"Except kill my mother." Why had he said that? Now Abby, the owner of Family Ties and committed to finding loving homes for needy children, looked at him with pity. Caleb didn't want anyone's pity. Ever.

"How long are you going to drag that around, Caleb?" Abby's dark eyes held sympathy, but her voice remained firm. "This is Lily's chance. Please don't let your issues with your father spoil it. It's time to get over the past."

Why did everyone keep telling him to get over the past, as if he could simply wipe his mother's cruel death out of his mind? *Maybe because Mia did it with Harlan's perfidy?* said an inner voice.

"Not forgiving Joel doesn't hurt him as much as it hurts you." When he didn't respond Abby sighed. "I need to go. Think about what I've said." She rose, handed him her written report, then left.

The intercom buzzed.

"Caleb, Mr. Joel Crane would like to speak to you." *I'll bet he would.*

Caleb knew he couldn't put off the confrontation forever, but as tension washed over him, he wanted to refuse to see his father. On the other hand, he wanted to face Joel and demand to know why he was still here in Buffalo Gap. But he was not going to do that in front of his secretary or any of his clients.

"Show him in, please," Caleb said, exerting rigid control as his secretary escorted his father into his office. He did not get up to welcome his guest as he usually did. Instead, he remained seated, jaw tight, waiting until his secretary closed the door behind her.

"Thank you for seeing me, Caleb. I know you're busy." Joel shuffled his feet when Caleb didn't answer, then asked, "May I sit down?"

"If you must." Caleb studied the man he'd despised for so long and noted his father looked old and tired. There was a droop to his shoulders that he'd not noticed before. Gray streaks covered Joel's head, leaving barely any of them the same brown shade as Caleb's.

"I wanted to talk to you about Lily's adoption," his father said quietly.

"I am not at liberty to discuss a client," Caleb informed him in a curt tone. "Is that everything?"

"Is it asking too much for you to just listen?" Joel said. "Please?"

Caleb exhaled, then shrugged.

"Thank you." Joel visibly relaxed. "I know you're her guardian, Caleb. I also know that you care about her very much. So do I. She's sweet and good, everything you think I'm not. I couldn't love her more if she were my own grandchild. I think Lily loves me, too."

"You don't deserve to be loved," Caleb said bluntly.

"None of us deserve that."

The words reminded Caleb of Mia and her comment long ago that no one "deserved" God's love. Joel seemed to read his mind.

"It's by God's grace that I live and breathe. I know that." He leaned forward. "I didn't kill your mother, Caleb. I know you think you saw me do that, but that is not what happened."

"I've heard all this—" Caleb began, but his father interrupted his brush-off.

"I was drunk, yes. I was angry, yes. In fact, I was in a rage. Booze did that to me. Most of the time I blacked out, but I didn't that day. I was arguing with your mother and I saw her step back. I reached out to grab her, to save her, but she backed away. And she fell." Tears coursed down Joel's cheeks, but Caleb ignored them.

"That's your story?' he said in his most scathing voice.

"That's the truth," Joel insisted. "I didn't push her, but in a way I did cause her death. She wouldn't have fallen if we hadn't been arguing. Nothing can change that. I will bear it on my conscience for the rest of my life. But I did not push your mother."

"What does any of this have to do with Lily?" Caleb said when the silence stretched too long.

"I love Lily. I want that precious little girl to have a home where she is loved. She loves you, Caleb. She believes you will do the right thing for her. I believe you will, too," Joel said, his gaze intense as it held Caleb's. "So let me help you help her."

Caleb's radar went up. What was his father after?

"If having me in Lily's life is a barrier to you allowing Mia to adopt her, I will leave Riverbend and Buffalo Gap. I will not allow anyone else to suffer because of my actions." Joel rose. Funny how he looked so dignified now, shoulders back, eyes clear, body poised.

On the other side of his massive desk, Caleb felt small.

"If that's what holds you back from approving Mia's adoption of Lily, say the word and I'll be gone."

"Really? You'd leave, just like that?" Caleb didn't believe it.

"Just like that. I love that little girl as much as I once

loved you, still love you," Joel said, meeting his gaze with a clear stare. "That's why I will not do anything to hinder her future."

"What about your vow that you wouldn't leave until what's between us is settled?" Caleb asked. Why did he feel that he'd lost the advantage here?

"I'll leave that to God. I can't do any more." Joel turned to leave, paused, then turned back. "I'm sorry I ruined your life, Caleb. I'm so sorry you lost your mother, your home, your life. But now you've been given a precious gift. Mia loves you. Don't throw that away because of our past, because of me."

There were a thousand things Caleb wanted to throw at him. And yet hadn't there been enough words?

"Let me know," Joel murmured, his eyes wet. "It won't take me long to pack." He quietly slipped out of the room.

And Caleb, who was used to being in control in his own office, knew he'd won his case but lost the most important battle of his life.

"I know you've been avoiding me." Three days later Mia stood, hands on her hips and she glared at Caleb. She'd bearded him in his office out of concern for Lily. At least that was what she told herself. "You can avoid me all you want, but there's a little girl who desperately misses you and I'm done making excuses for your absence. Go see Lily."

She turned and stalked to the door. But before she could grab the doorknob he spoke.

"I have been avoiding you. And it's been awful. Can we be friends again?" Caleb's amazing eyes twinkled, sending her heart rate into the stratosphere.

"What does being friends mean?" she asked cautiously, afraid to trust his words when he'd told her he couldn't love her.

"It means helping you get this Christmas extravaganza you're planning under way. Deal?" He held out his hand.

"Okay." Mia slipped her hand into his for a moment, then drew back. She'd exposed her heart and he'd rebuffed her. That hurt far worse than anything Harlan had done. She would not allow herself to be that vulnerable again. Caleb had been right. She was strong. She had to handle being around him without letting herself dream he was offering anything other than friendship.

"Thank you," he said quietly.

"You're a bit late getting on board." Mia loved the way he looked at her, as if she were more than just a friend. "We've already done a lot, but there's still the trip to the mall for Lily and Hilda."

"Monday? I haven't much on my schedule that day, so it's easily cleared. The crowds won't be so bad then, either. I'm pretty sure I can arrange a van rental in time." He lifted one eyebrow, waiting for her decision.

"Fortunately Lily's still doing her schoolwork at home, so yes, that works. Then we'll need to get a tree. Joel's rebuilt an old-fashioned sleigh so we can take Lily and Hilda for a ride to choose the right one."

"How's she doing?" he asked softly. Mia knew he meant Lily and not Hilda.

"Very well, according to her physiotherapist. It helps that she has a solo with the kids' choral group for the Sunday-school program they're performing on Christmas Eve. Lily insists she's going to walk onto the platform unaided. Joel built her an apparatus to help her manipulate stairs."

"Good." Caleb nodded. Mia's breath caught in her throat at his intense gaze.

"I'm afraid she's pushing too hard, but her physiotherapist says to let her work as hard as she wants." She was babbling and she knew it, but her mind was replaying his kiss and every part of her wanted to repeat that experience. "Joel and Hilda and I each keep a close eye on her."

"You haven't had your cookie-making session yet, have you?" Caleb looked so disappointed when she nodded that Mia made a snap decision.

"We'll need to have another, though. I'm going to throw a Christmas party at Riverbend after the Sunday-school concert. I'll invite anyone who wants to come." As she said it, Mia felt a rush of satisfaction. A party was exactly what everyone under her roof needed.

"Count me in for the baking day," he said.

"Okay, but before that I need to get my Christmas lights put up outside. I was planning to get some in Calgary, but the hardware store here had such a wonderful supply that I just bought a ton." She glanced at him sideways. "Joel and I are going to put some of them up tonight, I hope. I want the ones that hang from the eaves to go up first."

"You're not going up a ladder to hang Christmas lights, Mia," Caleb said, just as she'd hoped he would. "If you feed me dinner, I'll help hang the lights."

"With Joel?" she asked, studying him.

Caleb slowly nodded. "If he has to be there."

"He does. Thank you. I'll appreciate your help. Now

I'd better get home and start preparing dinner." She turned to leave. Caleb's hand on her arm stopped her.

"I spoke to Dr. Frank this morning, Mia. He told you Lily's recovery is a little slower than he'd expected?" He waited for her nod. "What if she doesn't get complete mobility? What do we do then?"

"Where's your faith, Caleb?" Mia heard the sharpness in her voice and modulated it. He was only speaking her fears. "Whatever happens, Lily will still be Lily and I will always want to adopt her. Is that what you're asking?"

"Not exactly, but thank you for clarifying." He shook his head.

"What?"

"That faith of yours, doesn't it ever weaken?" he asked.

If only he knew how hard it was to keep trusting God to work things out, to keep believing that He'd given her this deep love for Caleb for a reason.

"It's taken a hit lately," she said, holding his gaze with hers until she knew he caught her meaning. Summoning the faith he'd praised, she quoted, "'I know the plans I have for you, plans to prosper you and not to harm you.' God knows what He's doing, Caleb. Remember that." She waggled her fingers at him in a wave. "See you later."

As Mia drove the snow-covered road home, she recalled a sermon she'd heard long ago.

From time to time it's good to review the past so we can see what God has done, how He's worked things out in ways we could never imagine.

Mia thought of Harlan and the life of deceit she'd endured at his hands. That had ultimately led her here to Buffalo Gap, where she'd found joy and a child to love. That move had also given her the opportunity to make the house where she'd endured loneliness into a place of joy for Arthur and his kids.

Because of Caleb, Mia had not filled it with all the lovely furniture she'd imagined. Instead, she'd consulted Arthur about what he'd prefer and together they'd bought only a few serviceable pieces because he'd chosen to bring many of his own possessions. Some were damaged, but he'd insisted he could fix them. At first dubious, after her visit with him yesterday Mia realized those old things were what made the house exactly what she'd wanted—a home where old memories could be built on. Her former house was now a place where love prevailed.

"You worked it all out," she murmured, turning into her driveway and pulling into her garage. "So I'm trusting You with Caleb, too. Please work on his heart, work out his issues with Joel. And help Lily and Hilda recover fully. Please let this Christmas be a truly joy-filled one, for all of us."

It was up to God now. All she had to do was trust Him to soften Caleb's hardened heart so love could fill his life. Her love.

"I've eaten so much I don't know if I can climb up the ladder again," Joel said, pushing away from the table.

"Again?" Caleb frowned. Though it had almost melted now, sleet had pelted the valley earlier. He'd had to use his four-wheel drive to get to Riverbend. He couldn't imagine climbing a ladder outside in such weather.

"I hooked the clips on the eaves troughs to hang the

lights. I thought that would be easier in daylight." Joel met his gaze without rancor, then thanked Mia for the meal. As he hugged Lily good-night, Caleb watched his father's eyes close and saw the look of pure bliss fill his face. "Sweet dreams, sweet one," Joel whispered.

"Good night, Pops." Lily clung to his hand for a minute, letting go only after he kissed her cheek. Pops? When had that happened?

"I'm going to do the dishes," Hilda announced. "Without help," she insisted, shooting Mia a look that said *don't argue with me.* "I'm looking forward to seeing those lights up when I come back from prayer meeting tomorrow night."

"Our cue to get to work." Caleb rose, carried his dishes to the counter by the sink, then walked to the front door to don his coat, boots and gloves. To his surprise, Mia dressed to go outside, too.

"You didn't think I'd let you do this on your own, did you?" she teased. "I have a plan."

"Of course you do." With her masses of hair bound inside a knitted green cap that matched her eyes, Caleb thought she looked adorable. A matching scarf around her neck was tucked inside her cream jacket. On her hands she wore bright red mittens. "You look like a goofy Christmas elf," he teased as he tucked an escaping tendril of hair behind her ear.

"You may pay for that later," she warned with a grin, then went outside.

Caleb had dreaded this time of working with Joel. He'd only agreed because he knew how much Mia wanted to make her long-cherished Christmas dream come true. But in actuality, it was fun to hang the gazillion icicle lights.

"Did you buy out the store?" he asked when the strands were finally hung and sparkled their soft white glow into the night.

"Pretty much." She winked at him. "I had to. I have a big house."

"Understatement," Joel muttered with a sideways grin at Caleb. "What's next?"

"Lights on some of these gorgeous spruce trees," Mia said cheerfully.

Caleb insisted on being the ladder man. But the trees were huge. Even the extension ladder wasn't long enough to reach the top. It took some persuasion for Mia to agree to decorate the shorter ones. She reiterated her dream of lighting the large trees.

"Say, I met a fellow in town with a ladder truck who was decorating that big tree in the town square," Joel remembered when they'd finished decorating five smaller spruce trees. "Maybe you could hire him to string lights on your larger trees on either side of the house."

"Don't encourage her," Caleb begged, descending from the fifth and final tree. A second later he felt the cold, wet smack of a snowball against his neck. "Hey!"

"This is where I say good-night," Joel said, and quickly strode across the snow toward his bunkhouse.

"Good night, Joel. Thank yo—ach!" Mia spat out the mouthful of snow and glared at Caleb. "I warned you," she said before hurling a snow missile with incredible accuracy and speed. It caught him squarely on the forehead.

"Okay, I give. I give," he yelled after Mia had targeted him several more times. He dodged more missiles and finally threw up his hands. "You win."

"Yes, I do." She approached him, grinning from ear

to ear. "Just call me the queen of snowball fights. Let's build a snowman."

Caleb was chilled and ready to go inside, but he just couldn't deny her the simple pleasure. He would have slapped the thing together just to get it done, but Mia had precise expectations and produced a kitchen knife to make the snow creature fully rounded from all aspects.

"Good enough?" he asked, sure there was not an edge left anywhere.

"Almost." Mia pulled a soft black hat out of her pocket and perched it on the snowman's head. She added a carrot nose and something dark for snowman eyes. Finally she took her green scarf and wrapped it around his neck. Then she stood back and surveyed their work, her breath mingling with his. She linked her arm through his and tilted her head to the right so it rested on his shoulder. "Perfect. You build a good snowman for a lawyer, Caleb."

Somehow Caleb couldn't stop himself from sliding his arm around her waist and drawing her against his side.

"Teamwork," he said, now perfectly content to stand in the cold and stare at the light show he'd created with this most amazing woman.

"Look up," she whispered.

He did and saw Lily watching them. He waved and she waved back. Then her bedroom light went out.

"Minx. She's supposed to be asleep." Mia chuckled. "You probably woke her up when you bellowed over getting a little snow in your face."

"Probably." He knew what she was doing. She was keeping things light to avoid the intimacy they'd shared when they were last together. Part of Caleb was relieved, but part of him wanted to throw caution to the wind, pull her into his arms and kiss her until she asked him to stop. Part of him wanted to look forward to a host of Christmases to come.

"Tomorrow I'm going to build a fort," Mia said. "Lily wants one."

"And what Lily wants, Lily gets. You're going to be a doting mother," he said, surprised by how saying those words brought sweet delight to his heart.

Mia twisted to look at him, her face mere inches from his.

"Am I going to be Lily's mother, Caleb?" she asked in that breathy tone that told him she was thrilled by the prospect but afraid to let her hopes get too high. He guessed she'd feared he'd use Bobby's death against her. Because she didn't trust him.

"I think you're made for each other," he said so quietly she had to lean near to hear.

"Oh, Caleb, thank you." In a flash she curled her arms around his waist, stood on tiptoe and pressed her lips to his. A second later, much too soon for his taste, her kiss ended. "Thank you so much. I promise I will always love her."

"That's why Lily belongs with you." Her face shone with joy in the glow of the Christmas lights. No matter where he went in the future, Caleb knew he'd always remember the deep rich green of her eyes, the smooth curve of her cheek and the tendrils of hair that had escaped her cap and now framed her lovely face.

"I'm not sure about a lot of things," he admitted. "But I know with certainty that God brought the two of you together. No one could take better care of her, love her more deeply or work harder to make her happy. You *are* her mother."

"Oh, Caleb." Her sweet voice caressed his soul while her eyes begged him for—something. The temptation was too great.

Caleb bent his head and covered her lips with his, loving the tiny shiver Mia gave but knowing that taking the love she so freely offered was wrong. He would only hurt her again.

Slowly, gently, he broke off their kiss and stepped back, repressing the urge to reach out and stop her arms from leaving his waist.

"Hot chocolate?" she whispered, her voice slightly hoarse.

"I better go home." He couldn't stop himself from trailing a finger down her velvety cheek. "Thank you for a wonderful evening, Mia."

"Come again," she invited, her lips curving in a sweet smile.

He would. That was the problem. Caleb couldn't stop coming back to Riverbend, even though he knew he'd run into his father, even though he knew he'd have to struggle to resist kissing Mia.

But that wasn't love. It couldn't be, because love didn't intentionally hurt, and despite knowing how much both Mia and Lily cared for him, Caleb had every intention of asking Joel to leave Riverbend and Buffalo Gap. It was the only way he could expiate his need to avenge his mother's death.

But for Mia's sake he would wait until after Christmas.

Chapter Thirteen

"I thought you'd never get here, Uncle Caleb." Lily gave him a dark look. "Christmas is only seventeen days away."

"I'm sorry, sweetheart." He smoothed the dark hair and pressed a kiss to her forehead. Mia thought that was to avoid her condemning look. "I got busy."

"Too busy." Lily's dark blue eyes filled with reproach.

"Uncle Caleb is here now and Joel has the sleigh outside, so let's go get that tree." Mia avoided Caleb's glance, a little shy around him after his intense kiss by the snowman a week ago. She felt confused, at odds. One minute he was kissing her; the next she didn't see him for ages. What was going on?

There was no time to dwell on Caleb's odd behavior as she handed him a thermos of hot cocoa, a plastic container with treats and blankets to cover Lily and Hilda. Joel had cleared a wide path from the house. With him on one side and Caleb on the other, Lily and Hilda walked slowly over the path to the sleigh and with both men's help, sat on the backseat. Mia would have joined them, but Caleb insisted she sit up front between him and Joel.

As a buffer? she wondered. But since both men were working hard to avoid all contentious issues, she didn't ask.

"Isn't it fun, Mia? I never had a sleigh ride before." Lily chatted nonstop, clearly excited. She pestered Caleb by asking constantly if the tree they were passing was their Christmas tree. At first he tried to explain, then simply shook his head no.

"Wait, sweetie," Joel urged her. "We'll come to the best ones pretty soon."

Lily launched into her Christmas solo and then they all joined her in a round of Christmas carols. By then they were deep into the woods.

"Just a bit farther," Joel said almost under his breath.

"You've been out here before?" Caleb asked with a frown.

"I had to make sure it was okay for the sleigh," Joel said. "But I've walked almost every inch of Riverbend."

"Why?" Caleb demanded.

"Thinking, praying. Enjoying God's creation. Now, Lily, what do you think?" He drew the two horses Mia had inherited to a halt and smiled as Lily, wide-eyed and finally silent, gazed around the clearing. "See any Christmas trees you like?"

"All of them." Lily pointed left then right, her excitement growing. Mia touched her arm.

"Take a good look, honey, because we need exactly the right tree for our Christmas. Okay?" She smiled when Lily nodded.

Joel drove them around the clearing, turning this way

and that so they could see the trees from every angle. Finally Lily pointed.

"That one. Right, Mia?"

Mia nodded, unable to speak because of the joy she found in this moment.

"I'll come back tomorrow and cut it down," Joel promised. "While you're at the mall in Calgary."

"And next summer we'll come back here and plant a new one to take its place." What would next year bring? she wondered. Would Caleb have forgiven his father by then? Would Lily be able to run through the meadow among the trees?

Would God have answered her plea for Caleb to love her?

Thrusting away the doubt that bubbled inside, Mia asked if Joel could park the sleigh near their chosen tree.

"I think we should have a winter campfire," she said.

"I've never done that before." Lily's eyes grew huge when Caleb lifted her from the sleigh. "What if I fall, Uncle Caleb?" she said, her fear evident.

"Then, you'll get up." He chucked her cheek. "That's what we all do, darlin'."

Mia saw Joel glance at him, saw Caleb's expression tighten.

"If you men will build the fire, I have hot chocolate and some treats we can enjoy." She glanced at Hilda. "There's a bare spot under the massive pine tree. It might be a good place to collect those pinecones you wanted."

"It certainly is." Hilda pushed forward in the sleigh and held out a hand. "Joel, would you mind helping out an old woman?"

Joel almost sprinted forward to offer his hand. Mia

blinked, astonished by the sweet glance that passed between the two. She hadn't given a thought to Joel and Hilda building a relationship, but it was obvious as he escorted her across the snow and helped gather the acorns she wanted that they'd grown very fond of each other.

"That's your doing?" Caleb's mouth tightened into a grim line.

"Me?" Mia shook her head. "I had no idea. But I'm very happy for both of them."

"Nothing can come of it." He glared at her. "He's not to be trusted. I need to tell Ms. Hilda that."

Furious that he would allow his grudge against his father to ruin the happiness these two obviously might find together, Mia let her anger spill out.

"Are you so selfish that you can't allow anyone to be happy, Caleb?" She kept her voice low so Lily, who was making snow angels a few feet away, wouldn't hear. "Will that make your mother's death more palatable? Would she have approved of this vendetta you seem determined to carry out?"

Mia stomped away to join Lily. With that child's joy in life, goofy jokes and unstoppable laughter, Mia's anger quickly dissolved. She let Caleb build the fire, and when Hilda and Joel returned with their stash of pinecones, she spread out her picnic and poured a cup of hot chocolate for everyone. Though she sensed Caleb's glance, she refused to meet it. But her heart ached.

If only…

"'My help comes from the Lord,'" she reminded her sagging spirit.

The sleigh ride home was a lively affair. Hilda told them of her plans to use pinecones to make old-fashioned wreaths to decorate Riverbend. Lily fussed over what to wear for her solo performance while Joel pointed out chickadees, partridges, a snowy owl and a spruce grouse that flapped its wings angrily before moving out of their path.

Mia smiled and pretended nothing had changed, but for her the joy had gone out of the excursion. Caleb, too, seemed introspective. Joel disappeared with the sleigh after helping Lily and Hilda inside. By the time Caleb had brought in some wood for the fireplace Lily wanted lit, Joel had returned, the chosen Christmas tree in the back of the sleigh.

"Can we decorate it tonight?" Lily begged as she danced around Caleb and Joel, who had finally managed to get the tree inside the house and into its stand.

"Not tonight," Mia said, hating the disappointment that filled Lily's face. "The branches must warm up because they'll droop a little and we'll need to trim it."

"That's where the term 'trim the tree' came from," Hilda explained.

"Tomorrow?" Lily pleaded.

"Maybe, if we're not too tired when we get back from Calgary," Mia temporized, worried Lily might push herself too hard after a day at the mall. "We have to pick out your Christmas dress, remember?"

"Oh, yeah." Lily's face brightened. She turned to Caleb. "You're coming with us, too, right, Uncle Caleb?"

"I'm afraid I have to cancel. I've taken on a new case and I have a lot of preparation," he said to Mia over Lily's protests.

"On Sunday?" she murmured, arching one eyebrow, suspicious that he was simply trying to get out of his promise.

"Yes, because my client has been ordered to make a court appearance tomorrow morning," Caleb said softly. "I'm sorry, but—"

"You can't make the trip to Calgary," Mia finished, surprised by the rush of disappointment welling up inside. They'd had such a wonderful time on their last visit to the city.

"I really am sorry," Caleb said in a soft voice when Lily had wandered away grumbling.

Mia nodded as she struggled not to show how let down she felt. "I'll handle it."

"On your own?" His frown did nothing to mar his handsome good looks.

"I'm strong, Caleb. Remember?" she said to remind him of his own words. She shrugged. "Joel will come with us. We'll be fine."

"I do worry about you, Mia." His silver eyes met hers directly. She thought she saw a hint of softness there, but a second later it was gone and his tone was all business. "The van will be here with the driver at nine. He'll drive you to and from Calgary and anywhere else you want to go."

"Thank you." There seemed little more to say. Apparently Caleb realized it, too, because a moment later he was driving away from Riverbend while a hole opened up inside Mia's heart.

"Father?" she whispered helplessly.

Whence comes my help? My help comes from the Lord.

"This is my lesson on trust, isn't it?" she said, staring into the twilight outside, watching Caleb's taillights disappear. "Keep me strong, Lord."

* * *

Caleb deliberately did not visit Riverbend in the days following Mia's Calgary trip. Oh, he called several times during the week, just to make sure everything had gone well, that Hilda and Lily were no worse for wear. But mostly he called simply to hear Mia's voice.

"We're fine, Caleb. Preparing for Christmas. In fact, we're baking cookies this afternoon if you want to join us."

Did her careful, polite tone hold just a hint of longing? For him? She'd said she loved him. Did she still, or had she given up on him?

"Never mind," Mia said when he didn't answer. "I know you're busy. You can taste the fruits of our labors whenever you're able to stop by. Just call first in case I've taken Lily to practice her solo. You haven't forgotten the Christmas program Sunday night, have you? Or my party after?"

He hadn't forgotten. How could he? Everything about Mia was implanted on his brain: the way her hair curled and waved around her lovely face; the way she smiled, wholeheartedly, unabashedly inviting the world to join her; the wide-ranging plans she devised to bring as much joy to those around her as she could manage.

No, he hadn't forgotten anything about Mia Granger, though he'd tried to.

"Caleb?" Her gentle voice brought him back to the present. "I'm sorry. I'm prattling on and disturbing your busy day, aren't I? I'll let you go. Feel welcome to join us anytime." She hung up before he could tell her he would never be too busy for her.

Caleb avoided visiting Mia because seeing her and not holding her, not kissing her was too hard. He knew he would only hurt her. The desperate hunger in his soul to be part of her life had finally sent him to his knees, to beg God to take away the anger and misery his father's presence had brought. He'd prayed hard and long to be free of the past, yet the cold, hard lump of unforgiveness still sat in his stomach like a lead-weight reminder of all he'd lost.

Seeing Mia, being with her, watching her joy in life fill her lovely face only made Caleb realize anew that she was all the things he wanted. She made his life worthwhile. She made him a better man. But after hearing her voice today, Caleb finally accepted that for all his daydreams about a future with Mia, he would never enjoy sweet, precious moments with her again unless he could find a way to let go of the past and reconcile with his father.

"But how, God?" he said as the familiar rush of bitterness rose inside. "He doesn't deserve forgiveness."

He had to find a way, because Caleb suddenly realized that the law he loved was no longer enough to fill his heart. Mia did that.

Because he loved her? Yes, his heart screamed. He loved Mia. She made his world interesting, fun and worthwhile. He couldn't imagine a world where he couldn't see her, where he couldn't be near her to share her worries and her joys. This soul-deep yearning to share every one of Mia's tomorrows with Lily no matter what happened *had* to be love.

For a moment he dreamed it was possible.

Then Joel's face filled his mind. Joel embracing Lily. Joel sharing a smile with Mia. Joel and Hilda. In an instant indignation shoved out his love for Mia. What could he possibly offer her with this lump of forgiveness lodged in his throat? Nothing.

Except maybe some freedom from the past.

For a long time Caleb sat in his empty office alone. Then he got to work on a very special Christmas gift for Mia.

Chapter Fourteen

Mia sat in the darkness of the church sanctuary, heart in her mouth, as Lily hobbled unsteadily onto the stage. Glossy dark ringlets bobbed as she smoothed the skirt of her blue velvet dress and rearranged the lace. Then she lifted her gaze to the audience.

Fear darkened the little girl's deep blue eyes. Mia's heart squeezed with love. She could go up and rescue her, but Lily had practiced and anticipated her achievement for so long. Mia desperately wanted her to achieve her goal.

Help her, she prayed silently.

A rustle beside her drew her attention. Caleb. He was looking straight at Lily. He smiled and nodded, then sat down beside Mia.

"I hope you don't mind if I join you."

Mia shook her head but couldn't say a word. Sitting next to Caleb, his shoulder rubbing hers—why would she object to that? Feeling guilty for the rush of happiness suffusing her while Lily suffered, she returned her gaze to the stage and stared.

Lily was smiling. She nodded once to the pianist and

the music began. Her voice soared, sweetly announcing the birth of a baby who would save the world. Every note sounded perfect to Mia. She was spellbound by the joy radiating from Lily as her voice glided and dipped, strong and forceful, then soft as a whisper. As the last notes died away, Mia felt a tear trickle down her cheek. After a moment of pure silence, the church erupted in applause. As Lily walked regally from the stage, Mia was certain no one noticed her leg brace.

"She did it." Caleb grabbed her hand and squeezed it. "She was perfect, wasn't she?"

Mia nodded. With his beloved face mere inches away, the longing to touch him was overwhelming. But Caleb had made it clear that he could not love her.

As the music concert continued, with her heart breaking, Mia finally and completely turned Caleb and her love over to God. It wouldn't be easy. She still loved him desperately, trusted him and yearned to share a future with him. But Mia finally accepted that only by placing her total trust in God could she face life without Caleb.

When the concert was over and Pastor Don had praised everyone for their efforts, he reminded the congregation of Mia's invitation to her Christmas party. While Caleb spoke to friends, Mia collected Lily, Hilda and Joel and drove home, assuring Lily that her solo had been perfect while her heart begged God for comfort.

Caleb stood in the shadows of the sanctuary, listening to Mia repeat her assurance to Lily that she'd done a good job. He didn't need anyone to tell him; he could see how much the two loved each other in the way they looked at each other, touched each other. It was also evident that both Lily and Mia cared for his father. They easily included him in their group, smiling and laughing.

Envious of that love, Caleb let himself imagine he could be part of their world. But not with Joel, never with Joel. He walked out of the church, bitterness simmering inside him. Why did his father always have to spoil it?

"Honey?" Marsha dragged on his arm, stopping him from getting to his truck. "You're going to Mia's party, right?"

"I'm not sure." He hesitated. How could he go there, watch his father enjoy himself and not say something? That would ruin the party Mia had worked so hard to make. "I'm kind of—"

"Busy?" she demanded, one eyebrow arched. "Did it ever occur to you that you're too busy, Caleb? One of these days you're going to look back and realize that because you didn't grab the opportunity, you've missed the joy and love that God created especially for you."

"Marsha—"

"You listen to me, Caleb," she interrupted. Her voice had that stern tone that told him he was in trouble. "I'm your mother in every way that counts, so I'm going to tell you the cold hard truth."

"You always do," he said, trying to defuse her speech by making a joke. Marsha was not amused.

"Mia loves you. She doesn't care about your past or that bitterness you hang on to like a security blanket. Mia only wants you to be happy. That's real love, and it doesn't come around that often." She tilted her head. "But you know that, don't you, Caleb? Because you love her."

"It wouldn't work," he said, wishing she'd let it alone.

"You're God now? You know these things?" Her fierce glare pinned him. "Lara loved you and you tried to love her back but couldn't."

"I can't love anyone." Even to himself his words sounded silly.

"You don't love me? You don't love Bud?" Her scathing glower told him she knew differently.

Driven by her attack, Caleb did away with the niceties.

"I can't be around Mia when he's there. I can't stop the loathing and disgust I feel," he admitted.

"So? When I see chocolate, I can't stop wanting it. Does that mean I have to act on that feeling?" Marsha suddenly enveloped him in her arms and hugged tight. "I love you, Caleb," she said in a broken voice. "You're a good man who truly cares about helping people. You've achieved so much. But that sad little boy inside won't let you be free. He's keeping you from loving a woman who could enrich your life."

"Mom—"

"Let go of the past, Caleb. Please, before it drags you so far down you'll miss every wonderful thing God has for you." Marsha kissed his cheek, gave him one last hug and then, after a searching look, walked toward her husband.

As they drove away, Caleb knew he would go to Mia's party. He'd only been fooling himself that he could stay away from her.

For Mia's sake he would hold his tongue and endure his father's presence. But after the party he would seek Joel out and ask him to leave, as he'd promised. Maybe then Caleb could finally break free of his past.

* * *

Mia reveled in her teeming home, loving the sound of laughter as people mingled together. This was what she'd dreamed of when she'd first moved to Riverbend. But her dreams had grown and changed. Soon Lily would be her daughter in word and deed. But Caleb would never—

"Looks as if everyone's enjoying themselves." The object of Mia's thoughts suddenly appeared in front of her. "You've done a great job with the decorations and the food." Caleb held up a gingerbread man she and Lily had made. "I like the buttons best."

"Most kids do like chocolate," she teased.

"The tree looks stunning." His eyes glowed soft and warm. "I don't think all those stars came from the local store."

"Actually Hilda and Joel made them." She noted his wince at the mention of his father. "Excuse me. Some folks are leaving. I need to say goodbye, but please don't go. I want to ask you a favor."

Mia's hostess duties kept her busy for a half hour. By the time she saw Caleb again, her guests were gone. Joel and Hilda were cleaning up the kitchen with Lily when Caleb found her staring into the glowing embers in the fireplace.

"I think it's time for me to head out, also," he said.

"I'm glad you came." Mia couldn't stop staring into his eyes, wishing for the impossible. "I wanted to ask if you could drop Lily off at the Pembertons' in town. She's going for a sleepover. Ashley has the measles and according to her mom needs serious diversion."

"Which Lily can provide because she's already had

them." He nodded and wrinkled his nose. "I remember that occasion vividly. She tested all of our patience."

"That's why the Pembertons want her to come distract Ashley. I'd take her, but I'm really scared to drive on these icy roads after dark, though everyone else around here seems to take it in stride."

"We're used to it." He shrugged.

"Yes, well, maybe by next year I will be, too. Anyway, I hoped you could take Lily and save me disappointing her." Mia grinned. "She'll keep you entertained on the way. You know Lily. Always full of ideas."

"Believe me, I know. Sure, I'll drop her off." He looked at her, stared really. Mia's cheeks grew warm.

"Uncle Caleb, come get your goody bag," Lily called from the doorway. "I made it for you."

"Thank you, sweetheart." Mia walked with him, watched as Caleb took the bag and peeked inside. "Chocolate-chip cookies. Thank you."

"Welcome. Mia helped me. And Ms. Hilda. And Pops." Lily giggled when Joel appeared and tickled her under the chin.

Mia's heart broke as joy drained from Caleb's face.

"Go get your coat, Lily. Uncle Caleb is going to drop you off at Ashley's for the sleepover," Mia said quietly.

"Goody. I already got my backpack in the closet." Lily moved, stopped, then grinned. "You gotta kiss Mia, Uncle Caleb."

"What? Why?" Caleb looked as if he found the prospect distasteful.

"'Cause you're standing under the mistletoe. Me an' Pops put it there." Lily's smile never wavered. Her eyes sparkled with mischief, moving from Caleb to Mia, apparently oblivious to the tension in the room. "Kiss her, Uncle Caleb."

With no choice, Caleb bent his head and pressed his lips against Mia's. Though it wasn't the most romantic kiss they'd ever shared, the touch of his lips on hers brought back the hopes and dreams Mia had tried so hard to quash. She kissed him back, hoping he'd understand how much she loved him, how much she wished he would kiss her for the rest of his life.

But Caleb drew away.

"We need to get going." His voice was hoarse. "Mia will help you to my car. I need to talk to Joel for a moment. Alone."

The sharpness of that last word, the intensity in Caleb's eyes and the way he glared at his father caused a rush of worry in Mia's heart. *Do you trust God?* an inner voice asked.

"Come on, sweetheart. I'll get my coat and help you buckle up in Uncle Caleb's car." Mia glanced worriedly from Joel to Caleb. "You won't be long?"

"What I have to say won't take long," he promised grimly. "The car's running, so it should be warm."

Mia looked at Joel. He nodded his encouragement, so with no other choice, she grasped Lily's hand and left.

"You said you'd leave if I asked you to. I'm asking." Caleb kept his voice low so Hilda wouldn't hear. "Leave. Now. Tonight."

"Caleb, it's almost Christmas," Joel protested. "I've got a gift for Lily under the tree. I want to watch her open it. Just a few more days. Please?"

"You can't even keep your word, can you?" Caleb retrieved his coat. "Leave this place tonight. If you don't,

I'll make it so you'll wish you'd never come to Buffalo Gap."

To his surprise Joel didn't argue. He simply stood there in his faded corduroy jeans and washed-out shirt, looking dignified yet old. Finally he nodded.

"If that's what you want, I will leave. You'll never hear from me again," Joel promised. "But I'm not running out of here like a thief in the night. I am going to stay until Christmas. I owe that to Hilda and to Mia and to Lily. After that you'll be rid of me."

Caleb was about to argue when Hilda walked into the room. She glanced from him to Joel and frowned.

"Something wrong?" she asked.

"Yes," Caleb snapped, unable to control his fury that his father had won this round. "He is what's wrong. He's a murderer, a liar and a thief. Watch out."

Caleb stormed out of the house, said good-night to Mia, who backed away from his car and studied him with sadness. He climbed into the car, checking to be sure Lily was buckled in the backseat before he shoved the gearshift into Drive.

"What's wrong, Uncle Caleb?" Lily asked.

"Everything." He gunned the engine, then took off around the circular driveway, knowing he was going too fast but unable to stifle his building frustration.

Suddenly Lily said, "A deer!"

Caleb slammed on his brakes, putting the car into a spin on the icy road. He fought to right it and lost as his left front wheel slid off the road and sent the car rolling. Caleb's head slammed into the steering wheel. As everything faded he had only one thought.

Lily!

Chapter Fifteen

"Caleb? Can you hear me?"

The voice was Mia's, tender, oozing love. For him. Could she still love him after what he'd done?

"Lily?" he whispered, every muscle in his body protesting at the effort it took to say the word. But he had to know. Had he hurt her? Had his anger hurt sweet, precious Lily?

"Lily's fine, Caleb. Do you hear me?" Mia touched his cheek, her finger as soft as velvet against his cheek. "Lily is fine. Her seat belt kept her in place. But you have a concussion."

"Lily's okay?" Why couldn't he get his eyes open?

"She's fine. Joel got her out first, then rescued you," Mia explained. "I called 911, but they had to take their time because of the icy roads. Your car rolled and was leaking fuel. Joel thought it might ignite, so he pulled you out to safety."

"Joel?" Though Caleb finally pried his eyes open and saw Mia with her cape of red-gold hair, smiling at him, he couldn't make sense of what she was saying.

Joel had saved him? After Caleb had threatened him, ordered him to leave?

"I was so scared. You mean everything to me, Caleb. I love you so much." Mia pressed her lips to his, not asking for anything. Just offering comfort. And love. But how could she love him when he was so full of anger and hate?

Everything in his head felt jumbled, disjointed. Caleb opened his eyes again and found peace in Mia. Sweet Mia, holding his hand, loving him.

"The doctors want to talk to you, Caleb. I have to take Lily home. Rest well. I love you." She kissed his cheek, then disappeared. He wanted to go after her, but a hand pressed him down.

"You have a concussion, Caleb. You need to stay still for a while."

Caleb lay awake long into the night as images from the crash replayed in his brain. One cold, hard fact stuck out. Because of his anger at Joel, he hadn't been paying attention to his driving. He could easily have avoided the deer, had done it many times before. But with his mind clouded by anger, he'd nearly killed Lily.

What's the difference between your anger and your father's drinking, Caleb? his brain demanded. *Both led to a loss of control. You are as guilty as your father. It's only by God's grace that Lily's not badly hurt, or dead, like your mother.*

The truth finally pierced through his anger and bitterness to shine on the truth. Wrong was wrong. God didn't forgive by degree. He forgave. Period. Everyone made mistakes. Some were life changing, like his mother's death, but no less forgivable by God.

At last Caleb understood. His anger wasn't only toward his father, but also toward himself for not preventing his mother's death. He'd shifted the guilt he felt onto his father. He closed his eyes and let the scene replay. Arguing. His mother stepping back, falling while his father reached out. Was it Joel's fault?

Caleb didn't know anymore. All he knew was that the hate had to be over. He had to ask God's forgiveness, forgiveness willingly given for him *and* for his father.

Sun began to light the eastern sky while Caleb prayed for forgiveness. Cleansed and restored to his heavenly father, he finally drifted into sleep, his thoughts of Mia and the love she had. How could she still love him now that he'd endangered Lily?

"Father, You know this child far better than I do. I love him, but He's Your son, too. Take away his pain and heal him with Your love. In Jesus' name."

Caleb lifted his eyelids and studied the father seated next to his bed.

"How can you pray that?"

Joel simply smiled.

"How can you love me after all I've said and done to you?"

"Love is all I have to give you, Caleb," Joel said softly. "I've always loved you, since the day your mom put you in my arms. That will never change. I'll always pray for God's best for you." He rose. "I'm leaving. Goodbye, son."

"Wait!" Caleb struggled to sit up, wincing as his ribs protested. "I don't want you to go."

"I have to. I promised, and I keep my promises." Joel's steady gaze met his. "I'm sorry you can't forgive me."

"I don't have the right to forgive you," Caleb admitted. "It's you who should forgive me." The enormity of his actions replayed through his memory. "I could have killed Lily," he whispered.

"By God's grace you didn't. Lily only remembers the car rolling and hanging upside down. She doesn't have bad memories, except she's concerned about you. And the deer."

"By God's grace." Caleb mulled over the words. He had a father because of God's grace. He had a woman who loved him because of God's grace.

"Can you forgive me, Caleb?" Joel asked.

"I don't know. I've hung on to it for so long that I'm not sure I'll ever be completely free," Caleb answered honestly. He saw Joel's disappointment flare. "But I want to."

"Let's start over." Joel thrust out his hand. "Joel Crane, sinner saved by God's grace."

"Caleb Grant," he said, shaking his father's hand. "Also known as Caleb Crane. Son of Joel and Theresa Crane."

Tears filled his father's eyes as he said, "I'm looking forward to getting to know you, son. It will take time, but with God all things are possible."

"What?" Caleb asked, noting Joel's hesitation.

"Mia loves you, son. I think you love her, too." Joel frowned. "Love is the one thing that can heal you, but for it to do its work, you have to be vulnerable to it. There's no sure thing with love. But to go without it because you're afraid…that's wrong."

"I'm not sure I can love Mia as she ought to be loved," Caleb admitted. "I don't know anything about love."

"Sure you do. You know you'd give your life for her

and Lily. You know you want to be with her tomorrow and tomorrow after that."

True, but was that enough for someone as precious as Mia?

"Mia needs you in her life as much as you need her. Lily needs both of you." Joel shrugged. "Why don't you just enjoy that and leave the rest to God?"

Two nurses bustled into the room and ordered Joel out before Caleb could answer, which was all right because he needed time to think things through. And to pray.

He longed to see Mia, to hold her in his arms and hear her say once more that she loved him.

"Mia, will you please put on your dress and fix your hair?" Abby begged with a hint of frustration in her voice.

"But why? What's going on?" Mia knew Abby wouldn't tell her, because she'd already asked a hundred times. Finally she gave in, took the bag with the gorgeous black dress upstairs and changed into it. Abby helped her pin up her hair.

"You look so pretty," Lily told Mia when she returned downstairs. Her small arms hugged Mr. Fudge, the chocolate Lab puppy Mia had given her for Christmas. "Are you going to a party?"

"No." Caleb stepped into the room from the kitchen. "We're going to the ballet. *The Nutcracker*. It's a New Year's Eve tradition."

Mia's breath caught in her throat at the sight of him. He had a vivid navy bruise at the corner of his left eye, which only added to his handsome good looks. She hadn't seen him since Christmas when he'd stopped by to drop off the puppy, then left after sharing Christmas dinner. How she'd missed him.

"Tradition?" she whispered, soaking in his presence as joy filled her soul.

"Isn't it?" he asked, silver eyes aglow.

"Well, I usually go alone." Her gaze locked with his.

"It's probably time to change that part of the tradition, don't you think?" He held out her coat. Mia slipped her arms into it, clamping down on the rush of love.

This was Caleb being nice. It didn't mean anything, she told herself as Lily hugged them and Hilda and Joel promised to care for her.

"Go home, Abby. And thank you." Mia hugged her friend, so glad she'd made the move to Riverbend. That, like much of her life now, was due to Caleb. Dear, sweet Caleb.

She took a moment in the frigid winter night to admire his new vehicle. "A truck? How come?"

"I needed a change." He lifted her so she didn't have to negotiate the high step.

Oddly Mia found it hard to talk to him on the ride into Calgary. She felt shy, as if she barely knew this man who'd suddenly begun having long talks with his estranged father.

Dinner at a posh restaurant was nice, but Mia barely tasted the food, too busy wondering if Caleb was going to tell her he couldn't love her. She sat through the ballet on tenterhooks. Finally on the drive home, she asked, "Why did you do this?"

"You've been acting like a scared rabbit since we left. I guess this was a mistake." He turned into a lookout that gave them a view of the entire city, its lights sparkling in the night. "I need to tell you something."

Please, God?

"I love you."

She couldn't believe he'd said it or that he meant it. "What did you say?"

"I said I love you. I think I have for a long time. But I needed to be sure." He studied her with his amazing eyes, his words quiet but assured above the purr of the truck motor. "I've searched God for the truth. I've talked to Pastor Don and to my father. I'm pretty sure what I feel is love. For you."

"Oh." Mia broke his stare to study her hands. Dared she believe? Dared she trust?

"Is that all you're going to say?" he asked with a bark of laughter. "I've spent a week agonizing about this and all you say is 'oh'? Mia, come on!" The plea in Caleb's voice was her undoing.

"I love you, too," she whispered.

"Thank You, God." He leaned toward her and pressed his lips to hers, but the console came between them. Caleb grimaced. "Maybe it was a dumb idea to buy this truck," he said, threading his fingers through her hair, which he'd loosened.

"Why did you buy it?" she whispered, leaning in to his touch.

"Because when we get married, you'll need a truck on your ranch. And a bigger horse. I want to go riding with you, and those little ponies you have just don't cut it."

"You really are a cowboy at heart, lawyer Grant," Mia said, and then she didn't say anything for a while as Caleb kissed her. When he finally drew away, she asked the questions that plagued her. "When did you know you loved me?"

"I can't give you the exact day or time," he said. "You grew into my heart and became a part of me. Your grace, your beauty, the way you took on life and made sense of it— I admired you so much. Thanks to God's mercy, admiration turned to love. I love you. I love the way you care for Lily with all your heart. I want to share that with you, to build a home where love joins us. Will you marry me, Mia?"

"I love you, Caleb. I have for ages." She had to ask, "But what about Joel?"

"He's my father." Caleb sighed. "I'll never know exactly what happened and part of me will always miss my mom, but the day I rolled the car, the day I almost killed Lily—" He gulped, squeezed her hand hard. "That's when I realized that I am not qualified to judge anyone, that my anger could have hurt Lily just as his drunkenness hurt my mother."

Mia leaned over to touch his cheek with her lips.

"I haven't got it all down yet," he said quietly. "I have a ways to go. It will take time to repair the damage of anger and hate and bitterness."

"Love heals," she whispered. She smiled. "I'll help you work through it, Caleb, just as you helped me work through my problems. I'll marry you and help you be a father to Lily. Because I love you." After they'd sealed their love with a satisfying kiss, she leaned back in her seat and asked, "When will we get married?"

"Next year on New Year's Eve?" He lifted an eyebrow. "Isn't it time to start a new tradition?"

"But that's so far away," she mourned.

"I want that time, Mia. I want to court you, to talk over everything with you. I want to get to know my father. I want you to be absolutely certain that your marriage to me is what you want."

"Caleb, you don't have to worry. I know being married to you will be nothing like being married to Harlan," she said, tears in her eyes. "I love you. I never loved him."

"I know." He smiled reassuringly. "In a year, Lily's adoption will be final. We'll have had time to plan every detail of our future."

"Except the parts God will change," she reminded him.

"A wedding, one year from tonight?" he asked.

"A wedding," she agreed, and kissed him with praise in her heart to the Father who asked His children to trust Him, then chose the best gifts for them.

"By the way," Caleb mused as he drove her home, "I never gave you your Christmas gift. I have to tell you the first part."

"Okay." Puzzled, Mia studied his face and saw his smile. "What?"

"Bethany is back at Family Ties with her parents' blessing," Caleb said, a satisfied look tipping up his lips. "She's asked Abby and me to help her find a good family for her baby."

"If that's what she wants, I'm so glad. It's a wonderful gift. Thank you." She leaned over to brush a kiss against his cheek.

"But that's only part of your gift." Caleb pulled a paper from his pocket and handed it to her. "Merry Christmas, Mia."

Confused, she opened it and squinted to read it in the dash light. She blinked, gaped at him, then reread the entire thing once more. "Caleb?"

"You didn't kill Bobby, sweetheart. He died of SIDS, sudden infant death syndrome. Just one more thing Harlan lied about." Caleb touched her face. "Nobody knows why he died, but it was not your fault."

Mia wept all the way home. Then joy moved in as she and Caleb shared their news with Lily, Ms. Hilda and Joel. Riverbend Ranch brimmed with joy. That was exactly as Mia had prayed for.

Epilogue

On December 31 in a candlelight service at Buffalo Gap Community Church, Mia Granger married Caleb Grant. It was supposed to be a small, private ceremony, but who could say no to Mayor Marsha's constituents' desire to see her son tie the knot to the community's most delightful newbie? Unfortunately the event was running late because of the bride's lawyer.

"Harlan bought Riverbend because the mineral rights go with it," Bella told Mia as she held the bride's slim white heels. "That means that all royalties of oil and anything else they find go to you. Harlan commissioned a survey before he died. There is a vein with a precious metal in it. For as long as you live, the money will go to you. After your death, rights revert to the crown. You're a very wealthy woman, Mia."

"In many ways." She hugged Bella. "Thank you for telling me. Caleb and I will talk about it later. Right now I'm a little preoccupied with getting married. Can you straighten my veil?"

Bella complied, then took her place in a pew beside Mayor Marsha and her husband. The bridal party was small. Lily walked down the aisle first with no sign of a limp, resplendent in a creamy velvet dress with royal blue feathered trim. She held a dainty bouquet of out-of-season lilies that perfectly matched her eyes.

"Okay, Uncle Caleb?" she whispered loudly when she arrived at the front of the church. His thumbs-up made her smile.

The congregation rose when Hilda suddenly changed keys on the organ and began playing a familiar old hymn that had been Caleb's mother's favorite. Mia stepped into the aisle, her arm wrapped in Joel's.

Dressed in a hand-crocheted lace jacket and a long tulip skirt, she walked slowly toward Caleb, her green gaze beneath her long trailing veil concentrated on him. Her magnificent hair was held off her face with a silver band. She carried lilies in a sheaf mixed with cedar greens and tied with a silver band to match Caleb's eyes.

Once Joel had given her hand to Caleb, the couple turned toward Pastor Don to say their vows.

"I will love you forever, Caleb." Mia touched his cheek. "You will always be my beloved husband, a gift from God that I willingly accept. I can't wait to be your wife."

"I don't deserve you, Mia. But I thank God that He's blessed me with your love. You are the part of me that makes every day a blessing." Caleb's next words were for Mia alone. "When I was lost you came and drew me with your love so I could fully experience God's forgiveness. I love you. I always will."

Pastor Don said a few words, then with his blessing Mia and Caleb kissed.

"That's my mom and dad," Lily hollered, grinning

from ear to ear as Mr. Fudge came sliding down the aisle. "We're gonna be a family."

The bride and groom embraced Lily, holding her dog, and Joel and Hilda. It was clear to everyone that they already were.

* * * * *

WE HOPE YOU ENJOYED
THIS BOOK FROM

LOVE INSPIRED
INSPIRATIONAL ROMANCE

Uplifting stories of faith, forgiveness and hope.

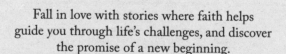

Fall in love with stories where faith helps
guide you through life's challenges, and discover
the promise of a new beginning.

6 NEW BOOKS AVAILABLE EVERY MONTH!

LIHALO2020

Get 4 FREE REWARDS!

We'll send you 2 FREE Books <u>plus</u> 2 FREE Mystery Gifts.

Love Inspired books feature uplifting stories where faith helps guide you through life's challenges and discover the promise of a new beginning.

FREE Value Over **$20**

YES! Please send me 2 FREE Love Inspired Romance novels and my 2 FREE mystery gifts (gifts are worth about $10 retail). After receiving them, if I don't wish to receive any more books, I can return the shipping statement marked "cancel." If I don't cancel, I will receive 6 brand-new novels every month and be billed just $5.24 each for the regular-print edition or $5.99 each for the larger-print edition in the U.S., or $5.74 each for the regular-print edition or $6.24 each for the larger-print edition in Canada. That's a savings of at least 13% off the cover price. It's quite a bargain! Shipping and handling is just 50¢ per book in the U.S. and $1.25 per book in Canada.* I understand that accepting the 2 free books and gifts places me under no obligation to buy anything. I can always return a shipment and cancel at any time. The free books and gifts are mine to keep no matter what I decide.

Choose one: ☐ **Love Inspired Romance Regular-Print** (105/305 IDN GNWC) ☐ **Love Inspired Romance Larger-Print** (122/322 IDN GNWC)

Name (please print)

Address   Apt. #

City   State/Province   Zip/Postal Code

Email: Please check this box ☐ if you would like to receive newsletters and promotional emails from Harlequin Enterprises ULC and its affiliates. You can unsubscribe anytime.

Mail to the Reader Service:
IN U.S.A.: P.O. Box 1341, Buffalo, NY 14240-8531
IN CANADA: P.O. Box 603, Fort Erie, Ontario L2A 5X3

Want to try 2 free books from another series? Call 1-800-873-8635 or visit www.ReaderService.com.

*Terms and prices subject to change without notice. Prices do not include sales taxes, which will be charged (if applicable) based on your state or country of residence. Canadian residents will be charged applicable taxes. Offer not valid in Quebec. This offer is limited to one order per household. Books received may not be as shown. Not valid for current subscribers to Love Inspired Romance books. All orders subject to approval. Credit or debit balances in a customer's account(s) may be offset by any other outstanding balance owed by or to the customer. Please allow 4 to 6 weeks for delivery. Offer available while quantities last.

Your Privacy—Your information is being collected by Harlequin Enterprises ULC, operating as Reader Service. For a complete summary of the information we collect, how we use this information and to whom it is disclosed, please visit our privacy notice located at corporate.harlequin.com/privacy-notice. From time to time we may also exchange your personal information with reputable third parties. If you wish to opt out of this sharing of your personal information, please visit readerservice.com/consumerschoice or call 1-800-873-8635. **Notice to California Residents**—Under California law, you have specific rights to control and access your data. For more information on these rights and how to exercise them, visit corporate.harlequin.com/california-privacy.

LI20R2

SPECIAL EXCERPT FROM

LOVE INSPIRED

INSPIRATIONAL ROMANCE

What happens when a beautiful foster mom claims an Oklahoma rancher as her fake fiancé?

Read on for a sneak preview of
The Rancher's Holiday Arrangement
by Brenda Minton.

"I am so sorry," Daisy told Joe as they walked down the sidewalk together.

The sun had come out and it was warm. The kind of day that made her long for spring.

"I don't know that I need an apology," Joe told her. "But an explanation would be a good start."

She shook her head. "I saw you sitting with your family, and I knew how I'd feel. Ambushed."

"I could have handled it. Now I'm engaged." He tossed her a dimpled grin. "What am I supposed to tell them when I don't have a wedding?"

"I got tired of your smug attitude and left you at the altar?" she asked, half teasing. "Where are we walking to?"

"I'm not sure. I guess the park."

"The park it is," she told him.

Daisy smiled down at the stroller. Myra and Miriam belonged with their mother, Lindsey. Daisy got to love them for a short time and hoped that she'd made a difference.

"It'll be hard to let them go," Joe said.

LIEXP1-120

"It will be," Daisy admitted. "I think they'll go home after New Year's."

"That's pretty soon."

"It is. We have a court date next week."

"I'm sorry," Joe said, reaching for her hand and giving it a light squeeze.

"None of that has anything to do with what I've done to your life. I've complicated things. I'm sorry. You can tell your parents I lost my mind for a few minutes. Tell them I have a horrible sense of humor and that we aren't even friends. Tell them I wanted to make your life difficult."

"Which one is true?" he asked.

"Maybe a combination," she answered. "I *do* have a horrible sense of humor. I *did* want to mess with you."

"And the part about us not being friends?"

"Honestly, I don't know what we are."

"I'll take friendship," he told her. "Don't worry, Daisy, I'm not holding you to this proposal."

She laughed and so did he.

"Good thing. The last thing I want is a real fiancé."

"I know I'm not the most handsome guy, but I'm a decent catch," he said.

She ignored the comment about his looks. The last thing she wanted to admit was that when he smiled, she forgot herself just a little.

Don't miss
The Rancher's Holiday Arrangement *by Brenda Minton,*
available November 2020 wherever
Love Inspired books and ebooks are sold.

LoveInspired.com

Copyright © 2020 by Brenda Minton

LIEXP1120